the EDUC
EPITOME QUIR

a novel by
A.F. HARROLD

published by
QUIRKSTANDARD'S ALTERNATIVE

To Peter.
An odd
book.
Enjoy?

Nov. 2013.

By the same author

Poetry
Logic & The Heart
Of Birds & Bees
Flood

Entertainments – Poetry, Prose, Pictures
Postcards From The Hedgehog
The Man Who Spent Years In The Bath

Poetry for Kids
I Eat Squirrels

First published in the UK in 2010 by

Quirkstandard's Alternative
1 Cranbourne Gardens
Reading
Berkshire
RG30 6TS

www.afharrold.co.uk
www.quirkstandardsalternative.co.uk

Copyright © 2010 A.F. Harrold

The moral right of A.F. Harrold to be identified as author of this work is
asserted in accordance with the Copyright, Designs and Patent Act of 1988.

Cover design and typesetting by Richard Ponsford

ISBN 978–0–9557081–4–5

Printed and bound by CPI Group (UK) Ltd, Croydon, CR0 4YY

Dedicated to Rikk Smith and Karen Stenner

with thanks to all those people who read earlier
versions of this story, in whole or in part,
or who listened to the first draft podcast,
and who passed comment one way or another.

Nescire quod antea quam natus sis acciderit, id est simper esse puerum; quid enim est aetas hominis nisi memoria rerum nostrarum cum superiorum aetate contexterit?

CICERO, *Orator Ad M. Brutum*

Quirkstandard, Breakfast & The Club

It was during the last years of the Great War that Lord Quirkstandard received the first inklings of an outline of a hint of the original idea that would one day, after wrangling, coaxing and much eventual help from outsiders, emerge into the dawn light of a brand new day of a fairly new century as the crowning glory of his only lasting accomplishment: *The Common University*.

However, as this pre-emptive shadow of a notion first passed across the creases of his cerebellum he was simply cursing to himself in the kitchen. The kitchen wasn't a typical place for Quirkstandard to be found, and the curses he used were the sort that might safely be used in the company of a lady without causing distress or embarrassment to either party since he was, without doubt, a gentleman.

Epitome Quirkstandard, Third Earl of Wainscoting, had woken up to find himself in a bit of a pickle. Owing to the ongoing war in France the last members of his domestic staff had been called away. Presumably, he thought, to do some tidying, dusting and cooking along the Western Front. This had left him all alone in his neat, but not overly large townhouse in the environs of Regent's Park, attempting to make his own breakfast.

The saucepan contained what, he believed with luck and perseverance, might turn out to be a soft-boiled egg. He had filled the pan with water from the tap and had found an egg underneath a ceramic chicken on the kitchen table. He had followed Cook's neatly written instructions and placed the pan on the stove, but now nothing was happening.

Cook had always liked him and had spent a little of his embarkation leave jotting down a variety of recipes and instructions for his employer to follow by himself until the new staff arrived.[1] Cook's instructions were detailed and various, but he had neglected, on the 'how to boil an egg' page, to mention where the matches were kept or, in fact, the need to light the gas underneath the saucepan at all. Fortunately for Quirkstandard's sake he had also neglected to instruct him to turn the gas on, so at least one tragedy was avoided on this warm summer's morning.

As he stood over the floating egg, timing it by the kitchen clock, Quirkstandard thought back to the evening before. Cook had taken him aside and quickly talked him through the pile of recipes, and he wondered just a little now, as he watched the egg coolly bobbing, whether, perhaps, there was something in what Cook had said last night that he should have noted down, something that Cook hadn't himself written in the notebook.

He remembered how, when he was a pupil at Eton, he

[1] The butler had placed a request with an agency who specialised in supplying elderly and/or inept domestic staff to stately homes, but he had told Quirkstandard that he didn't hold out too much hope, since the competition for staff was fairly fierce and their advertisement had arrived somewhat late in the war.

had been encouraged to make notes when the Masters spoke about anything. That was a number of years ago now and he tried to remember if they'd ever taught him about egg boiling, but he quickly came to the conclusion that they probably hadn't. As far as he remembered it, his schooling had been filled with things that had names like Classics and Latin. Well, not, he corrected himself, things with names *like* Classics and Latin, but things actually *called* Classics and Latin.

If only a man could have a decent education, he thought, filled with useful things, such as *How to Boil an Egg*, rather than the old Latin guff, which he had never even thought about until this very morning. The thought didn't occur, however, that had they taught him Egg Boiling, he probably wouldn't have remembered that either. It's quite likely that *anything* he had been taught at school, however useful it might have been, would have stuck to his brain like leaves on an autumnal oak.

He had been one of those boys who dutifully attended every class (possibly because he knew a letter might be sent home to his Aunt if he bunked off and he didn't fancy disappointing her (she was a woman he held in high esteem and who occasionally visited with a bag of sweets)) and had spent every lesson dozing in the back row, just as boys of his wealth felt, in that day and age, entitled to do. Occasionally he was woken by the noisy out-rushing of the other pupils at the end of a class, or by the sound of a board-duster as it bounced off the cranium of a slightly less well-off boy sat nearby, but even at these times he never felt the urge to write down what the master had been saying.

When it came to his final school exams Quirkstandard noticed that several of his classmates had sent along an Indian prodigy from a lower form who knew absolutely everything about everything. Little Perumparambil liked examinations so much that he would take your place for the price of a bottle of ginger pop and the satisfaction of a job well done. Quirkstandard, however, thinking he'd save the ginger pop for himself, sent his man along instead, dressed in his rather tight fitting school uniform.

This had seemed a remarkably smart idea at the time, and the extra hours he was able to spend in the bath instead of in the exam hall were, without doubt, several of the finest bathing hours of his life. However, when the results were posted a fortnight later he discovered that his valet turned out to have had as much grasp of the complexities of Classics and Latin as Quirkstandard himself had had.

He left school labelled a dunce of fairly significant proportions and had felt, in a place deep down inside which he couldn't quite reach to set a finger on, a slight but rising sense of failure. The fact that he hadn't even achieved the rank of biggest imbecile in the school (which would've been some sort of accomplishment) only helped to further widen his confused and salty gashes of lacerated pride.[2] His Aunt, on the other hand, had expected no better result from a school run by men

[2] The boy who was placed lowest in the school that year was a good friend of Quirkstandard's: a small schnauzer named Nigel Spiggot. (His parents had been hoping for a son but had only managed to acquire a pet. Since, however, they had placed their expected off-spring's name on the school's waiting list some years earlier the

4

(she held 'views' about that particular gender) and didn't even speak sternly to the boy about it. Instead she bought him a large cream cake in one of the little teashops of Windsor and sent him home on the train: this reaction from his Aunt (whom he looked up to and respected) mostly mollified his feelings of failure and very soon he thought nothing else about it.

If there was one thing Quirkstandard had learned from that exam fiasco, however, it was that one should never send a man to do a boy's job. And now that he was a man, a tall and attractively slim and healthy twenty-six year old example of one, with a flouncy moustache of his own drooping over his top lip (due to the absence, during the War, of the chap who popped in once a day to wax and prink the old topiary), he found himself coming to the sincere conclusion that boiling eggs really must be boy's work, since he seemed entirely incapable of doing it himself.

Abandoning the saucepan he decided that today (like most days) would be a fine day to go and dine at his Club in Town.

He had another look through all the rooms around his bedroom in an effort to find where his man kept his clothes. He knew he'd seen them all stored away once, neatly stacked and folded, but was dashed if he could find them now. So, drawing the cord of his dressing gown

Spiggots felt obliged to use the opportunity when it came up, and, it should be added, the governors of Eton College were not shy to the sound of money jangling into their Cash Office, even as old rope was seen leaving through the Porter's Lodge.)

.

tighter over the top of his pyjamas, and slipping his feet into two tall boots he found in the hallway, pulling a stick from the elephant's foot beside the front door and a hat from a nearby hook, he stepped out of his house into a gloriously sunny morning, fell down the steps and, after having gathered himself up on the pavement of Devonshire Terrace and dusted himself off, strode purposefully in the direction of Mauve's Club For Gentleman.

As Quirkstandard looked around the interior of the Great Room at Mauve's he was amused to notice that he wasn't the only gentleman who had arrived in his pyjamas. In fact, he noticed several proud, and pinkly Imperial, members of the club standing out in their full natal nakedness. These were chaps, he recognised, who had spent time in the Colonies and had got into the habit of sleeping, he chuckled to himself, in the altogether. Seeing them there he didn't feel quite so silly for not having been able to track down his daytime clothes. The War Office really hadn't thought, he thought, when they called up all these servants from across the houses of the Home Counties, that they'd be leaving the Home Front quite so exposed. He chuckled at his little joke and looked around to see if there was anyone about this morning who liked him enough to listen to it, but just then another thought popped into his old grey matter which quite chilled his spine.

If the Domestic Situation had reached such a pass in other people's houses too, then quite a few of them might not have had their breakfast either, which could well mean a run on the lunch menu.

He hung his hat on the appropriate hook of the hat-stand and strode purposely into the gloaming of the Club, straight toward the stairs that led to the Dining Room. As he ascended he noticed in a corner of the Great Room below him a gaggle of gentlemen in various states of dress and undress surrounding Snatchby, Mauve's elderly doorman. He stood at the centre of this quiet throng and Quirkstandard noticed how his hand would drift, with near tectonic grace, to point at the throat or the waist of a gentleman and exhibit or imitate some peculiar motion or other. Attendant on these movements was each gentleman's rapt attention. Quirkstandard was too far away to catch any of the dialogue other than his pal Harris Flirtwater's cry of 'By Jove!' as he pumped Snatchby's withered and dusty hand vigorously.

A few minutes later as they sat down to a big plate of bubble and squeak (which Quirkstandard noticed, was much more squeak than bubble) he engaged Flirtwater in conversation. It turned out that Snatchby had been instructing the gentlemen in the art of self-dressing. He had explained, named and identified each article of clothing, along with the usual and likely locations for clean and folded items in a typical household setting, and had then detailed and displayed the unique and precise movements, motions and actions required to fasten them onto appropriate parts of a gentleman's anatomy.

Quirkstandard felt a thrill pass through him as he saw, for the second time that morning, the value of useful and practical knowledge. No amount of Latin or Classics could ever help a gentleman to look dapper and respectable, but this, this wisdom that Snatchby had shared with Flirtwater and the others ... oh, that was the real business of education.

After spending the hour following elevenses with Snatchby, Quirkstandard relaxed into one of Mauve's famous lilac sofas. He felt better now with his digestive juices bubbling away (although he swore they were still squeaking a touch more than was ideal), and he felt the future was open before him, especially now that he had instructions on where he was likely to find his clothes. After all, there is only so much a gentleman can do in a dressing gown.

'You see,' he said to his friend Spiggot who was dozing on the floor beside the sofa, 'What a chap could really do with is a first rate proper education to prepare him, as it were, for the vicissitudes ... is that a word? ... for the vicissitudes (we'll assume it is, I think – it has a nice ring to it) of life. Without an education,' he concluded, 'one is required to rely on other people for everything, to do and to think, and at the end of the day, don't you think, Spiggot old chum, in the long run as it were ...' (Spiggot's ears jerked up at the word 'run' and he raised his head and yawned eagerly) '... well, what I mean to say is, other people simply aren't one, are they?'

Spiggot nodded in agreement, turned round, licked himself and then cocked his little leg against the corner of the sofa.

As he and Quirkstandard left the Reading Room the familiar distant clank of a mop and bucket approached slowly through Mauve's labyrinthine corridors.

Quirkstandard spent the evening, once he'd returned home, rummaging through the wardrobe he found behind a door in his dressing room, which, as it happened, was just off his bedroom, exactly where Snatchby had suggested. He examined row upon row of shirts, trousers, jackets, cravats, ties, long johns, underwear, bodices, girdles, socks, shoes, spatses, cummerbunds, waistcoats, vests and a variety of items he could give neither a name nor a use to. There were drawers filled with cufflinks and tiepins and novelty pocket watches, that he could only assume belonged to him. He had never dreamed he would be faced with such choice. He wasn't one of these dandies who're always playing about with their costumes and hairstyles, who read the fashion magazines day in and day out with one eye on next week's trend and the other on the competition. No, he'd prided himself on having little vanity and little interest in much besides the serious things in life, such as dinner, billiards and literature (which isn't to say that Quirkstandard read books, as such, but he did enjoy flicking through the reviews of books in one of the free newspapers he found lying around at Mauve's – the world felt a good place with books in it, and he always liked the smell of his father's library, which was the only room in the house, besides the kitchen, which remained even vaguely warm in the winter).

Passing his eye along the hangers and shelves and neatly folded piles that lay inside this large wardrobe was startling. Normally his man would simply place the day's clothes at the foot of his bed and help him into them after his bath and that would be the process of dressing dealt with for another day (unless he was visiting some-where that required the same thing to be done again just before dinner, that is). But now, faced with making the decisions himself, he felt daunted.

Some of the clothes hanging in the half-light had been his father's. He recognised the feel of the tweed, and he knew they had hung there untouched for years. As he ran his hand over them, with a touch of awe, he breathed in the memory-jogging scent of camphor.

Balustrade Quirkstandard, Second Earl of Wainscot-ing, had been born into a remarkably wealthy family. His father (Epitome's grandfather), Old Man Quirkstandard, the First Earl, had been a frugal but uncaring miser. It was rumoured that he had only ever parted with money freely on two occasions in his life. The first was on the day of his marriage. So pleased was he, the legend ran, with his beautiful young bride that he actually gave her a tip: a shiny threepenny bit. Many years later, at her funeral, so moved was he by the service that, when he thanked the vicar afterwards, he palmed a well-scrubbed ha'penny into his hand.

When asked about the truth of this legend Old Man Quirkstandard would pause, sigh and be heard to say, 'It was love, sir, love that made a man so impulsive.'

Within years of his wife passing away he opted to retire from both public and private life and the running of the family finances passed into the hands of his eldest and only son, Balustrade. Within six months the younger Quirkstandard had managed to lose the lot.

One Sunday afternoon he had ventured out across Regent's Park for his usual post-prandial stroll. He left the house one of the wealthiest young men in London and returned to it an hour and a half later a penniless soul. Even as he placed his hand on the doorknob a nagging doubt settled on his mind: he couldn't remember where he had put the family fortune.

As he opened the door and entered the front hall the doubt grew and he checked the hall table to see if he'd left it there. Of course he hadn't, and after checking every drawer in the house, behind every cupboard and between the cushions of the many sofas, settees and armchairs in the sitting rooms and bedrooms he reached the conclusion that he was an utter idiot and that he had, without doubt and quite possibly with irrevocable consequences, simply lost it.

He waited several months before telling anyone, just in case it turned up. But it didn't.

He was scared to admit his incompetence to his father, even by means of a séance, and he knew there was only one course of action open to him by which he might recoup his losses.

In the summer of 1890, Balustrade Quirkstandard got married.

He married Sarah Penultimate, one of the beautiful young heiresses to the Penultimate Aglet Fortune. Fortunately he had been engaged to her for a year prior to misplacing his own fortune, and so by the thinnest scrape of good luck he was able to pay off the butcher, the baker and the other clamouring tradesmen without anyone knowing quite how hopeless he had been.

Epitome Quirkstandard remembered his mother with some affection. She had always been so friendly whenever they had met and he knew that she had always insisted in the sternest terms that his Nanny dress him appropriately for the weather. There had even been a photograph of her in his nursery which he would think of in the darkness after he'd been tucked up and read to and kissed goodnight by that same marvellous Nanny.

Her hands had always smelt of carbolic soap, but he had loved her anyway.

Still looking into the wardrobe he realised it had grown late. He laid a selection of clothes out on the chair for the morning and, by the shaft of moonlight which blazed through the uncurtained window, he read once more the piece of card that Snatchby had given him. Were he actually serious about this education business, Snatchby had said (Quirkstandard had mentioned it to him in a flurry of excitement just after he'd mentioned it to Spiggot), then he, Snatchby, knew of just the establishment and just the gentleman who might be able to help.

Sat up in bed he read the card a final time before becoming sleepy and slipping into dreams where his dashing, handsome self, armed with self-confidence and a boundless natural intelligence, strolled with a firm and implacable swagger around Town. He almost always slept soundly.

The bed had belonged to his father years before who had rarely slept well in it, and certainly not in those last few cashless months before marriage. After the marriage he moved up to a bigger bed that he shared with

Lady Quirkstandard, and if he had sleepless nights there the reasons were usually quite different.

When, in that larger bed, he woke in a sweat and fright over the family fortunes (maybe from a dream in which he strolled around Town with a swagger and natural intelligence but no trousers and with the ghost of his father asking to borrow a fiver until next April), he could just roll over and look at the peacefully slumbering form of Sarah Penultimate-Quirkstandard and know that there lay the ravishing embodiment of a great big allowance (paid bi-annually), and this all by itself, was quite enough to stop him fretting further.

It was also in this larger bed that, shortly after their marriage, it is assumed that Epitome Quirkstandard was conceived, though in the way of newlyweds of the late nineteenth century it could very well have been almost any upstairs room of the house, or several noted knotted clumps of woodland within walking distance of their front door, or in that small passage between the kitchen and the scullery.

It was while Sarah Penultimate-Quirkstandard was pregnant with Epitome that she heard Balustrade Quirkstandard give a startled yelp one morning in the midst of their shared pre-natal exercises.

'What is it my dear?' she asked.

'My fortune,' he replied, stubbing out his cigar, 'It seems to be under the escritoire.'

And so Epitome was born, two weeks later, in the spring of 1891, into a family blessed with a lasting love and two quite large funds of money. He gurgled as contentedly then in his brand new cot with his Nanny gazing dotingly into his big blue eyes as he slept soundly now in his own old bed after his long and exciting day of discoveries at Mauve's.

2

Shops, Pavements & Strange Men

The next morning Epitome sprang out of bed with a new-born enthusiasm, splashed some cold water on his face (from the hot tap, but the boiler had run out of fuel in the night), rubbed it with a towel and stepped into his dressing room in order to dress. He looked at the clothes that he had carefully laid out the night before and laughed. His Aunt would be so proud, he imagined, to think that he had become so self-sufficient so quickly.

He pulled on a snug pair of long johns and a white vest, above which he buttoned a cool green checked shirt. A pair of navy blue plus fours were tugged up over his underwear and he buttoned the fly up at the front and slid his arms into the warm embrace of a brown hound's-tooth riding jacket and his feet into a soft warm pair of worn and comfortable russet-shaded carpet slippers. He failed to tie his tie but tucked it instead into his breast pocket, hoping he'd meet someone later on in the day who might be able to help out.

Picking up a walking stick and putting his father's deerstalker (what better to go and track down an education in?) on his head he closed the front door and strode once more in the direction of Town, feeling, this time, exactly like a proper gent.

The first thing he did was head to Mauve's for a spot of breakfast, followed by a rustle of the newspapers, a quick spell in the billiards room and then a bite of lunch, immediately after which he had a tiny smattering of dessert, followed by, since there weren't as many gentlemen in the Club that day as expected, seconds. After this busy morning and feeling significantly fuller than he had felt for literally hours, he decided to be firm with himself and to prevaricate no longer, to not draw things out, to neither avoid nor dodge the point or issue, because, frankly, the time had come, and there was no denying it, for which and with which and into which it could no longer be put off or avoided, however challenging it seemed, to embrace, enwrap and enter his future. He pulled out Snatchby's bit of card, drew a deep breath and grabbed a final brace of sandwiches before gathering up his hat and his stick and striking out into the streets of London in search of, well, an education.

Within half an hour he stood outside the premises in Charing Cross Road that Snatchby had recommended to him. He compared the name on the piece of card he had in his hand with the copperplate wording of the signage above the shop's windows and confirmed that they were the same – *Crepuscular & Sons: Educators To The World*.

For a moment he wondered what to do next and then reached out for the door handle. It didn't budge, neither the handle nor the door to which it was attached. He tried turning it both this way and that, as well as pushing and pulling, but it seemed, upon reflection, that the door was probably locked. Maybe, Quirkstandard thought, there's another entrance around here somewhere? He looked around.

To the right of *Crepuscular & Sons* was a very busy doorway leading into, what a sign announced to be, *The Café Coffee Shop & Cafeteria*. As he inhaled the scent of coffee, late afternoon breakfast and buttered buns, his stomach gurgled in sympathy (noticing the tiniest of corners which hadn't been filled at Mauve's and which were feeling left out), but he turned away from it, his mind overruling his body's mere physical desires. Oh, he thought, high-minded and more than little proud, I've reached a turning point in my life, which has hitherto been wasted in the vapid pursuit of billiards and the next hot meal or cold snack; no, I am a new man seeking new things and if that means missing an extra meal or two along the way, then stoic I shall be in the face of whatnot. It was quite the longest thought Quirkstandard could remember having had for years, and even if it trailed off a bit at the end and meandered a little in the middle, well, he still felt more than a little impressed with himself.

To the other side of *Crepuscular & Sons* was a shop whose sign read *The Charing Cross Woad Shop*. Once or twice a minute the tinkling doorbell tinkled as someone entered or exited the shop, and delivery boys on push-bikes came and went with bottles wrapped up in brown paper and string thunking dully in their baskets. It didn't seem to be quite so popular a shop as *The Café Coffee Shop*, but it still had a steady stream of customers and wobbling bicycles. It was only *Crepuscular & Sons* that seemed to maintain a steady business of nobody at all.

Quirkstandard returned his attention to the door handle. He wondered whether maybe he hadn't quite got the grip of it right the first time and gave it another few experimental twists. Nothing at all budged except for one trickle of sweat that appeared on his forehead. It was, after all, the summer and he probably hadn't actually needed to put the long johns on.

When dressing he had forgotten to pack a handkerchief in his pocket and so he wiped away this little dribble with a fingertip which he then turned his gaze upon. He had never really examined his own sweat before (nor that of any one else). Indeed the number of things he could remember studying in any depth at all could very well be counted on the fingers of one hand, and the hand wouldn't even have needed to have escaped minor industrial injury over the years. Curiosity was not his middle name.[3]

He held his finger up in the sunlight and marvelled as London reflected back at him from the glistening bead of sweat poised on its tip. As the light played across his retina, splashing electricity through his brain in miniscule but useful amounts, he was overcome by a bright wave of beauty. His knees wavered a bit and he felt giddy. Perhaps he should have sat down at this point, but he was entranced by the rapture of this close and deep aesthetic experience: the rainbow reflections of the world around him, held up on his fingertip as if he were a magician. But wrapped up in the aesthetics were a bundle of other questions of a more empirical nature: What is it, he wondered, that makes this bead of sweat glister so? (Indeed,

---

[3] It was Nebulous.

what is it that makes this bead of sweat?) From whence does this tiny rainbow vision arise? What makes London revolve so? These quasi-romantico-scientific thoughts (couched in just the language that Quirkstandard felt was appropriate but which was, almost certainly, unnecessarily florid) crept through un- and underused pathways in his brain, physically connecting axons and dendrites that had been strangers for years by sending snapping sparks across dusty synapses. Thoughts collected, stared at each other, sent out new thoughts and basked in the attention the brain they resided in was paying them for once and then Epitome Quirkstandard fainted.

Fortunately for him he fell onto the pavement and not into the street where a passing motor vehicle could have caused him serious injury. The only dangers he faced on the pavement were being trod on by passers-by, bitten by rats or territorially marked by passing dogs, but it seemed as if his luck was with him this morning as very few of these occurrences happened. The major immediate upshot was a distinguished bruise on his forehead which he must have gained either on the way down to the ground or immediately upon arrival there. In all other ways he was almost entirely unharmed.

Shortly after he came to he opened his eyes, and there, looming above him, was the face of a man he had never seen before in his life.

He shut his eyes.

He wondered where he was and tried to investigate what he could remember.

19

He remembered that he'd gone somewhere, and then he hit an impasse. It was a start though, wasn't it?

He tried to focus on where he was now.

He seemed to be lying on a table. Well, it seemed to be a table. It certainly wasn't a bed, divan or sofa: it wasn't soft for one thing and for a second thing he didn't have a blanket draped over him. So it had to be a table; you never had blankets on tables. Except for those tables that had tablecloths on: they were like thin blankets weren't they? Or more like sheets, he corrected himself. But is a blanket not just a thin sheet? He didn't know, and couldn't think who to ask. Oh, so maybe it's not a table? It wasn't a floor though. He could tell that because not only did he have an unaccountable sensation of altitude but the fingers of one of his hands twirled in the air off the edge of whatever surface was supporting him. So either he was lying on a table, without a tablecloth, or he was lying at the top of a flight of stairs.

He opened his eyes again. Still that other face looked down at him.

'You're awake then?' asked the voice of the face.

'Um, yes,' Quirkstandard managed to squeak. He was somewhat surprised when his answer came out an octave or two higher than he had expected.

'Good.'

'Um, yes,' Quirkstandard repeated, trying to get his voice down to more recognisable heights.

Pause.

'I was beginning to think you might've been a goner, mate,' said the face. 'We were gonna have to decide what to do with you.'

'Um, yes?' Quirkstandard said, cursing himself as his voice regained the falsetto through fear: he couldn't help but note a note of menace in his interlocutor's tone.

'That's a very high voice you've got there, I mean for a man of your build. D'you always speak like that?'

'Um, yes … I mean no,' ventured Quirkstandard, forcing his voice down lower than was natural in an effort to find some normality.

'Ye-e-es,' said his inquisitor with deliciously worried slowness.

The fellow drew the word out over several seconds for three reasons. Firstly he wanted to intimate his incredulity; secondly he wanted to create a bit of thinking time as he worked out whether the chap on the kitchen table was dangerous or not; and thirdly he rather liked the sound of his own voice.[4]

The man to whom the voice belonged was Rodney Crepuscular, one of the sons mentioned in the shop's name. His brother, Simon, had found the slumped and unconscious Quirkstandard propped up against their

[4] It was, to be fair, a nice voice. Smooth, rich and with just a hint of fruit hidden beneath the surface. He had spent some time modelling it in front of the bathroom mirror on two of his favourite music hall artistes, Big Tim Titch the French Hairdresser and Fritz Schmidt the Lancashire Prankster. Everyone said it was a nice voice, but it was most appreciated by his wife who had fallen deeply in love with it when she'd been woken up at three o'clock in the morning once by its shouting of drunken endearments underneath her mother's balcony. Her mother had, with a tired look tangled up in her curlers and dressing gown, asked her to do something about her gentleman friend and marriage had seemed the easiest way to smooth over the problem.

door when he came to open up again after a late long lunch and with the help of his father, who lived above the shop, had carried the somnolent gentleman through into the backroom-cum-kitchen, where he had, indeed, been laid on a table. Simon had then gone back out to buy some milk, while his father had returned upstairs to continue with his writing and Rodney had been left in charge of Quirkstandard's wellbeing.

While he had been unconscious in the street Quirk-standard had been remarkably lucky. Not only was he not beaten up, kidnapped or trodden on, but the only theft that had happened, in a city where cutpurses and handkerchief thieves were still persistent problems, had been to a small portion of his moustache. But since it had been getting a bit bushy this really wasn't any great loss. His deerstalker hat was gone too. Still, also and as well, he would think when he noticed it, no great loss.

Quirkstandard sat up.

Rodney took a step backwards.

Quirkstandard wobbled a bit and felt the blood rushing around his body and up to his head where it set in to aching. He lifted a hand to where it hurt most.

'Is this a lump?' he asked, in more or less his normal speaking tone. 'The old noggin feels a bit bigger here than there ... and it hurts. Ow. Crikey.'

'It's purple,' offered Crepuscular.

Quirkstandard thought for a moment as he prodded gently at the bruised area. He jokingly imagined it might blend in nicely with the sofas at Mauve's. He'd seen some of the younger chaps go so far as to buy scarves and gloves of various purplish hues in order to do just this, but this usually only led to swearing as they put their items down and then never found them again, so subtle and succinct was the camouflage effect. A bruised head, on the other hand (or on the other head, he corrected himself, ha-ha!) had at least one advantage over a glove: no matter where he rested it, he'd always be able to find it again, since it was attached, well, to his shoulders.

'It might blend in nicely with the sofas at Mauve's,' he said.

Rodney Crepuscular stared at him blankly. He was still trying to decide, from the little information he was gathering, whether his brother had dragged a lunatic or a gentleman in from the street. The way he was dressed he could easily have been either, and though his accent certainly sounded sophisticated Rodney had heard tell of plenty of upper class imbeciles wandering the streets after having murdered their families and staff simply because the crumpets weren't buttered just how they liked them. His mind was not yet at ease.

'It's my Club,' Quirkstandard said, seeing the blank face of his saviour and assuming he simply awaited elucidation. 'Well, when I say it's *my* Club, obviously I don't mean I own it or anything. In fact I'm not sure who does own it really or what it's all about or where it comes from or what it does or has done, frankly. Um, what I mean to say when I say it's *my* Club is that I occasionally have a drink there most days and sometimes a spot of luncheon or dinner ... or both ... and there are free newspapers ...' He was getting into the flow of this now, having steered the conversation, and indeed his mind, back onto a piece of turf he felt he knew something about, even if that something was not an awful lot as he was beginning to realise, and he continued, utterly ignoring or not noticing the look that had crossed Rodney Crepuscular's face, '... and I meet with other gentlemen there, of course, old Harris Flirtwater and Spiggot of course, and so on. Some of them I went to school with, you know, and it's so nice to keep in touch and find out what they're up to these days. Stiffy Tipminster, for example, is something biggish in the army, and old Fiddling Gingerfield has become an anarchist in the British Library ... I mean, none of us ever expected him to get a proper job like that, not old Fiddling, I mean, really!'

'An anarchist?'

'Yes, he spends all day scurrying around the bookshelves stacking things away and making little index cards and indexes and the like. Inky fingers, you see? He comes into the Club of an evening sometimes and talks about it for hours over billiards. I only ever really understood just about the gist of the thing, but he seems to enjoy it and really, that's what's so important in life, don't you think?'

'An anarchist?'

'Oh, yes. Loves it. I don't remember seeing you there though? Maybe you're a member of a different Club. I know some of the chaps belong to a few, but that always seemed a bit of a dud effort to me – I mean if you want to chat to them, they need to check their diaries to make sure they don't have to be somewhere else! I only belong to the one. It was my father's idea, he'd also been a Mauve's chap, I think, and well, I found, when I finished school, that there was a card waiting for me in the hall saying that I was invited to be a member and so, there you go, I've just been there, ipso facto as it were, ever since. Although I do go home, too, of course ... I don't want you to think ...'

'Prolix, ain't you?' interrupted Rodney just before Quirkstandard meandered to a halt of his own accord. He looked at his watch wearily.

'Er, Epitome, actually, Epitome Quirkstandard. Prolix was my great uncle. Maybe you're confusing us. Did you ever meet him? Although now I think about it he wasn't actually all that great. A bit of an ineffectual old duffer really, so they said, killed by a clematis as I recall ...' Quirkstandard paused as if struggling to remember something, 'a tragedy ...'

'Why, was he young?'

'Oh no, he was eighty-seven when he died, but he was a playwright. His most famous work, *The Black Eye Of Albert Hugginsbottom*, was a tragedy, that's what I meant.'

'It sounds pretty tragic. Does everyone die at the end?'

'Well, no, the play was actually a comedy, about a very short man who lived up to his name. The tragedy was it made its way to the stage at all. Wasn't a success, you see? Queen Victoria, she was the queen at the time, sent a telegram the very next morning declaring herself to be ... oh, what was the phrase she used ...? "Unenchanted" by the play. It had to be withdrawn after just two performances and great uncle Prolix was shamed. I hadn't been born at the time, you understand, but I heard about it all later on. Occasionally as a boy I'd be taken to a party and great uncle Prolix would be sat in his Bath chair at one side of the room, squeezing his little rubber duck, and splashing a little, while everyone else would sit on the other side of the room and whisper about him. It was all most pointless, like most family feuds I imagine, since he was practically deaf anyway. Until her dying day Queen Victoria snubbed him and she hasn't spoken to a Quirkstandard since, but I never really worry about that since garden parties can be so dull, don't you think?'

'Oh,' said Rodney, trying to wrestle the conversation back to something he understood or cared about. 'I'm not a member of any Club like that, but I do go along to the Charing Cross Road (& Area) Toad Fanciers' Group. It's kind of an informal club, you know? We meet twice a month in the Methodist Hall and compare toads we like. Sometimes someone fancies a frog, but like your Victoria woman, if they do, we snub them.'

Quirkstandard nodded at this and felt the room begin to spin. He decided to lie down once more.

'I'm going to lie down now,' he said, just before he passed out again.

'Fine, I'm going to have a sandwich,' said Rodney.

3

Sequins, Dreams & The Circus

The Crepuscular whose name was inscribed above the shop window and who was father to Rodney and his brother had been given at birth the rather unexpected name of Simone. Perhaps his mother had wanted a girl, or maybe the midwife had made a mistake when she opened her mouth intending to say the words, 'Mrs Crepuscular, you have a son,' or perhaps the vicar got confused when he was stood at the font ... Whatever had occurred, the fact of the matter was that Simone's mother dressed him in dresses and frilly lacy items up until his twelfth birthday, which was, the neighbours all agreed, a little later than was usual. He'd also been encouraged to help out with all the cooking, which was, perhaps, better than sweeping other people's chimneys or opening little doors to control the airflow through a coalmine, but was still, on the whole, hardly manly.

In the mornings, however, he was sent to the local village school. Whether it was to learn things or whether it was to help the local schoolmarm, with a view to taking over the job in years to come, Simone never discovered, since as soon as he was out of sight of his mother's kitchen window he'd skip off in the opposite direction. If the sun was warm he'd wander along to the local brook and the little bit of woodland that backed onto the farmland and, with a rod and a piece of string, he would annoy small animals. Sometimes he'd lie down in the sunshine, rest his forearm over his eyes to provide some shade and have a doze, since he'd been up at four o'clock baking bread and getting the hot water steaming for his father's wash basin.

Whatever he decided to do, he would, as soon as he reached the little stream, strip off his dress and his bloomers and hang them over a branch out of harm's way, to keep them clean and dry. Over years of missing school he created quite a cosy little den for himself, hidden there among the trees, with a riverside view, and he furnished it with a little lamp and a stool with a fitted umbrella which he could huddle under if it rained and get on with his embroidery ... and his daydreaming.

He daydreamed about The Circus. Always about The Circus. He had only ever visited a circus once in his life but that visit had left memorable marks in his mind. On that one special evening he had become so excited by the spectacle, so delighted, excited and overwrought by the experience that he had embarrassed both his parents by pulling off his dress, leaping over the barrier and running round and around the sawdust ring, singing and laughing and bouncing about at the top of his voice and his legs. Only a deft rugby tackle by a swift-thinking clown managed to restrain the boy. His parents had to collect him after the show from the ringmaster's office, since they were too ashamed to own up to owning him while the rest of the audience were still present. As it happened, the ringmaster wasn't all that put out and

offered what he claimed was a fair price to hire tl
out for the summer season, but Simone's parents
diately refused the offer on principle. The principles in
question being (a) surprise that the suggested price was
so miserly and (b) shock that the ringmaster was unwilling to haggle.

So, in his little den young Simone would close his
eyes and find himself transported to a big top filled with
clowns and elephants and girls in sequined leotards swinging back and forth high over everyone's heads and men
with enormous moustaches, muscles and dumbbells and
tiny little leopard-skin off-the-shoulder outfits. There
were seals in his imaginary circus who would flollop
their way across the sawdust up onto a plinth where they
would play God Save The Queen by squeezing the bulbs
of a series of horns. Lions would jump lazily through
flaming hoops, jugglers would dazzle and amaze with
their displays of virtuosity and their glittery balls, and
it would have taken a dozen white horses with feathery
headdresses to drag him away from the dreams he had of
a dozen white horses with feathery headdresses.

In 1862 Simone Crepuscular turned twelve and his
father, who had maybe wanted a son after all, slipped
a pair of trousers inside his birthday card. He pointed
at them and grunted something embarrassed in a kind,
fatherly manner, coughed, made vague buttoning
motions in the vicinity of his waist, muttered, 'Don't tell
your mother,' and went off to work. Simone was left to
attempt to put the things on all by himself. He tried them
first one way round and then the other. Neither way felt
right. It was all so ... well ... restrictive, he thought. But

at the same time he did feel a little tingle of normalness ripple up through him. Finally, he was a man.

The moment had come for him to run away from home, and from his mother in particular.

He packed his meagre possessions into a large hand-kerchief and his luxurious possessions into a rucksack and ran out the back door. He tripped as his trousers flopped to his ankles and tumbled headfirst down the steps, but he picked himself up quickly, the adrenalin coursing through his body, having bruised nothing but his pride and his head. After having another go at fasten-ing the buttons of his brand new flies he ran off down the narrow cobbled street in the direction of the village green.

As soon as he had made his way round the duck pond he saw that his intuition had been right. The green was covered with tents and mechanical apparatus. He stood under the eaves of the village tree and watched the burly men milling around in their shirt sleeves with grease and sweat wrinkling on their foreheads, smoking cigarettes and talking loudly and laughing carelessly. Occasionally a lady would pass by, walking across the green with a small puppy or dog on a lead, and she'd shout something crude at the men and make a sign with her free hand, at which point they'd quieten down and look a bit shy and embarrassed, being good chaps on the whole.

Simone became more and more sure, the longer he watched, that this was the life for him: this was what he wanted to do and to be. The cigarettes, the leaning, the whole 'having friends' business all seemed mightily attractive, if only in its novelty. So, he mustered up the courage to approach the most impressively moustachioed and extravagantly uniformed man around and followed him as he slipped into a big red tent, in the first chamber of which stood a large mahogany desk.

The impressive moustache began to examine some papers on the desk, his back to the entrance, and it was a minute or two before Simone summoned enough courage to announce his presence with a miniature cough.

'Excuse me, sir?' he added, meekly.

'What? Eh, excuse? Eh, what what?' sputtered the surprised gentleman, straightening his back and spinning round on his heel.

'Excuse me sir, I'd like to join up,' whispered Simone in a sheepish tone.

'Join up, eh? Eh? What?' replied the man, rebuttoning the buttons he'd unbuttoned upon entering the tent. 'This is most irregular, what? Do you have references, eh? A medical examination? What, eh? Most irregular indeed. Eh? What? What!? What, if I may entertain the idea for a moment, what is it you think you can do? Eh?'

'I want to …' Crepuscular paused, suddenly feeling a touch foolish. Young, shy, foolish and entirely out of his depth.

'Come on, eh? Out with it … boy? Come on, what?' blustered the big moustache with no let up.

'I'd like to …' Crepuscular's nerve failed him once more. What he had wanted to say, more than anything, was that he had longed all his life to fly on the highest trapeze, far above the crowds, high above the eyes and hats and sniggers of adoring audiences, freed from the ties of people's expectations and the reach of their long umbrellas. What he wanted to say was that he longed to be like one of the birds of the air, like an eagle, soaring, soaring proud and solitary through the high thin air, but at the same time that he desired, he longed to find a warm, secure place deep in the bosom of the heart of a loving circus family, because he believed that there was a bond of friendship and love holding together the very kernel of the heart of every circus.[5] He wanted to belong somewhere for himself, to be loved for himself, for who he was and not for some myth of gender-determined identity imposed upon him by a loving but misguided mother.

But he said none of this out loud, not his dreams, not his daydreams or his ambitions.

Seeing the gleaming buttons on the big moustache's bright uniform's chest he had a sudden flash: an image of himself in years to come in baggy tights. His sequins, badly sewn on, flapping loose on his chest. His leotard flicking desultorily under his arms in the breath of some passing breeze. Looking up he imagined he was stood at the foot of an immense ladder that stretched forever above him. He could hear the cold drip of grease falling from rung to rung, descending towards him, drip by drip down the years, and he knew that as soon as he reached out for that ladder he would climb, slip and fall, and that he would do it again and again. It seemed unshakeably inevitable. He couldn't share his dream with this marvellously uniformed stranger, with his giant, curling and

[5] Naturally, he was wrong.

officious moustache. All he saw was this little boy's face reflected back from a myriad of highly polished brass buttons.

'I'd like to help out,' was all he said, not denying his dreams entirely.

'Help out, eh? Very well, what? This is, you understand, most irregular though? Eh? What? But, I say, a boy with your sense of duty mustn't just be turned away, what? Eh? It would be a crime, a dereliction of my duty, eh? Normally I don't stand for folks marching into my tent and just demanding things, but you boy, eh?, I can see are just full of spunk and duty, what? Eh? We need boys like you? New blood, eh? But there are correct channels and offices, what, eh? Proper ways of doing these things, eh? But ... well, I do happen to have the appropriate paperwork here, look, so ... You can read, yes, what, eh?'

'A little, sir,' Simone lied.

'Well, that's all right, it's mostly small print anyway, what? Eh? You are sixteen, eh? Just say yes and sign here ...'

He handed Simone a pen, showed him where to place his signature and as soon as the cross was in place at the foot of the form he called for the Captain to come through. The Captain very kindly led Simone out of the Major's tent and showed him to the men's billets where he was given a bunk, a uniform, a handbook of military regulations and a lukewarm welcome. The very next morning the whole camp was packed up and posted to India. Simone Crepuscular had his first experience of the utter wretchedness of sea travel and swore to himself that if he ever survived this experience he would search in future for a circus that only travelled by land, or even better one that just stood still and let the people come to it.

So overwhelmed was he by the new and exciting world he had entered of peeling potatoes and polishing belt-buckles that it was nearly six months before he discovered he had joined the Army and this only occurred when he wondered out loud one day just when the girls with sequins would be arriving. One of his colleagues sat him down and read to him the contract he had signed by mistake and it was then that Simone learnt that he was indentured into the forces for a minimum tour of service of twenty-one years, with no time off for good behaviour.

'But there *are* elephants,' he said meekly, thinking it might make a difference, as he pointed out of the barracks window at India.

4

Moonlight & Pamphlets

When Epitome Quirkstandard opened his eyes he found that he was no longer lying on the table and there was no longer any light coming in through the window. Even in the darkness it only took him a moment to discover that he was now lying face down on the floor. The flagstones were cold under his new black eye. He must've rolled over in his sleep, he thought as he stumbled to his feet, that must surely have been it. It was a sensible conclusion to have reached based upon the evidence to hand and he felt a small curl of happiness at having reached it so swiftly.

He found his way, yawning and aching, to a chair and he sat down.

The night was quiet around him and the building was silent. A floorboard in the room above didn't squeak eerily and the drainpipe didn't rattle to itself in the wind outside the window. It was clearly quite late, Quirkstandard thought. He had arrived at the shop in the early afternoon and the natural assumption was that he hadn't gone far in the intervening time. Out the window he could see a small square paved yard, lit by a few stars and overhung by grey clouds that turned silvery each time they exposed the fat full moon.

In the distance he heard a faint tinkling. Listening close he counted two strikes. Two in the morning then. He liked London: there was something frightfully comforting in the sound of Little Ben in the long dark of the middle night.[6] He thought back to the many nights when he'd lain half-awake (or half-asleep, depending on whether he was feeling optimistic or pessimistic that night) on one of the guest beds at Mauve's after having eaten too hearty a meal or having drunk a tipple or two of port, and how the pale lavender curtains would waft in the summer breeze. Often he would sigh loudly with pleasure at the simplicity and quality of his life: a faint tinkle, a cool waft and what more could a gentleman possibly want? Often when he sighed particularly deeply he would receive a firm prod in the back from the gentleman in the bunk beneath his, who clearly wasn't feeling quite so contented with the world, but this was, Quirkstandard told himself, a small price to pay.

On a hook near the stove he found a cloth, which he held up to his bloodied nose and stepped through the door into the front room of the shop. He called out a speculative greeting, although not very loudly, it being so late, and received no reply. This time a floorboard did creak upstairs, but it was only the house settling and no further noise followed. It seemed he had been forgotten or abandoned and when he tried the handle of the front door he found it was firmly locked.

---

[6] Little Ben being the smaller of the bells held in the clock tower of the Houses Of Parliament, traditionally struck between 11pm and 6am so as not to annoy the neighbours quite so much.

Perhaps he might find a way out through the back door? But just as he was about to turn and head back to the kitchen to try it, a stray beam of moonlight rushed through the shop window and dimly lit the room. He noticed for the first time what it was the shop seemed to be stocked with. All along each wall were row after row after stack after shelf after pile after heap of bits of paper. Picking one up at random he saw that they seemed to be pamphlets of some sort.

He moved to the doorway where the moonlight was brightest and read the cover: *The Birds Of Hyde Park & South-East Iceland: An Enthusiast's Guide*. Inside it were sketches and descriptions of just what it had said, the birds of Hyde Park etc. Quirkstandard had visited Hyde Park a number of times (he had once spent a fortnight boating along the length of the Serpentine with his pals Harris Flirtwater and Nigel Spiggot) and naturally he recognised some of the waterfowl: there was a crested grebe called Walter who was well known to everyone, but then there were a number of others Quirkstandard thought he had only ever caught glimpses of. He read on and learnt more (although he wasn't quite sure where Iceland was). The pamphlet contained tips on the best ways to spot and identify different birds, on their feeding and breeding habits, annotations of their songs and calls, pictures from a variety of angles and a short snatch of history, both about the avian species in question and of the locales described.

By the time Dawn arrived Quirkstandard had read – *Fastenings Of All Description & Colorations, The Goodness Of Bread & Other French Cheeses*, and *A History Of The English-Speaking Porpoise*. Just as he finished this last one there was a rattle in the lock of the door and a small woman walked in with an enormous nose and a broom.

'Golly, um, good morning,' offered Quirkstandard civilly, if a trifle flustered.

'Good morning yourself,' she offered back without the least surprise.

'Er, I'm Quirkstandard,' said Quirkstandard.

'And I'm Dawn,' said Dawn.

'Very pleased to meet you.'

'Yes, they told me they had a gentleman locked away in here. 'Man with a weak temperament,' they said, 'Having a lie down,' they said, 'You be kind to him, Miss Dawn,' they said. 'Well, I'll be kind,' I said, 'If he's been tidy,' I said. 'You be kind all the same,' they said, 'He might have money,' they said. 'He might have money,' I said, 'But if he doesn't have manners then what's all the money in the world worth?' I said. 'Money's worth money,' they said. 'And bad manners means more work for me,' I said. 'For which we pays you money,' they said. 'When you remembers,' I said. 'You be kind to him all the same,' they said. 'If he's been tidy,' I said.'

Quirkstandard had begun to feel a little left out of this conversation and raised his hand. Miss Dawn stopped and looked him up and down for the first time, as if she could somehow sense how tidy he was by just such a cursory examination.

He coughed.

'I've been quite tidy,' he offered.

She stared a little harder.

'You've dripped blood on my floor,' she said, a cold eye flickering beneath a raised eyebrow.

'Oh. Where? I did try not to drip. I held this cloth to my nose,' he held up the cloth which turned out, now that daylight had arrived, to be an apron embroidered with a comic inscription suggesting the reader propose marriage to the cook.

'There's blood on the floor, just beside the kitchen table.'

'Oh,' said Quirkstandard, crestfallen.

'And ...' she said, drawing the word out, 'you've messed up the pamphlets. They're not going to like that, you know. They're not going to like that at all.'

She sucked at the air between her teeth as she shook her head.

'I'm sorry,' he answered, 'but I was bored and woke up in the middle of the night, or vice versa or whichever the other way round is, and I just found them here. I thought at first they might help me drop back off to sleep, but they turned out to be the most rippingly marvellous things I've ever seen. I just had to go on reading and reading. Did you know there was a dolphin washed up in Lyme Regis which could speak English, apparently most of them can't, and this one was arrested as a Spanish spy, but the magistrate, who was a learned man ...'

'Yeah, I heard that,' Dawn interrupted, swinging her boom to and fro on her shoulder.

'Marvellous,' Quirkstandard repeated, clutching a pamphlet in his hand.

'Yeah, ain't they just,' she agreed with a knowing smile spreading beneath her expressive, fat pink nose.

As Dawn fried bacon in the back room, Quirkstandard splashed water on his face in the outhouse. He dabbed at the swellings and discolorations on his temple and round his eye. The contusions weren't as violent or as violet as he'd expected, in fact they were more or less a thick pale dirty yellow. The swellings weren't as tight and tense as they felt from inside either. As he prodded the bruises, pulses of warming warning sensation flashed into his nerve centres. It wasn't something you could actively call pain, he thought. It didn't really hurt when he pushed at them, though it did feel particularly nice when he stopped doing it.

He prodded again and stopped. Oh, that did feel good. He chuckled at this. He must've been bruised and banged at some point when he was a lad, he supposed, but he couldn't remember when it might've been. Had he never fallen out of a tree or been tackled unexpectedly at rugger? He didn't recall any tree climbing exploits, so maybe he had just read about boys in books who had, and rugger was about the only subject that he got a pass in since his man, who he sent to sit his exams, was much bigger than most of the other lads, which had proved to be an advantage. So any bruises gained in a rugger match wouldn't have been his own, so maybe he had led a spotless boyhood after all.

He went to prod the bruise on his temple once more but was interrupted by Dawn calling out from the kitchen to tell him breakfast was ready. He wiped his face with the towel and headed indoors.

There, on the same table on which he had spent part of the night, were four place settings complete with crockery and cups. On each plate rested what even Quirkstandard recognised hungrily as a fat and fatty bacon sandwich. His mouth moistened a little. In the middle of the table was a variety of condiments and beside three of the plates sat steaming mugs of tea.

'I didn't know what your sort drank,' said Dawn, seemingly to herself.

Quirkstandard assumed the question to be directed at him, since there was no one else in the room, and set about answering it as such.

'Normally, to be perfectly frank Miss Dawn, I tend to drink whatever I am given. You see, I've not always been told the names of things or I forget them, and so sometimes it is difficult to make specific requests and informed decisions. I must say, looking at those papers and whatnots in the front room this morning made me more aware than ever that I seem to have learnt spectacularly little in my life. Oh, they opened up to me whole new worlds. Did I tell you about this dolphin they found once? Crikey Quirkers, I said to myself last night, there are so many of these things, so many of these brilliant pamphlets. Oh, I suspect that were I to look I could find a pamphlet in there, somewhere in there, that would teach me the names and distinguishing features of a vast variety of different beverages from all around the world – England, Iceland and beyond. And if I read such a guide, Miss Dawn, then I could answer your question correctly. I'd be able to lean back and look inside myself and tell you just what it was that I wanted right now, or maybe … maybe I'd just know, instinctively and without a moment's pause for thought, exactly what sort of drink is ideal for accompanying a bacon sandwich such as that which is laid out here this morning. I would be able to smell a glass of something from across the room and name it, not just name it, Miss Dawn, but know, inside myself, do you see …? I'll know where and why and when and how it was purchased and made. No more will I be reliant on other people to make …' At this point Quirkstandard felt the need to stand up to make his point, but since he was already standing up he stepped onto a chair and raised a finger in the air, clasped one hand over his breast and cast a turbulent expression into the future. '… no more will I be reliant,' he repeated, 'On other people to make my decisions for me, for I shall make them for myself. In this wide open future I see, I shall have the ability and the capability to choose my own drink whenever I choose to choose. I shall be my own master in all arenas of life, no more tossed on the prongs of someone else's dilemma. No longer a plaything of the fates. My own man. Do you hear me?' he stared through the ceiling and his raised finger swelled into a clenched fist. 'This is my dream, Mistress Dawn, I shall be a free man striding wisely through the world, shrinking from nothing and knowing everything, deciding everything …'

'Tea then?' she asked, rhetorically.

'Er, yes, I suppose so. If that's what you think I ought to have? I'm sure it'll be lovely, thank you. Oh, and sorry about the chair,' he said as he climbed down. He felt a little embarrassed by his outburst. He couldn't say where it had come from, it had certainly caught him off guard. He'd blustered and gabbled before, going on about things he didn't understand at length merely because nobody had thought to shut him up, but this had felt different. He'd meant it somehow. It was obvious that the germ of the idea that had struck him two mornings before, at that abortive attempted breakfast, had now taken root and was beginning to poke out shoots. There could be no turning back.

As his foot touched the floorboards some slight applause reached his ears. Heartfelt applause, but thin due to the solitary nature of the clapper. In the doorway that linked the back room kitchen to the shop stood, although at this point Quirkstandard couldn't even guess at his name, Simone Crepuscular, the proprietor.

'A fine speech sir, a fine speech indeed. I envy your eloquence and your passion. It is a fine day, today, on which to meet a man not afraid of his dreams. I think,' he paused to scratch his ear, 'that we may well be able to make each other very happy.'

Quirkstandard blushed nervously and nodded.

5

India, Elephants & A Bacon Sandwich

✺

It wouldn't be exactly true to say that Simone Crepuscular hadn't enjoyed his time in the army, because as he grew up it turned out that he had the sort of disposition which could turn to sunshine the most unlikely circumstances (except sea travel), but all the same it would be true to say there were a few specific things about army life that even he could never come to love.

The early mornings were one thing, as were the queues for the bathroom. Using a rifle was another: it turned out that they were heavier than they looked and when fired they made most astonishing noise right next to one's ear. Often he had himself noted down in casualty lists after training with a thumping headache. And uniforms. He never quite came to terms with the uniform. But all these things were, in the end, entirely surmountable when he looked around at the little patch of earth his battalion was encamped on with its sunshine and its elephants and its odd looking trees. Aside from all the marching up and down it really wasn't such a bad place at all.

The first four or five years were filled mostly with scrubbing potatoes and washing tea-towels behind the mess, but then he was promoted to the position of Camp Clerk.

When he first heard about it he assumed it was (just) a practical joke, since he'd long become accustomed to his mates making fun of his 'accidental enlistment through distinct illiteracy': to put such a man in charge of the entire battalion's paperwork seemed just the sort of lark he'd come to expect. However, as it turned out, it was nothing of the sort.

The Major, in his wisdom, had noticed that the previous clerk had died of a fatal encounter with some wildlife and that, therefore, it followed that the position needed to be filled and rather pronto. Not being one to delegate the important jobs he set about reviewing the files of each man in each platoon in order to find the most suitable candidate, and very soon grew bored. After all he'd written most of what was in the files at each man's annual review and he knew that he always wrote the same thing, which since the files were private and never consulted by anyone other than himself was not, in the normal course of things a problem. Eventually he spread a handful of files out on his desk, closed his eyes and scientifically jabbed with his finger.

When he posted the announcement most of the men and officers felt very similar emotions to those that Crepuscular felt, but then they noticed that the Major wasn't smiling, or at least not in the way that suggested he'd made a joke. In light of this no one opted to disagree with the Major, especially since, after all, he was the Major and they weren't, and so the promotion went through just like any other promotion.

For the next few years all correspondence, dockets, chits, chitties, memoranda, forms, documents, accounts, bills and divers other extraneous bits of paperwork in his unit consisted solely of Simone's impressionistic imitative squiggles, patterns and crosses. From a distance and through a squint in the dark these could be mistaken for some sort of writing, but close up they soon became a meaningless tangle of complex enigmatic quasi-pseudo-hieroglyphs. Even the British Army's enemies' most highly trained and intuitive cryptographers, strategists and accountants, who routinely intercepted the secret military post as it passed through their sorting offices in Berlin, Paris, Moscow and Washington, could cast no light on the presumed meaning locked deep within.

Nevertheless wages in the battalion were still paid, supplies still arrived (since no orders to the contrary were ever sent home) and the weather was warm and bright, with a cool breeze that rolled down from the foothills in the early evening and the camp became an oasis of peace in an increasingly fraught world. No orders to combat were ever received. Or if they were received nothing was ever done about them since Crepuscular simply pretended to read incoming post and filed it as the whim took him, and since the officers didn't want to look as if they were interfering with the Camp Clerk's work, no one ever checked.

In time Simone found that he could fit a whole day's work into just a few hours in the morning, 'copying out' orders passed down to him from the Major, scribbling on a half dozen official forms and filing the post. He'd squiggle artistically on a couple of envelopes, pop a few bits of paperwork inside them and then drop the sealed missives into the mail sack which was collected twice weekly by the military postman.

His role as Camp Clerk freed Crepuscular from all the menial jobs he'd been doing and now, once he had finished just as much 'paperwork' as he felt was necessary for any given day, he'd leave his hut and go get on with things that he thought to be more pressing. For example, he'd often go down to the bank of the local river, much broader and browner than any he'd sat beside before, and he'd strip off his uniform and hang it over a nearby branch of just the right height. With the wind on his skin he felt a freedom pump through his veins and he'd watch the world pass by from a seat somewhere halfway up some enormous foreign tree.

The world did pass by, most assuredly, but it went by slowly in this part of India, just drifting along, without making any fuss, allowing itself to be picked up and examined and put down again with a gentle touch. He found in it a meditation and a comfort after all the hectic squiggling he'd spent the morning performing on bits of paper.

The local women who came down to the river to wash their clothes would giggle shyly and coyly wave up at the naked Englishman in the tree who sometimes, if his mind hadn't wandered off entirely, waved back.

Quirkstandard looked up at the man who stood in the kitchen doorway praising him.

The first thing he noticed was the fellow's bald pate which the morning light glinted off. It was a shiny dome, surrounded by a fine haze of unkempt hairs that provided a sort of corona or halo to his face. He next noticed the man's excessive white and grey beard. This started just above and behind his ears, trailed woollily down the sides of his face, circled his mouth and spread down, down over his broad chest, before fading away, first into wisps and finally into air, somewhere just above his navel.

From his navel Quirkstandard's eyes continued their downward plunge and he noticed, almost instantly, that the man he was meeting wasn't wearing a waistcoat. He also wasn't wearing a shirt, a jacket or trousers. Or a kilt or a skirt, Quirkstandard added mentally, or, come to that, long johns (though it was high summer and such things weren't entirely necessary, he admitted). The man opposite had a white piece of cloth somehow perched around his parts and nothing else at all.

Epitome Quirkstandard wasn't sure where to look and scratched his bruises for something to do.

The man stepped from the doorway and sat down at the head of the table. He picked up his bacon sandwich.

'That happened to me yesterday,' Quirkstandard finally said, still standing up. 'Oh, no, actually it was the day before yesterday now …' No one interrupted him, so he went on, 'I was thinking, for a moment, that today was yesterday but that's wrong of course. It's just that yesterday passed in rather a haze and this day and that one have sort of blurred into one. It's a little as if, I suppose, yesterday was a mistake and had been rubbed out and we've started afresh this morning all over again. You see, I didn't sleep very well last night and I don't seem to have eaten since lunchtime, until this young lady made me this sandwich, and three meals are what mark days as being days, don't you agree? And so this sandwich seems to be catching up the meal I missed yesterday evening, because I didn't have it then and so it sort of slips backwards to fill the gap and so the day before yesterday isn't yesterday at all, and I wonder if there's a special word for it? Like yesterday but, you know, sort of one more than yesterday?' He paused for a moment and looked around. 'I'll just be quiet now. Sorry.' He felt a little foolish because the man with the beard was staring at him intently. Quirkstandard couldn't tell what the look on that face meant, hidden behind his beard like a child peering over the edge of a big salt and pepper rug.

'No need to apologise, dear sir,' the man said in a kind voice. 'Life is a confusion, and sometimes it does the soul good of a morning to express it as such.'

'Oh,' said Quirkstandard who was learning a lot of new things already.

'You see, sometimes you'll find, my dear sir, that days and days go by without you noticing them pass at all, and then one day you turn around and it is already years later and you can see, you can almost touch something that happened to you so long ago, and it seems so easy, so near. They might be days of joys, they could be happy days that are now long gone, or they might be days of darkness, days of horror and darkness. It doesn't matter, because there are some days that will live with you forever and that you can't shake off, despite trying, and then concurrent with those are patches of time that seem to vanish, to evaporate, that seem to slip out of conscious recall. Days and times and years grow dim and grey, rarely thought of, rarely recalled. But things don't remain static, dear sir, never do they remain static and you never know, can never say whether today is a day or not on which you might not yet turn around and find a year has gone by, or maybe two, or maybe thirty years have passed by, and suddenly every moment is clear once again, every bead of moisture sparkles on your brow, every flower's perfume smells strong in your lungs, every vanishing cry rings brilliant and shocking in your ears ...'

Dawn coughed gently from the sink.

'Ah,' said the great beard, taking a deep breath, 'my early warning. Apparently I am becoming verbosely stentorian again. It is my turn to apologise, dear sir. Sorry.'

Quirkstandard sat feeling a little dazed by the whole experience. He had never been spoken to in quite such a way, or held by quite so electric an eye as he had just been held by. He hadn't followed much of what had just been said to him, he had become a little lost around the second conjunction (something about turning round), but the tone in which it had all been said was so authoritative, yet kind, yet intense, yet quiet, yet strong, yet soft ... filled with humanity and a clear case of caring for another human being. It had struck Quirkstandard as being bright and intelligent and he'd recognised something of his own yearning for learning in there. For a moment, in just a moment, he had discovered a fellow traveller, but one who was, clearly so much further down the road than he was.

'Eat up your breakfast you two, it's getting cold with all this yapping.'

'Most certainly, dear Dawn. Sit down sir, please sit, and eat.'

Quirkstandard finally sat down and got on with eating his sandwich and drinking his tea. It was good stuff he thought and big portions too. As he chewed he happened to glance across the table where his eyes kept getting caught by those of his interlocutor. He couldn't decide whether to match his gaze or to look away, and compromised by blushing, coughing and shutting his eyes.

'What was it,' his companion asked between mouthfuls. 'What was it that happened to you on the day before yesterday that so reminded you of me?'

Quirkstandard liked being asked a question he knew the answer to and explained to this new friend the gist of his adventures so far, how he had woken up and been unable to find his clothes and how he had had to visit Mauve's wrapped in a hasty dressing gown and so on until he reached the breakfast table. The old man watched and listened closely, grinning ruefully and sympathetically. He chuckled when Quirkstandard had had difficulty with initially working the buttons and fastenings on his clothes, but not unkindly.

As Quirkstandard spoke the two Crepuscular sons, one of whom he hazily remembered having met the day before, came into the kitchen, sat down at the table and got straight on with their breakfast.

He finished his story by talking about the pamphlets he had read and as he spoke he remembered, once again, that there was a whole room of them next door, a whole room filled with knowledge that he had yet to know anything of, just next door. His genuine enthusiasm was clear in his face and he finished by mentioning his desire to better his education and to broaden his horizons.

'Mr Quirkstandard, sir,' said the bearded man, 'I am Crepuscular, Simone Crepuscular, and those were my pamphlets you were reading last night.'

'Oh,' said Quirkstandard, suddenly a bit awed. 'Did you know there was this dolphin that could speak …'

'Yes, I remember Mr Quirkstandard, I wrote that after following the unfolding tale in a series of newspapers I discovered dated to the early …'

'1760s, wasn't it?'

'Yes, that's most correct Mr Q. It seems you were paying attention.'

'Oh, rather. You see, the townspeople thought he was actually a Frenchman, but …'

'Actually, they thought he was a Spaniard, Mr Q., but, yes I remember, because, if you recall, I wrote the pamphlet you read.'

Quirkstandard looked up at him and nodded firmly (which he regretted a moment later when the inside of his bruised skull began to throb redundantly).

'Oh yes, of course you did, Mr …?'

'Crepuscular.'

'Oh, like the shop? Look I have a piece of card with the name of the shop on.' He patted his pockets. 'Oh, it's here somewhere …'

'And you, Mr Q., are here now – you're in the shop. Don't worry about finding the card, we trust you.'

'Oh, jolly good.'

'Mr Quirkstandard?'

'Yes?'

'I believe it is no coincidence that we have been brought together. I appear to have something you want,' he waved a hand toward the pamphlet room, 'and, I suspect, you have something, I'm sorry to say, that we need. That is, to put a blunt point on it, money.'

'Money? Is that all? Oh yes, I should think so,' replied Quirkstandard gaily. He felt relieved and light because for a moment from the portentous lowering of Mr Crepuscular's voice he had feared that the payment was going to be taken out in something much more onerous than cash, something that involved work or something. Now cash he could do, he had buckets of the stuff.

Simone Crepuscular leant across the table, his beard sweeping crumbs from his plate, and held out his hand.

'It's wonderful to meet you, Mr Q.'

'Oh, and you too, Mr Crepuscular,' he said shaking the older man's hand, 'you too.'

6

India, Literature & Poets

Alfred, Lord Tennyson spent two years toward the end of the 1870s working on a magnificent epic tragic memorial poem imaginatively investigating what had possibly happened to a famous battalion of the British Army that had gone missing in Northern India. Two whole years he spent in his study, dipping his pen in his ink pot, scratching away on the thick paper he preferred, crunching up sheet after sheet and throwing them at the waste paper basket which was several yards away from his desk.[7] When he placed the final full stop at the end

[7] As a writer it is important to get some exercise, since it is all too easy to fall into lazy, sedentary habits. Tennyson arranged his study like this for just this purpose – he was a remarkably bad shot and his housekeeper was a particularly stern old woman who had been with his family since he was a very small child. He lived in interminable fear of her, even though she was, by this point in time, almost a hundred years old and physically much, much smaller than him. Every screwed up piece of paper he threw missed the waste paper basket and knowing what she would say if she saw them littered on the study floor he felt obliged, each time, to get up, walk the few yards across the room and drop them in the bin by hand. Thus did he maintain a healthy exercise regime. He had read somewhere that this was how Shakespeare had done it, but that story was possibly apocryphal.

of the final stanza he heaved a great sigh of relief, pack-
aged The Lost Company up in brown paper and string,
addressed it to the Minister In Charge Of Military and
Commemorative Poetry at the War Office, and took it
by hand, himself, to the post box.

No one ever read the thing, which is believed to have
been full of dark mysteries and effulgent beauty and
danger, tigers and howdahs and maharajahs and magic
and gems as big as duck eggs and spells and curses and
dusky maidens dancing in the crumbling majestic ancient
palaces in the almost altogether while Tommy Atkins
watched with a dropped-jaw. No one read it because
it never reached the War Office, being lost in the post
almost immediately. This vexed Tennyson sorely, since
it had been the only copy and he couldn't remember
much about it (other than the above details, though how
they fitted together he could never quite say), and for
years afterwards at poetry readings he would begin by
saying, 'I once wrote a very good and very long poem,
harrumph, but thanks to that fat bastard Mr Anthony
Trollope I lost my only copy, so please, please don't
buy the man's books.' Trollope, of course, had invented
the pillar box and even when he died in 1882 Tennyson refused to be civil to him, going to his funeral with
the sole intention of reading (and rustling) a newspaper
throughout the service.

In India, however, things were going along much as
they always had. Although the battalion may have lost
touch with England and England with it, there was little consternation in the camp. With no orders arriving
they were never asked to fight, nor sent to quell uneasy

uprisings in the locals. In fact a lot of the soldiers, on their days off, married local girls and were busy getting on with raising families of lovely colourful children. It wasn't an unusual sight to catch kids playing hopscotch or skipping on the parade ground, nor for the men to be dressed in native style loincloths and dhotis (over the top of their uniforms, naturally). The camp itself grew organically, spreading a little this way, a little that, like a small township, and had merged on the eastern edge with the western edge of the local village. There was a warm friendly atmosphere here, with no one getting uppity and telling someone else what to do, which was the usual cause of colonial conflict. At night the jolly everlasting plucking of sitars mingled with the merry thump of pianos and a panoply of curious twinkling stars shone down on what was, in effect, a contented extended family.

Simone Crepuscular was most happy with it all. He hardly bothered with clerical work at all and would remove his clothes almost as soon as he'd had his breakfast, slip on his loincloth (at the request of the mayor of the village after several ladies had fallen in the river whilst washing clothes near his tree, for no reason they felt like explaining to their husbands or fathers, though their sisters and mothers tended to giggle quite a bit), and head off down to the river in the cool of the early morning. In fact he often didn't even bother to get dressed before breakfast either and if he wasn't up his tree contemplating the world and dreaming of being exactly where he was right now, he could be seen wandering round the camp as happy and as nude as the day he first wore a nappy.

Each morning the Major came out of his hut, stood on the veranda and looked across the hard parade ground to the fat red rising sun. He would wait a few minutes, tapping his swagger stick against his boot, just to see if anything military was likely to happen that morning, before turning and heading back indoors for his breakfast. Normally nothing military did happen, after all no orders ever arrived unless he pinned them up to the notice-board himself, but just occasionally he would come out to find the men lined up waiting for him on the parade ground in their smartest red uniforms and, with a tear in his eye at their thoughtfulness, he'd shout at them for a bit and they'd march up one way and then down the other and he'd wave his stick about and shout again and funnily enough everyone enjoyed it. Then he'd go indoors for his breakfast and the men would go off for theirs and they'd all feel quite justified in drawing their pay at the end of the month.

The Major's main interest was in polishing buttons. This had been one of the reasons he had sought promotion out as a younger man: the higher the rank the more buttons you were allowed. He liked the way they gleamed like little suns. Sometimes he would send his batman away on pointless errands for weeks at a time, so that he could take charge of his own polishing. (Normally the errands were so transparently pointless that the batman, not being an idiot, would spend the weeks in the mess talking, laughing, eating and playing cards.) Then the Major would sit out on his porch through the long sultry afternoons, when all the Indians were sensibly staying indoors, and he'd polish away, savouring the brassy glint of the bright sunlight as it flashed and dazzled across his retinas. Not only did he polish his own buttons, but the soldiers under his command would often, quietly, leave their shirts and jackets draped over the back of his rocking chair and he'd polish theirs too. Scrub, scrub, scrub he went, watching the dust devils swirl and listening to the hum of the heat haze. This was, he'd think to himself happily, not exactly what he'd expected when he'd signed up, but it would do quite nicely, what? Eh?

Crepuscular felt very much the same thing. Occasionally he thought about the circus, occasionally he'd feel a little thrill at the thought of a spangly leotard or a dancing tiger in a tutu, but then he'd look out at the beauty and quiet of the world around him and think, well, this isn't where I expected to be, but it's beautiful and quiet and I rather love it.

※

One day, a year or two after his thirtieth birthday in 1880, a friend of his, Jock Jones the Irish Quartermaster, showed him an advertisement he'd found in the back pages of the *Gagargarh Echo & Weekend Advertiser*. Crepuscular took the newspaper and looked at the page.

'Well, what do you think?' asked Jones, who was homesick for the steady rain of his homeland (not absolutely everyone, naturally, was as happy as Crepuscular or the Major).

'I'm not sure.'

'What are you not sure about?' asked Jones, grumbling a little in the heat, 'I thought it sounded perfect for you.'

'Well, the thing is, Jones, this advert here,' answered Crepuscular, pointing to the bit of text, 'well, I can't *quite* read it.'

Although everyone knew that the reason this battalion never did any of the things the rest of the army in India did was because of the chronic illiteracy of their clerk, Crepuscular never liked to admit it. He'd simply sidestep the question if it came up and whenever people asked him how work had been today he would say he'd been busy with all sorts of forms and whathaveyou and hope they wouldn't ask any more questions and let him get onto talking about the elephants he'd watched washing in the river that afternoon.

'Shall I read it out? You know mate, just so it's clear, like?'

'Please.'

'Can't read or write in English? Then why not drop us a line and join our simple, quick and easy correspondence course in learning to read and write in English? Then there's like an address you can write off to.'

'Oh, I don't know …'

'It'll do you good Crepuscular, it'll do us all good. It's nothing, you know, nothing to be ashamed of, reading and writing, like. I get all sorts of smart things from books. They're real sort of useful if you know how to treat 'em right.'

So, Simone swallowed his pride and asked Jock to write off on his behalf, claiming a little refresher course never hurt anyone, and within a few weeks the first instalment of the course arrived. When Crepuscular opened the packet and looked at the first instructional booklet and examined the pictures therein he felt a tingle of excitement arc up his spine. He found he was actually looking forward to the challenge; he felt the ineffable sensation of a world opening up to him, much as Epitome Quirkstandard would feel thirty-five years later perusing the first of the pamphlets. So, Simone sharpened his pen once more, dipped it in his inkwell and set about learning to mark marks on the paper which were neither arbitrary nor meaningless.

Within a few weeks he was reading and writing with the best of them. In his camp the best of them were a group of fellows who hung around under a great spreading banyan tree late at night reciting their poems to one another in shrill, hazy voices. They would light long cigarettes which perched precariously from the end of long ebony cigarette holders which dangled dangerously between dainty porcelain fingers and never seemed to be drawn on. Every week one or other of these figures was rushed to the infirmary with burns received when a feather boa went up with a woof and a scorched stink of singed ostrich. The remaining poets would linger under the tree, mincing in fear and shock, composing rhyming quatrains about the event and leaning in perpetual affectation. It didn't take Simone very long to realise that he was actually much better than the best of them and he soon drifted away, taking with him one important lesson that he would remember for as long as he lived – to never, ever, under any circumstances, write poetry.

A few days later he sat down at his clerk's desk and tipped up a small sack of post. Over the last fifteen years or so the post had dwindled until virtually nothing arrived at the camp each month, and today, for the month of May, there were just three items. He picked up his paper knife and opened the first envelope. He held up the sheet of paper and began to read it. He recognised the English letters immediately and soon managed to work out the words. With a mighty thrill he recognised an approximation of his own name – Sinone Crempatular – typed cack-handedly above a dotted-lined space on the pre-printed form. This was the first time in thirty-three years that he had seen his name (sort of) written down and a sudden tear of pride trickled down his cheek. It was his Discharge Paper.

7

Chequebooks & Mountain Walks

꙼

'So,' asked Quirkstandard. 'How much money do you actually need?'

'Oh, only what you owe us Mr Q. There's a tariff up beside the counter in the shop. Let's see ...'

Simone Crepuscular pulled a little notebook out from underneath his beard and a stub of pencil from behind his ear and licked the point.

'What was it that you read last night?'

Quirkstandard answered brightly, reeling off the names of the pamphlets as if they were exquisite items he had ordered from the menu in some particularly classy restaurant. '*The Birds Of Hyde Park & South-East Iceland, The Goodness Of Bread & Other French Cheeses, Fastenings Of All Descriptions & Colorations* and *The History Of The English Speaking Porpoise.*'

'Oh, very good. I am fond of that that *Bread & Cheese* one, though it makes me a bit peckish, I find. So, Mr Q., that's the hire of four pamphlets (on premises), one in Band A and three Band C, plus board and breakfast ...' he pointed at the empty plate in front of Quirkstandard. 'So ...'

His pencil performed the lengthy calculation in silence.

'So, that'll be two shillings, seven and a half pence. Is that agreeable, Mr Q.?'

'Oh,' answered Quirkstandard, a bit startled and patting his pockets, 'I don't actually seem to have any money on me, well, not that much anyway, would you perhaps take a cheque?'

'But of course, my dear sir,' replied Crepuscular, unfazed.

Epitome Quirkstandard reached deep inside his jacket and pulled out a large chequebook. He offered it to Simone.

'I can never quite remember how this thing works, but I brought it along today anyway, thinking that 'an education' might be a pricey affair. I wonder if you know how to work it?'

Simone Crepuscular took the chequebook from the offering hands and laid it on the table which Dawn had just cleared. He pulled a pen from the behind the ear that hadn't housed the pencil and one of his boys placed an inkwell in front of them. As he dipped the pen in the pot and wrote the requisite words on the piece of paper he made sure that Quirkstandard watched.

'I hate to think,' he said as he did so, 'that some people don't realise that every and any moment of the day can be an opportunity to learn new things, don't you feel that way too, Mr Q.?'

'Um, yes, you're exactly spot on the money there Mr Crepuscular,' said Epitome with more resolution than he felt. He'd had an immediate liking for this big bearded chap and had the strange presentiment that to disagree would be to let him down. Even the fact that

he'd obviously forgotten where he'd put his clothes the
evening before didn't dissuade Quirkstandard of his new
friend's fine qualities, in fact it seemed to remind him of
his own humanity and fallibility. It was just the sort of
mistake anyone could make, and, besides, Mr Crepuscular had listened to Quirkstandard talk as if he were
saying the most sensible or understandable things in the
world, as if his views actually counted for something,
and that was a most novel and gratifying sensation. Even
Spiggot hadn't been so supportive of his new quest for
education, and he was his best friend.

Oh, the chequebook! Quirkstandard woke from his
reverie with a start, realising that he hadn't been paying
attention to what was happening on the table.

'Um, could you repeat that please, Mr Crepuscular,'
he said, seeing that the cheque had writing in almost all
the spaces that had been blank a minute before, 'just so,'
he flustered a little, 'I mean, just so I have it absolutely
clear, again, you see? Yes?'

'Of course, Mr Q., of course.'

Simone Crepuscular pointed to each place on the
cheque in turn and explained which bit of information belonged there and how it should be written. He
then had Quirkstandard repeat it back to him with only
minimal prompting. After they both seemed satisfied
that something had been absorbed into the deep furrows
of the cerebellum (or some similar seat of learning, neither was feeling neurologically fussy) Crepuscular asked
Quirkstandard to sign his name down at the bottom.

Naturally this was something that Quirkstandard was
more than happy to do. He wanted to show his new

friend that he had pre-existing talents, that he wasn't entirely a hopeless case, because honesty and pride rub up against each other like that and blisters are never pleasant – it's good to admit your gaps and failings, but no one wishes to look like an idiot.

He had spent long winter evenings practising his signature (they required a gentleman to sign the register upon arrival at Mauve's and so it was a useful skill to have). In those days there were very few distractions available in the evenings, and even a gentleman of generous private means couldn't very well spend every night at the theatre, opera or music hall.[8]

Simone Crepuscular leant back in his chair for a moment and looked out the window at the camp which had been his home for the last twenty-one years. He'd made several friends during his time there. Sometimes he'd danced late into the night to the interminable weird keenings of the Indian musicians and he'd swum more than once with the young elephants as they gambolled among the early morning shallows of the broad slow river. Every inch of the impacted parade ground was known to him, was familiar to him, was a part of his soul, was a page in

[8] Obviously as far as it was a question of finances they probably could, but it was generally considered, among polite society, improper for a gentleman to be seen in the same building as actresses or singers more than once or twice a week, unless he was related to one of them, and even then it was not the done thing for a gentleman to actually be related to an actress or singer, except by illicit sex, which was not Quirkstandard's cup of tea at all.

the story of his life, was a beat in the thump of his heart. He stood up and stepped closer to the window to take in the wider view, leaving the freshly arrived post on his desk for a moment.

He wiped a cobweb away and waved back as a passing soldier saw him and waved up. Billy Smith, thought Crepuscular lovingly: a nice boy with no talents and no ambition, a lucky match. He didn't think this with bitterness, but with a little envy perhaps, since he now felt undeniable exhortations to move on stirring in his chest. The course Jock Jones had urged him onto had opened his eyes and his doors to a wider world. He knew he couldn't help but tread the pathways of that world, that there was no way forward into the rest of his life but through that unexpected and unexplored realm of everywhere – everywhere else, that is, everywhere which wasn't where he was right now. He didn't feel confident about it, didn't know whether he really wanted to follow this calling. The climb looked steep and the world so very wide and he felt small, small, small. But at the same time, how could he not move on?

He spun smartly on the ball of his foot, walked back to his desk, took his few personal possessions out of his drawer, popped them into a little rucksack and walked out of the door, leaving two unopened letters on his desk. Without hesitation he walked out of the camp and was a mile and a half up the dusty road that lead toward the distant mountains that sat pale and hazy on the northern horizon when he stopped. How could I have been so silly? he thought, as he turned on his heel once more and marched back to the camp.

Half an hour later he was back in his little office and leant on his desk. He scribbled a note on a piece of scrap paper, secured it to the front of his desk with a couple of handy nails and began walking, once again, toward the distant mountains that still hung pale and hazy on the far northern horizon.

The note just said *Gone Home*. If he had had any inkling of what lay in front of him, he may well have rephrased the note, but he didn't, so he didn't. Though with hindsight he did come to realise the rather irritating value of hindsight.

Crepuscular hadn't thought to sign that note because, he assumed correctly, that anyone finding a note attached to his desk in his office may well have been able to make a rather astute guess as to its origins.

On an object such as a cheque, on the other hand, which would soon be passing into the hands of all manner of strangers unaware, specifically speaking, of its provenance, such an identifying mark is welcomed, if not legally required.

Epitome Nebulous Quirkstandard enjoyed having such a long name. As he took the chequebook and laid it out on the table he flexed his wrist in preparation for the act of signing it.

When the paper was flat to his satisfaction he stood up. This was his moment. With the pen in one hand he leant over the cheque and made a few exploratory gestures, much in the way that an inexpert golfer will pretend that he missed the ball intentionally on several downswings before finally connecting with a solid thwack into the second cut of rough. Closing one eye he stepped back. Then he stepped forward again, like a swift swooping hawk, deadly and with one eye open, and quickly, fluidly he signed.

There was a blur of action. Quirkstandard's left elbow flew out to the side as his right hand impacted with the cheque. His tongue ravaged his lips, poked about in the inside of his cheek, flicked at the back of his teeth, and his one open eye flickered in concentration. The scritch and scratch of the pen as it changed angles, directions and declivities dominated the atmosphere – round and around it sounded, making letter after letter. D after R after A after D and so on. With a final flourish, much like a matador placing his tired foot on the haunch of a vanquished but worthy opponent, Quirkstandard stepped back, stood upright, with his hand on his breast, ink splashed across his cheek, pen at attention. Proud, handsome, triumphant.

Simone Crepuscular felt like clapping again, but didn't, just in case his new patron felt he was taking the Michael, which he didn't intend to do. Instead he just said, 'Well done, sir.'

'Er, well, actually,' said Quirkstandard, as he leant forward to examine his handiwork, 'I was rather wondering if we might go through that again ... I mean write another cheque that is, since I seemed to have gone and signed the wrong name on this one.' He paused before looking up and meeting Crepuscular's eyes. 'I must have been rushing. Sorry.'

He blushed just a little.

Crepuscular certainly didn't rush when he left the army. He walked away (for the second time) at a gentle pace, allowing the placid breezes to ruffle his chest hair and push complacently at the small puffs of dust his feet raised from the dry earth road. From time to time he'd sit down in the shade of some broad spreading tree and sip a little water from his canteen. Sometimes he'd stay under the tree for a few hours and read from one of the books in his rucksack or chat with peculiarly wizened old men. He carried with him a notebook and a stub of pencil and would practice his writing by taking dictation. When enough time had passed, for example when he'd finished a chapter or when the fakir had grown bored or boring, he would simply get up once more and carry on walking towards the north.

In the back of his mind was a general intention to return to England. It wasn't that he wanted to see his parents or his home again, and he didn't know anyone else who lived there, but somehow it seemed to him to be the right place to aim for. All those years ago he'd left it, but he hadn't *chosen* to leave it, and he wondered, had he stayed longer in England, whether he would have wanted to leave it of his own accord. So by going back he could restart his quest, in a way, reset the pedometer and be in a position to know or to discover whether he ought to go travelling again. These were the guiding principles of his journeying, and although some days they seemed to make more sense to him than they did on others, he stuck by them.

It took Crepuscular a while to get home, partly because the distance between India and England was quite large, but mainly because he didn't know the way. Walking north brought him, after a few weeks of meandering, into the foothills of the Himalayas. And a few weeks in the foothills brought him onto the lower slopes of the mountains. As the ground rose the air became cooler and he took a length of cloth out of his knapsack and wrapped it around his neck in a loose knot. It was a lovely scarf he had bought at a market in the last town he'd passed through. It smelt vaguely of patchouli oil and had glittery little bits of mirror sewn into it and an expansive tasselled fringe at either end. He thought it would keep him warm as he walked.

Sometime later he was trudging through snow and his feet were turning increasingly blue. He sat down wearily on a large flat rock and tried to bring some warmth to his shivering toes by breathing on them. Unfortunately he wasn't supple enough to reach them with his mouth[9] and had to make do with rubbing the exposed flesh between the thongs of his sandal with his fingers, but since they were almost equally cold the heat produced was minimal. As he held each foot between his palms he tried to think of a plan. He hadn't counted on the journey taking this long and for the first time began to have doubts about the direction he had chosen to head off in. His sandwiches were all gone and he knew that the nearest village was more days trek behind him than he cared to think about. As he sat, drooped

---

[9] Even after years of yoga classes in the camp he had never quite managed to rid himself of a natural English stiffness.

in dreary thought, he heard heavy footsteps coming up the narrow and rocky path he had been following, and suddenly a warm, wet, vegetable smell wafted over his shoulder and onto his cheek.

He turned around slowly to see a giant, shaggy, bovine face staring into his with deep black eyes that gazed out implacably from underneath a matted black fringe. It half-sneezed its hot digestive breath into his face and he reached out with one finger and prodded its enormous damp nose. With a speed that seemed at odds with its size the yak whipped out a long rough-edged tongue, pushed Crepuscular's finger away and lowed mournfully. It was a low low, a rumbling that echoed around Crepuscular's bowels, rising as slowly as a Buddhist's temper into his ribcage. Of course, he had seen the smaller domesticated relatives of this beast working in the fields down on the plains, but those animals, he realised in his pre-scientific manner, had been crossed with common docile cattle, bowdlerising the pure strength of the rugged true yak genes. Its eyes shone darkly and Crepuscular understood, instinctively, that he was not going to come to any harm.

As this realisation swept into him, causing his shoulders to relax and his lungs to exhale, the yak turned its gigantic broad shoulders and started to wander off along the ridge-path, leaving him behind. One horn caught the strap of Crepuscular's backpack and it swung away, tantalisingly out of his reach, dangling over the long fall down the mountainside below. There was nothing to do but follow.

With surprising grace the yak picked its way through

the icy rock fields, always seeming to find the easiest path, pausing only occasionally to tear up a stray stem of gorse that had nudged its way through the powdery snow and Crepuscular followed on behind.

By the time they settled down for the night, however, the excitement had ebbed away and his feet were just as cold as they'd ever been and his legs ached violently from the large steps he'd had to make to keep up on the last upward push. As he sat down in the sudden darkness, the sun having dipped below the other side of the mountain, the yak carefully ran his sandpapery tongue over Simone's feet in a gesture that was more friendly than useful.

As a rule yaks typically sleep standing up. Like horses they lock their knees into position, shut their eyes and fall into ineffable bovine dreams.[10] The yak, however, on this particular night decided to lie down. He had led Crepuscular to a shallow cave on the east side of the mountain, out of the wind. Snow had drifted out from one wall, which closed the cave off even more and as they lay down it seemed as snug a little exposed shallow cave on the side of a mountain as they could ever hope to find. Simone tucked his cold feet into the

[10] Obviously, to be scrupulously correct, very few (which isn't to say no) horses dream ineffable bovine dreams. The majority tend to dream quite effable equine dreams: they gallop over tediously green plains, manes and fetlocks glimmering freely in the dew of the morning; they imagine themselves to be in dappled woodland glades, beside a tinkling silver stream, with a single horn sprouting from their foreheads; and sometimes they hammer nails into the feet of blacksmiths.

belly fur of his hairy bed companion, covered his shoulders with his slight scarf and drifted into brilliantly untroubled sleep.

He was woken the next morning by the sun streaming into his eyes. His companion dropped a pile of shrubs at his feet and wordlessly suggested that they share breakfast together. As Simone chewed thoughtfully he gazed out at the view. In front of him, to the east, stretched the utter immensity of the mountain range, rugged rock and smooth faces of glinting snow silhouetted before the sun, as far as he could see – peak after peak, reaching to heaven. To his right he could look down into the distance of India, far-off blue-tinged India. A country he loved as his own, but which wasn't home. From up here, he thought, it looked flat and peaceful and quiet. He thought of the thick winding river he knew and of the smiles of the local girls as they washed their smalls in front of him, pretending to forget that he was perched in his tree.

As he finished his last bit of bitter-tasting (but slightly welcome all the same) root he stood up and stretched. The yak was already wandering off northwards again, along the ridge-path, and Crepuscular did what he had to do: he shouldered his rucksack and followed on behind.

When Quirkstandard had eventually signed the cheque correctly Simone Crepuscular led him back into the pamphlet room. He stood in the middle of the shelf-lined space and, turning to face Quirkstandard, opened his arms wide to the walls.

'This,' he said, 'is all my own work. Everything is here. I have written it all down, everything I've learnt, everything I've experienced. It's here. So, Mr Q., what is it you'd like to know?'

Epitome Quirkstandard didn't know what to say. It wasn't, he thought, that there was anything in particular he wanted to know, as such, but rather that he thought he wanted to learn about anything. And so after a moment's pondering he said as much.

'A wide and free-ranging autodidact, and in my shop too. Wonderful, Mr Q., just wonderful.'

'Where do you recommend I begin?'

'Well,' Simone answered after a second, 'why not begin where I began? Begin at the beginning, as was once traditional?'

He pointed with the index finger of an inky hand to a high shelf just beside the front door. Simon Crepuscular, the taller of the two sons, reached up and brought down a yellowed and much creased piece of paper. He handed it to Quirkstandard.

'*What I Did In India*,' he read out loud.

'Yes,' said Crepuscular, 'you see that's where it all began for me. I'm afraid that's one of the last copies now, so I can't let you take it out of the shop, but you are, of course, more than welcome, to take advantage of our browsing facilities.' He indicated a small table and chair in one corner that Quirkstandard hadn't noticed the night before. 'Please, sit down, have another cup of tea if you wish, and read away to your heart's content, Mr Q., I think you'll find that one an enjoyable start to the day.'

Quirkstandard sat down in the chair, which happened to be in an oblong patch of sunlight and already warm, and opened the pamphlet out on the table before him.

He stretched once, scratched at his bruises, smiled at Simone Crepuscular, and began to read.

8

Mountains & Monks

☙

After a week of following the yak, of sharing its food and bunking up with it at night, Crepuscular turned one final rocky corner.

There, below him, lay a deep living green valley. On either side jagged heights of jumbled rock reared up, grey-white and indomitable, but there, beneath his feet, down a single narrow path lay, verdant and smelling of early morning dew, a growing green valley.

The yak led him down this one last path, as he had led him along so many others previously, before leaving him in the care of a young sky-blue robed monk. A monk, moreover, who seemed to be expecting him and who bowed and smiled as he approached.

'Come with me, please,' he said in perfect but accented English.

Understanding his place by now Crepuscular followed this new host. He glanced over his shoulder just once as he began to walk and saw the large rear end of the yak (a sight he had grown fond of, since it had been the one unchanging view in his new and changing world) dwindling in the distance. The great beast paused, cocked its head to one side to sniff at a succulent, green-stemmed sapling, all fresh and juicy with new leaf growth. It

turned away without nibbling and wandered slowly
back to the near-barren mountainside in search of some
prickly, dry scrubby gorse bushes. Crepuscular smiled
sadly as he saw his silent friend vanish round the same
corner he had just turned.

He turned again and found the monk waiting for him
a little way down the path.

He was led down and down through the fields and
gardens of this hidden country, which was larger than
it had looked from so high up, and after an hour they
stopped outside a square yellow brick building that sat
in the centre of the small cluster of buildings that sat at
the centre of the valley. As they'd passed through the
fields curious faces had looked up from their hoeing
and digging and weeding. Crepuscular had noticed the
eyes of many different nations in those faces, rounded
eyes like his own, almond eyes like those of his guide,
dark eyes like the Indian friends he'd left behind at
the army camp. All their faces though were shaded a
dusky brown through long exposure to the sun, much
as his own had been after all the years he'd spent on the
subcontinent. He wondered how they had all found
their ways here. A few people had waved. They had all
seemed to smile.

Following the gesture of his monk-guide he walked
up the shallow steps of the yellow stone building and
was ushered along a short hallway, little more than a
deep doorway, into what he could only describe as an
inner sanctum. He felt the temperature, which had
been quite moderate outside in the sunshine, drop a
few degrees and his first breath misted in the shade. His

guide gestured him to sit on a reed mat that was laid on the swept stone floor.

In front of him, on a broad dais, sat an ancient old man. He was covered by a voluminous sky-blue robe, which rested on and around him as if it had been dropped in his vicinity from a great height and that it was only by the merest of good fortunes that the head-hole had landed square above his head, allowing him to poke out and look around.

For a minute everything was still. Simone heard the footsteps of his monk-guide vanish out of the little building behind him and then there was only silence. A silence that he didn't feel it would be right for him to break first.

The two men stared at each other for what seemed like minutes until finally the little man spoke.

'You have come a long way, Englishman.'

'Um, yes. You're right, I have, sir,' replied Crepuscular.

He had met fakirs and wise-men many times in his Indian life but none of them had been quite like this. It wasn't that he would have said they hadn't been wise, or even capable of strangely unnatural sleights of hand. He'd learnt all sorts of things from them, and had spent many long evenings listening entranced to the stories they told. One old man had cured his corns simply by rubbing a handful of elephant dung into his hair and chanting secret chants and another had taught him how to make bread. But none of them, it seemed to him now, had ever been quite like this old man. He felt, even after only seven words, that there was something undeniably special about this little fellow.

'Do you realise, I wonder,' the old man said, 'how far you still have left to go?'

His eyes were like deep pools of water. Like deep wells, somewhere in them stars were reflecting.

'I'm just going home, sir.'

Again, unhurried silence.

'Every step you take is a step both further away from and closer to that home.'

'How's that? ... Sir?'

'Listen.'

The Little Master held up one of his tiny hands. Layers of robe fell away to allow it access to the open air. From somewhere outside, somewhere distant, came the faint sounding of a clear deep horn. It was like a sound heard whilst dreaming, present but also absent, changed around maybe as it rolled around the steep walls of the lush valley. It was at once soporific and encouraging. Crepuscular wondered if maybe the altitude was making him dizzy.

'The note from the horn is a series of vibrations. Did you know that?'

'No, I don't think I did. What do you mean vibrations?'

'Vibrations in the air.' He paused. 'Englishman, picture the air divided into units, each so small that you cannot see it, but each one existing all the same, mindless of you or your belief in it or not. Sound is merely a connective series of these tiny units rubbing against each other, knocking into each other, do you see? Eventually this pattern, this sound, reaches your eardrum which is no more than a membrane attuned to these patterns of vibration, a stretched skin that can translate the hum into sound. Can you see that?'

Crepuscular tried to visualise this.

'Can I see that?'

'Yes, that was my question.'

'No, I can't see it. But I can hear it.'

Silence.

Then a grin spread across the flat tortoise face of the Little Master.

'I like that,' he said, 'I like that a lot.'

For a moment he giggled, to himself – a high childish giggle, his eyes flashing. Crepuscular smiled.

'Vibrations,' he prompted when the laughter died down.

'Yes, vibrations. As they travel away from the horn, away from their origin, they diminish in size and intensity. Do you hear that? Each subsequent vibration grows smaller as they use up the energy that began them. So the further away from the mouth of the horn the quieter the sound gets. But they are always finding their origin in the blowing of that one horn, blown by that one man, at that one time. They can never be anything else, no matter where or how they end up.'

'Yes, I see.'

'So, however far away that note sounds, however quiet it gets, it always carries with it the imprint of its origin, of its home if you will, and as it echoes, as it bounces from one mountain to another, sometimes it must, by chance, by fate, by luck, come back to exactly where it started. But it can never return home, as such. The conditions under which it began its brief life, the precise conditions of its creation have passed away, have moved on, have changed into something else. The man who blew it has moved on maybe, his horn packed away, perhaps it has started to rain, maybe he has an appointment somewhere else. Or maybe he is still there, but is pursing his lips differently, making new noises, starting new sounds off on their own quests. And the echo, the original note, grows smaller and fainter until eventually it is absorbed into stillness. Coming home is never, shall I say, coming home exactly. Do you see?'

'You mean I can't go home?'

'Oh, no, no, no,' chuckled the Little Master. 'You can go home all right, and I can see that you will. Oh to be in England, now that spring is here! Ha-ha! But just do not expect it to be home as such, for, always, remember that you yourself are no longer you. It is a simple lesson. Perhaps the simplest lesson of all and we have all had to learn it once.' He paused and drew a deep breath. 'Some of us,' he continued, 'have learnt it many times over.'

An impression of weariness crept into the room for a moment. But in less than a second he regained his air of authority, his eyes regained their liveliness and their well-like depth and he looked up at Crepuscular.

'Thank you Little Master,' he said, without knowing where the appellation had come from, but it seemed to fit. 'I wonder if I might stay here for a night or two, just to gather my strength up and get my bearings, before I head off again, you know, for England.'

'Of course you may stay. Stay as many nights as you like. That is what we are here for, we are a hostelry for those lost in the mountains.'

'Oh, no. I wasn't lost,' Crepuscular blurted, suddenly feeling defensive.

'You are right, of course,' replied the Little Master, 'I know you weren't lost. But others have been lost and others will be lost. And suffice it to say, that had you been ... well, no one remains lost for very long in these mountains. Not once we find them.'

After these words the Little Master closed his eyes and bowed his head. He looked as if he had fallen asleep in just that single moment, but he remained sitting upright. Crepuscular sat quietly where he was until he felt the hand of the first monk touch his shoulder.

'Come with me, please.'

Simone stood up and, still facing the Little Master, bowed. As he turned to leave he noticed something about the room that, inexplicably, he hadn't noticed before. The inner sanctum had no ceiling. Looking up he could see the deep blue of the high Himalayan sky, streaked with the thinnest white lines of clouds. As he watched a few snowflakes drifted down from heaven towards his face.

Before he left he looked once more on the Little Master who remained unmoved on the dais, cross-legged with his hands folded in his lap, his eyes closed in prayer, meditation or sleep. He smiled again.

He followed the monk-guide out into the warm valley and along a broad dirt road to a cluster of houses at its northern end. It was here that the mountain ridges rose and met at a triangular point as the valley floor sloped upwards to meet them. The wide southern end of the valley, he saw looking down the length, was open and sloped down toward the clouds. The late afternoon sunlight still poured across the land, though the mountains on his right pointed a few long fingers of shadow across the fields.

He was shown his lodgings. The room was sparse, but that was nothing new to Crepuscular, and the bed was firm, but for a man who had spent the previous fifteen years sleeping underneath a desk and then the last week or so tucked up with a yak, it felt like collapsing into a warm pit of feathers. Fortunately he wasn't allergic to the thought of feathers.

The next morning he met some of the monks and visitors over an early breakfast in the large refectory. Some had been, unlike him, lost in the mountains, and some had simply been passing through, and still others had actually sought this valley out after having heard a traveller's tale or having had a particularly impressive dream. Conversation was quiet and pleasant and slow. Nobody spoke with their mouths full, like they often did in the army, and no one felt in any rush to finish their stories. Crepuscular chewed his muesli and smiled.

After breakfast there was work to be done and he found himself left all alone. He took the chance to wander round the valley by himself, just for an hour or so, just to get the feel of the place fixed in his memory before he left. It would certainly be something to write a postcard home about, he thought, if only, he also thought, he had someone to write a postcard home to. Or a postcard. Or, for that matter, a home.

Later that afternoon, just after he'd packed his few possessions into his rucksack and negotiated with the man in the stores about taking some food for the trip, he started up the path that led out of the valley, on the opposite side to the path he'd followed in. His sandals were comfortable and having rested properly for a night he felt able to take on any journey the world threw at him.

However, after climbing the steep path for several hundred yards he turned around, strolled back into the valley, located the barber, had his head shaved and became a student of the Little Master.

Each day he attended a morning lesson, after spending several hours doing what needed to be done in the fields from dawn, followed by more fieldwork in the afternoon. There was nothing magical about this valley, it only remained viable through the hard work that everyone put into it. Crops didn't grow easily and required constant, but not cloying, care and attention. It was a delicate business. It would often be late in the evening before he found his way back to his small room, but however tired he was he rarely missed the opportunity, just before bed, to practise his writing by recording his experiences, his thoughts and his memories in the journal he had begun to keep. He kept track of what he believed he had learnt and was learning from the Little Master and attempted to record what was most important about his previous life by the thick slow river in India.

Three years, almost to the day, after he had first turned that corner into the deep green valley, he took, for the second time, that other path that led out of it and continued his long journey home.

The climb had grown smooth as it neared the mountain pass at the top and the light lay lazily and long across the late afternoon, and just before turning the final corner and heading out of that place forever he turned around.

Below him lay that glorious emerald valley, surrounded by the grey and white and black of the rock. Glittering in the sun he made out irrigation channels shining like silver threads, and there in the middle of everything sat the yellow-gold temple sitting solid and heavy. He thought, or maybe he just daydreamt, that he could make out a tiny figure in an open space at the temple's centre waving up at him. He didn't really believe that it was who he wished it to be, since his Little Master had been absorbed into stillness a fortnight before, but he smiled all the same, waved and walked on.

9

Horses & Bottles

꙾

By the time lunchtime came round Epitome had worked his way through five more pamphlets. Rodney Crepuscular, who was left in charge of the shop while his father went upstairs to write and his brother went off to do other business elsewhere, even sold him a small notebook and a pencil, with which he tried to make notes about what he was reading. Quirkstandard felt this was the appropriate thing to do, but since he didn't really understand what was important or what needed noting (taking, as he did, an indiscriminate pleasure in reading everything from anecdote, description, explanation to copyright notice) his notes were almost certainly rubbish.

Each time he finished a pamphlet he'd sit back with a big sigh and look up at the shelves that surrounded him and wonder where to go next. He made a neat stack of the pieces he'd read on the desk, as he had been asked, so that a Crepuscular could count them up later on and work out the fee. It wasn't that they were penny-pinching, but that Simone approved only of a scrupulous honesty and wanted to make sure that they only charged the exact amount due, especially knowing as he did that Epitome Quirkstandard would probably happily pay whatever they asked. That, he saw, was all the more reason to be precise and correct.

Quirkstandard began his reading that morning with Simone Crepuscular's autobiographical piece, *What I Did In India*. This had been the first pamphlet that he published and he remained justifiably proud of it. That had been in 1901 when he was freshly arrived back in England after nearly forty years of being elsewhere. After seeing the vastness of the rest of the world he had been surprised to find that the Shangri La of his childhood was just a tiny place, suffocating in mourning, swathed in black crêpe and sobbing gently into its handkerchief. This hadn't been what he'd been expecting.

Not only was the England Simone returned to much altered, but of course he himself was very different too. For a start he had two young sons in tow, who had to be fed, which required him to find some form of gainful employment. He briefly considered joining the Circus, but at the age of fifty-one he found that, sadly but honestly, it no longer held the thrill for him that it once had. He sat by the ringside with a chair in one hand and whip in the other and couldn't bring himself to tell the lions what to do for other people's amusement. He looked at these proud beasts with their prinked and perfumed manes and polished rubber dentures and felt that teaching them tricks was actually a slightly tawdry thing to do. It was all the ringmaster could do to convince him to not let them loose as he handed in his letter of resignation and left the big top for good.

He spent a week, shortly after that, singing sentimental ballads (which matched the mood he was in) in a small music hall near Exeter, but since, as the manager told him, he hadn't even gone so far as to bring a bucket in which to attempt to carry the tune, that job came to nothing either.

He eventually found regular paid work in a factory making and labelling bottles for the burgeoning bottle industry (all sorts of people needed bottles at just that time and a bottle factory was exactly the sort of place they went in order to get their bottles and so the bottle factory's business was booming). Simone worked in the printing room, where the labels were designed and printed before being pasted onto the bottles. Here he learnt how presses worked and how to set type and various related activities and he rather enjoyed it all. So long as he worked a twelve hour shift between set times and did exactly what he was told, he was free to do whatever he wanted, whenever he liked.

The drawback he found with this sort of work was that as a single parent of two boys of nine and eleven years of age, he didn't much like leaving them at the factory gates each morning. Other parents took their children into work with them, he noticed, but the rates of pay for minors were insulting, he felt, and besides Crepuscular wasn't an advocate of child labour. In fact he was something of a soft-hearted father and on more than one occasion[11] he was reprimanded by his foreman for staring out of the window at his boys playing conkers in the street instead of getting on with designing the new label for a bottle that, somewhere much further down the line, would contain an inferior grade tomato ketchup.

---

[11] That is to say, twice.

Sometimes, coming out of work of an evening he'd find that his boys had wandered off down the street — a mile in one direction was the town library, and a mile in the other direction were some gypsies who made them nettle tea. Simone didn't mind the boys doing either of these things, being broadminded and in favour of wide horizons and stretched brains, but they never left him a note to say which way they'd gone and the time he got to spend with them was limited already, and, besides that, it seemed unfair that they got to have all the fun and adventures while he was shut up indoors. And so he vowed to get a job where they could all stay together, and on making this promise they moved to London.

While walking to London, Crepuscular realised two things. Firstly, that the long journey he had thought had come to an end when he arrived at the docks six months earlier, hadn't in fact ended yet at all; and secondly, that the roads in England where much better than roads he had walked on almost anywhere else in the world. Walking with the boys through the mist and fog set his mind racing back over all the adventures (mainly walking, which doesn't always sound too adventurous, and is rarely all that exciting, but which, if you keep it up for long enough, can become an impressive anecdote all by itself) he had experienced on his long, long road.

When he had finally descended the northern slopes of the mountains, so many years before, he had found himself wandering in a strange, vacant desert land that seemed to stretch to every horizon (except the one behind him, that was still darkly ridged with peaks). Knowing very little of the skills required to survive in such a dry and harsh place he just kept on walking in a straight line, assuming that it was better to head somewhere than to stay still. He walked by night and into the early morning, drinking the dew that collected in the beard he had begun to grow and eating insects and lizards who were always surprised to see him.

Eventually the high dry desert gave way to high dry grasslands and he was able to supplement his diet with some high dry grass. As he kept on walking the desert became a faint memory and he grew used to the rolling heave of the slow slopes of the grassy steppe. It lent itself much better to walking than the long dunes had, and so he began to make good time (not that he had a watch or was keeping track of distance, but all the same he felt better about it). Each evening he'd build a little bivouac out of grass and make some grass soup in his little cooking pot and after dinner he'd lie out on the grass, rolling a blade of grass between his lips and staring up at the immense, starry heaven above him, with all its shapes and constellations looking a bit like grass to him, until he fell asleep. In the morning he'd wake up, rub his face clean with some nice dewy grass and start walking once more toward the rising sun. This was his new method for keeping his bearing (always remembering, of course, to swap over at lunchtime, so the sun was behind him (follow your shadow, Simone, he'd say then)).

After a week or so of hiking across the grassy plains he saw, on the horizon, in front of him, a settlement of some sort. From this distance it was merely a group of dark specks, silhouetted against the light sky, but the thin plumes of ascending smoke indicated either human inhabitants or particularly sophisticated gerbils. As he tucked himself up under his grass blanket he breathed an interested sigh of expectation. He liked his own company, without doubt, but the thought that tomorrow he might meet some people filled him with a thrill. New people, he thought, were always interesting, and he remembered back to the last new people he met, back in that hidden valley.

Even if he and these new friends had no language in common, he imagined, they'd be able to share other, more basic things: such as the simple joy at being human and alive in such a huge and beautiful universe.

The next morning he rose early and looked to where he'd spotted the settlement the night before, but couldn't see it. It should have been there, exactly there, he thought, pointing to the eastern horizon with his eyes. But it wasn't. It was as flat and dully grassy as all the other horizons he'd been staring at for weeks had been. He looked around him a shade confused, a touch disillusioned and feeling uncharacteristically grumpy. As he packed his gear away and prepared to head off for another day of marching toward nothing much, he wondered what might have happened. Had he simply been mistaken? Perhaps it had been a mirage. Or maybe something sinister had happened in the night?

As he slung his backpack over his shoulders he happened to glance away to the north and there, sat on the horizon was the same set of specks he'd seen the night before. They were the same, weren't they? They certainly looked the same, but it seemed they'd moved. From this distance, naturally, it was hard to be sure of their identity, but he had a good feeling that he'd refound his new friends. Maybe he'd rolled over in the night and had woken up facing the wrong direction. Yes, he thought inexpertly, maybe that was it.

He started walking northwards. All through the day he marched, never taking his eyes off the group of dark specks. Even when he stopped for lunch he didn't look away. By late afternoon, and he knew it was late afternoon because he could feel his legs aching and his back complaining, and besides the sun was sitting low on the horizon in front of him, he was a little closer to the specks and he could make out movement around them and smoke curling up from a fire. But hang on, he thought, the sun is in front of me? That would mean I'm facing west, but I started off going north this morning and just followed the specks. Maybe they'd moved?

Before the sun sank completely and before he tucked down for the night, he drew a line in the earth pointing from his camp to exactly where those specks were. When he woke up in the morning and followed the line of his line to the horizon he was hardly surprised at all to find nothing there. The sun was already quite warm and the dew was evaporating as he packed his things and slung his pack once more. If that camp wasn't going to play fair by staying still then he determined to spend no more time on it. He turned to face the rising sun and continue on his steady eastward trek. The sooner he reached a coast the sooner he could get home to England, he thought.

When he turned to begin his trek he saw the specks again. This time he could see that they were in fact round buildings which looked to be a cross between a tent and a hut. He could see that there were people milling around outside them and horses too and a thin blue wisp of smoke curled up from a fire somewhere amongst the encampment. He also noticed that the tents were only a hundred yards or so from where he stood.

As he stood there, looking at the buildings and at the children who were playing in the grass at the feet of an old lady who sat sewing a piece of leather onto another piece of leather, he wondered exactly what to do. They stared back at him with a disinterested curiosity, and continued getting on with the things they'd been getting on with, presumably, before he'd stood up. He could smell breakfast cooking on a fire somewhere, though he couldn't see it. Horses whinnied where they mingled and chewed grass and the day just got on with things.

Eventually a small man with a long drooping moustache, narrow shoulders, a furry hat with a spike poking out the top and little dark eyes, wandered towards him, holding, outstretched, in what Crepuscular took to be a traditional gesture of friendship, a loaded and tightly strung short bow.

Simone held out his hand and bounded over to introduce himself, delighted to be meeting someone after all this time alone. His rucksack bounced on his back and his loincloth flapped in the wind and a wide smile spread across his face.

So surprised was the Mongol Chieftain at the actions of this strange half-naked giant of a man, that he merely lowered his bow and shook Crepuscular's hand.

His grandfather had once met a French missionary who had left an educational book behind with the tribe of nomads. This book was being read at that very moment by the Chieftain's daughter in their ger. She was a simple, lovely girl, who had grown up with this one book, just as her father had, and just as all the members of the tribe had. It was a colourful book with pictures of all *The Civilised Peoples Of The World* in it, with little descriptions underneath, a variety of fascinating trivia and statistics, and a brief statement of why they were superior to the benighted heathens of, for example, the Mongolian plains. For this reason the Chieftain was able to put his finger on Crepuscular's nationality, if nothing else, with forthright immediacy.

He ushered the Englishman into his tent, sat him down on his favourite cushion and handed him a slice of toast (made from grass-flour) smeared liberally with horse-butter. Simone took it hungrily and, wrestling down a virulent coruscating wave of nausea, happily munched away.

They began to converse.

The Chieftain pointed at Simone's shaven head and lifted his hat. Underneath it was dark, straight oily hair, tied back in a ponytail, but which clearly displayed a receding hairline. They laughed at the similarity.

Crepuscular rubbed his hand over the shaggy growth of beard that covered his chin and then leant across and tugged, gently, at the Chieftain's narrow moustache. The two men chuckled at the similarity.

The Chieftain pointed at his guest's two legs and then

stood up and raised the edge of his long shirt to reveal that he too was blessed with a complete pair. Both men smiled at the similarity.

As the day went on they became close friends.

After a while Crepuscular married the Chieftain's daughter, who had watched them conversing on that first morning from behind a curtain. She had looked from the pages of the book to the real Englishman sat in her ger and thought to herself how much better the reality was, which is, of course, sometimes often the way.

Simone stayed with the tribe for almost three years. He enjoyed the nomadic life, which, after all chimed with the life he'd recently been living in so many ways. Every morning he'd pull back the curtain door of his ger and look out at a completely different (if indistinguishable) patch of Mongolian steppe. He enjoyed the variety and in time became able to recognise a wide range of different grasses from one another (and not just short grass and tall grass, but even more than that). He appreciated change that was very little change; to know that change was going on continually, but without ever changing much at all. This sort of change he liked. That was why he'd spent so long watching rivers flow, he thought – much the same, day to day, much the same. But then you never knew what might suddenly flow down to you, a dead buffalo or a golden palanquin: you never knew, but could easily find out, just by waiting a little bit longer.

He didn't marry the Chieftain's daughter straight away. First he travelled with them for some months and learnt a little of their language and their ways. He made himself useful by being taller than most of the men, and found he had an unexpected talent for actually being able to ride horses. They found him calming, the horses that is, and settled easily around him. He became particularly adept at milking them, which was a skill highly prized by the nomads, because of his long fingers and warm hands. He became a well-loved member of the tribe and, through working side-by-side with her, he came to love the Chieftain's daughter, which made her very happy indeed.

The wedding was a joyous occasion and in celebration half a dozen other travelling tribes descended on this one corner of the plains and the biggest party Crepuscular had ever been invited to happened. Dancing went on late into the summer and rich presents were bestowed on the happy couple. Mostly rich presents of horse-milk, horse-cheese and horse-butter, but which in a dairy-horse economy were generous gifts indeed.

Shortly after the wedding Crepuscular's beautiful young wife became pregnant and in the spring of 1889 she gave birth to a son. To his lasting sadness there were complications with the birth and in the absence of advanced medical procedures and sanitation his wife died a few hours after holding her little baby boy for the first time. All Simone had to remind him of her was their son, who, out of respect for her and her people, he allowed the tribe to name. They gave him the traditional nomadic name of Rodney, which meant 'Friend of Horses' in their tongue.

In time it became apparent that the grasslands were filled with too much melancholy for Simone to consider staying much longer and so, with the blessing of his father-in-law, who understood heartbreak as well as any man does, he resumed his homeward journey home.

With his rucksack stuffed with horse-cheese and washcloths to help with the baby he set out, Rodney bouncing on his hip, toward the rising sun and away from the happy interlude of a life spent wandering in wide circles on the steppes.

10

Education, Education & Education

❦

As Quirkstandard read *What I Did In India* feelings of
warmth and curiosity alternated through the grey matter
of that original alma mater, his brain. This was, indeed,
the thrill of learning – the best a man could get.

Unlike the pamphlets he'd read during the night,
which were all of a more immediately practical nature
(except for the one about the talking porpoise, which
was just a true and tragic tale of the triumph of greed,
villainy and pettiness over both human nature and
nature's unexpected miracles), the one he held in his
hands here this morning imparted knowledge that he
would most likely never be able to turn to his advantage.
Quirkstandard wasn't the sort of Englishman who was
likely to set out for the subcontinent, for instance, and
it is unlikely that, without doing so, he'd ever be able to
put to use the contents of a long paragraph he enjoyed
immensely, for example, about where best to stand in
order to remain dry during the morning ablutions of a
herd of elephants.

. Crepuscular's original pamphlet was filled with just
such useful paragraphs as that, some with diagrams, some
with drawings and all of them filled with quiet writing
which never strayed into the hyperbolic, but which all

the same managed to be gripping. It might've been his habit of becoming distracted in the middle of telling one anecdote and starting another, which in turn would become interrupted by a third, until finally a reader had no choice but to either read to the end with a breathless hopeful anticipation that the one particular story he or she wanted to discover the end of might actually be concluded somewhere, or to just let the experience of reading the pamphlet wash over them, as if Crepuscular were actually talking, and accept that you might never know the truth or the conclusion, but it's been a really rather nice hour in an interesting man's company all the same.

When the Crepusculars arrived in London they went straight to the Tourist Information Centre. Simone decided this would be a fine idea, following the advice he'd been given by a policeman who had grown tired of his questions.

He spent the morning waiting, with his two boys, in the waiting room thinking intensely. There wasn't a queue, but he didn't want to waste the opportunity. Every few minutes his face would light up and he'd stand and wander over to the little window behind which sat the Tourist Information Officer. She would look up from her desk, sigh and brace herself.

'Excuse me madam,' he'd begin, 'could you tell me who it was who had the greater influence on Kant's Theory of Transcendental Apperception? Was it Plato or Aristotle?'

Generally at this point the lady would remove her glasses, pinch the bridge of her nose, replace them and say, 'I'm sorry sir, but I don't know.'

'Oh? Well, thank you all the same.'

'Yes, thank you, sir.'

And Crepuscular would return to the bench, make a note in his notebook and resume his thinking.

'Excuse me, madam,' he would begin a few minutes later, 'could you explain the point of the letter 'C' in the English alphabet?'

'I'm sorry?'

'The letter 'C', madam. It seems to me, from just a cursory examination of the language, to have no real value of its own. I was wondering if you might know of some?'

'I must say, sir,' she'd reply, 'I really couldn't tell you.'

'Oh. Is that the same as saying you won't tell me?'

'I can't tell you, sir.'

'You're unable?'

'I just *don't* know, sir.'

'You don't know if you're able?'

'No sir, I am quite certain that I am unable.'

'Ah, so you mean you don't *know*?'

'No sir, I'm dreadfully afraid that I, with all due respect sir, don't have a clue.'

'Oh? Well, thank you for your time,' he would say as he resumed his seat and his thinking once more.

The woman would tidy her small pile of commemorative maps of the London Borough of Hackney and sympathise with the Greeks of ancient Athens who had become so irritated with the questions of Socrates that they made him drink hemlock. She wished she had a little book that might tell her just what hemlock was, where she could purchase it and how it should be prepared for maximum speed and efficiency.

After a whole morning filled with the garnering of almost no new information at all he wondered if maybe there wasn't a niche here that he could fill? He'd read a penny account of Socrates' life too, quite possibly the same one the lady in the Tourist Information Office had read, except she'd read all the way to the end and knew the final results, whereas Simone had got as far as reading about Socrates' endless questioning, the way he always helpfully pointed out the flaws and inconsistencies in his friends' suggested answers, the way they always ended up saying, 'Well, we don't know, Socrates, why don't you tell us ... what is Truth (or Value (or Justice)) etc.?' and how Socrates would always look at them sagely and say, 'Well, to be honest, I don't know either.'

Simone had put the booklet down at that point, astonished at the man's tenacity and his honesty. He thought he recognised some of the same values in himself. The curiosity and the humbleness to not always believe he knew better than anyone else. What he missed out on by putting the book down at that point was how all the gentlemen of Athens would go home each evening feeling mightily pissed off at Socrates, with his pointless pontificating and habit of making everyone else look like a fool. Of course, Socrates always slept soundly, for much the same reason.

Crepuscular knew that like Socrates he didn't know anything either, or rather that he didn't know the answers, but he had quite a clear bead on the questions and the sort of questions that fascinated him. Maybe, he thought, like the big S., he ought to try to spread some of these questions about, maybe someone would work an answer out, or maybe an answer would just come to him at some point – but there would be no chance of finding any answers by never asking the questions. So he decided to write down (or to organise all the writing he had spent the best part of the last twenty years making) his thoughts, his observations, his experiences, his questions, his troubles and his opinions in the hope that if they were interesting to him, then they might be interesting to someone else too.

So, he got up one final time and walked over to the Tourist Information Office's little window and asked the lady inside the booth whether she might have a map to hand which would show the premises of a printer of some kind. He knew that the world had changed since Socrates' day and that it wasn't possible to do what he wanted to do by simply talking to people. This was the age of mass communication, of newspapers, books, magazines and penny dreadfuls.

After she'd said 'No' out of habit, she listened closer to his question and realised that at last he had grasped the true nature of her job. Sometimes all it takes, she thought to herself, is for a man to wait long enough and the truth will bob up.

Smiling she pulled a map from her little pile, circled a few addresses and handed it over the counter.

'That'll be a penny,' she said, delighted to finally be earning her supper.

Crepuscular found a printer that same afternoon. He was happy to typeset and produce a pamphlet for a very reasonable fee. Now all they needed were some words.

Simone sat down on the Embankment with his notebook in his lap and stared out at the sluggish black water and the lights that reflected in it from the buildings along the far bank and the rising moon in the sky. All he wrote, for a time, was his name in the top right hand corner. But then a little later he got to work and added the date.

Watching the water and the slowly moving barges he wondered where to begin. There was so much in his head after fifty years of living and twenty years of jotting. He wanted to say it all, but he knew he had just a dozen sides of a single folded sheet of paper to fill tonight. He needed to find a method of ordering his life.

As the sun raised her first rosy finger above the horizon his great idea struck him with a flash. He would simply begin at the beginning and talk it through, all the way, he envisioned, to the end. And that is why *What I Did In India* began with a breathtaking description of a girl in sequined tights twirling high above the heads of a stunned and astonished crowd, flipping and twisting on a narrow trapeze with all the grace and beauty of starlight over the ocean and the thrill and danger of imminent death or paralysis at the merest slip of a finger. It then turned into a detailed, though cheerfully discursive, survey of the life, duties and observations of a soldier in Imperial India, with the customs, religions and weather of the natives, and descriptions of the flora and fauna and ruins that can be found round those parts. This information, which was as factually correct as Crepuscular could make it, was embedded in the seemingly autobiographical tale of an unnamed young clerk working in a curious battalion, headed by a handsome, brave Major and fenced in on one side by a thick brown river flowing slowly away.

What I Did In India was an immediate success, mainly, it should be admitted, though no one told Crepuscular this, to the presence on the first page of that beautiful girl in the sequined outfit. It was said that everybody in London bought a copy, or, if not actually everybody, then everybody who counted and had a spare penny. For a penny, from any one of three street corners (where Rodney, Simone and Simon each stood with a big bundle), you could transport yourself away from your dreary smog-bound London life to a world of sunshine, warmth and sequins, and share in the quiet but exotic life and dreams of a decent British Tommy.

Crepuscular had tapped a vein that, who would ever have guessed, was just waiting to be tapped, and at a price that made it popular with all classes. People would say things like, 'I heard my neighbours laughing all night and when I went round to see if they were all right I found them sat up in bed reading the passage about … And well, the next morning, naturally, I had to buy a copy for myself.'

It was even rumoured that a copy had found its way into the Royal Household and was perched on the side of the Royal Lavatory, with an inscription on it saying, 'Not for downstairs use. Ed.VII.'

By Christmas, Simone Crepuscular had published two more instalments of his story – *The Behaviour & Habits of The Mountain-Dwelling Cattle, Gorses & Monks Of The Himalayas* and *Things I Did In An Outer Mongolian Ger Or Yurt*. These sold just as quickly, despite the lack of any girls in sequins, and held the public's attention well into the New Year.

Within a few months of the sale of the first pamphlet they had earned a small fortune. Unfortunately it was a small fortune consisting entirely of quite large penny coins, which meant it was rather heavy. His eldest son, Rodney, suggested that he either invest the money in some sort of project, if only to get it out from under the mattress, or that they raise the price of each pamphlet to a pound. Pound notes, he argued, when accumulated in bulk would probably weigh much less and be much less lumpy than a similar quantity of coins.

Crepuscular *père* wisely had no faith in the Pound Pamphlet and so invested his cash in buying a shop. He hoped that with permanent premises from which to sell his wares his educational pamphlets might gain a respectable name for themselves. Instead of having to buy one from a grubby urchin on a street corner for a penny, a customer would now be able to visit an well-presented establishment and purchase a copy from a smartly turned out gentleman behind a counter, though still, Crepuscular insisted, for a penny. He liked the ring of value that price had about it.

Quirkstandard read these first three pamphlets and felt like he was really getting to know the large, bald, mostly-naked man he'd met in the kitchen, and at the same time was expanding the borders of his horizons with regards to knowledge of the world at large.

The other two pamphlets that he read he simply picked at random from the shelves for a bit of variety. They were *Gravity: What It Is, Where It Comes From, Goes To & What Colour It Might Be Were You Able To See It* and *How To Make Friends With Influential People Or Be Happy Not Doing So Should It Not Work Out For You*. As he finished this last one Miss Dawn brought him a ham sandwich and a cup of tea.

'Oh, thank you,' he said, realising that he'd grown hungry without noticing it.

Miss Dawn nodded imperceptibly (or maybe she didn't, Quirkstandard wasn't sure) and walked back out to the kitchen.

Rodney got up from his stool behind the counter (no one had been in that morning to buy anything) saying, 'I'm going out to have a fag. Watch the shop would you?'

He wandered out through the back room, presumably into the little backyard.

Quirkstandard was left all alone. He chewed happily on his sandwich and looked around. How long, he thought, would it take a man to read all this? It had taken him almost five hours to read just five. That was, he worked out in his head, approximately an hour a pamphlet. Looking at the walls he estimated that there must be thousands and thousands of pamphlets, and even though he knew that there were stacks of multiple copies of the same title, still it would work out at an absolutely tremendous number. His brain tried to engage itself in making some sort of further calculation but was thankfully interrupted by a knocking on the front door.

He stood up. The knocking happened again. He looked back to the kitchen to see if anyone was coming to answer it, but it seemed no one was. Then he remembered that Rodney Crepuscular had asked him, Epitome Quirkstandard, to mind the shop.

The knocking knocked again. It sounded quite urgent.

It really did seem as if no one was coming from the back room to answer it and so Quirkstandard walked over to the door, reached down for the handle, twisted the key in the lock, forgot to wonder whether that might explain the lack of customers throughout the morning, and opened the door.

11

Rafts, Stars & The Peace Of The Open Sea

As Simone Crepuscular island-hopped his way across the Pacific he often thought about all the things he had left behind (such as security, family (of sorts) and dry land). It was a lonely time for him. As much as he loved Rodney, he would readily admit (had anyone been there to ask him) that a baby was less than ideal company on a boat, and especially on a vessel that yawed and rolled as much as this one seemed to. Sometimes, for variety, it pitched and rolled, and at other times it would pitch and yaw. Occasionally (usually just as he was finally drifting off to sleep) it would roll, yaw, pitch and toss all at the same time, throwing him out of his hammock and onto the damp reed deck of the raft. All Crepuscular wanted was someone to hold onto his ankles as he vomited copiously over the side, and, of course, it was little things like this for which young Rodney was especially unsuited.

At first the Crepusculars had found passage on a real ship, sailing out of a port whose name had been written, on the sign they passed on their way into town, in strange pictographic symbols Simone had been unable to decipher. But that ship had been lost midway across the Sea of Japan when it was looted by pirates. The passengers had been stripped of their valuables and dumped in a lifeboat while the pirates repainted the ship and sailed off in the opposite direction.

The unnavigated lifeboat ran ashore a few weeks later on the west coast of Japan where a number of the other passengers had homes, family, friends and livelihoods to return to. During the ordeal in the lifeboat Crepuscular had been more than generous with the last few rolls of his horse-cheese, which had staved off starvation but had won him few friends.[12]

One man who hated him less than the others lent him enough yen to take a train across the island to the port of Shiogama where he was able to barter passage on a ship heading out into the Pacific. This ship too was soon attacked and sunk by pirates (Crepuscular's nautical luck always holding true) and the new lifeboat washed up on one of those uninhabited desert islands with palm trees, coconuts, a little rainy forest and more sand than a sand lovers' convention could ever be likely to need, even for the big finale. On this small island it didn't take too long for the atavistic impulses of the shipwreckees to rise to the surface and as soon as Simone spotted a fat lad eying Rodney up hungrily he decided to make a move. Under cover of night he slipped away from his companions and

[12] In part his shipmates were suspicious of him since whenever he wasn't offering the remains of his horse-cheese he was being hideously sick over the bulwarks and, quite frankly, they weren't sure (having smelt, seen and tasted the cheese) that he didn't occasionally get confused about which activity he was doing at any one time, but the Japanese, being a polite people, had conflicting feelings about which was worse: refusing a gift or consuming what might be 'reconstituted foodstuffs'. Good manners can be such a bind.

hastily lashed together a raft on a beach on the other side of the island and sailed away.

Navigating by the stars they sailed in circles until they bumped ashore on a completely different desert island. This one was also uninhabited and he stocked up with coconuts, fruit and fresh water and sailed on. For months they repeated this routine, just him and Rodney, one man and his son, scanning the horizon for signs of ships and islands and chucking up hearty chunks of coconut into the brine. Crepuscular hated every single moment. Seconds dragged by with nothing but the sound of the doldrums in his rigging, the stench of caked salt in his beard, the rare squawk of a seagull or albatross overhead,[13] but most of all he hated the endless, dreary lap of the waves all around his raft. The vast inhumanity of the ocean sank into his heart, oppressive and faceless, and he oscillated between deep depression and even deeper seasickness. Only the sight of little Rodney every morning, swaddled tightly to the mast, grinning at his daddy, kept him working.

He paddled when there wasn't any wind, ran up the sail when there was, and eventually, one night, the battered old raft shuddered ashore on its final beach.

When the morning arrived he looked one way and then the other and saw that the coast went on forever in both directions. This was not another island.

He had landed in America.

---

[13] Not being a reader of poetry he wished he'd had a gun with him to provide some meat as an alternative to yet another coconut. He hated coconuts just as much as he hated every other part of this voyage. He didn't care for the taste and the hairs always got stuck between his teeth.

12

The Aunt & The Doorman

Quirkstandard was briefly confused and then amused when he opened the front door of Crepuscular's shop. There, stood outside in the street, was Snatchby, Mauve's elderly doorman. Quirkstandard had never opened the door for the doorman before.

'Ah, Lord Quirkstandard, sir, I had hoped to find you here,' said Snatchby, cutting, with his usual deftness of conversation, to the point of the matter.

'Oh, yes, really? Well, here I am and no two ways about it, ha-ha! You've run me to ground Snatchby without a doubt and now here I stand before you, um … found, as it were. Yes. Um …?'

'Sir,' said Snatchby. 'It's your Aunt, sir.'

'Aunt Penelope?' asked Quirkstandard, suddenly worried. 'What's happened?

'Oh, nothing to be concerned about, sir. As far as I can tell she is in rude health and still enjoying her old tricks.'

'Oh, thank goodness for that. You did startle a chap just then Snatchby, with all this mysterious talk and trekking halfway across London to deliver the message that a fellow's Aunt is quite all right.'

'Well, sir. I came to deliver more than just that message, you see.' With this Snatchby reached a hand deep inside his coat, clearly seeking for a pocket that the tailor had never intended anyone but an astonishingly close friend to ever know about. 'Ah, here we go sir,' he said, pulling out a piece of card. 'She has sent another postcard to the Club, sir. I thought I would take the opportunity of using my post-luncheon break to pop it over to you. After all it's only two streets from here to Mauve's.'

'Just two streets?'

'Yes.'

'Oh, I thought it was further than that.'

'No, sir.'

'Oh. It seemed quite a fair distance when I did it.'

'Might you have taken a taxi cab, sir?'

'Well, I might have, yes, that's a distinct possibility.'

'It's possible, sir, that the driver of the taxi took, what I believe in the trade they call, the scenic route, sir.'

'Oh, well, maybe. I don't really remember all that much. Do you know, Snatchby, what has happened since we last met, back at the Club ... oh, when was it?'

'Yesterday, sir.'

'Oh, yes. That's right, but it seems like a lifetime. Oh, Snatchby the things I've read.'

'Indeed, sir?'

'Oh yes, they're enough to make a chap think, I'll tell you that. Why there was once this dolphin that was found by some people somewhere at some time and it spoke, well, English, just like you or me.'

'Goodness, sir.'

'Yes. That's just what I thought and there's no mistake – Goodness, indeed!'

'Ahem,' said Snatchby, indicating that his luncheon

break was only short and that he had other matters he wished to discuss before returning to Mauve's.

'Oh yes, go on, old chap. Ignore my wittering and just come out with what you want to say. You know I've never been one to stand on ... um, what is it I haven't stood on?'

'I couldn't rightly say, Lord Quirkstandard. But if I may be permitted to change the topic for a moment.'

'Of course, fire away as the Bishop said to the ... oh, who did he say it to?'

'The firing squad, perhaps sir?'

Quirkstandard thought for a moment.

'Oh, maybe it was, but I don't think so. I mean why would a Bishop be up before a firing squad?'

'Maybe they didn't like him, sir?'

'Oh, maybe. But you wanted to say something, Snatchby. Come on, out with it.'

'Well sir. It concerns your Aunt.'

'Oh, yes, you've brought a postcard.'

'That's right, sir. And that's the problem.'

'Hand it on over there, old chap. Don't just clutch it like a ticket ... I'd best read it, what?'

'Oh no sir, the message isn't what's important here. Rather ... well, sir, she sent the postcard to *the Club*.'

'Yes, Snatchby, and ...'

'Well, sir, this one is innocuous enough, but you know the view that the management take of postcards from, well, *certain ladies* being sent to the Club.'

'I don't believe I do,' replied Quirkstandard with uncharacteristic impetuousness.

'Sir ...'

'What?'

Snatchby gazed at Quirkstandard over the top of his half-moon spectacles and sighed.

'Snatchby?'

Snatchby continued to look, with what Quirkstandard could only describe as 'one of those looks'.

'Oh, all right. Yes, I know they disapprove, but Snatchby, really, what can I do?'

'Well, sir, you could ask her not to send postcards to the Club.'

'You know that I *did* ask her. I did. And she started sending more, and foreign ones, after that. You know the ones I mean, Snatchby, with the pictures of those foreign ladies with the fruit and ...'

'Yes, sir I remember very well indeed.'

The two men stood silent for a moment before Snatchby spoke again.

'The first one of her 'artistic' postcards gave Mr Lillytit an apoplectic fit, sir, and he turned quite puce in the face.'

'I thought it was in the hallway.'

'Ha-ha, sir, very good,' Snatchby said, without laughing. 'But seriously sir, he wasn't the only member of the management to take a dim view. Especially once they turned the card over and accidentally read the message she'd written.'

'Oh crikey, yes, I remember. She didn't keep her thoughts to herself, but then you've met Aunt Penelope, Snatchby, and you know she's never been one for keeping quiet about, you know, well, things that get on her wick, as it were.'

'Indeed not, sir.'

'I told her what effect her postcard had on Lillytit and asked her to apologise, but she refused. She's very stubborn.'

'Yes, and as I recall sir, her postcards started arriving ever more frequently after that.'

'Well, she does love me, Snatchby. I'm her only nephew and she's my only Aunt. What can I do?'

'Perhaps, sir, you could ask her to send your post elsewhere? I hesitate to say it, sir, and naturally I would never think to side with the management against a gentleman, but I believe the issue of her correspondence is beginning to have some effect on one's standing at the Club, vis-à-vis respectability, sir. Perhaps you could ask her to write to you at home, sir?'

'She is very much her own woman, Snatchby, and I did suggest to her that she write to Devonshire Terrace, but she persisted and insisted on keeping on writing to Mauve's in order to, oh how did she put it? Um, I think it was 'to chip away at the last bastions of the gentleman's world of undeserved and abominable exclusivity.' Or something like that. And besides, I think she enjoys it, Snatchby.'

'I'm sure she does, sir, I'm quite sure she does.'

The two men looked at each other.

'Do you want to come in, Snatchby?'

'No sir, I'd best be getting back to the Club now. You know what happens if I leave the door unattended for too long – there'll probably be a queue of gentleman halfway down the street by the time I get back.'

'Oh, jolly good.'

'Oh, here's the postcard, sir.'

'Thank you Snatchby,' Quirkstandard said as he took the card and held it up to the light. As he examined the picture side Snatchby spoke again.

'Sir?'

'Yes?'

'Do you really like it here, at *Crepuscular's*? You weren't just being polite earlier?'

'Oh no, Snatchby. I meant it. It's absolutely marvellous here. Did you know that in the Himalayas, which are mountains somewhere, there are these things like cows, but with, sort of, Astrakhan coats on? I forget what they're called, but it's not the sort of thing a chap just learns about and moves on – it absolutely changes his view of the world. And I've learnt so many things like that. Oh, Snatchby, if only you could pop in and see for yourself.'

'I have sir, many years ago. I'm very glad indeed that it's working out for you. Well, I'd best be off, sir.'

'Yes, cheerio then.'

As Quirkstandard closed the door he grinned to himself, simply pleased at being back in the shop, with his whole new future rolling out before him.

13

The Choice, The Town & The Pirate

When Simone Crepuscular and little Rodney first arrived in the Americas, they didn't know that they'd arrived in the Americas. In none of the places they'd been to, not in India, nor up the mountains, nor on the plains had Crepuscular ever seen a map or globe of the world. Oh, he was familiar with maps of local places, they'd had those in the army: big dusty papery faded things up on the walls with coloured shapes all over them, but he'd never studied them much at the time or cared: he hadn't known what they said, and until you know what's what on a map, which dot is the camp or which bright blue line represents that sluggish brown river outside, a map is just a sheet of variously coloured paper.

So, when they arrived in America he didn't know they were in America. Since there was no one waiting on the beach to give them directions he was faced with three options. Firstly they could proceed inland and see where that led them (which was more or less in an easterly direction); secondly they could go along the beach toward the north; or thirdly they could follow the beach southwards. Simone couldn't think which way would be best, couldn't see any overriding advantage to any one course over the others, not knowing, as he knew, what lay along any of them. He was just pleased to be on dry land once again, at long last, and his stomach had mostly settled.

He looked out at the sea, at the ocean. It was beautiful, he was quite happy to admit, when experienced from the land. So blue, so large. But that didn't help him decide. And faced with three choices he couldn't even flip a coin. Had he had one. Which he didn't.

In the end he lifted Rodney up in the air and spun him round and round, before dropping him onto the sand and seeing which way the dizzy little toddler would stagger and crawl.

He fell over facing south.

Sometime later they reached Ecuador. At first, Simone didn't know it was Ecuador either, but he didn't let that worry him.

The two of them stopped off one evening in a small seaside town and went into a bar. Rodney was walking now, but was still very short and liked to hold onto things. As he leaned against the edge of the bar Crepuscular tried to order a drink. He and the barman were, naturally enough, confronted by a language barrier, but Simone overcame this in the usual way by pointing to a bottle of something at random behind the bar for himself and then by pointing to little Rodney and raising an eyebrow.

The barman suggested with a clear and easy to understand gesture that they sit at one of the tables as he poured Crepuscular a glass of something vicious and viscous and gave Rodney a beaker of fish juice, which was, had anyone asked, not only a local delicacy but also one of several fish by-products that accounted for the modest poverty of this little out of the way town.

The barman brought the drinks over to their table and then scurried back behind the bar. Some of the locals stared at their table with undisguised interest. Crepuscular thought, as he looked round with a friendly smile, that he hadn't seen so many scars accumulated in one room in all his days, having never served in one of those parts of the army that ever saw any violent action. He sipped his vile drink, coughed, wept and patted his beard. He took another sip which turned out to be exactly as disgusting. If this rotgut was an acquired taste he didn't think he was going to worry too much about acquiring it, since he favoured both his sanity and his stomach lining.

Looking around the dim bar again, listening to the piano which had fallen silent as soon as they'd opened the swinging doors and remained so, Crepuscular began to think that maybe this hadn't been the ideal establishment to have a drink in, but Rodney seemed to like it and was contentedly slurping and spilling his fish juice in equal measure.

Suddenly, from out of the darkness, a metal hook came thudding into the table. Crepuscular looked up in startled shock. Rodney gurgled. Attached to the hook was a sailor. Crepuscular could hardly make out the fellow's face under the frown that covered it. In the gloomy dark of the room he could, however, make out the eye-patch across one eye, the glint of gold teeth from a troublesome grin and a voluminously feathered hat. The pirate (Simone felt qualified to be able to tell the difference between simple jolly Jack Tar sailors and mean, despicable, low-down pirates by now) extricated the hook from the table (with little difficulty) and leered at Rodney.

Rodney gurgled, giggled and leered back. The pirate reached out with the hook again and chucked the baby under the chin with the flat of its cold silvery curve. Rodney reached down and grabbed it and began to pull it towards his mouth, as he did with almost anything he got his little hands on. Just before the pointed barb passed his lips Simone leapt to his feet. His chair clattered on the floor behind him as the pirate easily ducked the fist that flew in his direction and responded with a jab to Crepuscular's gut which knocked the wind out of him and sent him stumbling backwards. He tripped over the fallen chair, and as he fell one of his legs came up and knocked the table over, which landed on the pirate's foot, leading to the eruption of a few choice Spanish expletives and the sight of a be-feathered hopping pirate, jewellery clanking and parrot flapping.

The room burst into strange Hispanic laughter. From every corner came foreign peals of pleasure. Crepuscular recognised a couple of words from his daze on the floor, but most of the chuckles, guffaws and bellows passed over his head. After a moment he felt a hand in his, helping him up and then a firm slap on his back as sailors and fishermen from all over the room came up and congratulated him. Well done, they seemed to be saying, you were very funny. Soon he was sat back down at the reset table with a dozen drinks in front of him. So this, he thought to himself, was how one went about making friends.

Rodney sat happily on the lap of the ruffian who had initiated the whole conversation, being fed bits of mashed up fruit by the pirate who had exchanged his hook for a little spoon. It seemed, as Crepuscular peered closer, to be a sort of Swiss Army Prosthetic and he thought, idly, how useful it would have been to have had something like that out on the plains of Mongolia, what with all those horses and all those little stones.

Since Crepuscular didn't speak any Spanish, as such, and since no one in this small Ecuadorean fishing town spoke any English, parts of the conversation that evening were long, slow and full of mistakes. It was one of those mistakes that led to Crepuscular finding himself made Mayor of the town and ushered up, as dawn was rising, to a large house on the hill overlooking the harbour. Here he slept off the worst hangover of his life and when he woke a day later found that there were people waiting to have a committee meeting.

The duties as Mayor weren't hugely onerous, the people were friendly and the mandated term of office was only three years, so he decided to stick at it. After that, when Rodney was old enough to be of some real help on a trek, they could set off again. It seemed to make some sort of sense, and, besides, he might actually be able to do some good while he was here, and that'd be a fine thing.

He appointed the hooked pirate who had started it all to be his deputy Mayor and when they had their first meeting after he'd finally shaken off the effects of the virulent fish spirit he'd drunk he noticed something unexpected. The fellow, in daylight, had a decidedly feminine air about him. And a decidedly feminine shape. And, come to think of it, a decidedly feminine voice. There was, of course, he soon learnt, a good reason for this, which was simply that the pirate was a woman.

Over the months that followed they worked closely together on plans for improving the town. They began the building of a reservoir up in the hills to provide clean, running water; they expanded the local school syllabus to include things other than fish, with Crepuscular even leading a few classes a week himself (having quickly managed to pick up the basics of Spanish); and they instituted a policy of casual days on board all ships operating out of the harbour on Fridays, as both a way of injecting a little fun into the hard lives of poor fishermen and also of raising some funds to cover their other civic projects.

As Crepuscular worked closer with Teresa-Maria (the pirate) on their plans they would often find themselves scribbling away late into the night, or into the early morning, and their arms would brush as they reached for this or that document or pencil or paperweight and soon they found that they'd catch each other's eye across the fug and babble of council meetings and share a little smile in amongst the chaos and sometimes, even when there was nothing to do officially, when projects were put to bed for the time being and complaints had been dealt with and disputes quenched, they'd meet up for a picnic or a cup of tea anyway. In short, they fell in love.

They were married around Christmas 1890 and in the autumn of 1891 Simone's second son, Simon, was born. And in 1893 when his term as Mayor came to an end he took his family and began to wander eastwards, toward the Andes. With his knowledge of mountaineering and survival skills they made good time and in just a few months found themselves descending into the Amazonian rainforest.

In his office Crepuscular had found an atlas and he'd memorised it as best as he could and so, for the first time in his life, he had an idea of where he was going. He knew which way England lay and how he could get there, and although it involved another long ocean voyage he was determined (since it had been three years or more since he'd been to sea and he'd forgotten just exactly how horrendous he found such experiences) to keep true to his original goal of going home.

Teresa-Maria had always hated her life in that miserable little fishing town, which had been, in part, why she'd become a pirate. Crepuscular had persuaded her to go straight (which included an end to robbery and murder on the high seas, not swearing in front of the children and letting her parrot go free) and much to her surprise she had enjoyed both her job in the council offices and her married life with Simone, and so she was more than happy to head out on an adventure leaving everything and everyone she had grown up with behind. While he was heading back to his childhood, she was running away, and they were both overjoyed.

She'd been less overjoyed, however, when he'd turned down her original plan which had been to commandeer a ship, kill its captain and sail to England via various buried caches of treasure she claimed to know about. Crepuscular wasn't the sort of man to put his foot down very often, but occasionally, when he felt particularly strongly about something, as he did in this instance, he could be quite persuasive and Teresa-Maria, grudgingly, but not despondently (after all, she might be able to persuade him to change his mind, she thought, once they reached the Atlantic), gave in.

And so it was they plunged into the noisy, dark heart of the rainforest: a man, a woman, a child and a baby. Prepared for absolutely anything, except, naturally, for what actually happened.

14

Aunts & Postcards

Epitome Quirkstandard turned his Aunt's postcard over in his hands.

He'd sat back down at the desk he'd been studying at all morning, but now he leant back in his chair with a less serious look on his face.

He loved hearing from his Aunt and wondered which exotic and exciting part of the world she had written to him from this time. She was exactly the sort of woman who was never still, always rushing off here and there, but wherever she ended up and whatever she did when she got there, she always thought of him, even now when he was all grown up and she had discharged her responsibilities toward him. He knew of chaps at the Club who were terrified of their Aunts (he also knew some chaps who were terrified of his, but that was quite a different story), who hid whenever they came calling and dreaded the tasks they were likely to be landed with by the dour sister of one or other, or in some cases both, of their parents. He shook his head with sadness and wonder at this, since his own Aunt had never been anything other than jolly special to him.

He loved getting post from her, though he preferred a letter to a postcard, because then he got the thrill of opening it, as if it were really a present. With a letter you never knew, he thought, what you were going to find inside, whether it would be sweet or savoury, plain or sparkling; you never knew how long it would take, whether there would be one sheet folded with big writing, or a bundle of sheets with all the words crammed onto them, as if there'd been a sudden late rush. Oh, he loved those letters. He'd hold the envelopes and look at the stamps and try to read the postmark. Sometimes he could tell what country she'd been in by doing so, but sometimes the ink was blurred or the stamps written in a foreign language and all he'd have would be a smudged idea, which would be confirmed or corrected by the contents.

A postcard, on the other hand, didn't have quite as much mystery. There was less deferred gratification possible. There was the picture and there on the other side were the words and, really, that was it. And the messages she would write on postcards differed to the stories she would tell in letters. Postcards tended to be short and to the point, often with a postscript for the postman and another for the management of Mauve's. With a postcard Aunt Penelope knew her wider audience and spoke to them all, often quite rudely (so that several postcards had never reached Epitome at all but had instead ended up in court, but fortunately a postcard leaves little room for a return address and so charges proved impossible to press).

This particular postcard wasn't as exotic as they sometimes were, featuring a pen and ink sketch of Arundel Castle on one side and short message on the other which

read: *E. Home for a month. Sun is shining gloriously. Walkies?*
P.P.

P.P. was Penelope Penultimate, his Aunt. E. was Epitome Quirkstandard, him. The rest of the message he understood just as quickly. She was home, but only for a month. She considered the weather to be very pleasant at the moment and was inviting him and Nigel Spiggot down to stay.

Immediately his heart beat quicker. He loved going down to the country to visit her. She had a small cottage, not one of these grand country houses where you had to dress for dinner and it took half an hour to walk from your bedroom to the dining room (if you could find it amongst all the doors), and so it made a very smart change. There was little ceremony at Aunt Penelope's house and, in fact, very little to do at all. They'd go for walks along the river and they'd read books in the garden and they'd drink tea and eat sandwiches and then they'd go for another stroll and he'd tell her about what had been happening in London, as far as he knew such things, and chat about what some of the fellows were getting up to at the Club and she'd swear and say rude things about them all and then they'd go off to their respective beds and get up the next day, stretch out in the sunshine, have some breakfast and do it all over again.

Aunt Penelope didn't approve of his friends. Not to say that she resented him having them, after all they were the boys he'd grown up with at school and who were his peers and always would be, but she didn't believe they added much in the way of value to the world. To be utterly truthful, she didn't think that Epitome added very much in the way of value to the world either, but she had a soft spot for him all the same. She knew, at least, that he wasn't actively making the world a worse place and that was something. She'd always steered him away from entering into politics or business and was quite happy for him to be a gentleman of leisure. The only friend of his that she liked was Nigel Spiggot who she believed needed the fresh air of the countryside from time to time. To have a run around a London park, she said, was all well and good as far as it went, but it didn't really go very far did it? The air was much cleaner down in Sussex, as was the river, and Spiggot vociferously agreed, and always showed as much by leaping into the water at the first opportunity he had and dragging out the biggest stick and chasing rabbits and collapsing exhausted long before bedtime.

Reading the message Epitome thought of how a jolly outing to the countryside might be just the thing to brighten his weekend, but then he suddenly remembered, with a thump, where he was, in the middle of all these brilliant pamphlets, surrounded by all this learning, all this reading. He felt torn in two. He wanted to go to the country and laze in the sunshine and watch Spiggot splash after ducks in the river, and, confusingly, at the same time, he wanted to stay here in the shop and read as much and learn as much and know as much as he possibly could. He'd never found himself on the prongs of two such disparate paths before and wondered how it might be possible to reconcile them.

Simone Crepuscular stepped out of the backroom.

'Was that the door I heard, Mr Q.?'

'Yes. It was for me. A postcard.'

'Oh, that's good. Can I have a look?'

'Of course. It's from my Aunt. Here you are.'

'Thank you.' Crepuscular held it up to the light and examined the picture. Without turning it over to read the caption he said, 'Arundel Castle, Mr Q. Is that what it is? I'm never very confident about castles, there's something very similar about them all.'

'Oh, yes. It is Arundel Castle. You see, that's where my Aunt lives. Well, not in the castle, obviously, I mean she's not a King or anything! But she lives in a cottage, just near there. In fact if the picture were a bit bigger and drawn from a different angle, you'd just be able to see her house, if there weren't all those trees in the way, of course.'

'Of course.'

15

Baby Names & Epitome's Plan

❧

As they hacked their way through the depths of the dark, lush Amazonian forests, surrounded by the noises of giant insects and vines and bats and rummaging things they never saw in the undergrowth and the dripping of old rain still making its slow fall from the canopy to the forest floor, it became increasingly obvious that Teresa-Maria was pregnant once again. According to Simone's time-table they would reach the Atlantic coast in just another month or two, long before her condition would become a hindrance to their hiking. He was so happy being a family, belonging to something that also belonged to him, with his two sons and his beautiful (if somewhat coarse) pirate wife, that he looked forward to nothing with greater anticipation than the prospect of having a third child.

They would toss names around as they made their slow progress through bunches of hanging ampelopsis and thick, prickly undergrowth.

'What about Jonathon?' Simone would say, for example, carrying Simon on his hip and holding Rodney's hand.

'Jonathon?' Teresa-Maria would reply, sounding a touch incredulous, as she hacked at a stubborn bit of vegetation with her machete attachment.

'Yes,' Simone would reply, seemingly unfazed by her tone, 'You see, I had an Uncle called Stephen when I was a boy, but he always asked us to call him Jonathon.'

'And did you?'

'Well, no. Father asked to see his birth certificate one day and refused to call him by any other name than what was on there.'

'And what name was on there then?'

'Oddly enough, it seemed the registrar had made a spelling mistake, or maybe granddad had made a speaking mistake, because from then on we had to call him Uncle Alberto.'

'How confusing.'

'Yes, mostly for his wife though.'

'All the same, Simone, I don't like Jonathon. It's a bloody dreadful name.'

'Why, what's wrong with it?'

'It just doesn't have what it takes to be a pirate's name.'

'Hang on. Cut-Throat John? That sounds all right to me.'

'Oh, well you *can* do that if you want. I mean, you can do that to any name, can't you? I think a name just needs to be more bloodthirsty all by itself. More ruthless.'

'Like what then?'

'Well, what about Blackbeard?'

'I've got to admit that *is* piratey.'

'You can't get much more piratey. It's good, it's solid, it's traditional.'

'I suppose you're right, but I'm not sure that it's the sort of name that's suitable, however lovely it might be in other ways, for a baby, I mean for a child, is it? It's more the sort of name one might assume in later life, as an alias perhaps or a sobriquet … something to strike fear and worry into the hearts of other pirates and into the officers of the law who are baying, romantically, at your heels, always one step behind your nefarious plans. I'm just not convinced that it would work, for example, for the first, well shall we say, fifteen years of a young lad's life. He'd be teased something rotten in the playground for a start.'

'A bit of teasing in early life is exactly what makes a pirate grow up to be a pirate.'

'Well, maybe that's true, but I still don't think Blackbeard should be on our list.'

'Very well. I didn't much like it anyway. I knew a Blackbeard once and he was a complete arsehole.'

'Teresa-Maria! There are children present.'

'I should bloody hope so, or it would mean you'd lost them.'

Sometimes the conversation would subside for a while as they navigated round some awkward obstacle or found an easygoing patch through which they could just stride comfortably, but sooner or later someone would say something else.

'Oh, Teresa-Maria,' Simone Crepuscular would say, for example, 'I've just remembered a joke I think you might like.'

'Is it about pirates?'

'Why, yes it is.'

'Very well, go on.'

(Teresa-Maria didn't have much of a sense of humour,

but she would pay attention to Simone's jokes if they were about something that interested her.)

'Here we go. How do you make a pirate angry?'

'Oh, well that's easy,' she'd reply. 'You kidnap her parrot, or you sink her ship, or you steal her treasure, or you insult her mother, or you ...'

'No, no, no. You're thinking too literally. You're not thinking about it like a joke, Maria.'

'No?'

'No. You see, what you do is you stop the pirate from having a 'p' and he becomes 'irate'.'

Teresa-Maria would stop, at a moment like this, and turn to look back at Crepuscular. The dew would glint on the blade of her machete in a sudden green shaft of sunlight. His grin would shrink. Her face would remain impassive, except for a twitch of the eye-patch. A shiver would surmount his spine as she turned back to slice through a harmless dangling vine. Dark plant juice would drip through the moment's silence.

'Don't you get it?' he would ask meekly.

'I get it,' she would say, 'I just think maybe it's time we stopped for lunch.'

'Oh, fine,' he would say, relieved. 'What have we got?'

'How about some vine leaves,' she'd say, 'stuffed with some other bloody vine leaves?'

'Lovely,' Simone would reply without a trace of irony, since he actually rather liked this rainforest staple.

The family would then sit down on a fallen tree stump or log, or maybe on the earthy floor itself if there was nowhere dryer to hand, after first, of course, having checked for bugs and scorpions. And for spiders, lizards, poisonous frogs, angry birds and bees. And for snakes, worms, giant butterflies, alligators, ants, fungi and sharp stones. And thorns. And giant fly-traps. And then they would tuck into their lunch.

'I think Blackbeard's probably better than Jonathon,' he would finally say, after chewing for some time on his vine leaf.

'See, I knew you'd come round in time,' she'd say, smiling, 'but really we ought to think of some other names too, just in case it turns out to be a boy.'

Epitome Quirkstandard spent the rest of the afternoon in the Crepuscular's shop, browsing more pamphlets, before going off to Mauve's for a spot of hearty supper. He spent the night there, since as Snatchby had said and as Simone had helped him to discover with a cheap pamphlet which happened to have underground and over-ground maps of a number of the great European capitals (including, as luck would have it, London), it wasn't far away. He slept in one of the guest bunks and woke fresh and refreshed the next morning. After a tiny spot of billiards with his pal Flirtwater, a larger smattering of breakfast and a quick sit down with the map and Snatchby, so that he'd be sure of the way (having noted that if you follow a path in one direction it's not always so simple to follow it back the other way unless you've been turning around and paying attention, since all the buildings look the other way round, as it were, when you go back and it's easy to end up faced by three roads and not know which one was the one you'd come out of, and you'd have to stand there and smell the wind and gauge the angle of ascent or descent and hope that by such clues you'll choose wisely, which isn't always the case) he went straight back to the Crepuscular's shop.

He worked his way through: *The Pacific Ocean & Other Great Misnomers (Including Rumoured Remedies For Mal-de-Mer); Keeping Clean In The Amazon Basin & Other Dirty Spots; Stamps Of The World (& Great Britain) & Their Apparent Perceived Relation To The Rainfall Patterns On The South Island Of New Zealand; Spiders, Pigeons & Carnivorous Trees Of The World*; and *How To Distinguish Pimples, Moles & Boils: A Spotter's Guide*. He sat and turned the crisp sheets over and over in his hands, absorbing every last bit of information (in much the same way as a sponge absorbs – that is: remarkably well at first, but with a lot of subsequent draining away, until eventually it will be, once again, as pristine and empty of water as it originally was). His jaw hung open, a distant gleam flittered in his eyes and a vein bulged in his forehead as his body tried to cope with the increased requests for oxygen arriving from his brain.

When Dawn brought him his lunchtime sandwich he put down *Horses & Houses: Not Merely A Difference Of Letters* and walked out into the kitchen. Simone was at the table with a large sheet of paper laid out before him, covered with his meticulous script and diagrams and he was pointing to a sketch in one corner, explaining something about it to his son Simon. They looked up at Quirkstandard as he entered.

'How has your morning been, Mr Q.?'

'Very instructional, thank you, Mr Crepuscular,

I never really guessed that there was so much to the world.'

'Oh, it's a wide place, and broad. That's certainly true enough.'

'I was wondering,' Quirkstandard began.

He paused.

'Yes, Mr Q., go on. If it's anything I can help you with, I mean anything within reason, then you know, sir, that I shall.'

'Well, you see, I was wondering, because I know a lot of chaps who're in just the same posish as I was on Monday – you know what I mean, Mr Crepuscular, daft as a plank and about as likely to understand an equation as a horse is likely to marry the king. So, I thought, since I'm here and they're not and since the front room isn't all that big really, whether I might, well, take a couple of the pamphlets away and show them to a few chums back at my Club? Sort of give them the boost up and maybe they'll come and read the next one themselves?'

'Why of course, that sounds a jolly enough idea. You know, Mr Q., as well as I do that these pamphlets (except for a few particular ones of which that we've only the one copy left) are as much for sale as they are for reading here, and even if you don't want to purchase we can always rent off the premises. All that takes is a small deposit and whatever you wish from the shelves can be yours for the day.'

'Oh, smashing.'

Quirkstandard returned to the front room and began to make a small pile of what he saw to be the key pamphlets that would turn an idle gentleman's head. He knew he faced a struggle with some of his pals, but he thought if he could find the right angle of attack on each of them then he might be able to start something special.

He soon found that his pile included all the pamphlets he'd read thus far and this was clearly too much to get through in one evening's assault on Mauve's. Sadly he began to whittle them down to just a couple. As he picked each one up to examine it and to make a decision he turned them over and read facts that he'd only read a few hours earlier, and he was surprised to discover that some of them he already knew, though some were (once again) brand new. But the fact, he told himself, that some of it had stuck ... well, that had to mean he was getting smarter, yes?

'What about Veronica?'

  'It sounds a bit girly, don't you think? A bit weak.'

  'Bertha?'

  'A bit too manly.'

  'Hieronymus?'

  'Too much like a Dutch painter.'

  'Sebastian, then?'

  'Too much like a man I killed once in a fit of wrath.'

'Oh, he must have been a bad man to get you angry dear,' Crepuscular said, treading carefully through the jungle.

'Yes, a truly dreadful man. He was a pirate from a different ship to mine, you see, and we were drinking together in Pedro's Bar, late one night, when he suggested that his ship was bigger than mine. What did I care about that? It wasn't my ship, as such, since I was only crewing on her over the summer holiday to pay my way through Pirate College. What did it really matter if his ship was bigger? He was only crewing for the same reason as me. We'd had a couple of classes together that term and he'd always been a bit full of himself. I'd watched him in the Swaggering Lectures and he was rubbish, but had a big brass buckle on his hat, with feathers and beads hanging from it, which always distracted the lecturer who had this thing for cheap baubles, so he'd come out of there with decent marks when he should've, frankly, had to do Swaggering re-sits. And it was the same in other classes too: all talk and no trousers. Anyway, I tried not to let his bragging get to me that morning and so when he continued to go on about the size of his ship versus mine I leant over the table and slapped him on the cheek. Just gently enough to make him shut up. But, when he got up off the floor, he picked up his drink and threw it straight in my face.'

'I'm surprised, Maria, that he'd managed to live this long.'

'Well, he'd been drinking mineral water, you see, and those bubbles can sting a fair bit if they get your eyes, which they did, and so I stood there half blinded by the fizzing and I just pulled out my pistol and shot him. It was all I could think to do.'

'Bang. Bang.'

'Yes, a bit like that Rodney darling. Except I had a revolver and so there were six bullets.'

'Bang, bang, bang, bang, bang, bang,' Rodney shouted into the rainforest canopy. A flock of toucans erupted from the trees high above and flew off squawking noisily.

'Except, of course, being blinded I couldn't see so well and every one of those bullets missed him. One of them, though, was reflected off the mirror behind the bar and flew back down the barrel, which exploded and left me with this.' She held up her hook hand.

'So, you didn't kill him then?'

'Not then, no. But I pushed him down a latrine the next night when he'd been drinking harder stuff. He drowned.'

'Golly,' said father and son together.

'Well, it turned out to be a blessing really. I'd not been doing too good in my classes either (I was never academically gifted), but when I got back to Pirate College after the summer break I graduated immediately with flying colours. All because of the hook, it gets you on a sort of fast track, you see. So here I am.'

'And then I met you …'

'… yes, later on, long after that, you met me.' She leaned over and kissed him, seeming to be genuinely happy for a moment.

After walking a little further Simone paused and asked, 'That pirate, that student, was he called Sebastian then?'

'Do you know something,' Teresa-Maria said, after a moment, 'I can't rightly recall. I think that might've been the name of his ship. It's all so long ago now.'

They walked on, further into the forest.

16

The Shop & The Browsers

❧

After the astonishing success of his first three pamphlets Simone Crepuscular set up *Crepuscular & Sons: Educators To The World*, his shop.

The moment he did so the bottom dropped out of the pamphlet market. Demand simply dried up, along with sales.

At first it seemed that no one was ever going to come into their shop. Then, one day, almost three months after he first laid out his wares on the counter, unbolted the front door and counted out his float, the little bell tinkled and a man entered. In silence he looked at the three titles on the counter, looked around the otherwise empty room and then went out again. Quite swiftly.

Another three months of uninterrupted quiet passed by before the doorbell tinkled again. Simone looked up expectantly from where he sat at the counter, putting the finishing touches to a drawing for a new pamphlet. It was the same chap from three months earlier. Once again he looked around, didn't see anything he wanted and left without saying a word.

This teasing lack of appreciation so upset Simone that he hurriedly set aside his drawings, pulled out a fresh sheet of paper and wrote in his finest large script *THIS*

IS NOT THE SHOP YOU WANT; PLEASE TRY ELSEWHERE.

This, naturally enough in a city like London where the extraordinary soon becomes ordinary and the ordinary evaporates to humdrum in a matter of minutes, immediately attracted the attention of passers-by, who came in and started browsing, wondering just what it might be that they didn't want. In a moment of pique Simone tried to usher them out. He was mostly successful in this endeavour but failed, however, to clear the shop entirely before one of these gawkers bought a pamphlet.

As he placed the penny in the till Simone Crepuscular finally felt the satisfaction of a shopkeeper surge in him. It's not a question of greed or caprice, but rather a more benign warmth that comes from fulfilling one's chosen role. In the same way as a baker takes pride in baking bread (and more so when the bread is eaten by someone who gets pleasure from bread) and a train driver takes pride in driving the train (and more so when passengers are moved from one place to another on time), so a shop-keeper is fulfilled, qua shopkeeper, not when he merely keeps a shop which is, of course, a start, but only when that shop is used as a shop by the public. Of course, cash in the till drawer isn't to be sniffed at either.

As those first six months of shopkeeping had passed by he had been toying with a number of ideas for subsequent pamphlets. Some were further autobiographical tales, bringing his story, more or less, up to date in the series he had begun so successfully, but he had other ideas too: to investigate some Eastern philosophies that were close to his heart; the mystical experiences and beliefs of other cultures and species (he wasn't exactly sure what this meant, but was willing to think about it); or, to write about the geography, geology and natural history of various countries around the world that he hadn't actually visited himself. He had heard of many things, tales and rumours from the people he'd met in his long peregrination, and on Wednesday afternoons, which was half-day closing, he'd made a habit of visiting the British Museum and sitting in the Reading Room, studying anything that came to light. He realised he wasn't bound by his own experiences, and he realised that not everyone had the time or the patience to sit through some of those abstruse tomes that were brought to his desk, but he could summarise, précis and concatenate the best bits to make them palatable.

By the end of those first six months he had plans and sketches prepared for the next 23 pamphlets. What he now needed however was some cash with which to pay the printer to print even one of them. And all they had to do to raise the money was to sell the remaining stocks of the originals.

He called a meeting with his sons.

Rodney waved a hand in the air in the backroom to get his father's attention.

'Yes Rodney?'

'Daddy, I think I have an idea.'

'Go on.'

Rodney, aged 12, explained his theory and Crepuscular found himself sadly agreeing with the boy. They had alienated their clientele by trying to better themselves. The sort of people who had ceaselessly bought the pamphlets from small boys hawking them on street corners were reluctant to go and seek them out in a quiet shop, under a pristinely painted sign and with a gentleman stood behind an imposing counter. By removing themselves from the passing foot-trade of the hurly-burly on the street it was as if, Rodney suggested, they had (unwittingly) cocked a snook at their loyal customers. And even though their work was, at heart, about bettering oneself, they had thoughtlessly attempted a step too far too soon.

So the boys went back out onto two street corners, with bags full of the first three pamphlets and began singing out their hawkers' songs once more.

When they returned in the evening they each had a bag of pennies, but also a half full sack of papers. They'd sold some, but not all.

'I'm not used to bringing any home, dad,' said Simon, aged 10.

'No, but times change, son,' said his father, 'We have to be adaptable.'

'Daddy?'

'Yes, Rodney?'

'There was this man on this corner right near me, right, and he was selling cakes fresh from inside a little portable oven thing that he had, and people kept coming up and buying them from him, all steaming and buttery.'

'Yes ...'

'Well, I heard him say to a gent who came along and who asked how, you know, how trade was, right? And he said to this bloke, to the gent, he said, you know, about his hot cakes ... he said, 'They're selling like new pamphlets, mate', is what he said. Does that mean us?'

'It meant us, I'm afraid Rodney. Past tense. It *meant* us.'

A small tear came to his eye as he remembered the golden days of the previous autumn.

'Ah, my boys,' he said wistfully, 'Once, we were the best. But now, we're just us.'

'You're still the best to us, daddy,' said Simon, very sweetly, though a little sickly too.

Through a careful use of promotions, two for the price of one offers, free toast and limited editions (available upon presentation of the appropriate number of coupons snipped off previous pamphlets' back covers) they managed to gather a small but loyal base of regular readers. The spread was never as large as it had been in the beginning and occasionally someone would be overheard in the street saying, 'I wonder whatever happened to that bloke with all those bits of paper?' but those who still read the things, well, they knew.

Crepuscular sold pamphlets by mail order and various libraries and mutual improvement associations around the country subscribed. The growing boys would still take new pamphlets out onto street corners for a week each month, as they were freshly printed, and they had a few loyal browsers in the shop and Crepuscular ran the place as a lending library. It all served to keep the family's heads above water, if not ever allowing them to get out of the pool, as such.

In the long run though, Simone was happy, scribbling away, researching, drawing and writing. His world was circumscribed by the British Museum on Great Russell Street to the north and the galleries on Trafalgar Square to the south, and in-between were all the varied bookshops of Charing Cross Road. He rarely went outside of this area, but, as he thought to himself, he had seen so much of the world before this, that he could spend the rest of his life sat in a single chair and not have time to consider everything he'd seen. Unexpectedly he had found happiness in his writing, in his life and in his study.

Buying the shop hadn't been the first mistake that Simone Crepuscular had made, and not all of them had ended up turning out quite so well. Nine years earlier he had made another one, which became something of a shot albatross to him.

Whether it was through the inadequacy of the maps he had examined or whether it was due to subtle tectonic movement or voracious plant growth or shifting political borders, he had found himself intractably lost in the Amazon Basin. To a certain extent and looked at from a certain point of view he wasn't lost at all. If someone had asked, 'Where are you?' he would have been able to answer, 'In the Amazon Basin,' without a moment's hesitation and with tragic ease. However, the detail was lacking. This jungle all looked the same to him. There were some trees and bushes and hanging things over there, some upright greenery and shrubs over here, and always the noise of things living, eating and multiplying all around them.

He tried his hardest to maintain an eastward march each day, but often they had to change direction, or double back, due to impassable bits of undergrowth or sudden cliffs or small shrunken heads mounted on poles, and they often ended up making their progress in the opposite direction entirely.

By now the highly gravid Teresa-Maria was finding it hard going to keep up with her tall, stridingly fit husband. Simone found this frustrating and naively kept believing that in just a few more days they'd be out of the jungle and on the coast, where they could find a room in an inn and maybe even a midwife. He saw no other alternative but to keep pushing the family onwards. His eternally optimistic open-minded, shut-eyed but conversationally cheerful outlook on the world only caused Teresa-Maria to writhe, when she wasn't huffing with the effort of walking further. She was clear-sighted about their predicament and when her time of confinement drew too close to ignore any longer, she did the only thing she could in order to make Simone face up to the truth.

She sat down, with her back to a tree, folded her hands on her round, tight belly and refused to move any further.

Simone was about to argue the point, explaining how 'lost' was a relative concept, and how, besides, better people had been lost before, when he really looked at her.

In the dim light of the evening, with the occasional shaft of sunlight running almost horizontally under the canopy, she was a sad, small figure, dark amongst the undergrowth. Then, suddenly, one of those shafts struck her face, after having rushed many millions of miles through space, and as the photons reflected off the moist spheres of her eyes Simone saw himself reflected there too. They were joined by this, joined together, in this together, lost together. How far would they have to travel? Millions of miles too? How could anyone ever know? Then, somewhere above them, a branch shifted in the wind and the beam of light was blocked, a few hundred meters suddenly removed from its journey, by something as simple as a breeze. Her face fell into darkness and he fell into her eyes.

One moment he was standing still, staring down at his beautiful but weary and teary wife, the next moment he found himself fainting away, as if drugged. He collapsed to the leafy ground and into a troubled dream-filled sleep, in which he was visited by the yak he had met so many, many years before high in the Himalayas. In the midst of the humid jungle it stood, chewing insolently on a mouthful of cud. As Crepuscular looked at it, as he reached out a hand to touch it, as he ruffled his fingers through that thick, rough hair he remembered so well, that had saved his life once before, it shrugged.

He was silent.

The yak looked up at him and shrugged again.

It looked all around it, as if looking for the path home, and shrugged for a third time.

A shrug from a yak is not something that can be ignored. A yak has enormous shoulders, humped, muscular, certain and strong, and in a moment Crepuscular found himself shrugging along with them. Following the yak's lead.

When he woke he found his head was resting in Teresa-Maria's lap and Rodney was holding a sponge (made out of chewed-up vine leaves soaked in a nearby streamlet) to his brow.

As he looked up into his wife's face he said three words. Three little words he should have said to her, he realised, long ago, but had never had the courage or the clearness of mind, had never quite had the faith in her to believe that she would understand, that she might be able to help, even. He looked up, into her eyes and said, 'We're lost, Maria,' before slumping back into a feverish, though dreamless, sleep.

17

Jungles, Telegrams & Tips

In another jungle, some ten years later, Penelope Pen-ultimate, Quirkstandard's Aunt, also received some bad news.

She was on an expedition with a gossiping gaggle of schoolgirls exploring the uncharted rainforests of the small island of Dominica in the Lesser Antilles. They had been wandering purposefully for three months (purposefully only in the sense that the girls were taking turns navigating, in order to learn basic orienteering and map reading skills, but such skills were, she was almost ready to admit, slow in coming this trip), subsisting on rainwater, hummingbirds (she always carried a butterfly net for catching just such light snacks) and the ubiqui-tous forest food of vine leaves, stuffed with other vine leaves. The girls were becoming restless.

Miss Penultimate was becoming restless too. She was a professional expedition leader, a teacher and educator of young ladies in the more abstruse skills of world-survival (skills which she argued were transferable into the lives her wards were likely to face upon return to England: marriage or a season in London), but this group of girls, as warm-hearted and friendly as they all were, were the most hopeless bunch of incompetent young ladies she had ever happened to take under her wing. They tried, and kept trying, but they also kept failing.

Miss Penultimate hated few things more than giving up on a girl. She believed the world, and what laughingly passed under the name of 'civilisation', would do that for them, or to them, by itself. She wanted to see her girls capable of kicking back at the outmoded, uninteresting lives that were being prepared for them back home, where they were expected to be nothing more than pretty accompaniments on their husbands' arms and perambulatory factories for churning out heirs. She knew that most of her girls would end up in marriages just like that (since she only dealt with the nice upper middle class and lower upper class families who could afford her fees) and she wanted them to have something else, even if it was only a slight, unfulfilled sense of their own worth as individuals, their own beauty as unique creatures in their own rights, even if they never did anything more than occasionally think about those four months spent in the rainforest. That's all she really expected, to sow a little seed of dissatisfaction in their humdrum, day-to-day, carbon copy lives. If she'd done that much for them she'd be happy-ish. Of course, if they went on some demonstrations requesting the vote or demanding better working conditions and equal pay for women in factories and service industries and if they let their maid wear the pearls once in a while, then Miss Penultimate would feel even better.

But, as far as she could tell, this present gaggle were just looking forward to getting home, even though not a one of them had the faintest clue in which direction home lay. But they were nice handsome girls and none of them actively simpered anymore, which was a step forward from the first night they'd all spent in their tent. So at least, in a small way, that was something, she thought.

It was just after supper, on this particular night in this particular jungle, and the sleeping mats had been unrolled and the cocoa was being boiled, when there came a knocking from outside the tent.

Drawing her dressing gown around her, handing her pipe to one of the girls and checking that her knife was tucked in her boot where she could quickly reach it, Miss Penultimate drew aside the tent flap and stepped outside.

'Telegram for Penultimate, ma'am,' said the telegram boy.

'That's me, thank you,' she said, taking the envelope from his hand.

She opened it quickly and read it through twice. It wasn't long.

'There's no reply, thank you.'

'Ma'am.'

Before she turned to duck under the flap and re-enter the warm fug of the tent, she looked back at the young chap, his hand still half-outstretched.

'Oh, can I give you a tip, young man?'

'Please ma'am. That would be kind.'

'Very well. My tip is to stop calling me 'ma'am'. I'm not the bloody queen.'

'Yes, ma' ... Miss,' he said as she vanished behind canvas.

'That's better,' she called from inside, with more gaiety than she felt. 'Well done.'

As she stood just inside the tent she read the note one more time, before becoming uncharacteristically self-conscious. She glanced up to see the half dozen young ladies staring up at her expectantly. They looked up to her, she knew, and not just because she was taller than them, but because she was their leader who could be relied upon to solve any fix, to undo any mishap. She'd applied splints and insect repellent, sucked the poison out of more than one foot, arm or thigh and had turned Gertie's map the right way up just before they walked over the cliff. She was their strong and correct leader, who could talk on any subject and be interesting, who could answer any question and who was staunchly confident in the face of even the most credulous vapidity.

But now she felt her lip tremble. Damn it, she said to herself, what's happening? Pull it together Penny, these are only girls, they shouldn't have to see weakness in a woman. Pull it together! And she did. Her lip stood firm, unquivered, and, without one word that might have given some sign of her sudden grief, she walked through the tent to her own sleeping mat over in the far corner, slumped down, pulled a blanket over her shoulders and drifted into unpleasant dreams.

The girls, naturally, not being total idiots, knew there was something wrong. After all, supper hadn't long been over and although darkness had fallen quickly outside, they usually spent this time playing games or wrestling or, at the very least, practising a little swearing.[14] But tonight, while Miss Penultimate slept miserably in the corner, the girls were forced to amuse themselves.

In the morning they began packing up the tent and all their equipment and before lunch they were marching in the direction of the nearest seaport, ready to head back to England and the future. They were leaving a month ahead of schedule (not to anyone's great chagrin,

---

[14] Miss Penultimate didn't particularly approve of girls swearing, but for just that reason she took it upon herself to instruct them in appropriate terms of abuse. Had they been left to their own devices, she reasoned, they would pick up vulgar gutter words from their brothers and husbands, and men had very little idea of how to swear creatively or with flair and charm. It was all genitals, defecation and copulation with them. She instructed her wards in more imaginative modes of exclamation, more piercing insults rich with colour and diversity, but free of the easy slurring of her own gender or her own gender's personal parts. She also steered clear of religion, as much as was possible, arguing that it was just another patriarchal institution bent on cowing women in subjugated, subservient and subhuman positions.

Swearing, uncreatively, was unladylike, she argued, and if there was one thing Miss Penultimate liked it was a lady. (Naturally she also wished that men would be more ladylike (and indeed, conversely, that ladies would be more gentlemanly (in the sense of being 'cultured, courteous and well-educated', not in the sense of being 'oafish, boorish and tedious in extremis' which seemed to be the common understanding of the term in the streets of her day)).) She stood up for politeness, gentility and proper etiquette as much as she could. It does no harm, she would say, to the cause of Universal Suffrage, for a lady to know the correct knife to use when stabbing a violent, arrogant and megalomanic husband to death.

153

it should be noted) and Miss Penultimate finally, grudgingly explained why.

'Girls,' she announced. 'My dear sister has passed away.
This was the gist of the telegram I received last night.
And although we are all sisters, in a way, she was the
only one for whom I cared utterly and unconditionally,
the one with whom I grew up and who I loved. She has
passed away, back home in England, and I ...' here she
had to pause to find the correct way to approach these
difficult, unexpected words ... 'Girls,' she began again,
'my dear girls, I appear to have inherited ... a *boy*.'

18

The Baby, The Lost Temple
& Simone's Good News

Simone Crepuscular had a fair idea of what to do when it came to giving birth. He was exactly the sort of man who couldn't help but pay attention when something as interesting as that happened on, for example, the wide and often unexciting grasslands of Mongolia (even when the horse-doctor barred his entry he had listened very carefully through the tent wall). He thought that the moment had now come, here in the rainforest, for him to take charge, since Teresa-Maria was sitting down breathing deeply and looking flushed. Had she not been otherwise preoccupied she might have taken charge herself, having done this once already, but she didn't really care who thought they were in charge, just so long as it didn't take long.

Rodney kept Simon at a safe distance and lit a fire so that his daddy could heat some water up. Crepuscular had impressed on his boys the importance of washing one's hands, especially at a time like this. Rodney sat with his arm round Simon as they watched their mother and stepmother groan and swear and sweat and their father mutter to himself from between her legs. Naturally Simone had explained to both boys exactly what was about to happen, but they didn't entirely believe him. They leant closer to get a better view.

After a fairly short and pleasingly trouble free time their father stood up and showed them their new sister and the two of them gasped in amazement. She really was a breathing and squealing little baby girl, with tiny hands and feet and face and everything: everything that is, except a winkle, as Rodney observed. His father washed his hands and explained certain things about the world, including girls.

Teresa-Maria held her daughter to her breast, in the deep nest of leaves that Simone had made for her to rest in. The two boys snuggled up beside her, desperate not to be left out and, shuffling across, she made space for them. Only Simone remained outside the familial bed. He hadn't made it quite big enough for the five of them and so, as they all dozed, sighed and whimpered, he sat up through the night beside the fire, keeping a weather eye out for jaguars. And for alligators. And for vultures, insects, snakes and all the rest. None came near.

He had hoped that on the next morning they might be able to start moving again, but Teresa-Maria wanted to stay in bed. She was too tired to move. As Simone rustled up some vine leaves, larvae and berries for breakfast the boys played with their new sister as if she were the best toy they'd ever had. Rodney sat her in his lap and jiggled her about, while Simon sang her songs that he made up on the spot. She ignored them and cried and wriggled quietly all to herself.

Teresa-Maria spent the morning alternately sleeping, nursing, napping, nursing and sleeping. The boys carried the little girl about, picked her up, snuggled beside their mother and chewed on their berries. Only Simone felt less than an essential part of the family. He'd hardly had a chance to hold his daughter, the rest of them had been so greedy for her, and to his surprise he found himself grumbling that there were, in fact, more important things to be getting on with than dandling babies.

No one noticed when, halfway through the day, he wandered off into the jungle to see if today, just by chance, he might be able to find a clearing or a hilltop from which to spy the lay of the land and chart their course onwards to the sea and to home.

'I'm failing them,' he said as he brushed the brush to one side and ducked under a narrow corkscrewing horizontal branch, 'I know what I'm doing, I know exactly what I'm doing, for once, and it's failing, that's what it is. Failing them.'

He tried to cast his mind back to that deep green valley in the mountains, that place where he'd once begun his spiritual growth, where he'd learnt to look at the world with eyes that were open to wonder and which weren't concerned with success. What would his Little Master have done had he been in this same situation? What had he taught Simone that could be applied to this place? To this time?

'When a man is lost,' he remembered the Little Master once saying, 'He has simply found somewhere else instead. To find there what he was looking to find is impossible, unless he is hoping for something else. To get where he wants to go he must turn around and forget about where he is going. Then he will arrive somewhere, and wherever somewhere is, somewhere else is always close to hand. The two are indivisible.'

After saying this he had hit each of his students with the long staff he kept beside his mat specially for the task. Since Simone always sat at the front, eagerly taking notes, hanging on each of the Little Master's words and movements, he found the beatings with the staff to be an insistent but passing nuisance (they tended to jog his writing hand). If one was sat at the back of the room, however, the tip of the staff would be moving at a considerable speed and packed quite a wallop. But those who were furthest away often needed the biggest reminder, as the Little Master occasionally pointed out. With a thwack.

'If I'm lost, as I seem to be,' muttered Simone to the rainforest, 'then I must look at where I am, because maybe it's where I'm meant to be after all. Perhaps it's not that I haven't got to where I wanted to be, it's just that I didn't know where it was I was actually wanting to go ... and if that's the case, then how could I possibly know that I've arrived?' He paused, one foot raised in walking, and leant a hand on a gnarled old trunk, before sighing and talking into his beard once more. 'Goodness,' he said, 'the Little Master did talk some nonsense sometimes.'

He felt better admitting this to himself. He'd loved the old man, and had hung on his every phrase and utterance and had jotted as many of them down as he could, but he'd only followed half of them and of those he only thought he really understood half of them. The rest, he admitted, seemed like insoluble conundrums designed to make your brain ache.

He thought about heading back to the camp now and in a moment all the misery of his failure, of his lost path, of his lack of a plan forward slumped down onto his shoulders. How could he go back? How could he go back now? More of a failure than ever.

He let the foot that had been dangling in the air complete its step forward and lowered it to the ground.

His foot touched stone.

It didn't feel, to his toes, like a pebble or a random bit of boulder. He could feel a distinct edge to it. He could trace a step, a level surface and six inches in, a riser of stone.

As he peered through the darkness he made out the shape, dark against the patchy sky, of an old stepped pyramid. It was covered with vines and moss and had clearly been abandoned and forgotten for centuries, but he could see from where he stood at its base that the platform at the summit of its steep side poked out above the canopy. He could see sunlight glint brightly on the grey stone.

In ten minutes he had climbed the hundred-odd steps and stood out in the fresh air, breathing hard and half afraid to look. He bent over with his hands on his hips drawing his breath until finally he straightened up and using a hand as a visor looked out across the sea of greenery. Feeling a little nauseous he quickly changed the metaphor and looked out across the rolling cloud-scape of the forest canopy. Yes, it was like looking at green clouds from above, the way they undulated, the way here they were thicker and darker; how here they climbed, stacking massive and thick, as they covered some hidden hillside like dark cumulonimbus; how there they fell lower, like looking through a break in the clouds at the forested earth below.

Far to the east he could see a silver glittering. There, like a sliver just beyond the horizon, was the ocean. He'd seen it. He could see it. It was a long way, but now he knew which way. And there, oh joy! ... There, not two or three miles distant, was the telltale gouge through the green canopy that could only be the great river, the Amazon itself, or one of its many tributaries. All he had to do was find that river (just over there, two or three miles to the north) and then follow it as it flowed unhesitatingly to the sea, because that's what rivers do, every time. Except, of course, he thought deflating a little, for the ones that just go to lakes and stop.

He made his way back to the family camp a much happier man. Hope had bloomed and he longed to see his beautiful little daughter.

By the time Simone Crepuscular made his way back to the camp evening was beginning to fall. In the early shadow, through obscuring trunks, he caught glimpses of Teresa-Maria up on her feet hunched over a fresh fire, the black bottom of their travel kettle swinging in the orange flames. Little Simon was curled up in the leafy nest with his little sister, quiet and bleary, and Rodney was stood beside his mother, a hand firmly on his hip as if he were commanding nations.

When he emerged from the undergrowth, nervous for having been away so long, he found he was greeted with a smile and no questions. Rodney skipped over and took his hand.

'We're making tea, daddy,' he said.

'Oh yes?'

'Did you have a nice walk, darling?'

'Oh yes, thank you dear. Did you get some rest today?'

'Yes.'

Crepuscular let himself be led over to the fire where he kissed his wife on the forehead as she lifted the kettle off the fire with a stick and gently thumped it down on the mud. There was a hiss and sizzle and among the scent of steaming dirt Simone caught a pungent whiff of the vine tea. He remembered the glorious tea he'd drunk in India and instead of letting the comparison get him down, he held it up before him as simply another good reason to leave the jungle. He pictured again that slow loop of river he'd seen from the top of the temple and glanced through the shrubbery to the north, the way they needed to go, as if he might be able to see it from here.

He decided that he wouldn't mention his good news straight away. He'd wait until they'd all had a nice cup of tea ... well, until they'd had a cup of tea at any rate, and then he'd just slip it into the conversation as a casual aside. He knew he'd be risking life and limb by doing it this way, Teresa-Maria wasn't really the sort who took surprises well – either because they spoilt her plans or because in her excitement she'd swing her arms around and, depending on which attachment was strapped to her right wrist, several different levels of injury suddenly became available. But all the same, the look on her face would be worth a little risk, he thought. He wanted to feel loved and not just as her husband, but as someone who was actually proving himself to be capable, but at the same time, he didn't like to boast, so just a casual mention as if it were nothing …

They sat down with their mugs of vine tea and everyone inhaled the coiling steam that twirled up from the surface. It certainly cleared the sinuses and if anyone had had a cold it wouldn't have lasted long under such a medicinal assault. That's what this is, he thought, it's more like medicine than real tea. He tipped his mug to one side and then to the other and watched with unending fascination as the liquid gloopily followed the Earth's pull, slowly settling down to the new equilibrium as if gravity and the trend for a liquid to keep its surface perpendicular to that of the Earth were merely guidelines, rather than rules. It was like treacle, perhaps, or particularly aromatic mud.

Teresa-Maria sat with the little baby girl tucked in her lap and the two boys sat by her side and everyone huddled over their mugs. No one drank. After a minute of this Simone could contain himself no longer and he burst out with the news about the pyramid he'd found and how the river swept round so close to where they were and how he could see it heading off to the ocean, which he'd glimpsed on the very far horizon.

He spoke excitedly, and at length even though there wasn't that much to tell, but he described the way he'd stumbled onto the old stone steps and what he imagined the temple must've been used for in years gone by, but as he went off on archaeological speculations his family focussed on the most important bit of news – that, at last, they knew the way out.

Teresa-Maria jumped to her feet, filled with energy and delight. She danced around twirling their little daughter in her arms, animated in just the way that Simone had hoped she would be. All verve had been returned to her, all vim, all vigour. The merry eagerness, the cutthroat daring ruthless pleasure at life that she'd had when they'd first met, suddenly whooshed back up into her cheeks and she began to sing to their girl as she danced.

'We're all saved, we're all free,
daddy's saved us, you shall see!'

Crepuscular stood stopped in the middle of his ongoing oration and grinned from ear to ear as she swirled and twirled. He hadn't seen her so happy since they'd first climbed down from the Andes, months and months earlier, and had walked their first few steps into the dense, patchy dark of the rainforest. The first thing they had seen, high in the nearest branches, had been parrots, a whole flock of parrots just sat there watching them with intelligent beady eyes. She loved parrots and these ones were beautiful, green like emeralds and red like rubies. He spontaneously gave them to her as a gift, and although she was a little disappointed when he explained that it was a symbolic gift and that if she actually wanted to keep one she'd have to climb the tree and capture it herself, she saw the generosity in it and laughed with loving eyes. She'd hugged him and kissed him as Rodney made gagging noises behind their backs. She'd looked up at those first parrots and with a slight glint of sadness in her eye had said that she didn't do that sort of thing anymore anyway, but how lovely it was to see parrots happy and free in the wild.

'We're near the river, the river's near the sea,
we're going to the ocean, you shall see!'

She was beautiful as she danced, he thought. And he began to tap his foot and sway his hips too.

'We're going home, we're going to be free,
over the ocean blue, you shall see!'

And then, all of sudden, she wasn't there anymore.

There was silence in the jungle as three pairs of eyes stared at the space where she had been. It was empty now, as if she had simply vanished into the air. And then, after that suspended moment of peace, the scream reached them and Crepuscular jolted awake and into action.

He ran in two strides to where she'd been stood, and was lucky that his hand gripped a trunk instinctively when he got there, because there, just beyond the edge of their camp, of their *terra cognita*, was a cliff. It plunged down for maybe five hundred feet, vertiginous, huge, vertical, sheer and brown. He could see the canopy of the jungle dip and spread away below him, far below him: a deep valley, a rift valley perhaps, stretching away to the south. And there, in the air, far below him was his Teresa-Maria falling, spinning round and round. Her scream, a constant thread of sound, was diminishing now, in a moment he could hear nothing of it. And there ... oh, there, just beyond her was a tiny speck, the baby ... his girl, slipped from her arms, whipped away and flying free, falling free. Falling into the unknown depths of the distant, deep rainforest.

He watched until Teresa-Maria, his Maria, reached the forest canopy. She punched a tiny dark hole in it, breaking branches, tearing off leaves. A powdery flock of birds rose like dust from her point of entry, startled and scared into mindless flight, but they soon calmed, circled, descended and vanished back into the green blanket of trees again.

He had lost sight of the baby girl, she had been so tiny, and he had no idea where she had fallen. And the gloom was increasing. Soon the canopy was dark, soon the night had fallen entirely and then the rain began.

He stepped back from the edge of the muddy ledge as a great roll of thunder cracked the humid air. He turned his back on the view of that black valley and walked over to his boys. Fat drops of warm rain were splashing on the leaves above them, drumming like native telegrams, breaking up into smaller droplets at each level, until they reached the forest floor like a mist. Before Simone reached his boys his face broke down, his hands reached up and tore at his beard, yanking, tugging at it. Scraps of hair came loose, as tears rolled down his cheeks. From above them leaves began to fall; little twigs snapped off sturdier branches and a few fat drops, fat like a man's thumb, found their way to earth. As his lips and eyes turned red and ran with raw tears he fell to his knees, trembling, misshapen.

His boys were as scared by this as by their mother (and step-mother)'s sudden disappearance. They didn't know what to do, what was expected, what reaction was correct in this situation. As their father lay in the mud, getting wetter and shuddering they huddled together, sucking their thumbs and joining in with the crying. After a while they grew cold, so they dragged, step by step, urging by urging, their father over to the leafy nest he'd built for them. There he lay curled up and the boys lay beside him, sharing all their warmth against the oncoming chill of night.

They pulled a few giant leaves over themselves in a not wholly pointless effort to keep out the rain.

The storm finally blew itself out some hours before dawn, but the jungle echoed with the continual dripping of water long after the sun had risen. Exhausted by his impotent weeping, and with a pounding headache forming somewhere inside his shaven skull, Simone finally got up. He fed his boys a breakfast of fruit that he found in the bottom of Teresa-Maria's shoulder bag. He'd found it snagged on a tree-root nearby, muddy, torn but still full of oddments. Everything else in the camp, his cooking pots, his rucksack, the notebooks he'd been keeping for years had all vanished. They'd been swept away by the water that had washed across the sodden sod of the thick muddy ground all night.

Once the boys had eaten he followed some of these diminishing streamlets and found how they all flowed to the same point, a narrow lip of rock that pointed out over the cliff edge. He watched the small waterfall fall and evaporate into mist a hundred feet below him. Looking around in the daylight he could see no way down the cliff: it seemed sheer and smooth and unclimbable. He couldn't even make out which one of the dark spots in the canopy was the hole that Teresa-Maria had made when she fell. He cursed himself for not having paid closer, better attention at the time, for not having made a quick sketch map in his notebook. Was it that one there? Or that break in the green a little further on …? He couldn't say. The more he looked, the more holes appeared to him, the more possible gravesites made themselves known.

He realised he didn't know what he was doing, standing there, toes on the lip of rock, looking down into the valley. Or rather he knew what had happened, what had brought him here. He understood what he was looking at, but what eluded his brain right at this moment, what seemed hazy and hard to grasp, were the facts of how and when he had made his way to the cliff-edge, how he had fed the boys, how he had got up before that. It was as if his body were operating without him; he was in there, but so exhausted, he was still curled up, sucking his thumb, unable to embrace or face his loss. He peered over the ledge of his body, watching it move around, watching it manipulate the world, just as he peered over the ledge of the world itself. All he wanted to do, trapped inside, was go back to sleep (which presupposes that he had actually slept during the night, which was not entirely correct), or perhaps to topple forwards into the deep open air.

Suddenly his eyes jerked him awake. His head swung, he stood up straight, caught his balance, leaned back. He'd spotted something, whilst only half-aware … something that now looked like a way down the sheer face, further along the cliff to the west. Something inside urged him to get down there, into the sunken forest. It wasn't the belief that his wife might still be alive, never for one moment did he delude himself with such a hopeful, wishful fantasy. He had seen the results of falls from much lower heights in the mountains and knew that gravity, velocity and the human body were not close friends. But still he needed to find her. He needed, perhaps, to touch her body, to hold it in some farewell gesture, to dispose of it in a dignified manner, not just to leave it unmarked and unnoticed for the rats and the panthers and the carrion birds. Perhaps he just longed for a farewell more ritual and more perfect than the frantic and unmeaning wave she'd given as she fell.

An hour later he'd found himself down in the well of the valley. The cliff had been *just* traversable to the west, down a series of broken natural pathways. Some hours after that he had actually found her body. It had lain broken at the foot of a tree he had no name for. He'd straightened her buckled limbs and smoothed her hair and piled stones around her to keep off the predators. He was happy to leave her to the smaller processes of the world, to let her sink back into the soil in the jaws of insects and through the stomachs of worms and larvae, slowly as the seasons passed. That was dignified, he thought, more dignified than being ripped at by pumas or tapirs or vultures.

After sitting with her and burying her and leaving her he had wandered the jungle around the foot of the cliff and gathered up what he could find of their belongings. He'd walked miles round and round and found his rucksack (it required some tree climbing to reach), with all his notebooks intact and mostly dry, and he'd found a cooking pot, which he wasn't sure was actually one of his, but which he claimed anyway. What he hadn't found a trace of, was his baby. It was as if she had been lost on the wind, or more simply that the jungle was so huge and she so small and he only one man searching it. He'd sworn, but had known that he had to climb back up the cliff before night fell and get back to his two boys. They were alive and he loved them and could locate them, therefore they would be, they must be, his focus now.

Only once, while climbing the narrow path out of the valley did he think he heard the sound of a baby's cry. It was a thin and distant sound, carried by the high fast wind that alternately pushed and pulled him on the dangerous cliff path. High and thin and then gone. Perhaps, he thought to himself, it was some aural illusion created by the wind whipping through a tree or driving through a hole in a rock. Maybe it was just an animal. He convinced himself, in no short time, that it must've been a natural sound of some sort that merely played with his sense of wishful thinking. But for a moment there, for one terrifying hopeful moment, it had sounded shockingly real.

19

Penelope Penultimate &
The Lawyer's Office

When Penelope Penultimate arrived back in London she went straight to the Quirkstandard family's lawyer's office. There she met the man who had been entrusted with the safekeeping of her sister's will. Her brother-in-law had died three years earlier in slightly mysterious circumstances, which after some investigation by the authorities were deemed to be 'still fairly mysterious'. Whatever the precise circumstances had been, and the rumours were varied (not that Miss Penultimate listened to rumours and her sister hadn't liked to talk about them, even to her), the fact had been established beyond doubt that Lord Quirkstandard was dead. Now that Sarah Pen-ultimate-Quirkstandard, Lady Quirkstandard, had also departed that left their only son as sole heir. Balustrade had no siblings to quibble over the details and on the Penultimate side Penelope was the only relative, there-fore she assumed that the procedures would be fairly straightforward, legally.

Ivor Funicular was a small man, hardly five foot two when barefooted and barely an inch or so taller in his boots. His hair was dark, his nose offensive in an indistinct way (not only couldn't you put your finger on just what it was, but you wouldn't have wanted to even had you been allowed) and his eyes glistened like Brilliantine.

When Miss Penultimate entered his office he was sat in the chair at his desk giving dictation to his secretary. He (the secretary) was sat with a notepad on his knee on the desk. When Funicular saw Miss Penultimate in his doorway he gestured the secretary aside with a flick of his hand and stood up, becoming momentarily shorter, before climbing back into his chair.

'Please, have a seat, Mrs ...?' he said as he did so.

'Miss.'

'Oh, I do apologise, Miss ...?'

'There appears to be only the one chair,' she observed, after briefly glancing around the small room.

'There's always the desk?' Funicular offered.

'I think I'll stand, if you don't mind.'

'As you wish, Miss ...? The marble is rather cold.' He smiled in a grimacing sort of way, as if he had made a joke which he felt needed pointing out in the silence.

'Yes, quite.'

'Indeed. Indeed.'

A silence passed between them. Funicular gazed and Miss Penultimate waited. Nothing happened. He seemed content to just look at her over the top of his spired fingertips. Eventually she gave in and spoke.

'Is there something you wish me to sign, Mr Funicular?'

'Oh, maybe. Are you famous, Miss ...?'

'Famous?'

'Yes. I do have an autograph book, but as a rule I do only collect signatures of the great and the good, and sometimes actors too. And you, Miss …?'

'No, I'm not famous. I meant, do you want me to sign some paperwork? Is there something that requires my signature, legally?'

'Oh. I see. Well, that would depend, wouldn't it?'

'Depend, on what?'

'On who you think you are.'

'Really?'

'Most sincerely.'

'Surely sir,' Miss Penultimate felt a pedantic twitch rise in response to this little man's quiet but persistent obstreperousness, 'Who I am and who I think I am are not necessarily statements of common identification. Are you really suggesting that the latter, a mere belief in who I am, is in fact pertinent to the question in hand; or do you, as I suspect, wish to know, as a contingent fact in the external world, what it says inside, for example, inside my hatband? You wish to know, I imagine, who the rest of the world believes me to be, and if I claim to be Napoleon or Joan of Arc that would merely be an accidental confirmation of my inappropriateness to be signing legal paperwork of any kind.'

'Ah, so true, so true, Miss …? Um? Who do you *think* you are? An intriguing and revealing question indeed as you point out. A fount of inappropriate knowledge for this office. One that we may investigate, perhaps, at our leisure some other time. So, madam, assuming you claim to be neither Napoleon nor Joan of Arc (which would be unfortunate since I don't keep a straitjacket handy in the office, anymore), would you be so kind as to tell me, just who it is you are?'

'I, Mr Funicular, am the sister of the late Sarah Penultimate-Quirkstandard. I am Miss Penelope Penultimate and I believe you have something for me.'

'Oh, Miss Penultimate!' he shouted gleefully, 'You've come all the way from the jungle to see me! I should've guessed from your hat, of course. Forgive me for my rudeness and lack of detective intelligence. Oh, I would be delighted if you *would* sign my autograph book before you leave. I have worn your aglets ever since I was a lad.'[15]

'How lovely. I feel obliged, however, Mr Funicular, to point out that I haven't come straight from the jungle, and nor have I come, strictly speaking, to see you.'

'All the same, all the same, here you are in my little office.'

'Yes, it is quite small isn't it?'

'Ah, you make a joke.' (Miss Penultimate didn't think that she had.) 'I adore a woman who can joke. And such a funny woman, wisely cracking wisecracks in my office. My office!'

'Yes. This conversation (which would be far better, Mr Funicular, were it shorter) would be very awkward were I in someone else's office. That is why I am here.'

'Ah, yes. Shorter is always better. That's one of my mottos. Would you like to know what the others are, Miss Penultimate?'

---

[15] The Penultimate Fortune was founded on the sale of aglets. Miss Penultimate found the fame that came along with the name (which was known around the world, wherever aglets were sold) to have been both an aid and a hindrance (sometimes at the same time) on her wide travels.

'No.'

'Oh, very well. One of them is *Size is unimport* …'

'Mr Funicular, to business, please. Now. I believe you have something for me?'

'Oh yes.' He scooted his chair forward and plunged his hand into a pile of papers. 'Yes, Miss Penultimate. There are, of course, some formalities to be observed first.'

'Of course.'

He leant back in his chair, clutching a sheet of legal paper in his hand and stared at her for a moment.

'Over dinner, perhaps?'

'I'm sorry?' said Miss Penultimate, uncharacteristically thrown.

'The details, Miss Penultimate, I thought we might discuss them over dinner, maybe this evening?'

'No.'

'Tomorrow night, then. Or the weekend? In fact, I'm quite free …'

'No.'

'Oh.'

'Here and now, Mr Funicular.'

'Well then, let me at least send for a couple of glasses of wine. I mean, civilisation can hardly be said to exist without the fragrant juices of the grape to fill the gaps. Let us whet with wine our palates …'

'No. Mr Funicular it is a quarter past nine in the morning. I left work early and travelled almost four and a half thousand miles to be here and I am in neither the mood for your risible ideas of romance, nor for further, if I may speak frankly, fannying around. Stop it at once and show me exactly what it is that you have relating to my late sister's will. Thank you.'

If Miss Penultimate had not already been standing she would have stood at this point. As it was she simply stood straighter, if such a thing were possible, and stared.

Penelope Penultimate was a handsome lady, not beautiful in any classical sense, but decidedly eye-catching. Much of this had to do with her deportment and posture, but no small part came about from her eyes. She had a number of stares which quickly silenced people, men and women, and she knew exactly which one to use in which circumstances. They captivated, quietened and could inculcate loyalty, adoration and fear. Oh, most especially fear. She was not a woman to cross, that's what those eyes could say, as the blue in them turned icy cold and as they narrowed their beams to sharp, penetrating arrows. There was no messing. With those eyes she had once dissuaded a jaguar from pouncing in the Amazon and had on another occasion quieted a whole horde of revolting mutineers in the South China Seas after a week with no fresh water and a dicky compass.

It was one of these stares that she turned on Ivor Funicular now. But to her surprise he appeared to remain unfazed by her steely glint. Whether it was a sign of a strong will, of idiocy or of severe myopia she couldn't tell.

'To business then,' he said. 'Do you mind if I sit on your lap, Miss Penultimate?'

'What?'

She was not used to be being so wrong-footed, but this little man, this annoying little man, was zigzagging about too quickly. She felt tired with the ship-lag and had rushed to visit the lawyer without having any breakfast.

'We need to go over the text of the will, just quickly. I mean it's all quite straightforward.'

'That's not what you just said, Mr Funicular. Repeat what you said before that.'

'The will, Miss Penultimate, we must just look over it ...'

'No, before that ... There was something about my lap?'

'Ah, dear Miss Penultimate, as you correctly noticed upon your entrance, there is only one chair in this little office. I'm only a junior partner you see and such extravagances as having two chairs are quite beyond my means at this point in time. What I was suggesting, which is, I can assure you, quite standard procedure in a situation like this, in which we both need to be able to see the same document from the same angle, is that you take the chair and I hop up onto your lap ...'

Miss Penultimate had not heard such offensive drivel for years and years, not since she encountered a pair of Prussian missionaries in the Belgian Congo. But even then they'd simply been surprised by her and her girls (who were somewhat taller than the pygmies they'd been sent to talk to), and what followed was more along the lines of an embarrassed misunderstanding than the sort of pointed, purposeful nonsense that Funicular was spouting.

'Just tell me what it says,' she said coldly.

'You could sit on mine, if you prefer.'

'No.'

They paused for a moment longer. A clock ticked.

'Are you definitely sure you won't sit down? A slice of cake perhaps? Some tea?'

She tried increasing her stare and raised an eyebrow half an inch. What had never failed to quell an imperious man before, failed now.

'The will, Mr Funicular.'

He looked up, straight into her eyes and didn't shudder at all. He did pause for a long moment though.

'Yes, of course,' he said, finally.

He laid the piece of paper he'd been waving around down onto the desk in front of him and pulled a pair of reading glasses out of his suit's breast pocket. Miss Penultimate recognised the gold flare of the Quirkstandard letterhead at the top of the sheet.

'Your sister, Lady Penultimate-Quirkstandard, made this will merely hours before she passed away. But it was signed and witnessed, and is entirely in order, replacing her previous will which had been made in 1897, well before her husband's untimely death. When she was told that the verrucas had spread to her brain she became calm and called for us to set her affairs straight. I was with her shortly before the end, my dear Miss Penultimate, and I can say that your sister was not in very much pain, despite the size of the growths ...'

'Get on with it.'

'Oh, yes ...'

'The will.'

'The will says two things. Firstly, that everything that was hers passes to her son, Epitome Quirkstandard; and, secondly, that, until he reaches his twenty-first birthday, she entrusts the boy, and all his financial, educational and moral affairs, into your care.'

She sighed. It was exactly as she expected. She couldn't have imagined it playing out any other way. She *had* inherited the boy. A son she had never wanted, had never thought about, barely ever met and had never much liked. What was she going to do with him?

'Here,' said Mr Funicular, having climbed down from his chair and walked round to the front of the desk, 'Are the keys to 23 Devonshire Terrace.'

He handed her a set of keys from his pocket, before spinning on his tiny heel and marching toward a giant safe in the corner of the room.

'And in here,' he said reaching up with a key of his own and twirling a combination lock at the same time, 'Are Lady Penultimate-Quirkstandard's jewellery, cutlery and documents. We felt it best not to leave them lying unaccounted for in a house full of servants. I'm sure you understand.'

As he swung open the heavy door which led, not so much into a safe as into a small room filled with shelves of miscellaneous paperwork, various boxes, and assorted boxes of paperwork all tied up with fancy legal ribbons, Miss Penultimate caught sight of a small boy.

Her thin, pale twelve year old nephew was sat on a little wooden stool, reading a magazine. She noticed a candle burning on one of the shelves just to his side.

'Oh, and here's the boy,' added Funicular, apparently as an afterthought.

As the lawyer stepped into the safe, climbed a stepladder and pulled down three small boxes from a high shelf, Epitome stretched and stepped out into the office. It took him a moment to recognise his Aunt, since it had been at least a year since she had last visited and he'd been busy idling at the time, but when he did see her and realised who she was he ran over, flung his arms around her waist and buried his head in her bosom, something no man had ever dared do before.

'Auntie, Auntie!' he cried, as if in joy.

Something unexpected stirred in Miss Penultimate's heart at this great welcome, and as she prised his head away from her bust and looked at his big teary eyes she patted his cheek and said, 'There, there, dear, your Aunt's here for you now.' Perhaps it was simply having spent a quarter of an hour wrangling with Funicular that improved her view of Epitome (as if he proved that not all men were as vulgar, smarmy and idiotic), or perhaps it was the emergence of long buried maternal instincts,[16] or maybe just that her overpowering moral sense kicked in and wouldn't leave one of her own family behind. Whatever it was, she was determined from that moment on, that what she could do for the boy, she would do.

She ruffled his hair in a way she imagined might be comforting. But who knew with boys?

Funicular placed the three packages onto his desk.

'Jewellery, cutlery and important documents,' he said, 'Could you just sign the docket there to say you've picked them up?'

[16] It might be worth noting that it wasn't the warm glow of a maternal instinct that led her to gather together and care for groups of young ladies, as she regularly did; it was cash.

As she signed, he walked back to the safe and closed it, locked it and spun the combination wheel. Miss Penultimate was fairly sure she'd memorised the numbers and she knew which pocket Funicular kept the key in. You never know, she thought, when such information might come in handy.

'Are you sure,' Funicular said, apropos very little, 'that I can't tempt you with just a small glass of wine, or perhaps, seeing what time it is, a quick breakfast roll?'

His eyes flickered devilishly.

'Mr Funicular,' Miss Penultimate answered slowly and evenly, 'may I speak candidly with you a moment? Stepping outside the usual bounds of normal and good society? Outside the conventional mores of usual London decency, if you see what I mean? Only, what I wish to say to you … may be … upsetting.'

'Miss Penultimate. I think we both know I am a man of the world. I can guarantee that not only is whatever you say to me in this office obviously covered and bound by my lawyer's oath of confidentiality, but also that I am almost, shy of a few exceptions, quite entirely unshockable.'

He stepped with her over to the large window which dominated one wall of the office, leaving Epitome sat on the other side of the desk shuffling his heels.

'Very well, Mr Funicular,' she began, bending over him like an awesome, beautiful leaning tower and speaking in a low soft hushed voice. 'In my time I have killed only three men. All of them, it must be said, were taller than you, broader than you and possibly more intelligent than you, although one of them was a Bavarian, so who can say? He was despatched with a paperweight, a very large and heavy paperweight. Another vanished mysteriously in the night from the deck of an ocean liner, and the third I strangled to death with my belt.'

Funicular blanched.

'Does this shock you sir?'

'I must admit to a little unsettledness,' he said, looking out of the window at the roof of a passing cab. 'That a woman should remove her belt in the presence of a man … quite unthinkable.'

Miss Penultimate looked at him pityingly.

'Sometimes,' she leant and whispered into his ear, 'Mr Funicular, sometimes I wear trousers.'

His eyes flicked from the view of the street to her legs which were, here in England, covered up with a simple, plain brown skirt.

'Do you know, Mr Funicular, what those men did to encourage me to take such drastic steps?' she asked, while straightening herself up a little and returning to the topic she most wanted to impress upon him.

'To make you wear trousers?'

'No, to kill them, you little fool. Trousers are simply much more practical in many parts of the world. For riding camels and so on. And for having pockets. No, Mr Funicular, do you know what those men did that made me take such drastic action with regards to their deaths?'

'No.'

'They overstepped *the mark*, Mr Funicular.'

'*The mark*?'

'Yes.'

'Oh.'

'And can I give you a piece of advice, Mr Funicular.'

'I expect so, Miss Penultimate, you are most wonderfully generous.'

'Mr Funicular.'

'Yes?'

'Be very, very careful in the future.'

'Yes?'

'If we were to meet somewhere that happened to neither be your office nor surrounded by witnesses you may well find yourself at a slight disadvantage.'

'Disad-?

'Disadvantage, Mr Funicular. Unless you had a pistol, of course. In which case things might be evened up a little. But I wouldn't recommend it.'

'Disadvant-?'

'Mr Funicular?'

'Mmm?'

'Do you understand me?'

He gulped and nodded.

'I was,' she added, 'Going to say 'Do we understand each other?' but then I realised that I could never possibly understand quite what it is that makes a repulsive worm like you get up in the morning. Which may or may not be a pity. Though I suspect 'not'.'

To her delight he started to cry. Not loudly, not blubbing and groaning, but a silent tear trickled down his cheek and landed with a little splash among the dandruff on his collar.

'I don't like you, Mr Funicular. Pray, let this be an end to it.'

Epitome had watched the two grown-ups talking by the window and although he hadn't been able to make out any of the words he could see that his Aunt was strong and brave and upstanding and beautiful and he felt that he loved her very much. He'd been sad to hear that mama had died, but she'd never had the mysterious something that Auntie Penelope had and he looked forward to spending the rest of his life with her. He certainly wasn't sad to see the back of the lawyer's safe.

'Come boy,' said Miss Penultimate, her voice warm once more, the icy glint banished from her eye. She took his hand in hers and helped him down from the desk where he'd been sat. 'Let us leave this place and find something to eat.'

'Iced cream?'

'If that is what you want, Epitome, then, today, that is what you shall have. Did I ever tell you of the time I was in Florence, oh! The iced creams they had there ...! Of course, they call them something quite different, but the flavours, my boy ...'

Funicular stood, hunched, staring out of the window and after a few minutes watched Penelope Penultimate and the boy cross the street below him. He watched the swing of the hem of her skirt, remembering the steel in her voice, her breath in his ear, the ruthless threat she'd uttered to him, just to him. Deep inside his chest he felt the stirring of an emotion that he dared hardly put a name to. He cancelled the rest of his appointments for the morning, in order to think about it all, and about her, for a little bit longer.

20

Crepuscular & The View Out To Sea

꙳

Crepuscular and his two boys found their way to the banks of the Amazon and from there they paddled and drifted their way along to the Brazilian coast.

The further they went the wider the river grew, until they lost sight of the other bank entirely. It reminded Simone uncomfortably of the sea, but to his mild surprise he found the fresh water and the smaller waves combined to make him only slightly violently ill.

It was the thought of those two boys by his side, or in his arms, that gave him the strength or the desire to continue. As he lay, pretending to sleep, at night, there was no desire in him stronger than the one which bade him remain lying down, that said to him, 'Stay here in the jungle, here with your heart.' But each morning they'd wake him up, from the shallow version of sleep he'd eventually drop into, and seeing their hungry faces, so reliant on him, so entirely reliant on him, he'd make them breakfast out of whatever grew close to hand, in a sort of hazy half-trance, and they'd start walking or boating. As much as possible heading eastwards.

He'd detached Teresa-Maria's multi-purpose prosthetic before he'd left her, since it was the only sharp instrument they'd brought with them. Holding it made him feel as if not everything was lost, and as he looked at its shining, reflective surface he sometimes imagined that his eyes weren't the only ones that were looking back at him.

When they finally reached a small estuary town, a few weeks later, he sat down on the quay and stared out at the ocean. Far away, way beyond the brown outflow of the river and the dotted clumps of land that littered the delta, he could see a razor thin slate grey line which represented the deep salt sea. Looking at it he sighed deeply. Thinking about it he slumped visibly. He remembered what the Pacific had been like. He knew what the river had done to him, and now he was faced with this second great ocean, without his mariner-bride. She had always claimed great cures for seasickness, and although she had never revealed them (since they'd never been to sea together) and even though he suspected (knowing her deeply piratical nature) that they probably involved keelhauling or plank-walking, he so, so wished she were here to tell them to him.

She had been the steady point on his horizon, the smile he aimed for but which was always mysterious, always not wholly explored yet. There was so much future before them, so much she had yet to tell him. She was reticent, secretive, oddly quiet and he longed to find everything out, but he'd never pushed her when she stopped an anecdote halfway through, saying, 'No, I don't think I want to go on.' He knew there'd be a time – in a year maybe; maybe in thirty years – when she'd come back to that story and finish it off. His pirate, his beauty, his bride. His mystery.

So, Simone Crepuscular sat on that quay, looking out at the water and once again, as if it might change things, he sighed deeply. He had been travelling, on and off, for ten years and had come many thousands and thousands of miles. He wondered how it was that the Simone Crepuscular he was today was so different from the Simone Crepuscular he had been at the beginning, the one that had walked out of that army camp in Northern India, and had even less in common with the Simone Crepuscular (the boy) who had tried to join the circus. Oh! He hadn't thought of the circus for years, he'd forgotten about the clowns and the sea lions and the burning hoops. He'd seen real seals in the wild since then, gazing up out of the foaming seawater at him as he lay on his boat, with their giant brown eyes like particularly sweet puppies, as they dodged the falling vomit.

How strange the path has been, he thought, how little of it I could ever have predicted.

He was wise enough to know that the Simone Crepuscular who finally set his foot back on English soil would be yet another, newer, Simone Crepuscular, one that he hadn't met yet.

After watching the ships bobbing in the tide for some days he stood up, called his boys to him and walked over to the quayside. He scanned the flags that dandled from the stern of each boat, trying to recognise what they represented, but he'd never really given any time to studying flags so he simply picked the one that looked most cheerful.

As he walked up the gangplank, in order to offer his services to the Captain in exchange for board and transport, he felt his stomach perform its usual nautical flips and he wished he'd never eaten anything, ever before, ever in his entire life. Ever. Ever. Ever.

21

Quirkstandard Searches for Gentlemen

❦

On Friday morning Epitome Quirkstandard went back to Mauve's. In his hands he carried a folder containing a dozen of his favourite Crepuscular pamphlets. He nodded at Snatchby as he strode through the doors, for the first time in his life marching like a man with a purpose. Down corridors he stalked at speed, not stopping to talk, not even checking his pigeonhole for post; no, he had more important things on his mind at last. At last, a real purpose.

As the doors to the Great Room swung shut behind him, he peered into the gloom. This set him back in his tracks somewhat. After spending the last few days in the bright shop front of *Crepuscular & Sons* he had forgotten quite how dim they liked to keep the lighting here at Mauve's. It was Club policy to not excite the gentlemen with intense stimuli, and so the windows were kept shuttered and the gas lamps hissed quietly on the walls where they were turned to the lowest setting.

Gingerly he paced to the very middle of the room. Away on either side, in front and behind him, were deep leather armchairs and a few purplish settees. Whether they were all occupied or not was hard to tell in this light, but he coughed quietly to get their potential inhabitant's attention anyway.

Another thing he had forgotten about this place, living out, as he had, in the real world for a few days, was how sound itself seemed muffled, as if the distance it travelled before tailing off was curtailed in the close dimness. As he thought this, the image of Crepuscular's Little Master and what he had said about sound popped into his mind. Something about vibrations. Quirkstandard hadn't quite followed that bit, but there had been a very nice drawing of a yak that had stuck in his mind. He'd been impressed with the breadth of the animal's horns. A yak, he thought, would've made a noise that these old men would've noticed.

Of course, many of the gentlemen who were members of Mauve's were no older than Quirkstandard, but he couldn't help but think of them that way now – as ineffectual old duffers – stuck in their ways and unable and unwilling to poke their head out from behind the barricades of their wealth, privilege and ignorance in order to learn new tricks: ergo, old men.

Quirkstandard coughed once more, ready to begin his lecture. There was no response.

He wished he'd brought a glass and a fork, because he thought that would make a more immediately noticeable sound. They did that, he'd noticed, at banquets and weddings and things to get everyone's attention.

Putting his folder down on an occasional table he marched back up the corridor to where Snatchby was waiting in the hallway.

'Snatchby?'

'Yes, sir?'

'Do you know where there are any wine glasses?'

'Yes, sir.'

'Oh, super. Can I get one?'

'Yes, sir.'

'And a fork, I think. That should do the job, yes?'

'Indeed, sir.'

Quirkstandard followed Snatchby up the passage to a cabinet just outside the Great Room in which were glasses and cutlery. He selected a pair of items, thanked Snatchby and re-entered the room.

Having strode over to where he'd left his papers he stopped, coughed gently and then tinged the glass.

A clear note shone through the room, beautiful and glittering and rousing entirely no response.

Quirkstandard tinged again.

This time he either hit too hard or had found by chance the undetectable focus of the glassblower's stresses, the sweet spot as it were, and with a cracking tinkle the glass shattered into a thousand pieces in his hand, leaving him holding a jagged stem and a fork and looking rather worried.

'Oh dear,' he said, knowing that breakages were added onto a gentleman's subs at the end of the month.

'Don't worry, sir,' said Snatchby, appearing by his elbow, 'I brought a dustpan, just on the off-chance. And a brush, sir.'

'Oh, very good Snatchby, old man. Always one step ahead, eh? Smashing.'

'*Smashing* indeed, sir.'

'Ha ha. Yes. I see what you mean.'

Quirkstandard looked around the room.

It seemed that no one had stirred.

Not one gentleman had come forward to hear what he had to say, not one newspaper had been folded away with a fresh noisy crunching. Nothing. In his hands (well, on the occasional table at his side) was the most explosive, eye-opening, world expanding material that had ever passed through the portals of the Club and they weren't paying the scantest bit of attention to him or it. He only wanted the chance to share it. That's all.

He took a step forward and leant into the gloom. The nearest plush leather armchairs were, it turned out, quite empty. He walked over to some more, a little further off, only to discover that they were empty too.

'Snatchby?' he said.

'Yes, sir?'

'Snatchby, are there any gentleman in this Club?'

'As you know sir, much to your Aunt's chagrin, there are *only* gentlemen in this Club.'

'This is no time for jokes Snatchby, this is important. You know what I mean. Are there any gentlemen in this Club today, right now?'

'You mean are there any gentlemen here at present, sir?'

'Yes.'

'There is one sir.'

'Just one?'

'Yes sir, just the one.'

'Well,' said Quirkstandard, feeling a little crestfallen, 'I suppose one is better than none. I had hoped to make a bit of a splash with this material. It really is top-notch stuff – thrilling, funny, informative and rippingly intelligent – really good stuff, and I'd rather hoped there'd be a little crowd here to hear it.'

'I'm sorry, sir.'

'Yes, well, I don't suppose it's your fault, Snatchby, old man.'

'Indeed not, sir.'

'Well, Snatchby, you'd best lead me to this solitary gentleman so that I may enlighten his life with the glow of education.'

'Ah, sir. I believe I must have been unclear in my pronunciation.'

'Oh?'

'Yes, sir. The one gentleman present this morning, well sir, it happens to be you, sir.'

Quirkstandard looked around.

'Really?'

'Really, sir.'

'Just me, then?'

'Yes, sir. Just you.'

'Crikey. I must look rather a dunce, Snatchby, to not have worked that out myself. I'm rather glad now, I must say, that there aren't any other chaps around to see me be so thick.'

'My lips are sealed, as ever, sir.'

'Thank you Snatchby, you're a card.' Quirkstandard paused for a moment. 'So,' he began again, 'Where is everyone today?'

'You must be forgetting, sir, with all the excitement of your new hobby perhaps, that this is the third Friday of the month.' Quirkstandard looked none the wiser. 'And on the third Friday of the month, sir, the gentlemen of this establishment like to play a game of hide-and-seek. I believe a book is run and there is a tournament cup at the end of the year.'[17]

'Oh well, you know I've never much gone in for sports, Snatchby, I'd forgotten about that. Blast it. So there's no one here at all?'

'No, sir. There is you, and there is me. I believe Mr Lillytit is in his office, but you weren't counting the management were you, sir?'

'No Snatchby. I don't think he'd appreciate having his brain stretched, do you?'

'I couldn't say, sir.'

'No, I didn't think so either.'

'Oh, and your friend Mr Spiggot is here, sir. He's in the garden. Cook gave him a bone just before going off duty.'

'What?'

---

[17] Early that morning (early at Mauve's meaning sometime after ten o'clock, but before lunch) Snatchby had stood in the corner of the Second Lesser Room, where post-breakfast cigars were traditionally consumed, and had been asked to count to one hundred while keeping his eyes closed. As he counted, the gentlemen went and hid and once he had reached one hundred it was his job to look for them.

This was a Mauve's tradition which had continued unchanged and unchallenged since time immemorial (meaning about 1909). Snatchby played his part with good humour since he was paid well-enough at the end of each week to not worry about being a little silly. However, since most of the gentlemen (and on this particular Friday, all of the gentlemen) would by now be sniggering behind laden clothes-horses or inside pantries in a wide variety of town houses and stately homes across the Home Counties, Snatchby tended to put very little effort into his seeking and spent the quiet time catching up with his newspaper.

'A bone, sir.'

'No. Of course a bone. What else would cook give out? What I meant was, did you say Mr Spiggot?'

'I did sir. Mr Spiggot, sir.'

'Well yes, Snatchby, I thought I heard you the first time. But I also thought I heard you that I was the only gentleman here? How could you forget Spiggot? You silly chap.'

'Quite so, sir. I am berating myself for the omission even now, sir.'

'And so you should, Snatchby, so you should. Now he's in the garden, you say?'

'Indeed, sir.'

'Well, I shall go read one of these pamphlets to him and see how he likes it.'

'Very good, sir.'

Later that afternoon Quirkstandard and Nigel Spiggot went to Victoria Station in order to buy their train tickets to Arundel in advance. This was after Spiggot had listened, yawning lengthily, to Quirkstandard read from *Cardinal Compass Points & Other Directions Of Ecumenical Interest*. Spiggot had been unimpressed and had spent most of the lecture thinking about the bottom of a girl he'd met the day before in Hyde Park. It had been an impressive bottom, full of fascinating and informative scents, redolent with individuality and personality and his little tail wagged as he remembered it.

Naturally Quirkstandard had felt disappointed by his best friend's reluctance to share in his enthusiasm for the new learning, but the thing was they were pals despite their differences and not even something as important as this could dent that friendship. He'd known that Spiggot wasn't really the academic sort ever since they'd first met on the playing fields of Eton – when Spiggot was running with the ball between his teeth there was no one who could bring him down (not that he scored any tries, but, at least, the games master said, he showed some interest). Nowadays Spiggot didn't run so much. Unlike Quirkstandard he hadn't held onto his youth quite so well and one of his legs was a bit gammy and his eyes were a bit misty. His nose, however, was still sharp and his hearing, when the dinner bell at Mauve's went or when a stranger approached the front door, was better than ever.

Following the disappointment with the pamphlet Quirkstandard had walked with Spiggot round to the Spiggots' house and rang the bell. The butler had answered and had gone and found Mrs Spiggot.

'Ah, Lord Quirkstandard,' she said, 'Is everything all right?'

'Oh yes, Mrs Spiggot,' he answered brightly, 'I've had a postcard from Auntie Penelope inviting me down to her place in Sussex for the weekend, and I wondered if Nigel might be allowed to come too?'

'Does your Aunt say he's welcome?'

'Yes. She used a special code word just for Nigel.'

'Very well, I should think that would be all right.' She leant down and stroked Spiggot behind the ear. 'Would you like a weekend in the country, darling?'

Nigel Spiggot answered with a woof, a snuffle and a wag.

'I'd best just ask Mr Spiggot, just to make sure, but I don't think there's anything Nigel needs to do here.'

She went away into the house leaving the two gentlemen stood on the doorstep.

'See, I knew she'd say you could come ... I bet your governor says the same thing. We're off to the fresh air and the country, Spiggot old pal.'

Nigel Spiggot looked up at his friend Epitome Quirkstandard and gazed with the big eyes of a dog who actually seems to understand what a human being is saying to him. He wagged his tail a little.

In a minute Mrs Spiggot returned to the door.

'Of course it's all right,' she said.

'Lovely, we'll be off tomorrow morning, and probably come back in time for lunch on Monday, if that's all right? And can Nigel stay the night at my house, Mrs Spiggot please, so that we're all ready for the off in the morning?'

'That sounds super, Lord Quirkstandard dear. Are you going to get your tickets in advance, just in case you're running late in the morning?' (She was familiar with the habits of young men.)

'Oh, that's a super idea, Mrs Spiggot. Thanks a lot. Come on Nigel, let's get to the station.'

'Victoria, isn't it?' (Mrs Spiggot thought it wouldn't hurt to remind the boys.)

'Yes, that's it.'

And so, forty minutes later the two chaps strolled in a jaunty men-about-town manner through the station right up to the little ticket window. The jauntiness of their walk was indicated mainly by the length of the pendulous swing of Quirkstandard's stick and by the way he looked loftily about in every direction except that in which he was moving. Spiggot held his head high, swayed his hips wide and nodded at all the ladies he passed. They looked like a couple of dandy swells off on a train trip somewhere rather pleasant, which was, if only the observers had known it, surprisingly near the mark.

It would have been much nearer the mark, however, if they hadn't been told at the ticket window that, due to engineering works just south of Clapham Junction, there were no trains running toward the south coast this weekend at all.

'Oh,' Quirkstandard said.

He looked down at Spiggot and Spiggot looked up at him and Quirkstandard raised his shoulders in a shrug. Spiggot panted a little and wagged his tail, before sitting down and licking himself.

A minute later the two gentlemen walked out of Victoria Station with a lot less swagger and swell than they'd taken in with them. Spiggot trotted over to a little tea shop-cum-butcher's he knew across the way and they pondered their next moves over a cup of Earl Grey and a slightly grisly bone.

22

Simon Crepuscular & The Big Plan

❦

'Of course I will,' said Simon Crepuscular. 'A weekend in the country is just what I need, and maybe dad will want to come along too. He's not been out of the city for ages, I can't think when the last time was. Some fresh air, a clean river to walk beside. Oh, it'll do us all the world of good.'

Quirkstandard and Spiggot looked at each other and nodded happily. They were sat in the kitchen at *Crepuscular & Sons* and were enjoying a cup of tea and a biscuit respectively.

'That's smashing. You see the trains are an awful nuisance …'

'Yes, you said. Rodney, are you going to come?'

'No. I've got to paint the bloody hall this weekend. Rose's mother's coming to stay next week and she always expects the hall to be a different colour. Thinks a husband's not doing his duty if it's the same shade of peach from one visit to the next.'

'Oh well.'

'Yeah, 'Oh well' indeed. You go and enjoy the sunshine and the lazing about watching ducks and newts and things. You'll probably see some fancy toads while you're there.'

'Oh, there's all sorts of things like that where Auntie Penelope lives. Frogs and dragonflies and rabbits and all sorts.'

'Yeah, well I don't care much for the frogs, but if you see any toads, Simon, do a quick sketch for me would you?'

'I'll try my best, oh brother of mine.'

Rodney picked up his paper and put down his empty teacup and made excuses to leave.

'I've got the paint on order, I'd best pick it up before old Jones sells it by mistake. You know what he's like, anything for a quick profit.'

'Cheerio.'

'Yeah, 'bye.'

As Rodney shut the front door with a jingle behind him, footsteps shifted about overhead and creaked their way down the stairs.

'Oh, Mr Q., I thought I heard your voice,' said Simone as he emerged into the kitchen. 'How did your lecture go this morning? Many chaps buck up and listen to you?'

Nigel Spiggot yawned in his chair.

'Well, to be honest, Mr Crepuscular, it was a bit of a no show. Only Spiggot here showed up and he doesn't really pay much attention to education. He prefers sticks. But I'm going to try again on some of the other chaps next week I think. I'm sure someone's going to catch the bug.'

'Well, that's encouraging. You're not a quitter Mr Q., I'll give you that much. So, this is Mr Spiggot who you've talked so much about.'

Simone Crepuscular looked down at the little schnauzer who sat at his kitchen table munching on another of
Dawn's biscuits.

'Shake hands Spiggot,' said Quirkstandard by way of
encouragement.

Nigel Spiggot looked up at Crepuscular's outstretched
hand and raised his right front paw up and plonked it
down in the open palm.

They shook.

'It's a pleasure to make your acquaintance, Mr Spiggot,' said Crepuscular.

Nigel Spiggot barked once in a friendly manner.

'We're going to visit Mr Quirkstandard's Aunt in the
country and I'm going to drive a Rolls-Royce,' said
Simon.

'I think it's a Silvery Ghost.'

'Mr Q.?'

'Um, it's a sort of Rolls-Royce.'

'Yes, I know the Silver Ghost, Mr Q., there's a rather a
good illustration of one in a pamphlet I wrote a few years
ago on the influence of the supernatural in the motoring
industry. More what I meant was ... What does Simon
mean when he says we're going to visit your Aunt? And
then, subordinate to that first question is, of course, a
clarificatory addendum pertaining to the motorcar, it's
origin, ownership and his capabilities as a driver.'

'Oh, you see Auntie Penelope has invited Spiggot and
I to head down for some japes and dinner this weekend
and the trains were all of a dither, well, I mean to say,
there weren't any, and so I came back here not knowing
where else to go on a Friday afternoon to ponder the

problem, you see I've already sent her a telegram from Mauve's to say we're coming, and then I asked Mr Crepuscular – oh ... I mean *this* Mr Crepuscular – if he had any ideas and he asked if I had a car, and I realised that I do, although I don't have a chauffeur since he's gone off to give the Germans what for, and he said (Mr Crepuscular that is, not the chauffer) that he could drive it for me. And so I said, well why doesn't he come and stay for the weekend too. I'm sure Auntie Penelope will be happy to have another guest.'

'I see.'

'Oh, she's only got a little cottage, Mr Crepuscular, but she puts a tent up in the garden for me and Spiggot to sleep in and I'm sure she can find another one for you two if you wanted to come? She's got oodles of tents around the place. That's sort of part of what she does, you see. Camping and all that.'

'Well, if Simon thinks he can drive this contraption ...'

'It's a Rolls-Royce dad, I think it's probably more than a contraption.'

'Well, if you think you can drive it, then I'm sure a few days in the fresh air won't be a bad idea at all.'

'Well, after my mother and father died, Auntie Penelope looked after me. I was only a boy, you see,' Quirkstandard explained later to the Crepusculars, 'And I don't think anyone thought I'd be able to look after myself and so they sent her a telegram and whoosh! She came and saved me. She bought me iced cream, I remember that, and then we went home and then I got sent back to school. She had to go back to work, being an explorer and whathaveyou, because that's what she does, she travels round the world a bit like you did in those pamphlets, do you remember? Except she takes girls with her, little groups of girls that she teaches things. I never really understood what it was they learnt, but then I never had much of a penchant for education, at that time anyway. I mean I rather flunked at school, which is why I'm so grateful for your help now. I think once a gentleman has had a chance and some time to mature, then he's much more suited to knuckling down with the schoolbooks and wrestling with the big questions. Education's probably wasted on children. I mean it was wasted on me when I was a child. But she'd take these girls off with her to Africa or Austria or Australia, I always get those three muddled, and they'd trek in the jungle and all live in tents and all that. And while I was at school she always used to send me these long letters, filled with stories and adventures and a whole lot of stuff I skipped about politics and history and the sort. I only wanted to read the bits about her fighting the crocodiles and the pygmies. And she'd scribble little pictures in the margins of the animals and butterflies that she'd seen or the shape of the moon or a mountain or something and sometimes she'd sketch some of the girls she was sharing the tent with. And those letters, especially those ones, actually made me some friends at Eton, I mean besides Spiggot here who was a chum from the first day we met each other and who never much cared for pictures of any sort. All he's ever wanted is a stick and a walk and a scratch behind the ears, eh, old chum? But she used to come back when school was out and she'd take me to the seaside and to the zoo and things like that. Oh, we had such fun. And sometimes she'd come down to Eton during term and arrive on a Saturday afternoon and normally the porters were very strict about visitors and boys weren't actually allowed any, not on a Saturday because that was against the rules, but I'd watch her walking up the street from the window and see her meet one of the porters and talk to him and they'd always let her in, they liked her that much.[18] And she'd take me out to one of those little tea-shops in Windsor and we'd have cake and tea and buns and I'd feel really sad when she went away again, but then a week later a postcard would arrive or a letter and that'd make me feel better again. She was brilliant, Mr Crepuscular, she was super. I saw her loads more than I ever saw my mother, I mean before she was dead. Not that I'm saying mother was bad, but Auntie Penelope really cared. And then I left school and did that university thing and finally I turned twenty-one and came into my inheritance, as they say, and she gave me the keys to the safe where the family fortune was kept and moved her things out of Devonshire Terrace and bought this little cottage of her own down in Sussex, on the Downs. A place called Arundel. It's very nice, there's a river and trees and all sorts there. Spiggot likes it because there's a whole lot of sticks lying around and ducks and things to chase. It's smashing isn't it? She still writes, you know,

[18] Naturally they didn't, in fact, like Miss Penultimate at all, but they did fear her, which brings its own sort of respect.

and I still don't understand half of what she talks about, but I like the pictures and I like the adventures. She's not like a normal Aunt at all. You hear some dreadful dull stories at Mauve's about other Aunts. She never expects me to do anything much and has never asked me to marry anyone. I think you'll like her, Mr Crepuscular, you remind me of her, I mean your pamphlets do. Not that she has a beard or anything …'

23

Nancy Walker &
Miss Penultimate's Kitchen

※

Like so many children in the late Victorian age Nancy Walker had been found as a baby and handed in to an orphanage where she spent some time growing up. She was not the most cooperative of orphans, not only asking for seconds but also punching other girls, refusing to do her schoolwork, refusing to do her homework, bawling when being made to have a bath, spitting at Matron when she combed her hair, punching the Governor when he tried to reason with her and whispering after lights out.

By the time she was ten years old the orphanage authorities had had quite enough of her obstreperous and disobedient ways and sent her into service at the most harshly disciplined, tightly controlled and unlikely of domestic situations – in the house of the Duke of Norfolk, that is to say Arundel Castle.

Nancy wasn't the most obliging of employees either. But her position as Fourth Scullery Maid meant she was never seen by the masters and rarely by the daylight. So her foul language, temper tantrums and tears went uncommented on outside the kitchen and, as such, little harm was done. Naturally she tried to ensure that little work was done either, but both the Butler and the

Housekeeper took a fancy to her backside, the former with a slipper and the latter with a spatula. After she'd learnt that all the doors and windows were kept locked at night, Nancy eventually made a grudging show of knuckling down and got on with grudgingly getting on with her work.

It was never particularly good work. The cutlery rarely sparkled after she had polished it and the potatoes were rarely entirely naked once she'd peeled them, but she did just enough to keep her out of real trouble. She even managed to almost make some friends amongst the other Scullery and Parlour Maids, but for the most part they lacked the vital sparkle that Nancy had, and were content to giggle about amusingly shaped vegetables and whether the Stable Boy's trousers were tight enough. Nancy found this tedious and stupid and longed through the long days to get up to her tiny shared attic room and indulge her secret vice: reading books.

She liked Robert Louis Stevenson and imagined sharing Jim Hawkins' adventures on the Hispaniola and on the desert island. She swore she would've shown Long John Silver and his mutineers a thing or two, and often lay awake in bed dreaming of what she might do with her share of the treasure.

'I'd get out of this business, for one thing, Betty,' she'd say to the Third Scullery Maid as they scrubbed carrots in the dark little room off the kitchen.

'What?' Betty would say, tugged out of a daydream about Ted the Stable Boy's tight trousers.

'If I had an hundred pounds, I'd quit. I'd tell Mr Waters where to stuff it.'

She would wave a carrot threateningly and demonstratively as she spoke.

'Oh, he wouldn't like that,' Betty would answer, wondering if, on the other hand, Ted might. After all the carrot was nicely tapered and of a good healthy size.

'Well, I don't care do I? Do I look like I care? You give me an hundred pounds right now, right, and I'd go out there into the kitchen right now and I'd say to Mrs Fatty, "Stuff this in your ugly gob, I'm off," then I'd go up to Mr Waters and I'd wave my hundred pounds in his face and tell him to bog off right and proper and then I'd just keep walking up the stairs and out them big front doors.'

'You'd never.'

'I would and all.'

'But why?'

'What d'you mean, 'Why?''

'Why would you leave here, Nancy? I mean a job's a job, ain't it? And in a couple of years you could be a Chamber Maid, with a frilly apron and a lovely dress and touching all them pearls and things and you know how everyone loves a Chamber Maid?'

'Well, maybe I will do that, an' all. But I'm just saying, right, give me a pile of cash and I'll set meself up, somewhere else, like. I'd be a lady of leisure and I'd give you a job, one where you could see the sunshine more 'an just on a Sunday afternoon.' (This was always one of Nancy's bones of contention. The scullery had no windows and her working day started in the dark before dawn and ended in the dark after dusk.)

'Really? You'd give me a job?'

'Yeah, course I would. You're a big girl ain't you, got great strong arms like an ox, yes? Well, I'll have so much money, you see, there'll be more veggies for chopping than you've ever seen. And you can do 'em all.'

'Oh, that's real kind Nancy,' Betty would say, with no trace of guile.

'Yeah, I suppose it is,' Nancy would answer, keeping her thoughts to herself.

Betty wasn't alone in not having any ambition beyond a specific set of narrow expectations, and Nancy found this hard to understand. She'd read Jules Verne's stories of adventures under the sea and inside the earth and wanted to fight dinosaurs and discover unknown tribes and bring home the biggest diamond she could find – not because she liked diamonds, but because no one had done it before. She wanted to be Alan Quartermain and Jim Hawkins and Captain Nemo all rolled into one, but instead she scrubbed potatoes, was occasionally spanked half-heartedly by Mr Waters, the Butler (once the first hundred beatings had had little effect he rather lost interest, but felt obliged to continue as appropriate), and was asked impolitely to put out her candle by the girls she shared her little attic bedroom with. She would extinguish it and then sit up staring out of the window at the moon. To think, she thought, confusing fiction with fact as she was wont to do, men have walked on that far off shiny globe and those insect-like Selenites live their mad lives under its surface – and here I am, stuck, not just on earth, but in this bloody castle.

Then one day she found that she began to think less of the adventures she didn't have and more of how tight

Ted's trousers were, and also how tight Betty's blouse was, and indeed how tight her own clothes had grown. She had turned fifteen and the imaginary company of Jim Hawkins was no longer quite enough to keep all of her attention.

After Epitome Quirkstandard's twenty-first birthday Miss Penultimate left London and bought the small cottage on the outskirts of Arundel that would serve her as an English base to return to between expeditions. It was a pleasant little place, with a healthy-sized garden that ran down to the River Arun which meandered into the countryside on either side. The ground floor of the cottage had a large kitchen powered by gas, which also lit the rooms, a hallway and a front room, and upstairs there were two bedrooms and a study, which she immediately filled with accumulated junk from around the world. In the garden was an outhouse and a tin bath hung in the kitchen. Everything, Miss Penultimate thought when she looked around it, that a woman could want from a home.

The previous owner had been an elderly lady with few friends who had died in one of the upstairs rooms. When the milkman thought to look inside the cottage searching for the money she owed him, he found that her body had mostly been eaten by her cats, so a little tidying had needed doing, but in all other ways the house was in good order. The business about the cats, who still roamed the garden on occasion, had put a few buyers off, but Miss Penultimate wasn't the sort to worry about a bit of bony mess, ghosts or stray pussies making a nuisance of themselves. However, she did feign a little womanly distress in order to get the price knocked down. She had high principles, but she also had common sense.

The previous owner had a gardener who came once or twice a week to tend the place and Miss Penultimate chose to retain his services, since he was quiet, polite and considerate. But the house didn't come with a house-keeper and she needed someone to take charge of the domestic business and keep the place warm and tidy when she was away, so she placed an advert in the *Arundel Evening Advertiser & News*.

Every single one of the two women who came to be interviewed were either elderly, decrepit or enormous, things that Miss Penultimate didn't necessarily hold against them. However they were also ignorant, unintel-ligent and dull, faults which she took as personal affronts. However, on the third hand, as it were, they were also the only two applicants and she had to somehow choose between them.

She was sat at the kitchen table trying to figure out some test for them to compete at (maybe firing an arrow through a series of … no, that wouldn't do) when there came a knock on her back door.

Glancing up at the clock she said, 'Come in.'

'Sorry I'm late, ma'am,' said a soft voice.

Miss Penultimate looked up toward the door and, seeing a nervous looking face poking round the edge with large dark eyes and a swirl of swooping black hair, stood up.

'Oh, do come in and sit down,' she said, an unexpected excitement fluttering in her heart.

'I'm sorry I'm late,' the girl said again, 'but it was getting dark and I took the wrong street and besides, it's not really that late, is it?'

Her voice seemed to blend the best parts of honesty and heresy together. There was something edgy but innocent about it that caught Miss Penultimate's ear.

She gestured the girl into a chair and sat down in the opposite one herself. She studied her face with a calm look that masked the sudden perturbations thumping in her breast. It was a remarkably pleasant face, which seemed paler than it actually was due to the blackness of the thick hair that fell either side of it. For a moment, before she flicked it away over her shoulder, half of her face was hidden by that hair. A normal girl would have had it tied back, or put it up, thought Miss Penultimate, before chiding herself for having such a conservative thought. Why should a girl wear her hair in any particular way, simply because it was usual? It was the twentieth century now, after all.

That pale face continued to strike her. When she got closer, later on, she noticed that there was a touch of colour about it after all, certainly once she'd been out in the sun a bit, a slight wheaty inflection which suggested that the English sky was just a touch too overcast. She had thin, pink lips which parted in the moment before she spoke, as she thought to speak, revealing damp, straight teeth in a dark mouth. As she tucked her hair out of the way once more, Miss Penultimate noticed how long and delicate the fingers were, and the calluses that masked them. A few stray strands of hair remained crossing that face, and she refused her immediate thought, which was to reach out and move them aside herself.

After a few moments Miss Penultimate remembered to speak.

'Do you want the job, my dear?'

'I saw the advert in the paper, I brought it along …'

'I know. I saw it in your hand. It has my address which is how you came to be here. Now, would you like the job?'

'Don't you want to see my references? I mean, ma'am.'

'Do you have any?'

'No. Not really. Not as such. But I could get some if they was important. I mean, but they mightn't be any good.'

'I'm sure that's not a problem.'

'It would be a relief to me, ma'am, if it weren't. I do rather need a job right now and I'd take just about anything.'

'Then the job is yours.'

Miss Penultimate explained the chores that were necessary and Nancy saw how straightforward they were and how kind Miss Penultimate seemed to be. This seemed to be going well, she thought to herself. After she'd lost the job at the castle, leaving under something of a cloud (in the rain, with lightning, thunder and the promise of no let up to the storm in sight), she'd been at a loss quite what to do. Fortunately she'd had just enough money saved up to buy herself a fish and chip supper and there, underneath the lump of cod, was the advert for this job. With nothing to lose, but a wasted evening which would've been wasted in any case, she'd made her way to the cottage. Not having left with the fortune she'd once dreamt of, she was a sensible enough girl to know a job was essential, and preferably one with a roof over her head would be best.

After the details were ironed out (the chores were less onerous and more interesting than in her previous job (never having, in nine years, advanced beyond First Scullery Maid (who was the one who decided which maid would chop which vegetable, but that was exactly as far as the responsibility went)), with a bit of variety and sunlight and the likelihood of some spare time, if it was just going to be the two of them in the house) Miss Penultimate slid a piece of paper across the table and asked Nancy to sign it. It was when doing this that she realised she hadn't even asked the girl her name yet.

'Nancy Walker?' she repeated, a little surprised.

'Yes, ma'am.'

'How old are you, Nancy?'

'I'm nineteen, ma'am.'

'Nineteen? So, that's ... oh.'

Miss Penultimate paused and looked even closer at Miss Walker. Nancy blushed at the scrutiny and wondered what she'd done now, or what she'd got herself into.

'Ma'am?'

'Oh, do stop calling me 'Ma'am', I'm not the bloody queen, you know. It's making me feel so awfully old.'

'Yes, of course. Er, sorry ... Miss?'

'Thank you, yes. Now, Nancy, my dear, I have

something to tell you. Oh no, first I ought to ask ... Um, did you grow up in an orphanage?'

'Yeah, until they got rid of me. They were a right bunch of ... Um, I mean ... yes, Miss. I did.'

'Very well. Nancy? Let me tell you a story.' Penelope Penultimate laid her hands on the table, smoothed the wood out as if it were a tablecloth before drawing a deep breath, looking up, looking away and going on. 'Nineteen years ago I was in no way prepared to be a mother. I had so much before me, whole vistas were open wide and I was enjoying looking at them, planning to pass through them and to see what further vistas might lie on the other side. I had begun my own business, I was working for myself, at last making my own living by doing something that I loved to do. My father was dead, my sister was married and I was free – all off by myself. It was a beautiful time, Nancy, I want you to try to remember that. I was travelling the world.'

'Um. It sounds lovely. Miss.'

'But I, er, I found I had a baby, Nancy. I found a foundling, if you will, and I felt, suddenly, a conflict swell up inside me. I had very rarely felt conflicts open up in me before and so maybe this time I chose the wrong path. You must understand, dear Nancy, how complicated things threatened to become all of a sudden. There was only one time before that when I had felt so torn in two different directions: when I was deciding whether to stay in the family business. That was before my father died. After he died our Uncle made it quite clear that he didn't believe women had any place on the Board, so that was that; but I'd decided to go my own way before then anyway, and my father had put his hand on my shoulder and gladly watched me spread my wings.'

'Mmm-hm?'

'Yes. He was proud to see me setting out for myself, he had always had faith in me. Oh Nancy, he was that rarest of men, a gentlemanly gentleman, but he was also nervous on my behalf too. He'd tried to make his own way, a number of times and failed, had had to come back embarrassed and humbled. I remember as a little girl passing him his handkerchief as he blew his nose after another failed invention. But in the end it worked for him, he made aglets, you know?'

'Penultimate Aglets? You're one of *those* Penultimates, Miss?'

'I am.'

'But I'm wearing some of your aglets on me boots right now!' She grinned in excitement as she said this and pulled her skirt up to reveal, not only her boot, not only her ankle, but also several inches of young, black stockinged calf.

'I'm pleased to hear it, Nancy,' Miss Penultimate answered, trying not to look, or trying to not look like she was looking, 'By doing so you're contributing, in a tiny way, to your own wages. You see I get a dividend twice a year from the company's profits, which is very useful in keeping everything running.'

'Oh, I didn't buy them, Miss. I got them in me last job. They was part of the uniform, you see?'

'Ah yes, of course. By the way, who was your last employer?'

'Oh, that was the Duke. Well, Mrs Fatty, the Cook,

she was the one that told me what to do, her and Mr Waters, the Butler. But the Duke paid all the bills and it was his house upstairs. Well, his castle.'

'Oh, you were at the castle?'

'Yes.'

'And why did you decide to leave? I mean, not that I'm not grateful for your moving on, but this must be something of a step down for someone used to the grand style?'

'Oh, no. I didn't have nothing to do with the grand style, Miss. I was just a Scullery Maid and I just did the washing up and chopped the veggies. I mean you mustn't worry, I can do all the rest. I read and write, you know, I learnt that before I was ten even, and I can do me sums and I know the names of all the grocers and butchers and whathaveyou because I used to hear Mrs Fatty talking to them and the delivery boys. So I can do all that stuff that you asked. There's no problem there. Miss.'

'So …?'

'Miss?'

'Why did you … move on, Nancy?'

'Oh, well. I got into a bit of trouble.'

'Oh?'

'Yes. I'm not sure I ought to tell you, Miss. You might not want me here afterwards.'

'Well, Nancy you've just signed a contract with a minimum six month term. So I think we're stuck with each other, whatever you say next. Go on …'

'Well, you see, if you must know, I got one of the Parlour Maids pregnant.'

Miss Penultimate looked blank for a moment,

assuming she'd misheard or misunderstood something that would very shortly become clear.

'I'm sorry?'

'Well, *I'm* not that sorry. I mean it finally got me out of that place. Oh, it was a rotten kitchen. I mean it was a good kitchen, Mrs Fatty could cook, but it weren't no place to live, you know?'

'No, Nancy, I meant ... How ...? Well ... Unless ... You did what?'

'Oh, yes, well I got Peggy pregnant. And do you know something? If I'd been the Duke then it all would've been all hushed up and not a word said about it. Peggy'd be out with a little purse of cash and she'd be better off, you know. But because it was us servants doing it ourselves, we're *all* out on our arses, with a big to do and not a 'cheerio' in sight.'

'You got a girl pregnant?'

'Well, sort of. You see there was this Page Boy, Cyril, who happened to have a bit of a fancy for me, but I weren't interested. And so, to cut the long story short, after a bit of messing about, and a practical joke too far, late one night, well, Cyril has a bit of a nervous breakdown and starts yelling out in his sleep and is afraid to be left alone with any of the women – oh it's 'Mr Waters, don't leave me alone ...' every five minutes – and eventually me and Peggy are kicked out of the castle. And he can't look at an ice cream spoon the same way again. And he sits all awkward-like whenever he sits ...'

'Nancy?'

'Yes?'

'I think we should move on.'

'Of course. Yes. Miss.'

During her little speech Nancy had begun blushing with the memory and excitement of the anecdote and Miss Penultimate had watched the blush rise up from under her smock, up her throat and round her cheeks. Where her hair was tucked behind one ear it revealed that her ears were glowing too. This was quite charming, although she didn't approve of the story in itself, since it had left a poor girl in a troubled situation, although the discomfiture caused to the Page Boy didn't cross her mind in any other way than with a small chuckle.

But she had to steer the conversation back to other things.

'Nancy?'

'Yes?'

'I was … twenty-seven years old and I wasn't prepared to be a mother.'

'Oh yes, the baby.'

'That's right. I was in conflict. Did I keep this babe, this little girl, this beautiful but rather tearful child I'd found, or rather, to be more precise, that one of my girls had found and given to me, or did I give her away? It wasn't an easy decision Nancy, but then again also it wasn't a particularly hard one. I didn't have any room in my life at that time for a baby daughter, do you understand? I had to give her away. I had my business to keep going and that was hard enough as a lone woman, let alone one with a baby on her hip. So … I had to give the baby away.'

'I see,' said Nancy quietly, suspecting that she might be beginning to understand, and to wonder whether maybe she shouldn't have turned the piece of newspaper over, earlier, to see if there might not have been another job on the other side.

'But before I took her to the Adoption Agency I named her. If you don't do that, you see, they give the baby a name out of their big book, um … the Bible … and frankly I preferred to take some responsibility myself. I gave the girl a name, a good one, one that had strength and dignity and bearing.'

'And I am … I mean, I was, that baby? Is that what you're trying to tell me?'

'Yes. That's really the truth of the matter.'

'So, you're my mother then?'

Miss Penultimate looked startled.

'Oh God no! Nancy, you really were a foundling, my dear. A girl called Veronica Higginsworth-Smythe found you and brought you to me.'

'So, do you mean *she's* my mother … with two surnames?'

'No Nancy, I've no idea who your mother is. You really were a foundling. She wasn't pregnant, not Veronica. Very ugly girl, and besides she'd been in my tent for three months. We would've noticed.'

'Oh.'

'Nancy, you have to trust me.'

For a moment Miss Penultimate felt a deep drag of fear in her belly, as if she had already lost the girl. And it wasn't the worry of losing a housekeeper, it was something harder than that – something that felt like a fishhook or barbed arrowhead under the skin. But then Nancy Walker looked up, met her eyes, a bright dark dazzle in her pupil where the gaslight caught on the moisture.

'Do you know what, Miss? I think I do trust you. I trust you better than anyone I've ever met before. You just told me the truth, didn't you? And you didn't have to, did you?'

'No, I suppose not.'

The room hung in silence for several lengthy seconds, as Nancy rocked her head to one side and looked intently across the table.

'Ah, but Miss, that's where you're wrong, isn't it? Because, do you know what? Because I think, perhaps, you *did* have to tell me, didn't you?'

Nancy wanted the job, she needed the job, but her words weren't entirely motivated by that thought. She found herself actually wanting to say them, because of what they said, not, necessarily, for what they might achieve. She looked at this older woman, with those funny little streaks of grey on either temple, whisking off into the rest of her hair, which was tied back, not all that neatly, but energetically. She sat up straight, but her hands were folding and unfolding in her lap.

'I do hope,' she said, 'that your life hasn't been tragic, Nancy. I do hope you've been happy.'

'Oh, I've been happy enough,' Nancy lied. 'The orphanage wasn't bad. They fed us and then I went to work for the Duke. So you know, not that bad.'

'And now, you're here with me,' said Miss Penultimate. As she spoke, almost without thinking, she laid a hand over Nancy's on the table.

'Yes, Miss. I seem to have come full circle, don't I? Without even knowing that that was what I was doing. How curious.'

They both pondered the unlikely coincidence in silence for a moment, maybe two.

'Strange indeed. But that's the world, Nancy. That's the world exactly.'

'Yes, Miss.'

The two ladies smiled for a time in the warmth of the kitchen before Nancy slid her hand away, got up and put the kettle on.

24

Simon & The Silver Ghost

That evening Spiggot helped Epitome pack his small weekend trunk. Together they chose several changes of clothes from his dressing room, some ablutionary necessities from the bathroom and Epitome put in the folder of pamphlets he'd borrowed from the Crepusculars that morning but which he had forgotten to return to them. He was sure the old man wouldn't mind him holding onto them for a little bit longer. He also packed a pillow and some blankets, knowing his Aunt's ideas of comfort, and wished that Cook was still here to give him some sandwiches. Nevermind, he thought in a moment of wholly unwarranted prandial optimism, maybe Auntie will have hired a cook of her own by now. Left to her own devices, her ideas of a suitable meal could remind a gentleman, used to society and its niceties, of her sleeping arrangements.

Nigel Spiggot watched all this packing, all this stuffing and forgetting and shutting and remembering and opening and restuffing and locking shut and remembering something else, with a sense of bemused detachment and doggish superiority. He travelled light and had nothing with him except the small bag his parents insisted he take, which contained a long lead, a waistcoat (in case, unlikely as it seemed if you'd ever met Miss Penultimate, that he needed to dress for dinner), an India rubber ball and some biscuits for the journey which he and Quirkstandard had already eaten.

That night they both slept soundly, although the excitement of going away was clearly in Quirkstandard's sleeping mind because he rolled over more than was usual in his dreams and kicked out at some vision or other, quite knocking Spiggot off the end of the bed with an angry yelp. Although, in actual fact, he was half lost in dreams too, and climbed back onto the blankets (with a little difficulty, owing to his short legs and his dicky bladder) imagining he was chasing the scent of some cat or other. He growled, ground his teeth, snorted loudly once, farted quietly and drifted back into a more contented slumber. Quirkstandard woke dozily at the noise, the damp patch and the smell, apologised, rolled over and snuggled back into sleep himself.

After breakfast the next morning, which consisted of two very hard-boiled eggs,[19] they assembled in the street with the two Crepusculars and looked at the car that was parked there.

---

[19] Miss Dawn, had taken Quirkstandard aside for a few cookery lessons, but upon discovering the precise depth of his natural talents she set about teaching him to appreciate what he could make, rather than attempting to make what he claimed to like.

'Golly, that's nice,' said Simon, who had an eye for design.

His father ran a hand along the white bonnet and looked at the wheels appreciatively.

'It's a car,' he said. 'That's for sure. Can you drive it Simon?'

'Oh, it's more than a car, dad. Look at it, it's a Rolls-Royce. It's the sort of car that other cars dream about being.'

'It's got cobwebs.'

'Ah … well …' said Quirkstandard, as if he were about to begin an explanation.

'As long as they're not so big as to clog the works,' said Simon, 'I think we'll be safe.'

'It's not us I worry about,' said Simone Crepuscular, leaning down and hooking a strand of cobweb on the end of his finger. A tiny spider tried scuttling to safety but found his entire world transformed to whooshing air and this small pink hillock of land: the fingertip.

Crepuscular scraped the spider off on a railing and went to investigate the other three wheels.

'Are you sure you can drive this, Mr Crepuscular?'

'Oh, yes. I've read all about it.'

'Well, jolly good.'

'The rest of the wheels are clear now, I think we can probably be going, don't you, Mr Q.?'

And so the four of them climbed up. Quirkstandard and Spiggot sat in the back and the two Crepusculars sat in the front. Simone Crepuscular had brought along a map and unfolded it expansively as Simon started the engine up. Once it caught he turned around and advised the passengers to hold onto their hats.

And within seconds they were off and speedily reversing into a lamppost.

'I think,' said Simon's father, 'We need to be going in the other direction, unless I've got the map upside down.'

'Two more? You mean there's three of 'em, Miss? And the dog,' complained Hugh Nerrin, Miss Penultimate's gardener. 'Where are you expecting me to put 'em all?'

It was Saturday morning, the Crepusculars had set off in the Silver Ghost and Penelope Penultimate had just read her nephew's telegram.

She stood outside her back door with Nerrin and surveyed her garden. At the south end stood the little two man tent that Nerrin had erected beside his tomato frames. It had aired nicely overnight and didn't smell quite as musty as it had the day before. It wasn't Miss Penultimate's best tent, she had much smarter and larger ones, but it was the only one that fitted on that patch of lawn.

'Perhaps we could put them in the shed, Nerrin?' she said eventually.

'Yes, Miss.'

He didn't argue and just made his way over to the shed and opened the door. He flicked a dark straggle of loose hair out of his eye, before unbuttoning his shirt and slipping it off his muscular, powerful torso and hanging it on a handy hook.

'If you'll excuse me, Miss,' he said, politely.

225

'Of course, Nerrin, don't mind me.'

He began shifting his tools out of the shed. Although he didn't move them far, merely leaning them against the shed's outside, carrying all those forks and trowels and hoes and spades and watering cans and the rotary mower and tins and pots and cardboard boxes of chemicals, seeds, bulbs and paint, and rugs for kneeling and protective gloves, soon caused a misty sheen of sweat to break out between his strong flexing shoulder blades, which moved under his skin like finely honed tectonic plates, though much quicker. He covered everything up with a tarpaulin, just in case it rained and then leant against the door, wiping his glimmering, dark brow on the back of his hand.

'There you go, Nerrin,' Miss Penultimate said unnecessarily. 'They'll be safe enough like that. All we need to do now is find something for these men to sleep on in there.'

'Miss?'

'Let me pop upstairs. I must have a spare couple of sleeping mats. I do hope they've thought to bring some blankets.'

'It's a warm day, Miss.'

'Ah, but does that mean it'll be a warm night?' she said as she watched Nerrin slip his thin shirt on over his swarthy chest and his taut biceps. He fastened the buttons carefully with his powerful, but precise, fingers.

'Who knows, Miss?'

A few minutes later, after she had retrieved two thin padded sleeping mats from her attic, they heard the distant thunder of a motorcar driving somewhere in the countryside.

Nancy came out from the kitchen and stood with Penelope, standing on tiptoe trying to see where the noise was coming from. Nerrin assiduously got on with some weeding at the far end of the garden, not particularly interested in folk from London.

From down the lane came the noise of breaking shrubbery, an internal combustion engine and the scrape of paintwork, and the two ladies wandered over to the gate to see what was coming. Around the corner jerked Quirkstandard's Silver Ghost, somewhat closer to the afterlife than when it had set out. It lodged one wheel in a ditch and a headlight in a robin's nest and shuddered to a halt.

'There we are,' said the younger of the two men sat in the front. 'Parked.'

Spiggot was the first out of the beached motorcar, leaping ashore like a mariner who had just discovered that he didn't much like ships. With surprising agility for his age he bounced across the lane, and leapt at Miss Penultimate, landed short, and waddled the last yard and a half to finish slumped against her ankles.

'Good morning, Mr Spiggot,' she said bending down to stroke him behind his ear, just the way he liked.

Ah, Spiggot thought, this is why I come here, she knows just how to treat a man. He was, quite probably, the only gentleman ever to think such a thing about Miss Penultimate.

'Auntie,' Quirkstandard called out as he wandered over in Spiggot's wake. 'Auntie!'

'Here I am,' she called back, wondering if the boy needed the extra clue, and then feeling just the tiniest bit guilty for having thought such a thing about her own flesh and blood, but then adding a wave all the same.

Quirkstandard fell into her arms, and, even though he was a good few inches taller than her and a little broader, she hugged him in a warm embrace that made him stand up straight and feel loved.

Spiggot edged out of the way of his feet and wagged happily, while casting a wary eye back toward the Rolls-Royce.

'Auntie,' Quirkstandard began, letting go of his Aunt and stepping back, 'I want to introduce my new friends, Mr Crepuscular and Mr Crepuscular – well one's Mr Crepuscular, and one's a different Mr Crepuscular, it's a bit confusing at first, but I can tell them apart, because … well one has a beard and the other one is much younger.' He waved his hand in the direction of the two of them who had now climbed out of the car. 'There's another son, but he's not here. He had to paint his wife this weekend.'

'Oh, how lovely,' his Aunt said, looking at her two new guests.

She held her hand out and shook the proffered hand of the younger of the pair. Her eyes, however, kept glancing toward the elder.

'It's a pleasure to meet you, Miss Penultimate,' said Simon as he extracted his hand from her grip. 'I've got a pair of the *Basic 01*s on right now. It's an honour.' He glanced toward his shoelaces as he spoke.

'Really, um …?'

'Simon. Simon Crepuscular.'

'Really, Mr Crepuscular. I believe the *01*s are still the

best selling line – stylish in a popular sort of way, cheap and of reasonable quality – but I really have nothing to do with the business anymore.'

'Thank you.'

Simon had freed his hand and stepped back, backwards, as if he were being ushered out of the presence of royalty. He found himself bowing a little for no reason at all.

Simone Crepuscular stood, like his son, with his hand proffered, at attention. He was a tall man, even in his advancing age, and his shoulders were broad. His head had long since lost its original fine covering of hair, and he no longer needed to shave it to keep it looking that way. All it required was a quick wipe over with a cloth in the morning and he was ready to face the world. He had been wearing a sunhat in the car, with a little stringy chin strap to keep it on in the wind, but now he'd taken this off, feeling uncomfortable wearing such a thing in the presence of a lady. His beard, which was white and grey and long, had been combed out especially that morning and he had scrubbed as many ink stains off his hands as he could without removing skin at the same time. They were long-fingered and pink. His eyes, which were of a very deep blue, so deep they sometimes seemed black, glittered brightly, full of intelligence and brimming over with curiosity. All of this Miss Penultimate took in with a keenly trained first glance.

Her second glance took in the sandals that Crepuscular habitually wore. They had clearly been associated with him for some time. The leather was pliable and moulded around the contours of his feet with remarkable consistency. They reminded her of the similar comfortable familiarity that her own favourite pair of boots had with her feet. Of course, she thought (the remnants of the business woman in her popping its head up for a moment), sandals don't require aglets. She didn't feel sorry about this, or feel any resentment towards this man who refused her father's fine offering to the world, but rather she found herself amused that, moments after chiding the young man for mentioning the aglets at all, here she was, unable to repress the thought of them in her own observations.

After her second glance had taken in Mr Crepuscular's footwear, and her first had looked him in the face, her third quickly took in the rest of him. She wasn't so impressed with this. As a rule she didn't invite men to her house (they certainly weren't allowed inside the cottage), and if she had made a habit of it, then she would certainly have expected them to wear more clothes than this. That was just a suspicion, but like most of her suspicions, she suspected it was reliable. Mr Crepuscular was wearing his usual loincloth, looped over, round and under his belt and nothing else, unless he had other items of clothing, say a tie perhaps or a scarf, hidden under his voluminous beard.

'Ma'am,' he said as he stepped into the space before her that his son had just vacated.

'Mr Crepuscular, really there's no need to call me that, I'm not the bloody queen,' she snapped, feeling annoyed out of habit. But then when his hand met hers and she felt the firmness of that grip something in her softened just a touch.

There is nothing quite so unfortunate and unpleasant, she thought, than shaking hands with a damp squib, a wet fish or a piece of blancmange. Such occurrences, which crop up throughout life, could well be viewed stoically, or perhaps with a dash of compassion or pity on the side, but they can never be enjoyed. What would it be like, Simone Crepuscular and Miss Penultimate thought at precisely the same time, to be the owner of a hand that behaved in just that way, that was no more firm than a sock full of custard, a piece of boiled lettuce or a jellyfish? They both shuddered a little at the thought. They were each thankful, and pleasantly surprised to find that the other had a handshake as firm as their grip was strong. This did mean, however, that they were also the sort of people who were reluctant to be seen to be the first to break off, in case that was interpreted as weakness, as if, maybe, the strength of their grip ran out of strength and just gave itself up, melting away like whipped cream in a light breeze.

Eventually Crepuscular, realising he was the guest and should offer the first branch of peace and humility, let go and Miss Penultimate followed his lead.

'What should I call you then?' he asked.

She thought for a moment, as her eyes once more flickered over his entire length.

'I think Miss Penultimate will be fine for now.'

Meeting Mr Crepuscular in his curious state of dress, a state which she imagined must cause some consternation up in London where she knew there were many people who took such matters as calves, thighs and midriffs (not to mention anything else) with awful seriousness, reminded Miss Penultimate of a trip she had taken with some girls at the turn of the century to a resort in the Austrian Alps. It had been an early naturist establishment, although this hadn't been entirely clear from the literature she had read in advance (otherwise she might have hesitated about escorting six such plain and unimaginative young women there), but Miss Penultimate had found the air and the light to be persuading and pleasing enough to encourage her to try it out.[20]

At that time of year, the tail end of the long warm Autumn the whole of Europe had been experiencing, there were few people around and for the most part she and the girls had the run of the chalets and could walk for whole afternoons in the high pine forests without seeing anyone. She had been much younger then, she thought ruefully, and the fresh air whistling all over her skin had been the sort of silly thing she might enjoy, being carefree and happy, although responsible for six grumbling fully-dressed young women. She had felt a bit irked at first when they had all refused to take up the opportunity to let the wind run its fingers through their hair, but since

[20] It is an interesting (and entirely truthful) aside to note that the very first official Naturist Club was set up in 1891 in Thana, in what was then British India, by a District and Sessions Judge of the Bombay Civil Service, one C.E.G. Crawford. According to contemporary records the only other members of this club were Andrew and Kellogg Calderwood, the sons of a local missionary. The club was dissolved in 1892 when Crawford, who had been a widower, remarried. It is not recorded what happened to the Calderwood brothers.

they were the ones missing out, and since she believed forcing girls to do what they weren't happy to do was more than a touch dubious, she let them be, although she did have to stretch her German vocabulary to the limits with the resort authorities in order to allow them to stay there whilst staying clothed. But she appreciated stretching her vocabulary now and then, since, she always said, only a complete idiot didn't savour a challenge.

Although she was irked at first, later on she was, for once, relieved that her wards hadn't followed her example, for one afternoon as she was leading her girls down a wooded path, dressed in only her sturdy, companionable walking boots and her rucksack, she heard someone whistle. Now, she knew that whistling was a common enough pastime or entertainment in Austria, even after the invention of the printing press, but this particular whistle had been of the most coarse sort, which carried with it a very obvious meaning and implication. As if the meaning weren't clear enough from the wolfish melisma of the thing, she watched as one rotund little German twenty yards ahead on the path made a suggestive leer, wink and hand gesture.

She stopped her girls with an outstretched arm. They'd already seen the jolly fat man, with his jolly alpenstock and his jolly little belt with its numerous pouches slung underneath his jolly round belly and just over his jolly little out-of-doors winkle which jiggled comically as he walked. Had the girls not spent the last few weeks following Miss Penultimate around and being educated they would have been aghast at such a sight (one which may well have caused their mothers to faint), but they were now somewhat blasé about the whole thing, and, besides, it was a very small winkle. All the same when he winked lasciviously they drew their breaths, wondering just what her response would be.

What Miss Penultimate had done next was something she was not proud of: she had reached into her rucksack and pulled out a wrinkled, though carefully folded, plain dress and pulled it on over her head. One of the girls helped with the fastenings at the back and in a moment all her modesty was restored. She had assumed, when she acted, that her dignity would be restored too, but that wasn't the case. Even as the German shrugged disappointedly (though lewdly) and walked off she knew that what the portly foreigner had made her feel was shame, shame about being who she was, naked or not. Shame for being Penelope Penultimate. And this feeling had arisen as a direct consequence of his actions, and she hated having her freedom infringed like that, and she hated, even more, being swayed by such feelings. If she, Penelope Penultimate, wanted to be naked, especially in such a sweet little Alpine resort specially set aside for just such a state of being, then she should be able to do so, without worrying what anyone else thought or felt about it; it was her business and no one else's. It was the twentieth century now, after all. And if fat, sweaty, German machismo-addled hikers couldn't see that in an unaffected manner, if they had to bring their own sweaty sexual neuroses and hang-ups along with them, then that was their problem and not hers.

She took small comfort the next morning as she strolled naked to the dining chalet to have breakfast that at least that one particular disturbed hiker wouldn't be disturbing anyone else, having had an unfortunate encounter in the night with a large glass paperweight. Later she partly regretted having been so impetuous.

But all that memory passed by in a moment, just a flash across her cerebellum that made her smile ambivalently. Now her attention snapped back to where she was standing.

Mr Crepuscular had just asked her a question.

'I'm sorry?' she said, 'I was miles away.'

It turned out he had just asked where the lavatory was. Well, she thought, he certainly isn't the usual stuffy gentleman with the normal shames about bodies and their functions and what can be said in front of ladies one has only just met. It made a nice difference. She pointed to the hut at the end of the garden.

'Thank you, Miss Penultimate, you're very kind.'

He bowed his head and wandered away.

Yes, she thought as she watched him go, he's an unusual chap that one.

'Auntie,' said Quirkstandard, 'I almost tied my tie all by myself this morning.' He pointed to the piece of silk that was clumsily knotted around his neck. 'Spiggot did try to help, but he's no good at knots.'

'Well done, dear,' she said.

※

Ah, thought Simone Crepuscular, Miss Penelope Penultimate!

She reminded him of something. Or of someone? There was something that fluttered just at the edge of his memory when he looked at her. What was it? It was something to do with the way she spoke, the certainty of it, the surety. The way she held herself. She stood up straight, but at the same time there was something flighty, something impulsive about her. He noticed how her attention had wandered, how her mind seemed to flit about, not always present in the present. This was just like him, just like his mind, he thought, I'm always wandering off, following trains of thought that lead from this to that to that, making connections. That's why he did what he did, wrote the pamphlets he wrote: one subject would lead to another, would suggest another, would encroach on another, and one pamphlet would turn into two or four or more ...

And then it struck him. That handshake. Those eyes. And suddenly he found he had thought of Teresa-Maria.

It had been twenty-four years, he realised, almost a quarter of a century, more than a third of his life, and he still woke in the night seeing her fall away from him; still thought to ask her advice, to ask her his questions. He hadn't slept a full night since that day in the jungle. He could close his eyes now, just where he sat, and see her shrinking, rushing away from his hands. It was a helplessness that had enveloped everything he had done, that had coloured everything with just a touch of grey.

The pamphlets, he felt, the business was just something to keep him busy, something he had invented as an occupation for himself and the boys. Had she been with them ... well, he had no idea what they might be doing now, though he was sure it wouldn't be this. He was a ponderer, a slow thinker, a ruminator and always had been, and he was intimately aware of these facts. Of course, at its best the business was wonderful. When they were suddenly a success it had been the first thing to have really gone right in years, and there was just nothing to compare with it. But since then the hum and the drum had combined and the peaks, the exciting moments, were rare. Mr Q., Lord Quirkstandard, was one such peak – to see someone so honestly open and accepting of the work, of the life's work that Crepuscular had extended through the pamphlets, well, naturally, that gave a man a boost. But when the pamphlets weren't read, when the weeks went by without a customer and it was raining and the streets of London were paved with yesterday's newspapers, well, then the façade was revealed to be the façade it was and the hollow fallacy echoed and the clock slowed and slowed until the spaces between the tick and the tock lasted an afternoon and he couldn't stop himself from thinking about his wife; about his dead wife.

Ah, Teresa-Maria.

The reason he'd just thought of her, he remembered, pulling himself back onto a logical path, devoid of diversions, digressions and yet other digressions, was that he was comparing her with Miss Penultimate. No. That wasn't true. He felt a twinge of guilt even at the thought that that might've been what he was doing. In the years that had passed he had dedicated himself to his boys, to his work, and had hardly noticed a woman (at least, not in the way that the phrase suggests), let alone compared one to his beloved, to his lost Maria. What was it, he tried to think, that had reminded him of her?

It took a moment but it came to him.

The handshake. That was it. Miss Penultimate had had this delightful strong grip, this assuredness, this self-confidence, this implacable trust that the world was under her control, or if it weren't then, at least, that she was above its control. This was what he thought he intuited from that handshake. But more important than that, he had enjoyed it simply for what it was, for the contact it made between two strangers, between two people who had never met one another and who, in all likelihood he admitted, would probably never meet again after this weekend. But the handshake would be something that remained, inviolable. It existed and could be remembered. Ah, he said to himself, now it is that I finally see, now it is we finally come to the rub.

With a certain guilt and with a certain heaviness of heart he remembered that never, in the few years he knew her and loved her, never, not once in those three and half years (was that all it was?) that they had been inseparable companions, lovers and parents, not on a single day while they worked side by side in his Mayoral office or slept side by side in their galleon-sized bed, had he ever shaken hands with his dear, his darling Teresa-Maria. Of all the attachments on her ingenious silver stump there was nothing suitable for such a gesture of greeting. It wasn't, to be honest, a common gesture amongst pirates who preferred to spit heartily, so he could see why such a device might have been missed off, but the sheer sadness of the fact of the absence, a fact he'd never noted before, that only this morning, only in the last few minutes had become alive for him … the sadness of it seeped down his spine and accumulated in his cold feet. He wiped a tear away from his eye with the back of his hand and looked around.

This was a very nice lavatory, he noted. It was a flushing design, plumbed in with an upraised cistern and a sweet little seahorse motif carved on the chain end handle. To his right was a stack of old magazines. He picked one off the top – *Gentleman's Relish* it said. Simone hadn't seen this publication before (he rarely read anything other than what he'd piled up for reference material), and as he flicked through he noticed all sorts of nonsense. Advice for gentlemen on the best way to curl their moustaches and how to keep their ladies satisfied.[21] As he flicked further nothing remotely more sensible or less offensive appeared. Here was a page filled with vapid questions asked by 'readers' which were answered by what the magazine referred to as an 'agony uncle' (agony for obvious reasons, though whose uncle he was supposed to be remained unclear). He offered ridiculous advice as some sort of 'solution'. Presumably, Crepuscular thought while reading a few examples, the solution to each gentleman's problem was to make them look like an idiot. There was also an article in which government ministers and other distinguished gentlemen were asked pertinent and fawning questions by simpering journalists. Is this,

---

[21] 'Why not let the little lady in your life spend one afternoon each week in the kitchen with the servants? There her natural affinity for washing up and baking will be satisfied and she will be contented. No more fraught moments upstairs as she struggles to find some meaning and fulfilment for her little mind. Just one afternoon though, we don't want to tire her out – she's only a lady after all!'

Crepuscular frowned, what we fought the Enlightenment for?

The front few pages of the magazine had been torn out and with a smile he realised what it was that Miss Penultimate collected them for. He rubbed the paper between his finger and thumb – it was a nice quality, thick but soft stock, quite ideal.

He tore a few sheets out, used them to his satisfaction and then reached for the seahorse. After a few moments, to check that he had cleared his face of all trace of tears, he stood up, adjusted his loincloth, opened the door and rejoined the lunch party.

25

Nancy & The Lunch Party

Once she'd seen the car come to a stop in the hedgerow and had seen the men disembark Nancy Walker went back to the cottage to get the kettle on. She didn't hang around for shaking hands and all that sort of thing, since, whatever else she was, she was also still the housekeeper and it probably wasn't her place.

Once in the kitchen though, and once the kettle was filled and sitting snug on the gas, she thought about what it was she had seen. There was Lord Quirkstandard, a young man of around her own age, who was as thick as the dictionary. For some reason Penny seemed to care for him, even though he was hopeless, gormless and about as interesting as a bout of Shakespeare. Naturally Nancy had met him a number of times during the previous five years that she'd been employed in the household and he had never noticed her once. This, perhaps, was what actually irked her most, since had she been pressed she would have admitted that he was harmless and not really worth the sorts of knots that she felt. As far as he was concerned she was a servant and servants all looked the same to him. He rarely remembered her name.

With Lord Quirkstandard came that funny chap, Nigel Spiggot. Nancy liked Spiggot, who may have been a Lord as well, she couldn't remember, and he seemed to like her. But he *was* a dog, she thought, even when certain other people seemed to forget this fact, and as such she didn't feel threatened by him. (Was that what Lord Quirkstandard made her feel? Threatened? Did she have the feeling that he could somehow put the scuppers on her situation, because he was a Lord and she was a housekeeper? Or was it just that she'd become quite fed up with the very idea of the aristocracy long before she'd left the orphanage to go and work for one?[22])

And then there were the two strangers. One of them was a big old almost naked man and the other, so she gathered, was his son. She'd always found almost naked old men a bit creepy, especially ones with long grey and white beards. (She had a flash in her memory of the Santa Claus who visited the orphanage late at night shortly before she was sent off to the Duke.) Beards in themselves unnerved Nancy. They made men look like they were hiding something, probably a detrimentally ingrown inbred chin. But this beard was long and wild, making the old chap look a little less than sane. It reminded her of beards she and Penny had seen in Madagascar, where certain tribal elders stopped plucking their chins once

[22] There had been a Sports Days every summer at the orphanage and local dignitaries would come and place bets on the children. Nancy was quite a fast girl and not above a few dirty tricks if it meant she might get an extra portion of grub at dinner, but because none of the winnings that the nobs made off her speed returned to her – she'd see them tucking wads of notes into their inside pockets and tipping their hats at her before buggering off to wherever it was they'd come from – the whole event left a sour taste of frustration in her mouth.

they became too weak in the knees to continue hunting. Some of these old blokes lived for years after they had stopped being useful to the tribe. All they did was sit around and tell stories, like respected elders were supposed to, except, according to Penny who understood a little of the local tongue, what they actually did was mumble into the mass of curly grey hair in a way that made any meaning indecipherable. What was the point of them?, Nancy had asked, and Penny had had to agree that these old men were rather a waste of resources. But they didn't travel in order to make judgments on or make changes to the traditional cultural practices of the indigenous peoples: that was one of Penelope's rules. When she explained to the girls, however, about the folly of keeping elderly bearded men alive beyond their use, and one of the girls pointed out that under at least one beard she could see a pair of withered breasts dangling, Penelope had at once stormed into the chief's hut and insisted that elderly women be treated with respect and dignity and should be shaved at once.

That was probably enough reason, Nancy reflected, to be a little unnerved by the old man's beard. But then add to that the fact that here, two decades into the twentieth century in a civilised country, someone should wander around in a loincloth and sandals, well, that just made her blush and wonder what he thought he was doing. Penny had hardly blinked at the unusual get up and so Nancy determined not to mention it or let it affect her politeness when serving tea, but all the same, it wasn't normal, and however iconoclastic Nancy felt herself to be, she certainly retained something of the set of standard mores she'd been taught as she grew up. Admittedly she had spent, and still did spend, some time exploring outside of them – but she knew that she was transgressing and usually there was a good reason for it – but for other people to play so fast and easy with the morals of the time, well, that was just a step on the road to anarchy, surely?

The other chap, the son, was dressed properly and looked quite nice. He didn't have a silly moustache like Lord Quirkstandard and didn't have a silly beard like his father. He could almost drive a motorcar and had probably dressed himself and he did have a smart haircut. In short, she decided, he was the only normal person to climb down from the car this morning. And he'd looked at her. She'd noticed that. He'd blushed when he saw her, but that might've been something to do with the exertion of parking the car in such a narrow lane. But all the same, a blush was a blush. How sweet. How idiotic.

If Nancy had taken that moment, just as the kettle boiled and she turned away from the washing up she'd been doing in the sink under the window which looked out into the garden, to look out of the window, she would've noticed that Master Crepuscular was looking at her again. In fact, she'd've noticed that his fair, though slightly Latin looking, eyes had hardly left her. He'd been watching her as if the window between them had been no barrier at all, which of course, in a way, it wasn't.

Having turned the gas off underneath the kettle, filled the teapot and set the cups, spoons, milk jug and sugar bowl out on the tray, she turned back to the sink to get a teaspoon from the draining board. She happened to glance up through the window and accidentally caught his gaze. For a moment their eyes met and locked, just for a moment, before he blushed again and looked away.

Nancy chuckled. The boy was probably a freak, hanging round with the rest of the party, but he had a nice smile and a little bit of attention from a stranger now and then was quite sweet.

'May I ask you a question, Mr Crepuscular?'

'Of course you may, Miss Penultimate, of course. Please go ahead.'

'Are you by any chance (Epitome, do put that down, you don't know where it's been) related to the author of those educative pamphlets? Do you know the ones I mean?'

Simon Crepuscular's eyes flickered to his father and Spiggot stopped licking himself on the lawn.

'Why, Miss Penultimate ... those humble pieces? I thought you must know ... I thought Mr Q. might've said ... why, those pamphlets, well ... I ... I write them myself.'

Miss Penultimate peered closely at him. Simone Crepuscular blushed and ran his hand through his beard and made noises like a Madagascan elder for a moment to fill the silence.

'You?' she said, her voice refusing to show the surprise she felt. 'You write them?'

'Yes. Me. I write them. I mean, of course, sometimes one of the boys helps out with an apposite phrase or an idea or two and Simon here,' he waved a hand in Simon's direction and smiled, 'is a good little artist and he often does some of the illustrations or maps, but the text of them ... well, really, the text of them is all my own work. Generally speaking, as a matter of course. Usually ...'

'But I thought?' she began, nonplussed.

'Madam ... Miss Penultimate ... you have shown me the highest compliment by exhibiting such disbelief, and I thank you for it.' He blushed much as his son had been blushing on and off all morning. 'But please ... do stop it now ...'

'But, Mr Crepuscular,' she went on, 'I was under the impression ... I mean, I have shown those pamphlets to my girls for ... oh, for years ... and I always thought ... I mean, I have ...'

Simone Crepuscular picked the dessert fork from his plate, pushed a few cake crumbs around into a straight line, then held it for a moment between finger and thumb, touched it to his lips absently and set it down.

'But, sir, I thought they were written by ... a woman. And you, I can't help but notice, are rather definitely of the ... uh ... opposite gender, shall we say?'

'Ah, my dear lady,' at this Miss Penultimate raised an eyebrow, 'my dear Miss Penultimate, therein lies the one gift I received from my mother. My given name *is* Simone and I have borne it for the last, oh, sixty-seven years, man and boy. Or more correctly, chronologically speaking, of course, as boy and man. I quickly grew used to it and so have the people who are my friends. It is only from a distance that it still causes confusion. I quite forget that. I should apologise, but extend the hope that in time you will be used to it too.'

'Hang on a moment,' said Quirkstandard, lifting his dessert fork in the air, in not quite the same way that Crepuscular had, though clearly in some sort of imitation. 'Isn't Simone a girl's name?'

'Yes, Epitome, it often is,' his Aunt answered. 'But, sir,' she continued to Crepuscular, 'for many years now I have regularly shown your pamphlet, *Voting Practices From Abroad That Leave The English In Shame*, to my girls. It's a most insightful and moving tract ...'

'Thank you, it's a delight to hear you approve of it.'

'Approve? Oh, Mr Crepuscular, it is incendiary and truthful. How could a woman with any sense of justice not approve? And well written too. So many political tracts are well-meaning but illiterate, don't you think?'

'Well, I don't know that it's a political tract, Miss Penultimate, I just jotted down the picture as I saw it ...'

'Which is one of flagrant injustice to more than half the population of Great Britain, Mr Crepuscular ...'

'Well, I suppose that's true, I just thought that the confused system of voting in New Zealand was an interesting story to try to disentangle and explain ...'

'A system in which women have already been voting for twenty-four years, Mr Crepuscular. That fact must put Mr Lloyd George to shame and force him to force the issue ...'

'But, it was, to be fair Miss Penultimate, the Maori question that was most confused ... and still is, I believe.'

'And you also wrote the pamphlet, *How Birth Happens & Where Chocolate Comes From*?'

'Oh yes. That was me too.'

'I've shown that to girls around the world, Mr Crepuscular, and they're always astonished. But your descriptions and explanations and diagrams are so clear. None of that obfuscation or dithy-dathering that you find in the text books. I have recommended that pamphlet ... oh, to hundreds of women. And you wrote it?'

'I did, madam.'

'Well sir. I have had to re-evaluate my impressions of you more than once today (Epitome, don't go so near the pond) and each time I find that you come out on top.' She smiled. 'You're a most interesting man. I congratulate you.'

'Shall I take the lunch things away now, Penny?' said Nancy who had just come out of the house. She glanced shyly at Simon as she said it and he stared, as subtly as his blushing countenance could manage, at her apron front.

'What very charming lace,' he said, for sake of something to say.

'Yes, please do Nancy, dear,' Miss Penultimate replied, resting her hand on the small of Miss Walker's back as she bent to fill the tray. She left her hand there for a few moments before replacing it in her own lap.

Nancy collected all the crockery, straightened up, smiled as a splash was heard from the pond, and went back into the kitchen where she had been listening to the others' conversation all along.

26

Garden, River & Picnic

Hugh Nerrin watched the small party leave the garden and finally he was alone. He listened with one ear as they faded into the distance further along the river. He filled his watering-can from the pump. Once it was full, and he hadn't heard the others for a few minutes, he put it down, beside the vegetable patch, and walked over to the table on the patio. He sat down on one of the benches and pulled a small tin out of his pocket.

Having rolled and smoked a short, narrow cigarette he felt inclined to get back on with his work. He had been with Miss Penultimate long enough to respect her work ethic, which was that, in short, if someone says they're going to work, then they jolly well should, and if they're not going to then that's fine but we'll find someone else to do the work that needs doing. He didn't mind that. He liked the work he did. He'd first come to this garden as a boy, helping his old dad with it on the weekends, and now he tended it alone. He'd never really considered doing anything else, oh maybe doing this in a different garden perhaps – his skills were eminently transferable in that way – but he'd heard tell of jobs in offices and things and didn't like the sound of them at all.

He'd spent enough time indoors when he was a lad. At

school. And he hadn't got on with that very well. Oh, he could read some and make a good stab at bits of writing, but all the talk had bored him. What did he care about things that always seemed to have happened so far away and so long ago, or in made up books, when he could kneel in the mud and finger the roots of a wilting rose-bush to determine what was wrong? That was living right in the present, with no distractions, no prevarications. Yet at the same time, there was very little in the realm of horticulture that couldn't wait five minutes for him to have a cigarette and a ponder. That was something about teachers, wasn't it? They always wanted answers now. They'd ask a question and if a boy didn't have his hand up in a second then they were already failing. Some-times things took longer than that to work out, but by the time he put his hand up the teacher would have said the correct answer anyway, which made Nerrin wonder why she was asking in the first place.

He'd left school with a certificate that he later showed to old Mrs Wickloft who lived in the cottage before Miss Penultimate. The headmaster had been an educator far in advance of the staff he employed and had believed that each child deserved to take away from his or her education a bit of self-confidence, an understanding of exactly where their particular skills and abilities lay (highlighting their successes, not their failures) and an absolutely smashing certificate. To this end he always took extra time to soak the paper he used in tea before drying them, crumpling them lightly, and writing out each pupil's achievements in an impressively large and scrolling hand. Nerrin's had simply read '*Good with plants'*. That had seemed to satisfy Mrs Wickloft that he should carry on the work his father had done[23] and so he became something of a fixture at the cottage.

Miss Penultimate never told him what to do in the garden. So long as he kept it looking fairly neat and tree roots didn't undermine the cottage she was happy. Besides which, she was often away for months at a time, so Nerrin would simply potter and experiment along whatever paths his green fingers took him down. The only downside to the job, if it could really be considered that, was that, because he was a man, he was no longer allowed inside the house. Mrs Wickloft had often invited him in for a cup of tea, especially if it was raining or windy or sunny or overcast or early or late or lunchtime or teatime or some other, less prandial, time of day. She was quite a lonely old widow and Nerrin had been young and an employee, and so he drank the tea that was offered to him whenever he was invited.

Miss Penultimate, on very much the other hand, didn't hold with having men in the house. She claimed it was nothing personal, she'd never spoken harshly to Nerrin or decried him on account of his gender, but men were by nature dirty, filthy, inconsiderate and not the sort of thing she wanted indoors. He didn't mind so much, because she never begrudged him a cup of tea. He just had to drink it outside. Sometimes that pretty Miss Walker would bring him a slice of cake, usually when

[23] It was assumed he died in 1901, when he volunteered to fight in the Second Boer War and never returned, although it may well be that he just liked the sunshine and stayed away. His letters were unclear on the point.

he had his shirt off and was digging in the sunshine. It wasn't a great hardship, not being allowed in to make himself tea. If it rained he could always go and sit in his shed and look at the pictures in his seed catalogue. He had his certificate hanging on the wall in there and his mum gave him some sandwiches every morning, so he could always eat those. It wasn't a bad life at all.

And a few years earlier he'd shown Miss Penultimate a letter he'd had from the War Ministry, asking him to report for a physical examination with a view to his taking a short trip to France. He'd been stuck on some of the longer words and when he'd shown the letter to his mum to get her to read them out she'd burst into tears, so he turned to his employer who he knew full well was the smartest person he'd ever met. She took the letter from him and sent him back to work and that was the last he heard about the war (except for what mentions it got in his seed catalogues over the next few years). Exactly what she'd done he never knew, but he was thankful for it. He couldn't speak French and had secretly been afraid that they might make fun of him when he got there. His mum had sent Miss Penultimate one of her inedible cakes, but he never delivered it, being, as he said, grateful.

Now he stood up from the bench, tucked his cigarette tin back in his shirt-pocket and began to wander happily over to where he had left his watering-can. Before he got there he was distracted by a cough. It was one of those attention-seeking coughs – not a hearty bronchial type that was necessary to do a job of work such as clearing an air tube, but a dainty, little discreet hand-wave of a cough, designed solely to make someone look in its direction. Nerrin looked in its direction.

There, leaning on the garden gate, was a short little man. He was stood with his feet on the bottom bar and his arms resting on the top. He was dressed in a dark suit, such as one might wear, Nerrin imagined, in an office. It was tightly buttoned up and had a drift of snow on the shoulders. Nerrin wondered if he was a Russian freshly arrived for the war, but then he remembered that that was something to do with boots, not shoulders, so this chap couldn't be one of them. The quickest way to clear this matter up, he thought, was to ask this fellow who he was and what he wanted, but just as he opened his mouth to do so the stranger spoke.

'Excuse me, sir?' he began. 'Am I by any chance stood at and upon the gate of the thrilling Penny Penultimate?'

Nerrin looked at him. He considered for a moment trying out one of *Miss* Penultimate's stares, but then decided not to, since (a) he wasn't her and (b) he had the feeling it mightn't work anyway. He was aghast that this complete stranger (he'd never seen the bloke before, so he had to be a stranger, yes?) should use such a familiar term of address for his employer. Nerrin would never even have dared to say 'Penelope', let alone the shorter form. Only Miss Walker ever said that, and that, Nerrin admitted, was a special case; a situation that he was fairly sure this little man was not ever likely to be a party to.

'Yes,' he answered after a minute. 'This is the house of Miss Penultimate. She's not here right now.'

'Wonderful. That's all I wanted to know, dear sir, dear chap. Now I'll be off. Good day.'

And with that the stranger straightened himself up, climbed down from the gate and jaunted off up the lane toward town.

It was only after he had gone that Nerrin thought to ask his name and his business and whether there was any message. But, he added mentally a minute later, he would have suggested leaving a message himself if he had wished to do so.

Nevertheless, something in the air made Nerrin feel uneasy about what had just happened. As if the sun had gone in for a moment he felt a little colder.

He looked up. The sun had gone in. That would explain it. Within a minute or two the cloud passed and he was bathed in glorious solar warmth once more. He wandered over, picked up his watering-can and, finally, got on with his job.

It being a sunny and warm day, with bees buzzing round the garden lazily and the coots and moorhens fussing about with twigs in the shade, they had decided to go for a walk along the riverbank. Nancy packed a basket with ginger beer and lemonade, some apples, a tin of home-baked biscuits and a few spare rounds of sandwiches and Miss Penultimate had given it to her nephew to carry. Quirkstandard had then left it behind on the lawn and Simon had gone back for it as soon as Spiggot had wanted a biscuit, which had only been a few minutes into the walk.

They walked arranged in this manner (although the order was free to change and from time to time did): at the front of the party Quirkstandard and Spiggot skipped and gambolled. They had often, over the years, visited Aunt Penelope here and they knew the countryside around the cottage quite as well as they knew anywhere. Spiggot would occasionally run up ahead, tug at branches that were clearly a dozen times his own diminutive size, jump up and down in excitement, run back to where Quirkstandard was, catch him up, run ahead, scrabble at the earth, tug at the branch once more and refuse to be satisfied until Quirkstandard had extricated the log from the bracken and brambles and had it tucked under his arm, at which point naturally (perhaps having something of a cat's fickleness in him) he would become much more interested in the smell of a duck, leap in the river, paddle furiously and ineffectually before climbing out of the cold water, scrabbling noisily up the muddy bank, where he'd wait for Quirkstandard to get up close before shaking himself dry and panting in exhaustion for a minute, before repeating it all over again. In short, Spiggot rather enjoyed the freedom of nature compared to the amenities of civilisation that surrounded him up in Town.

Occasionally Miss Penultimate's voice could be heard shouting, 'No swimming here boys, save it for later.' And although Spiggot respected Aunt Penelope as one of the finest, most generous and nicest smelling of all human beings, he didn't pay very much attention to this ruling. Quirkstandard, on the other hand, did. He was still drying out after Spiggot had helped him into the garden pond and was striding along in the sunshine in his long underwear and vest, with his trousers and his shirt and jacket draped over his arms drying. Normally, had he been forced to do such a thing in, say, The Strand or up Bond Street, he would have felt something of an embarrassed idiot, but here in the countryside he felt nothing of the sort. He loved getting out of Town for just this reason: the constraints and confines of polite society were loosened here; no longer was he expected to be the superior, to be an example of wit, wisdom, manners and morals to the lower classes – no, here he could just be human, dignity be damned! So, striding along with his clothes steaming gently in the sun and the breeze he felt like a nature boy, like one of those chaps he might've read about in Classics and Latin if he'd done the reading at school – he felt sure there was probably something relevant in there, he just had that sort of feeling about it. Maybe I should ask Mr Crepuscular about it, he thought, he's smart and will almost certainly know what's what, and besides he dresses a bit like I do, or rather I'm dressed a bit like him, I suppose. Yes, he's the chap. Wandering along Bond Street in his underwear would have had Quirkstandard worrying that some ladies might spot him and be shocked – he cared about not shocking ladies – but here by the riverside there was only his Aunt, who really didn't count among the shockable people of the world, and her housekeeper who was only the housekeeper and so didn't really count as a lady. He felt quite at ease.

Behind the two gentlemen of the party walked Simon Crepuscular and Nancy Walker. They walked together only because they were next in line. Miss Walker was very quiet and initiated no conversation. She kept glancing back to the couple behind them, looking back at

Miss Penultimate, even turning around and walking backwards for a few paces with her hands crossed across her lap. Simon could hardly bring himself to glance at her, feeling a blush rush into his face whenever he did. He cursed his capillaries and wondered why today of all days they were behaving quite so ludicrously. Maybe it was just the heat of the day, or perhaps it was the weight of the picnic basket he was carrying, which didn't get noticeably lighter even when Spiggot had eaten all the biscuits. He also felt nervous: there was an unevenness in his heartbeat and a flutter in his lungs, or maybe his stomach.

As they walked he kept up a light patter of conversation, hoping that he might say something that might possibly be perhaps somehow of some sort of possible interest to her. When he, very occasionally, did look in Miss Walker's direction, not only did he blush but he also lost track of just what it was he was saying. At times like this, in order to regain his thread, or pick up a new one, he'd look out at the river and make an observant and perceptive remark about it, which always seemed to come out sounding like, 'Oh, a duck.' Miss Walker would look at him in these moments and feel a strange compassionate confusion, for although what the young fellow was saying was clearly stupid and obvious and dull (and long before she ever met Miss Penultimate, she had formulated her own opinions of worth concerning stupid, boring and obvious people), the way he said it – the flutter in his voice, the question, the hesitation, the tone (somewhere between a squeak and a baritone) – was oddly striking, his eyes actually dark and intelligent, his hair dark and attractively flicked behind his ear. Noticing these things Nancy would feel a strange mixture of guilt, jealousy and internalised warmth. She would turn and look back at Penny talking with the old man, try to steady her beating heart on that calm and imperturbable rock of womanhood, and her jealousy would well up a bit further, spilling, sometimes, over the brim. It was all most unwelcome.

Apart from occasionally saying something like, 'Yes, a duck,' she remained quite quiet as they walked along in the dappled sunlight by the river.

Bringing up the rear of the party were Miss Penultimate and Mr Crepuscular. As they walked along, a little slower than the rest of the group, they found themselves sinking deeper and deeper into conversation. They found they had both visited, over the years, many of the same places in the obscurer (or at least, less English) corners of the world, albeit usually at different times, and they were happily swapping notes on all of these. But their conversation ranged further and wider than that. Crepuscular's mind was sharp, fast, broad and shone a clear light wherever he pointed it and Miss Penultimate tried harnessing it for her own purposes. She suggested topics of thought that had snagged her over the years, questions of politics, equality, philosophies and the things one sometimes had to eat in extreme circumstances out in the field – these things that had sometimes confused her or left her ever so slightly uncertain whether she was in the right (although she'd rarely admit to such a thing). She steered him round to offering his thoughts and opinions and sometimes they agreed with hers, sometimes they overlapped, sometimes he saw things with a new eye and sometimes he was infuriating. Sometimes he claimed to have no opinion about something, even after she had outlined the facts of the matter (as she saw them), and she found this most peculiar, but slightly charming. All in all he was a good experience, she decided – talking to him was a fine clarifying experience.

Between the end of lunch and the beginning of their walk Miss Penultimate had returned indoors and gone up to her bedroom. Having now met Epitome's new friends she decided it was time to change her attire. Not knowing who they were going to be, or exactly what his relationship with them was, she had dressed modestly and formally, in a nice plain full dress, with sleeves and petticoats. However, once she had met and spoken with Simone Crepuscular she realised that there was no chance of her upsetting him with anything she could possibly wear, and so she changed into a pair of slightly battered, but perfectly serviceable, comfortable and twice-patched shorts, which came down to just above her knees. They'd served her well in the tropics and did just as well with a Sussex summer. On her feet, as usual, she tugged those old walking boots that had been with her for twenty years or more. They'd been resoled more times than she cared to remember, and several parts of the leather uppers had had to be replaced, along with lace after lace after lace. She rolled a pair of white cotton socks over the mouth of the boot once she'd done them up and holding her feet out before her (as she sat on the end of the bed) she thought that they looked quite dapper. She pulled a cream-coloured short-sleeved light cotton shirt on, buttoned it up and tucked the tails into the top of the shorts, did the belt up on those and once she'd grabbed a sturdy stick from the stick-stand by the back door, her battered old hat from the hat-stand and popped a picnic blanket into her rucksack was all ready to go out walking.

Simone Crepuscular had smiled when he'd seen her come out of the cottage dressed like this, 'A right adventurer,' he'd said, and she'd been all ready to scold him for saying, 'Adventuress,' with a lecture on the patronising use of feminine endings, which, by and large, act as substitutions in fact for diminutive suffixes, but then she noticed what he'd actually said and thought to herself – this man keeps surprising me, in good ways; how unusual – and smiled.

So Miss Penultimate and Mr Crepuscular kept up the rearguard, chattering enthusiastically. Every now and then Penelope would smile at Nancy, who was walking a dozen yards in front of them talking quietly with the younger Crepuscular (she couldn't make out any of their conversation, not that she really tried, being quite consumed by her own). She smiled when Miss Walker turned round and smiled back at her. Whenever she did so she found a proud swelling in her chest – Nancy was beautiful, there were quite no two ways round it, her dark eyes stirred things in Penelope that felt more than quite delightful. She realised, at moments like this, when all sorts of wonderful happenstances came together, just how terribly happy she was.

'It's a wonderful world really,' she'd say to Simone Crepuscular.

'Indeed, madam, but we were discussing the pitiful state of the pay structure in medical facilities on the front line of the western front, not to mention the …'

'Oh, I know, but, Mr Crepuscular, look around you …'

'Oh, the world is beautiful, I wouldn't want to live anywhere else.'

'Well, that's lucky, Mr Crepuscular, because you won't.'

'Indeed, Miss P., are you not a religious woman?'

'No, not really. This is it, Mr Crepuscular. Not only is this as good as it gets, but this is all we get. Which is why those nurses really ought to be recompensed in a manner that isn't insulting to the work they put in, especially when compared against the pay scale that not only the doctors but the male orderlies and stretcher bearers are …'

And so she went on, talking about her life with a man who seemed to understand, who seemed to genuinely care and be interested, as the warm air of a lengthening summer's afternoon played across her arms and legs and face, carrying the scents of the river, of the fields, of the blossom, the flowers, while locking eyes with her sweetheart, as somewhere further ahead her nephew played like a very tall child and the sounds of nature – the occasional trill of a coot; the deep, distant honk of a goose – lapped around her sensorium. Days didn't get much better than this, she thought.

Although, of course, she was still barred from voting in General Elections, but she buried this bitter thought as she turned once again to pay attention to this treasure that Epitome had brought her.

Simone Crepuscular, for his part, shared very much in the feelings that were coursing through this remarkable woman by his side. He listened as she spoke of islands and jungles and forests and deserts she had been to, of the peoples she'd met or spoken to, and the rituals she had taken part in and the rites she had witnessed. His eyes glimmered and he found himself interrupting her, often, not because he wanted her to stop, but because he had something to add, and then he'd be going off on one of his stories, one of the stories of his life, of his travels, of his adventures or misadventures and then he'd remember that she was still in the middle of her story and he'd become quiet, apologise, ask her to go on. But he found as he told his tales she'd interrupt him too, go off on new tangents that had just occurred to her, that arose from something he'd said and he'd have to try to pick up his threads three minutes or five minutes further down the line. And so, as the afternoon went on, they each learnt half of the story of the other, learnt about halves of each others' lives. He found it a most remarkable meeting. He hadn't felt so alive, so involved for … well, he couldn't remember quite the last time he'd talked for so long without growing bored of himself.

He had, of course, talked with his sons about his travels, for much of them were their travels too, but since they'd been there at the time, however small they were, some of the thrill of explanation, of exclamation, of exploration was removed. They'd heard the stories often enough in childhood, and they didn't always need to hear them told yet again. Reminiscing with them, was different to storytelling. Talking with Miss Penultimate was something different again. Of course, he had written it all down (in one form or another, as autobiography or as objective documentary, as reportage or as fiction), published most of it, but writing was an active act that held as its object a passive audience: it was without dialogue. He'd received some praise in the early years and letters from readers with questions but nothing had stimulated the follicles of his brain, he thought, quite like Miss Penelope Penultimate did.

As he thought about these thoughts, in a rare moment of quiet that afternoon, there was a loud splash from up ahead where Mr Q. had become overexcited about one of Mr Spiggot's sticks. It had looked as though the two had been having a tug-o-war competition. Spiggot had admitted defeat with a jaw-opening bark, sending the still tugging Quirkstandard down into the silvery stream.

Nancy Walker and Simon Crepuscular worked together to get Quirkstandard out, Spiggot not offering much assistance at all, even though the soaking had been his doing, and as they dangled a long branch for him to clutch their hands touched. It was just an accident, they only brushed against one another for a moment, and Simon blushed and apologised, but in that very singular moment as flesh touched flesh Nancy looked up at his mouth and wondered what it might feel like against hers. It was only a passing thought, no sooner glimpsed than it was gone, but all the same she was a little shocked and surprised to see that it had existed at all.

As they helped Quirkstandard ashore Nancy looked back and watched as Penny and the old man came up to them. They were still chattering, Penny's hands gesturing wildly and widely, her eyes bright with life, with light and his looking straight into them. She walked sort of half-sideways for a moment, facing the old Crepuscular, explaining something or other with arms working and rucksack bouncing. Nancy could hardly remember the last time she had seen her Penny looking quite so animated.

Miss Penultimate flicked out the blanket and they all sat down. Crepuscular opened the picnic basket, handed round the goodies and they each opened a bottle. They sat quietly as they ate, and just watched the river passing by. After a while, bottles of fizzy pop finished, apples munched and sandwiches swapped and eaten, Penelope pointed to a tree that grew out, at an angle, from the opposite bank of the river. There, in a low branch, sat a flash of emerald, a dash of blue. A tiny black eye regarded them for the merest of moments before deciding that they were not fish and were therefore not of interest. It returned to scanning the river. Then, in a dart of movement too fast for anyone to understand entirely, the kingfisher dove into the water and returned to its branch with a small silvery wriggle in its beak. With a cock of its head the fish vanished.

'So beautiful,' whispered Simone Crepuscular.

'Oh, we're lucky to have an Aunt in the country like mine,' Quirkstandard whispered to Nigel Spiggot, 'I've always been quite adman ... adamun ... adam-thingy about that point.'

Nigel agreed whilst swallowing the crusts of Quirkstandard's sandwich.

Aunt Penelope smiled at the pair of them. Mr Spiggot was always polite and never any bother and his enthusiasm seemed to be, somehow, catching. She was pleased Epitome had made at least one friend at school, though she wondered and worried a little what would happen when the inevitable happened to Mr Spiggot in the next few years. Dogs do get through their lives that much faster.

Quirkstandard stood up and reached for his underwear, which were hanging on a nearby branch drying in the sun. His moustache was drooping a shade and it was most fortunate that it had been trimmed recently, otherwise he thought it might have looked very silly indeed.

He didn't notice the pondweed in his hair.

He pulled his long underpants on just as a pair of huge white swans landed on the river, causing the kingfisher to vanish. He got dressed as the others threw the swans the few final crumbs of their afternoon picnic and they started back, slowly, in the direction of the cottage.

27

Charades & Moonlight

✿

That evening they sat in the garden. The sun was sinking and the shadows trailed long across the fading view, but the warmth held its ground in the air and only Venus and the pale paring of the crescent moon shone out of the deepening sky.

Nancy poured the wine and everyone, except Nigel Spiggot, was drinking it in a convivial manner. That is to say, as it was poured they'd sip, hold their glasses for a moment as conversations fluttered around, then sip some more, paying more attention to the words being spoken, the game being played and the faces flashing than to the vintage, but it was good drinkable stuff and no one was being polite about it.

Simon Crepuscular stood in the middle of the little semi-circle and everyone's attention was focussed on him.

'One word,' someone said in response to his hand gesture.

Simon nodded and began to trace another, more intricate sign with his hands.

'A play, or a … No, a play. Yes?'

He stood there for a moment, obviously thinking quite hard, but seemingly unable to come up with any way of continuing.

'Um ...' he said.

'No talking.'

'Come on.'

'What about the syllables?'

'Yes, syllables Simon, come on ...'

He counted these out on his fingers as he half mouthed the play's title and then held all four fingers and the thumb of his right hand in the crook of his left elbow.

'Five syllables?'

He nodded and went on, tapping just one finger in the same place.

'First syllable.'

He lifted his right hand up as if he were holding something: a ball, a pineapple, a very small Christmas pudding ...

'Um? Ball?'

'Pineapple? No, that's too many syllables ...'

'Pud?'

He shook his head impatiently, trying to make it known that he hadn't finished this particular part of the mime. As he shook his head he began to realise he'd maybe had enough of the wine. Anyway, he lifted the thing he held in his hand up to his mouth and pretended to bite into it.

'Eat?'

'Bite?'

'Bit?'

'Ate?'

He bit again and made a show of turning the item around in his hand, so that he took a chunk out of different sides.

'Simon, you're making chomping noises ... Is that allowed?'

'Chomp?'

'Is it a ball?'

'No, Epitome ...'

'Hungry?'

'Greedy?'

'No, Mr Crepuscular, it's still only one syllable ...!'

'What's he doing now?'

Simon was holding up, between his forefinger and his thumb (the former raised above the latter), the remains of his mime. He pointed at the space that simulated the existence of whatever it was he'd been eating. He pointed as if it were important.

'What?'

He moved it to his lips and took one small nibble from the edge to make the imaginary thing neater.

'Is it an apple?'

'Don't be silly Nancy, that's two syllables. He only wants one.'

'Yes, I know Penny, I'm not stupid. But I think it might've been an apple before he started eating it, that's what I mean.'

'Well, if it was an apple before he started eating it, then it's still an apple now.'

'I didn't see an apple.'

'No Epitome, he was pretending. Nancy meant to say 'an imaginary apple'.'

'Oh, so it's a core now.'

'Well, 'an imaginary core', yes.'

'Penny that's what I meant, look ...'

Simon was trying to get their attention by hopping up and down (which also reminded him that he probably shouldn't have another glass of that wine) and was grinning and pointing at Quirkstandard, while keeping a finger of his other hand on his nose.

'Aha!'

'Yes, so, five syllables … first syllable 'core' …'

'See that's what I was going to say Penny, 'core', I knew it was 'core' …'

'Well, Epitome got it first.'

'Only because I said it … I gave him the clue … he wouldn't've got it himself if he'd had to try to think about it.'

'She is right Auntie …'

'Yes, but Epitome got it Nancy, do stop complaining.'

'Let's wait and see what comes next, shall we, ladies, gentleman … the game's not over yet,' said the elder Crepuscular trying to calm the situation down.

Simon was stood tapping two fingers in his elbow.

'Second syllable.'

'Oh, goodie.'

Simon tugged at his ear …

'Sounds like …'

… and pointed at his knee.

'Knee.'

He nodded. Quirkstandard beamed.

'Oh, I'm doing good tonight …'

'It only sounds like knee, Mr Q., you're not quite there yet.'

'Tree.'

'Bee.'

'Sea.'

'Dundee.'

'No, Epitome, it's only one syllable. Look …'

Simon was holding his forefinger and thumb up again, this time the space they measured was horizontal. He moved the fingers together repeatedly.

'Does that mean smaller?'

'Yes, I think so.'

'What's smaller than a knee?'

'Um, an acorn, or a very small orange …?'

'No, I think it means a word smaller than 'knee' … like 'nn' …?'

'Or 'ee'.'

'Oh, Mr Q., I think you have it again, look how he's nodding!'

'Well done Epitome,' said his Aunt, 'You're sailing with a tailwind tonight. Bravo.'

'I was about to say that,' said Nancy.

She was sat in-between Lord Quirkstandard and Penny, with Mr Crepuscular the other side of Penny and Spiggot curled up at Quirkstandard's feet. Every now and then a loud snore came from his floppy lips and he twitched a bit. That was quite sweet in a chocolate box sort of way, she thought.

'So, 'core, ee' …'

Simon tapped three fingers in his elbow and made a surprised look with his face.

Nancy refilled her wine glass and slurped at it. This game was beginning to piss her off. She didn't much like games anyway, except cards, and even then she only really liked the sort that involved matchsticks, because she had a sneaky, underhand method of cheating that nobody, in all the years she had played cards up at the castle, had been able to work out. They knew she must be cheating somehow, because she always ended up with more matchsticks than an excitable arsonist, but no one ever caught her. But she didn't know any plays. This game was weighted against her. And when she turned to look at Penny, her usual recourse in unpleasant situations, she was appalled to see her seemingly enjoying the evening, and what's more she was whispering something to the old guy in the loincloth. Good God! What was that all about?

And then, as she was looking at Penny, the old Crepuscular noticed her and smiled at her. She gulped her wine and turned back to look at the younger chap. Maybe she could win this game after all. If the idiot nephew was getting there, then surely, resourceful, pretty, charming and witty Nancy Walker could get there first …

'Coriolanus,' said Quirkstandard.

'Shush, Epitome, we're only on the third syllable – that's far too long.'

'Actually, Miss Penultimate …'

'You shush too, you're not allowed to speak.'

'Simon, you know better than …'

'Dad! Miss Penultimate! Mr Quirkstandard has it.'

'Well, he's got something.'

'Nancy?!'

'No, I mean he's guessed the play.'

'Really?'

'What was it?'

'Coriolanus.'

'Is that what you said, Mr Q.?'

'Oh, er, yes. Just something I remembered from school.'

'It's Shakespeare.'

'Oh, golly. I didn't know that. I just remembered the sound of it. It sounded like what Mr Crepuscular had spelt out – 'core, ee, oh!' – you see?'

'Yes, we see.'

'Well, Mr Q., it's your turn now.'

Simone Crepuscular turned to Penelope Penultimate and said quietly, 'He's really come on, you know. I hate to boast, but he's been reading my pamphlets all week and I notice a difference from when I first met him on Tuesday. I can't claim the credit though, he's done it all himself, Miss Penultimate, but I do feel some modest satisfaction in it.'

'I've noticed something too, yes. I'm so pleased you've got him reading, Mr Crepuscular, and I'm so pleased it's your marvellous pamphlets that he's found. There's a lot of trash around, but you've … well, you know, I think you have something special there … I really must read some more. Maybe when you get back to London you could make a little selection for me, of things you think I might like. You could send them down, or even bring them yourself if you wanted to come back for a bit more fresh air.'

'Thank you, Miss Penultimate, that's very generous, very kind. I shall set my mind to it as soon as I'm back to the shop.'

Nancy snorted, spilling some wine on her dress.

'Oh do be more careful Nan,' said Penelope turning and patting her arm, 'you know how hard wine is to get out.'

Nancy knew. Of course she knew. Of course I know, she thought, standing up and pouring the last few splashes of the last open bottle into her glass. Of course I know, that's what I do, wash and scrub and apply the soda water, apply the vinegar, sprinkle the salt – I know the stains, I know the solutions. That's my bloody job.

She thumped back down in her seat.

Quirkstandard stood up from his and took Simon's place in the middle. Simon sat down in Quirkstandard's seat, next to Nancy.

'Five words,' someone said, in response to some raised fingers.

'Yes.'

'No, you're not supposed to talk.'

'Oh, sorry. Yes. I forgot. Um, but it *is* five words.'

'Yes, we got that.'

Quirkstandard stood there for a moment, still with his hand raised.

'Um?'

'Aren't you going to tell us what it is?' asked Nancy.

'Oh,' said Quirkstandard, suddenly looking confused, 'I thought that was sort of the point of the game. But I could tell you if that's …'

'No, I mean what *sort* of a thing it is.'

'A book or a play, Mr Q., that sort of thing.'

'Oh, yes, it's a …'

'Sshhh.'

He stood for a moment with both his hands out in

front of him and tried to decide what to do with them. After another moment he lowered them again and spoke.

'How do you do a pamphlet?'

'I don't know,' said Miss Penultimate. 'I don't think I've seen anyone do a pamphlet before.'

'I think it's a sort of unfolding motion like this,' said Simon, making a sort of unfolding motion with his hands.

Nancy nudged him and smiled.

'Thank you, right, spot on,' said Quirkstandard as he approximated a version of Simon's unfolding gesture with his own hands.

Nigel Spiggot snorted, barked and rolled over in his sleep.

'No,' said Quirkstandard, looking at his pal with confusion, 'it's a pamphlet.'

'Shush dear.'

'Sorry.'

'Mr Q., no more talking.'

'Yes, I know, but people keep ...'

'I know, but maybe this once you don't need to apologise ...'

'Oh, sorry, right.'

'Sshhh!'

Quirkstandard held up his first finger.

'First word.'

He lowered the hand and looked puzzled.

'Um, how does one do a 'what?'' he asked.

'Mr Q.?'

'Yes?'

'Is it by any chance, *What I Did In India*?'

'Yes. Oh well done Mr Crepuscular. That was jolly quick and jolly clever of you. I'd hardly got going at all, and there you are steaming in.'

Nancy muttered something. Simon Crepuscular leant in so he could hear what she said when she repeated it.

'What the bloody hell is that? I've never even heard of it.'

'Oh, that? That's one of dad's ... I mean my father's ... pamphlets. It's very good, it's all about India and the circus and all that sort of thing. It's funny and informative. You'd like it.'

Nancy leant back and looked at the old man. So, he'd been able to guess his own pamphlet when the idiot Earl had spent all week reading it. Big surprise, she thought. Doesn't make him the bloody winner though, does it?

Penny had rested her hand on his arm as she congratulated him and was laughing at something Nancy hadn't heard.

'I've had enough of this,' she said suddenly, standing up with a wobble and a whoosh in her head. 'If you need me anymore tonight, ma'am, I'll be in bed.'

She curtseyed crudely and opened the kitchen door.

'Nan?' said Miss Penultimate in a tone that conveyed additional information, maybe a question, that was only apparent to her and the girl. One of her eyebrows raised an eighth of an inch, but Nancy ignored it and went indoors.

'Very well then,' Miss Penultimate said to the closed door, 'I probably shan't be late up myself.'

The door said nothing.

In actual fact she was quite late going up to bed, since she spoke for a long time more with Simone Crepuscular. They wandered out into the lane to take the noise of their conversation away from the others who had climbed into their sleeping bags shortly after the end of the game of charades, all (except Spiggot) feeling light-headed and happily dozy.

In the lane, as the thin bright moon shone down, silvering the hedgerows, they talked about the Amazon and the Pacific. Miss Penultimate tucked her arm through one of Crepuscular's, to stop him from getting lost in the dark, she announced, even though the stars were blazing now with a bright pale luminescence and the road was clearly lit between the pitch dark of the hedgerows.

'How did you come to be doing what you do, Miss Penultimate?' Crepuscular asked at one point. 'I mean, I ended up wandering as a result of a poor education. I was something of a stupid boy, but I can't imagine the same was …?'

'Oh, it's a long story. It's hard to say where it begins. Where it began. I went on my first adventure, my first expedition, in … oh, when was it? 1887? Thirty years ago? Goodness, but, yes … Yes, that was the trip. I had just turned twenty-one and I wanted to do something away from the family. You see, well … isn't that where these things always begin? Sarah and I, she was my sister …'

'Mr Q.'s …?'

'Yes, Epitome's mother. Well she and I didn't have what you'd call a normal childhood, as such.'

'Few of us do, Miss Penultimate.'

'I suppose so, but ...'

'My boys, both of my boys were brought up, for the most part, on the hoof. Across Asia and South America. Where's the stability in a life like that? Where's the normality? I feel sorry for them sometimes, when I think what they might've had – a secure home, a mother who loved them, proper schooling – they both missed out on all that. The only constant in their life – the only thing they knew would not change from one morning to the next was me. That's no life really. Not a childhood anyway.'

'I'm sure you did your best, Mr Crepuscular.'

'Oh, please, call me Simone. I've never held with excessive formality between friends.'

'Friends?'

'Yes, I think we've come that far today, Miss Penultimate, don't you think?'

'Oh yes. Friends it is then. And Simone, you may as well call me Penelope.'

'I think I'll call you Miss Penultimate, Miss Penultimate, if you don't mind. It's how I best think of you. I've never really been a Mister, not a gentleman as such, but you ... well, you deserve a bit of respect and I want to pay it.'

'Very well.'

'Thank you.'

'I'm sure though, Simone, that you did the best for your boys that you could. I've only met the one but he seems to be a perfectly civil young man, as far as a young man can be, that is ... I mean, he takes after you.'

'You don't much like men, Miss Penultimate, I know that, but yes, both my boys turned out well, in spite of everything. And I think most people do. My childhood was as unorthodox as any. I had a mother who'd wanted a girl. Well, you can tell from the name. I guess I have her to thank for everything – for forcing me to run away in the first place, and later for the chance of you reading my works, my writings ...'

'Oh, I'm sure ...'

'Would you have though? If there'd been a fellow's name on the front, instead of mine?'

'Well ... maybe not.'

'Of course not, you're a woman of deep principles, Miss Penultimate, and I respect that.'

'It's strange isn't it?'

'Isn't it?'

'There your boys are, growing up with you and no mother, and there, on the other side of the world, twenty years earlier, there were Sarah and I doing just the same.'

'You mean growing up without a mother. Not growing up with me.'

'No. Quite so. Our mother left our father just before I was born. I was the elder, Sarah came six years later. I always looked out for her, from the start. But my father's sister never thought we would be able to ... well, cope with a baby, and she insisted on coming in and poking about. Well, helping out, she said, but it always seemed like poking about to me.'

'Sorry, did you say your mother left *before* you were born?'

'Yes. It's a bit silly really. I can see why she might have wanted to leave my father, he wasn't, well, he wasn't very good at bringing home the bacon, to use a colloquialism. She ran off, I never really heard how or why, or with whom for that matter, but one day there was a knock at the door and my father opened it and there I was in a little basket with a note telling him to deal with the consequences of his own mistake for once. And then six years later there was another knock at the door and another basket and there was Sarah.'

'That is …?'

'Odd?'

'Yes.'

'Yes, well I suppose it is, unless it's your life, in which case it just is what it is. Which it is.'

'What did he do? Your father.'

'Well, he took us in and looked after us, what else could he do?'

'No, no. I meant in general – what did he do?'

'Oh. Yes, of course. Well, he was an inventor. And he did odd jobs. But really he was an inventor and, as far as I can guess, that was what drove our mother away. He had the most brilliant ideas. He was like Leonardo da Vinci, except none of his ideas ever worked. None of my father's that is. I think da Vinci's worked …'

'Sometimes. Some of them.'

'Oh. Well, the house was full of mechanical apparatuses that fell apart when you touched them or which automatically sliced carrots and fingers and shirtsleeves.

It was a dangerous place at times. And me and Sarah were growing up in the middle of it. I mean we soon learnt not to fiddle with things and our Aunt, who was just a busybody as much as anything, left when I was ten and Sarah was four after she had caught her elbow in an automatic mangle he'd built for mashing potatoes. Fortunately for her it didn't work very well. It didn't have the pressure it needed to crush them, the potatoes, otherwise she would've lost her arm. But it scared her enough that she finally left and let the three of us be. And so then it was just Sarah and myself.'

'And your father.'

'Well, he was busy. If he wasn't drawing or building some new contraption that was sure to fail to make our fortune, then he was out doing whatever work he could find, at the market or at the docks, in order to buy food and materials – not always in that order. Sarah and I went to school, and to the library. We were really in charge of ourselves.'

'Lots of children, Miss Penultimate, are left in charge of themselves, and certainly were in those days, and many, many of them have not turned out to be half as witty and smart as you.'

She smiled.

'Well, we had a stroke of fortune. That's really all it was. Otherwise I might still be roaming the streets looking to better myself somehow. Do you know, we used to steal fruit?'

'Really?'

'Yes. Sarah would go and cry, being only little, and I'd stuff apples and whatever else there was into my bag. I used her as a distraction, Mr Crepuscular ...'

'Simone.'

'... I used poor Sarah as an accomplice and I never even asked her. Do you realise that? She was only a little girl and I told her to go and cry where everyone could see her. And she always did what I said.'

'You were only a girl, Miss Penultimate ... only a little girl too.'

'No, I don't think so. I was never *only* a girl. Not really. We grew up so quickly.'

'Some of us never quite grow up. Which is worse? Which is better?'

'Oh. I don't really know what I'm saying, Mr ... Simone. I don't normally drink quite so much wine.'

'Ah! No, me neither.'

'But you see he discovered this plant, a bush. It was oriental and it grew these little fruits. He bought it from a traveller ...'

'Who?'

'I never knew, he only said it was 'a mysterious traveller' ...'

'No, I meant who are you talking about?'

'Oh, my father.'

'Ah, yes!'

'So, he had this bush with these little fruits and he knew ... oh, he had a feeling and this time it was a good feeling, this was going to be it, this was going to be the invention to make his fortune ... but, of course, he'd had that feeling a hundred times before and they'd come to ...'

'To nothing?'

'Usually even less than that. He only had two fingers left on his right hand. Those were the sort of mistakes he'd made. But this time, he was sure it was going to work out. But he didn't have a clue. I really could see why our mother left ... he wasn't stupid by any means, but certainly he had no luck and no common sense. He submitted patents for all sorts of products to be made from these fruits, but none of them ever made a penny, because they were all impractical, unnecessary or just lunatic. Then one day I heard him complaining about his shoe laces.'

'His shoe laces?'

'Yes, you remember how, back before the seventies, they were always fraying and you could never get them through the holes, the eyes of the shoe? The eyelets?'

'I've always worn sandals I'm afraid, but I think I know what you're going to say ...'

'What?'

'That it was at that moment he had the eureka idea that lead to the invention of the aglet? That in a flash he saw that if he popped a little thing shaped like one of these fruits on the end of the lace it would no longer fray and would always go through the hole?'

'No.'

'Oh.'

'No. He didn't have the idea. But I did. I was twelve years old at the time and a child can't register a patent, so my father had to register it in his name. He didn't want to. He was kind (which was one of his problems) and it took me a whole night to convince him that he had to do it. And once he did, well the aglets took off and we never looked back. We moved to a big house, he hired a nanny to look after Sarah, I was sent to a boarding school, and his brother finally remembered that he existed and became a partner in Penultimate's Aglets.'

'*Your Penultimate Aglet Won't Be Your Last.*'

'Yes. I came up with the slogan too.'

'I remembering seeing it on a packing crate in Lío, in about … oh? … 1892.'

'Lío?'

'Oh, a small town, in Ecuador as it turned out, that I spent a few years in. The slogan stuck with me. I never quite knew what it was for … I'd not seen an aglet in Asia, and they were only just catching on there then in Latin America. But I always remembered the slogan.'

'Such a small world.'

'Yes, but it still takes a long time to go all the way round.'

'Yes.'

They walked in silence for a bit, scuffing their heels and listening to the scuttling noises that came from the hedgerows all around them.

'When I left school, I was eighteen then, I did the usual things a girl of my nouveau riche class was meant to do, but I never did them very well. I used to get into scrapes and my father had to bail me out once or twice. He was embarrassed, because it meant his name was in the papers again, but I think secretly he approved. He'd always wanted adventure. But his brother didn't like me. Asked me to keep quiet and sit at the back, if you will. And so I decided to do something stupid that would get me away from arrogant men like him and I became a governess in a big house on the Isle of Wight, looking after three girls. I had a good grasp of languages and could exert a bit of discipline and so I rather enjoyed my time there, the weather made a lovely change to London smogs, and the accent was of course delightfully quaint to my ears, and the girls were charming, but in time I got bored. It was just too much of the same, day after day.'

'But, so much of life is like that.'

'Ah, but you can do something about it, Mr Crepuscular. You know that. And so I went back to London and put an advert in the paper advertising my services as a sort of governess 'with field trips'. You give me your girls, I take them away for six months, improve them and then give them back, in exchange for your money. That was the idea and it has worked all these years. Thirty years! Oh, I really don't feel that old … do you?'

'No. Not tonight anyway.'

'Well, yes. I'm never quite sure whether the parents believe we actually visit half of the places their girls must tell them that we've been to, but that's not my concern – just so long as I get to travel and get paid I'm happy.'

'Do you know, I haven't left London, not more than a dozen times in more than that number of years?'

'Really?'

'Really. And I don't miss it. Travelling, I mean. I did so much of it. I saw so much back then, that I'm happy now to have my four walls and my unchanging view. Maybe it'll come to you too, in time, Miss Penultimate.'

'If it does, Simone, you have permission to shoot me.'

'I'm afraid you shall have to find another assassin on that day, Miss P., I couldn't pull the trigger.'

'I killed my father.'

'I'm sorry?'

The moon slid behind some thin cloud, dimmed the lane, splintered its light into faint narrow shafts and then she was herself once more, proud and unique and immemorial, shining white like a sliver of heliographic mirror hung 300,000 miles away and holding steady. They idled in silence for a few moments.

'Well, not actually. But I might as well have done. I was away when he had his last heart attack. He'd grown fat and prosperous. A new waistcoat every time I saw him.' She paused. 'I hated it. Hated what he'd become. That one idea had worked and he'd stopped trying anything else. He'd relaxed into success and just let other people build the machines to churn out the wretched things, commissioned other people to design the packets … ten years earlier he would have done it all himself, late at night on his drawing board, knocking tea over his drawings, setting fire to his dressing gown … all that business. But now he had become a name at the top of a bit of cardboard and he'd stopped reaching out. And that was his brother's fault. He was a bad influence. He liked money, you see. That's always a bad sign, once that becomes more important than high ideals and ideas.'

'I couldn't agree more. Sometimes Rodney complains … well maybe 'complains' is the wrong word, because he doesn't do that, but he certainly mentions it sometimes … he says we ought to charge more, we ought to investigate what it is the public wants … I ought to focus my writing on certain criteria that he's identified. But he has a wife, you see, Miss P., and they have a baby on the way, and the pamphlets were never built to support more than just me and the boys, so maybe he's right.'

'Ideas are important, Mr Crepuscular, as is money ... but a balance must be found.'

'A balance, yes ...'

'I sent him a letter while I was away (I was only in France, this was, what? 1890?) saying that I thought his brother was a pompous, unhelpful, arrogant, idiotic, greedy, pig-headed businessman. Oh, I'd had a glass or two of this fine Chablis, and I hadn't learnt the perils (or if I had, I'd forgotten them) of writing letters late at night and a little tight ... So the next thing I know I had a telegram calling me back, saying my father was ill. Well, he was only young, he was fifty I think, and I thought another week won't make any difference ... he hadn't been ill when I went away. And so I finished the trip as planned, left my girls at Victoria Station as normal to be collected by their parents, and went to the house and I found that I'd missed not only his dying, but the funeral too. My Uncle hadn't thought to send a second telegram. And when I saw him, well, I noticed my letter was in his in tray. He saw me in his office. I had to make an appointment. He didn't mention it, but I knew he'd read it, and well ... that was the moment I could've taken over the company, I mean at least become a partner ... but my Uncle didn't think it was woman's work, wouldn't hear of it.'

'You wouldn't have liked it ... business, I mean.'

'No, of course not, but that wasn't the point. The point was that I was told by that wretched man what to do. By my own Uncle? As if *he* knew best for *me*. God, I hated him for a while there Mr Crepuscular. But ...'

'What?'

'Oh …? Nothing. No, I don't know what I was talking about all that for. It's very ancient history. He died shortly after that anyway. A tragic accident, it said in the newspaper. I …'

'There are many tragic accidents in this world. Some are more tragic than others, perhaps.'

'Yes, I suppose that must be true.'

'And there are some small miracles. Moments and events that balance out the tragedy.'

'Yes?'

'Yes.'

Simone Crepuscular sensed that Penelope had said all she was likely too. He thought for a little before speaking again.

'When I left the army I found one of those miracles. I walked into the Himalayas, not having any idea what I was doing. Have you ever been there?'

'No. It's not somewhere I've been. I don't quite know why. Maybe because there's so much elsewhere, that it's hard to see it all.'

'Maybe.'

'It's not by the coast is it, Mr Crepuscular?'

'No, not really.'

'Well, there's another reason. I tend to travel by ship.'

Simone felt a little queasy at the word.

'In the Himalayas I met these people. Well, I met this one man, who made all the difference.'

'A man?'

'Yes. There was this valley, you see. It was high up in the mountains, but it was green. I learnt about agriculture there. It was like being in the cradle of the Tigris and Euphrates thousands of years ago, I mean for me that is. We planted and we grew and we irrigated, and I was taught all this by such quiet monks, such humble, beautiful people, that they seemed to have come from somewhere else. Or somewhen else. I don't know if any of this makes sense, but they seemed to be not quite of this earth. When I look back now, and it's been such a long time, it all seems a bit like a dream, do you see?'

'Yes, I can understand that.'

'When I look back they seem as if they weren't quite connected to the world, as if they walked just a little beyond it, a little above it … just an inch or so … and yet, at the same time, they were utterly rooted in the soil. They knew every potato we planted, almost by name as it were. It was most peculiar. I was reminded of it earlier, actually, when I was looking at your garden, at your vegetable patch and the herb bed.'

'Oh, that's not me …'

'I don't have a garden in London, I haven't ever had a garden of my own. Not since I was in the army, and then I wasn't thinking about things like that.' He paused and they walked on in silence for a way. 'Do you want to know something?' He stopped walking and looked at her, lit as she was by the moon, pale and so near to being unreal that he sighed. 'Do you want to know something that I've thought about for years and have never quite come to terms with?'

'Only if you want to tell me, but yes, Mr Crepuscular, I would like to know.'

'Miss Penultimate, I haven't written this down because

I've never been quite sure, but tonight, walking with you here, listening to you, well, I feel a calmness that gives me an idea that I may have been right ... I might've been taught the right things all along.'

'Go on.'

They were both silent for a moment more and then Simone started walking again, although slowly.

'When I was studying with the Little Master ... he was the man I met there in the Himalayas who taught me everything, taught me all about being still and about moving and about listening and ... oh, about everything ...'

'Like a guru?'

'I suppose so, yes. Though that word comes from the Sanskrit, it means 'weighty', and he was just the lightest man I've ever known. But if you mean 'Was I his student?', then yes, and he was my Master. When we were studying with him we would meditate. Do you understand meditation, Miss Penultimate?'

'Enough to follow you, I'm sure.'

'Well, he told us that we had never, and in all likelihood would never (he was a blunt teacher, but good) that we would never *truly* meditate. Someone asked what he meant, asked him to explain. I expect they still have the bruises from his stick. Ha! Sometimes he was very blunt. It's funny, Miss Penultimate, but in all these years that have passed since then, I've never wondered what became of those other students. We weren't friends as such, we didn't speak much, but we all shared the same vision. I expect most of them are dead now. Many of them were older than me, even back then, and I'm quite old enough now. I wonder whether they stayed there, or whether they left, like me, and took their little memories of that place out into the world … scattered seeds of it around the globe. I wonder if that valley exists now, not just in the space between two mountains, but in widely spaced minds around the world. It's a thought. Oh, it's a curious thing, time, isn't it? I mean what it does to us, how it changes us?'

Penelope nodded affirmatively, not wanting to speak, but watching the thoughts move across this man's face in the moonlight.

'He said that we didn't meditate, and we could tell this because if we ever really *did* meditate we would become (that is the person doing the meditating) would become invisible. He said that we only see one another because each soul creates vibrations, sort of mental vibrations in the world. Every thought that passes through our brains, every ripple of soul, as it were, creates disturbances in the stuff, in the substance, in the matter that makes up the world. When we puzzle about something, again there's a disturbance made. When we think something, or think about something … there's a disturbance. When we fear or worry or smile or laugh, it disturbs the world. When we love,' at this word he pointedly didn't turn to look at Miss Penultimate, 'it sets up a disturbance in the world.'

He was quiet for a moment and again stopped walking.

A fox paused in the road before them and Penelope touched Simone's arm with her hand to point it out. It vanished into the hedgerow on the left hand side, although for a moment she wondered if it had, perhaps, just vanished, just turned invisible as it ignored them. It was very dark here, under the shade of the overhanging trees, and as the fox slid out of the streak of moonlight it had been caught in, she felt it really could have, in that moment, done anything, even disappeared.

'These disturbances,' Crepuscular continued after a moment, 'are what we sense of each other. It is these disturbances, these ripples through whatever the substance of the world, of reality, really is that allow us to see each other, to know each other. When a man, or a woman of course, meditates they still these disturbances. Calm then. When they truly unfocus, which is what meditation is, then their disturbances diminish and, eventually, at some point they would vanish from our world.'

'Is that true?'

'I don't know ... I think I believe it is,' replied Simone. 'At that point, when a sort of spiritual entropy, to use a negative sounding but perhaps accurately descriptive phrase, sets in, the person who is meditating is absorbed into the universe, not as themselves, but as nothing. That is the goal, I think, of life.'

They started walking again, this time back down the lane towards the cottage.

'I was in the Little Master's temple-room one day. We were all sitting in silence, you know cross-legged, just gazing off into the distance or with our eyes closed, *pretending* to meditate, as he would have said, when something happened. And this is what I haven't spoken about before, so don't laugh. Please. I was sitting there, I had my eyes open and was watching a snowflake that was drifting down from the open ceiling. I often did that, I found it aided my concentration, and, although I was focussing on something, it helped me to eliminate a lot of other things from my mind while I practised the non-meditation. But this day I noticed a sudden light, and I saw the snowflake melt, in the air, in front of my eyes. Time seemed to slow and my eyesight seemed to become acute. I watched as each of the six prongs of this tiny delicate and perfect artefact turned to water. It happened one at a time, first the one at the top and then the one sticking up on the left and then the one on the right. It was miraculous to watch, as if time had slowed or was slowing. I turned my head and turning it seemed to take such an effort, and an age, but I turned just as the last point of the ice-star vaporised into the air, into the light and I saw the source of the light. It came from where the Little Master had been sitting, right before us. In fact he was still there, but as I watched he faded away. I could see through him! I could see through him to the floor he sat on, I could see the far wall, and it was becoming clearer, and at the same time this light was pouring out of his skin. It was a glutinous light, it moved slowly and as it reached me I felt warmed with a vast and deep sense of compassion, there was so much love in that light, I knew I could never turn away from it. And then it was gone.'

Penelope put her arm around his broad shoulders and rested his cheek upon hers. He wasn't crying, but he was filled with something that tensed his body, that made it awkward for him to continue. Once again they had stopped walking.

He lifted his head and looked into her eyes. It was dark but the slim crescent moon was behind him and her face was lit palely by the light from that distant reflecting globe. She showed some concern, she showed some love, she showed some curiosity. He continued, because, he felt, this was what was important, everything that had gone before had been to set the scene, had been merely necessary educative information.

'He smiled.'

She looked at him for a moment before asking, 'Your Little Master?'

'Yes,' he said, seemingly happy to have said it.

A few more moments went by. This seemed to be a time of moments and of pauses, he thought to himself reflecting on this part of the evening later on.

'As that light reached out to fill the room, to calm the room, as he disappeared from sight, as the room became utterly visible through him, I saw him smile. It was like the Cheshire Cat, you remember in that Alice book?' She didn't. He didn't attempt to explain. 'I just saw the faintest hint of that smile in the air, it hung there for a moment. I had watched his mouth move from the straight line he usually wore to one where the corners pointed upwards. It was a smile, I can't say it any other way. And then the light vanished and he ... his body slumped forward on the dais. He just crumpled up and collapsed forwards.'

Penelope raised her hand to her mouth. 'I thought he vanished? I thought he slipped away into Nirvana or whatever it is?'

'He failed, Miss Penultimate, that is the secret I

have carried for so long. Or one secret at any rate. My Master failed.'

'How …?'

'I never got to speak to him after that, he was dead when he hit the floor. It became apparent I was the only one who had seen what had happened, I don't know, maybe everyone else had had their eyes closed. But they heard the crash, and it was as if time restarted with the thud of his body on the stone, a blur of activity burst out. Someone rushed over and checked for a pulse, opened his eyes, put a mirror by his mouth. He was very dead. They put it down to a heart attack or something, you know, something non-mysterious and I never mentioned what I'd seen, not even there, not even then.'

'What was it you saw, what does it mean? I think I understand it, but … just to be sure …'

'Miss Penultimate, he achieved what I can only dream of achieving, in fact what I am somewhat afraid of achieving. He became, just for a moment, invisible. Really. He unfocussed himself so much he faded away, he found that perfect equilibrium and was ready to be freed from this wheel of living. But he realised this, in that ultimate moment, he understood what was happening and it seemed *good* to him, that's why he smiled. But that realisation, that final understanding, that feeling of satisfaction, of self-satisfaction was a disturbance, you see, was an imperfection. And so he became visible again, he came back to us, his meditation was flawed, as are all of ours. As for the heart attack, maybe it was … maybe he was just disappointed … maybe what he had experienced overpowered him. Maybe he had seen enough, lived enough, done enough. Maybe it was his time. Some Masters have that ability, just with a thought, you know.' Here a tear trickled out of Simone's eye and traced a line down his cheek into his beard. 'When they turned his body over, the smile was gone.'

They had reached the cottage once again and Penelope opened the gate.

Simone lay his hand on top of hers as it rested on the latch. They stood for a minute like that, just listening to the night around them.

'You know,' he said, finally, looking at her hand under his, feeling her fingers, cold under his warm palm, 'I am an old man. But inside my breast beats a young man's heart still. And I grow foolish ...'

'Shush,' she said quietly, laying a finger over his lips, 'I think I know what you want to say, but I am not the person to whom you should say it.'

Simone stood in silence. He looked at her lips and then up at her eyes.

'I don't know where she is, I'm afraid, the woman you should be saying this to. I don't know where to find her for you; I get the feeling, though, she is lost somewhere ...'

Simone nodded, almost imperceptibly. In that moment he was overwhelmed with a desire to tell her everything, to tell her about Teresa-Maria and about his daughter ... about all his losses. He wanted to lay his head on her breast and dampen it with his tears. To tell her everything, to tell yet another story, another secret he had never shared. A secret he, perhaps, never could. He saw his Maria's eyes staring at him from Penelope's face, for just a second – it was the way the shadow struck them in the starlight. But he didn't say anything to her. The night had long passed the moment in which telling that secret, telling that story would have been possible. It had grown too late.

'Miss Walker is waiting for me upstairs. She is my world, Mr Crepuscular, and I could never turn away from that, not even for a minute. I am lucky to be loved so well, I know that, and I am happy. She is more than I deserve, sir, much more. But I am also sorry, please believe me when I say this, Simone, I am so sorry to be unable to give you what you need.'

She withdrew her hand from under his and, standing on tiptoe, laid a single kiss on his brow before walking slowly into the cottage.

Simone Crepuscular, with his young man's heart beating sadly and wildly in his old man's chest, walked slowly across the garden to the shed where his bed was waiting for him. He didn't have a watch to look at but knew that it was very late indeed, and he, perhaps, had had two too many glasses of wine that he now, really, really needed to sleep off.

28

Bedknobs & Sunrise

He didn't want to disturb Simon by clumping about in the shed they'd been billeted in so Simone Crepuscular decided to sleep out of doors. It was a beautiful night, still warm, and as he lay his head back on his folded hands he gazed up at the swirling universe above him. The grass that was broken by his weight was releasing its comforting, apologetic smell and he was sadly at aching ease. Until, that is, he was jerked upright by the sound of a scream.

He really hadn't been expecting a scream.

Immediately a fearful, fretful barking burst out further down the garden. Nigel Spiggot had heard the scream too and was now expressing his disapproval, maybe trying to scare off whatever monster had caused it, by running around inside the tent and yapping in all directions at once.

With a speed that belied both his age and his size Crepuscular climbed to his feet. The scream had come from inside the house, inside the cottage – that much had been clear. He strode across the patio, banged his shin on a bench, cursed quietly, took a deep breath and opened the kitchen door. It was very dark inside, the pale moon and starlight that his eyes had grown accustomed to didn't make any difference to the kitchen, and he paused on the doorstep for a few seconds trying to get his bearings.

There were noises upstairs, up above his head. Creaking floorboards and what sounded like sobbing. Crossing the kitchen he pulled open the inner door and found himself in a hallway. Off to one side was a door that must lead into the front room, ahead of him was the front door – he could make out the stained glass pattern of some twining roses glowing faintly in the night – and on his left, facing the front door, were the stairs. He marched forward and spun up them, taking them two at a time and in a second he was tripping over something heavy and unmoving at the top. That's dangerous, he thought, someone could trip on that and fall all the way down. He had his usual involuntary vision of Teresa-Maria falling away from him, hands outstretched, mouth moving. If only, he whimpered, if only I could tell what she was saying to me …

But no, that's the past, that's over and dead and lost, he reminded himself, picking himself up from the floor, this is the now. Concentrate Crepuscular, concentrate on the now. Be useful *now*.

What he had tripped on, he realised, was Miss Penultimate. She was lying on the floor. Was she breathing? He knelt beside her and held a hand in front of her face. Yes, she was breathing. He sighed a relieved sigh. And look, he thought, the vein in her neck there, that's thumping away like mad. It seemed she had simply fainted. As he stood up he noticed what hadn't struck him before – that there was a source of light on this landing, unlike downstairs. That was how he could see these things. It made sense once he thought about it.

Behind him was a doorway, facing the head of the stairs, and he could tell that it was from through there that both the sobbing and the light was coming. He slowly turned round to look.

Yellow candle light fluttered and flickered. Shadows moved back and forth with the draught. Framed, through the doorway, was a wrought iron bedstead, whose curlicues cast strange shadows across the floor before him. In the bed, sheets clutched up to her breasts, face a streak of tears, was young Nancy Walker and beside her, sat on the edge of the bed red-faced and pulling his shirt on haphazardly, was his son, Simon.

As far as she could remember Penelope Penultimate had never fainted in her life. She was simply not that sort of woman. And yet this sudden shock, coupled with the headiness of the wine she'd drunk and the lateness of the hour, late even for her, had all combined to so knock her back that she had presented to the world a very good impression of fainting. Nor was Simone Crepuscular the sort of man given to fainting fits, by he too felt strangely attracted by the possibility.

He staggered in the doorway as if reeling from a physical blow. He clutched at the doorjamb and closed his eyes. 'I'm sorry, Miss Walker,' he said, out of ingrained politeness. But it didn't help.

Behind him he heard movement.

At the top of the stairs Miss Penultimate had climbed to her feet, and from downstairs he could also hear the noise of someone in the kitchen. Mr Quirkstandard must've got up, he thought, but at least Mr Spiggot has stopped all his noise.

A hand laid itself on his shoulder and turned him round.

'Let us go downstairs, Mr Crepuscular,' said Miss Penultimate, her eyes dimmed.

As they descended Nancy burst into a sudden, loud shudder of tears.

'I'm so sorry,' she moaned, between heaving breaths and violent sniffs, 'I'm so sorry …'

Penelope and Simone walked into the kitchen where the two gentlemen were waiting for them. Quirkstandard had somehow managed to light one of the gas lamps above the sink.

'What is it?' he asked with a quiver in his voice, clearly distressed by seeing his Aunt upset.

'A mistake,' said Crepuscular, on everyone's behalf.

'Let's go back to the garden, boys,' said Penelope.

Quirkstandard led the way, opening the back door and wiping his feet on the mat before stepping outside.

They righted the bench that Simone had knocked over and sat down at the table where, twelve hours earlier they had had such a civilised, pleasant late lunch.

'You look after your Aunt, sir,' he said to Epitome.

'Yes, of course.'

Quirkstandard sat beside his Aunt and wrapped his arms round her shoulders. The role reversal was upsetting to him. She had always been strong and implacable, was that the word? He had never expected to have her leaning on his shoulder, weeping quiet tears into his dressing gown. He patted her absently and stroked her thick dark hair and cried a little himself. Spiggot sat on the bench and rested his head in her lap. She twined a finger through his hair.

Simone walked back into the kitchen and found Simon lingering sheepishly in the opposite doorway.

For the first time in his life Crepuscular had to bite his tongue and even more worryingly found he had to restrain the urge to step across the room and slap the boy. But he did restrain it and settled for looking disappointed.

He gestured to the front door and the two Crepusculars walked into the hallway.

The door was locked, but the key was in the lock, so in a moment they stood out in the lane. Without saying anything, without really knowing what to say, Simone pointed to the car and Simon sloped off to try to find some sleep in the back seat. The elder Crepuscular watched his stupid, unfortunate boy walk into the darkness. He walked in a straight line and Crepuscular noted how they had all seemed to have sobered up now.

In time Quirkstandard took his Aunt through to the front room, where the dew wouldn't dampen them, and she slept on the sofa while he held her hand, wishing that someone would tell him what had happened or what was going on now. It had been such a nice visit, up to this, and he was confused, scared and worried. Was it something he had done wrong? Had he spoiled that game they'd been playing before bed by not really knowing quite how to play it properly? They'd never played it at Mauve's.

Spiggot dozed on the floor, shivering, twitching and half-yelping as he liked to do as and when his dreams directed. This was something normal, Quirkstandard thought, amongst all this unusual business. He's a good friend, really the best.

Simone made his way to the bed he'd been given in the shed and failed to sleep for almost the entirety of the one or two hours it took for the sun to rise and the world to wake.

Nancy did not come downstairs but sat up in the arm-chair in the bedroom watching her thoughts parade in front of her. She had a good view out of the window and a little later saw the sun rise, and a little after that finally slumped into an unpleasant, shallow but dream-filled sleep.

29

Church Bells & Breakfast Conversations

✹

Morning brought with it little sense of peace. Miss Pen-ultimate woke early. She dried her eyes before splashing them with cold water and drying them again. Then she carried the sleeping Epitome out and laid him down in the tent where he'd been meant to spend the night.

Her head ached and her mouth felt thick with the accumulations of the morning. She thought, with sour distaste, of the number of men who had traipsed and tramped in her cottage during the early hours as she swirled a cupful of soapy salt water round her mouth. She had never expected a weekend like this. She was tempo-rarily unable to attach an accurate label to the state of her feelings. She knew, however, that they weren't good.

Simone Crepuscular had also risen early. He was sat beside the river, a short way away, clutching his head between his two large hands which were leant, in turn, between his knees. He was specifically wondering just why the world had chosen this morning to be so damned bright and noisy – even the earthworms seemed to be chewing their mouthfuls of soil with particular vigour. There should be some peace on a Sunday morning, he thought, in such an ostensibly Christian country as this one. Surely. And then the church bells began braying across the fields and he clutched his hands closer over his ears.

Penelope sat on the bench outside the kitchen door smoking her pipe. She hadn't picked it up for some months, after Nancy had complained that it looked like a pretentious affectation and made the cottage smell like an old man's cardigan. She'd hoped the tobacco might soothe her, but she found it to be of little help. She tapped the bowl too often on the table, fiddled incessantly with her matches and had been biting down so hard on the stem that not only had she cracked it, but she'd also given herself a sort of preliminary toothache, a muscular warning, as it were, incipient numbness presaging the pain soon to arrive.

She didn't feel like breakfast and didn't go indoors to make herself any. Besides Nancy got shirty if she touched the frying pans without asking. The kitchen really had become her domain and Penelope was usually sent upstairs with the newspaper or some maps when dinner was being prepared. Penelope wasn't even sure she knew where everything was kept anymore, but since she didn't want any breakfast this wasn't a problem.

As the sun crept higher in the sky the day drew on. She sat a while longer, occasionally chewing absently on the end of her little finger. The trees swayed in the small breeze that shifted round the foot of the hills. The church bells were still chiming and that sound, at least, was something distant and unconnected to her thoughts, which was what she needed more of. The local vicar had called on her once, shortly after she'd moved into the cottage. Having attempted to fulfil his duty of care to a new parishioner he never came back. Penelope almost smiled at the memory of him scurrying away up the lane, coat tails flapping indignantly in the wind. She didn't care much for the church (or the Church), but its bells had always fitted into her ideal of an English countryside, so she had mostly refrained from writing stern letters about them to the local press, bishop and MP.

✹

Later on Crepuscular came back to the garden, having finally grown tired of watching flotsam float by and his head finally having shrunk back to something close to normal size. As he stepped into the garden he was followed by eleven faint peals from inside the church's belfry.

He sat down at the table beside the kitchen.

Miss Penultimate didn't look up at him as he approached, or as he sat, but once he was settled she spoke.

'How could she do it?' she said quietly, possibly to him, possibly to the garden at large, or possibly simply as the continuation of a conversation she'd been having all by herself. There was a flint edge to her tone – it was knapped, a bit ragged, but still painfully sharp.

Crepuscular went to lay a sympathetic hand on her shoulder, not really sure what else he could do other than listen, but she shrugged it aside before it even touched her.

Now she looked up at him. Her eyes were in shadow where the few stray strands from her dark fringe fell across them.

'Oh, it's you. Ahem. I'd appreciate it if you could all leave as soon as is practicable, Mr Crepuscular. Thank you for bringing my nephew for his visit, but I think there is nothing much left for us to do here. I fear Sundays are awfully dull in the country.'

'Madam ...'

She stopped him sharply with a glance and then followed his eyes round as he looked up and over her shoulder.

In the doorway of the kitchen stood the most bedraggled little thing. A creature of pity and remorse, in this moment, and in this moment alone, no longer beautiful. If she'd been held under the pump and drowned like a kitten she couldn't have looked more sorry for herself. Her eyes and cheeks were puffy and raw, her dress was unironed and just pulled on, her hair was still down and uncombed. Her hands were held out, weakly, as if in supplication, and although her mouth opened nothing came out of it but air.

'Nancy, oh,' began Penelope, standing up as if she had just uttered a complete sentence.

Simone looked from one woman to the other, feeling suddenly peculiarly uncomfortable. This wasn't a feeling he had felt often enough to ever grow accustomed to. He'd always, throughout his long travels and even sat at home, fitted in wherever he'd ended up, bending just enough (metaphysically) to still be himself but to also be just what was wanted. But right now, right here, he felt as if he didn't belong, as if something were unfolding that he had no right to be party to.

'Nancy,' Penelope began again. It wasn't at all clear

what she wanted to say, nor how she wanted to say it. There was a wobble in her voice, but it wobbled along a razor's edge; a blunt, cold razor. Rusty. Her hands moved under their own compulsion, floating in the air before her breast, one hand tugging at the fingertips of the other, as if they might come off with the appropriate twist and reveal the answer to her prevarication. In her thoughts she cursed those hands – showing her up like that. But then – oh! – those thoughts, what were they all about? They raced here and there, through and across all the years that she and Miss Walker had known each other, holding up the pictures of unexpected happiness here and then crunching them up; holding up images of sadnesses and arguments there and all those obstacles they'd overcome, and then crushing them up too, before her eyes, as if they'd been of no point.

Her lip trembled.

A noise came from between Nancy's lips, which could have been, 'Ma'am.'

And then something inscrutable snapped, some tipping point was reached and Miss Penultimate tumbled free down the other side.

She slapped Nancy across the cheek, leaving a red glow in the shape of her hand. Besides the expected and impulsive stagger Nancy didn't move. She didn't lift a hand in response; she didn't even lift her eyes up.

'How could you? How dare you? How, Nancy, how? Just tell me that. What made you do it? Why?' – these are a tidied and ordered sample of the sort of questions Penelope threw at her young companion, battering them like hailstones against her breast. They're neatened and condensed and rationalised on the page, but in that Arundel garden, through that warm Sunday lunchtime, her railing took longer, was less ordered, much less thought through.

Nancy sat down, slumped down, on the doorstep under the rain of questions. It seemed to her to be a torrent, to be a physical beating. She became weak, feeling put upon and, staring up at the wrath pouring down on her, could only open her mouth, gasp at the air, scrabble to get some into her lungs and say, again and again, 'I'm so sorry,' and 'Love,' although what she meant by this latter statement, whether it was a noun or a verb, a command, request or plea, was unclear.

Simone Crepuscular was distressed and deeply saddened by the scene. He understood human emotions as well as the next man (or probably better considering Quirkstandard had just woken up and was emerging from his tent) and knew how deep they could hurt. He still had an empty space at his core.

'Auntie?' Quirkstandard cried, though not loud enough to break in above her own shouting. Crepuscular saw he had tears on his cheeks, which in turn had grown ashen.

'Never before has a man set foot in that house, and now what is it? A cottage of sluts? Is that what you've made it?' This still shouted, still rambling, still much less coherently stated than writing it down must make it seem. Penelope had never been so angry before, never been so hurt. This burnt her insides, this twisted her heart, thinking that Nancy had been touched by a man, might even have enjoyed it, had done it for some

inscrutable reason she couldn't fathom just to hurt her
… well, hurt her she had. It was as if she'd taken a fist-
ful of shards, hot from some gigantic symbolic kiln, and
thrust them into Penelope's guts, twisting them once for
despair and twice for desperation. What was this?

Crepuscular took his opportunity to slip away, walked
quickly to Quirkstandard and took his arm. He was
pointing at his Aunt, his mouth open, her face covered
by clouds of anger, of loathing, and his own displaying
his innocence, his entire and magnificent lack of understanding. If life's a game, then what was this? His lower
lip trembled, even while his upper one remained stiff,
and Simone wrapped him up in his broad arms.

'Hush now,' he said as he began to hum a Mongolian lullaby he'd learnt a lifetime before. The horsemen
had used it to calm foals who became fraught out on the
broad grasslands, as they sometimes did when being, for
example, branded or milked for the first time.

'This is how you pay me back,' continued Penelope,
'acting like a common slattern in our bed …?'

'Penny?' this single imploring word, drawn up out of
Nancy's chest. It carried the subtext of '*Stop, please stop,
don't you think I know what I've done, and can't we just have
a cup of tea now, get back to the way things were and never talk
about this again – haven't I suffered enough?*'

'If it hadn't been for me you'd've been wandering
the streets now,' Penelope's vehemence was terrible to
behold, and perhaps even more so now that her eloquence was returning. 'You know full well that only I
would have taken you in, would have given you a job
just like that. If you weren't here, you'd be out there

somewhere, selling yourself like a million other victims of this dreadful trammelling masculine world we inhabit ... and I don't even know if you'd be able to make enough money for bread ... damn you ...'

Crepuscular held Quirkstandard in his arms. The boy, the young man, was gentled now, but he could feel his tears still flowing. His heart was shaken, his world was shaken, by his Aunt's lack of decorum. If she could be like this, he was thinking (though not in words, not consciously), with the housekeeper, how might she be with me one day; what if I don't please her, don't live up to her expectations? Crepuscular tried not to listen to Miss Penultimate's words as best as he could. Her wrath had certainly stilled his schoolboy crush, but he still felt compassion for her, he still liked her, but his deep caring was scarred by her anger, scared by it too.

'In fact,' she continued, 'if it hadn't been for me you wouldn't even be alive at all. If I hadn't brought you back from that blasted jungle as the tiny puking, mewling babe that you were, you wouldn't have had any life at all, except maybe co-habiting with some pygmies inside some alligator's bloody stomach. If I hadn't already saved you twice, my dear, you might already have been dead.' She stopped.

The storm suddenly blew itself out with this realisation, with this sudden summoning up of a world with no Nancy Walker in it, a world bereft of love and of her lover. She looked down at Nancy and her eyes softened. How could she, she thought in a swift reversal of mental states, have ever been angry with her? She knelt down by the step, in front of Nancy, and held a hand out to her still red cheek. Even as she did so a chasm opened in her heart. She had, it was suddenly true, in that very moment forgiven Nancy Walker for every crime she had committed (as she had forgiven her before, and would again), for every stupid mistake she'd made in the long darknesses of the night … of all nights everywhere. This forgiveness was entire, unconditional and she could never, *would* never (she understood immediately), take it back. But what − she dreaded to articulate the thought − what if Nancy would not forgive her? Or what if it hadn't been a mistake? What if she went off, that afternoon, that very minute, in Epitome's Rolls-Royce with the Crepuscular boy? What if they drove off? What if Nancy had changed her mind, had changed her heart? How would Penelope cope then? What could she possibly do then?

Attendant upon these thoughts came other thoughts of equally dark content. What if, for example, she was still loved but wasn't forgiven? That is, what if Nancy couldn't forgive her for the way she had just treated her (she'd never laid a hand on the girl in so violent a way before), for the language she had used, for the names she had called her? What if Nancy didn't forget the horrors of this morning? Penelope was willing to forgive and move on, but wasn't it *she* who had wronged Nancy? Didn't she need to be forgiven herself and what would happen? What chance did she have of living, if that forgiveness was not forthcoming?

She held her hand out to touch Nancy's cheek. She wiped away the tears, touched her lips. She brought her face close and kissed her eyes, which were closed and screwed up. With one hand she neatened the loose hair, brushed it away from her face, traced the outline of her ear, of her jaw, her neck. Every contour, every line on the girl's face she had known so well. Had she, she asked herself, thrown all this away with her wrath, with her unthinking and unhesitating anger?

In a flash she realised that what she reminded herself of, by acting like that, was a man. As retribution went it had been swift and righteous, meted out upon the innocent. She shuddered later, but now the thought simply worried her. Like the last bolt keeping one of Brunel's great bridges upright, all the strain was on her and she knew at any moment, at any moment soon, it might just pop, she might explode and the world would suddenly be falling. In fact, she could see the sky above her as she fell backwards, as the world spun, a vertiginous coiling in her stomach, in the pit of her stomach, and then ...

And then Nancy's arms were around her neck, her cheek pressed against hers. Penelope felt their bosoms press against one another, warm and full of life, the blood beating faster through those veins than ever before, capillaries working overtime to contain the situation, to shed the heat. Penelope half sat on the ground as Nancy's mouth found hers and her arms clasped her back, the back of her head, held her close.

Crepuscular let go of Epitome, allowing him to stand for himself. Now Miss Penultimate's shouting had stopped, now the storm of her wrath had calmed itself, Quirkstandard too felt calmer. Crepuscular looked at him.

'Do you have a handkerchief, Mr Q.?'

'Er, no, I don't believe I do,' Quirkstandard answered, patting his pockets.

'Here, use mine.' Crepuscular handed him one he produced from under his beard, saying, 'Blow your nose, Mr Q., and wipe your eyes, or the other way round if that seems better, then maybe step down to the outhouse to splash your face. We want you looking your best for your Aunt don't we? Run along.'

Epitome followed his friend's advice. It seemed sensible and filled with no ulterior motives. However, had he noticed the slightly distracted look in Mr Crepuscular's beard he might have thought twice about the question of motivation, because it was looking ever so slightly ulterior. Crepuscular wanted the young man out of the way. He needed to discover something that it would be easier to discover, easier to discuss with as few people around as possible.

'Father,' said a voice by his side.

Simone looked at Simon and Simon looked at him. He, for one, had washed and shaved this morning, thought his father. And, he added, he should stay for this.

His thoughts were interrupted by the emergence of Mr Spiggot. He yawned and yapped and squeezed past the two ladies on the kitchen doorstep. He looked around the garden with quite the normal carefree expectation of someone who'd slept well for the rest of the night after a brief nightmare had woken them early on and was now just looking for a handy tree and maybe a spot of breakfast. When he saw Simone he wandered over.

'Mr Spiggot,' Crepuscular began, squatting down so as to be more on the little gentleman's level, 'perhaps you'd be so kind as to go and help Mr Q. with his ablutions, you know how muddled he gets sometimes, and then perhaps you'd like a little walk along the river? Just for half an hour or so. I doubt I'll need much longer than that.'

Spiggot looked up at the big man as if he understood every word. Quirkstandard probably didn't actually need any help with his abluting, but the sound of a walk did sound good, especially where there were ducks and water and maybe even a vole or two. So, intuiting the glint in his eye as being one that suggested the suggestion he had just suggested wasn't actually much of a suggestion, per se, Spiggot toddled off toward the outhouse where the sound of splashing water could be quietly heard.

'Simon …'

'Yes father?'

'Come with me.'

'Yes father.'

The younger Crepuscular looked towards Nancy and felt his heart sinking. He hadn't expected her to come to him, not last night, and if he hadn't been quite so light-headed with the unaccustomed extra bottle of wine she'd offered him after the charades had ended he would never have acted quite so out of character when she had. He'd noticed her during the afternoon, of course, there weren't many pretty girls of a similar age who came into the pamphlet shop and so he was always reduced to a blushing imbecile when he met one. Rodney had always had the luck with women, he thought, it was something to do with those exotic eyes he had, that and the fact he was, off the bat, more sociable, joining clubs and things while Simon stayed at home copying out the old man's handwriting.

And after the mess he'd made of last night (what he remembered of it) before his father stormed upstairs and rescued him, he hadn't really expected Nancy to come back to him this morning. And, of course, she hadn't, and now it was quite clear that he was right to assume she wouldn't, and in amongst everything else it was actually a nice feeling to finally be right about something, even something as sad and untidy as this.

'Father, I'm sorry,' he said. 'I'm so sorry to have embarrassed you like this ...'

His father silenced him with a gesture.

'Simon,' he said at last, after a sigh, 'these next few moments are more important than anything, son. Just be quiet and come with me. Whatever happens, please, do not say a word. You were there, but you were too young to remember, to know ... Only I know what happened.'

Simon didn't understand, but followed.

'Miss Penultimate,' began Crepuscular as he approached the ladies, his hand held up as if he were a schoolboy wishing to ask a question.

Penelope turned away from Nancy's face, where she had been contemplating the crinkled lines that had formed at the edges of her young eyes.

'Mr Crepuscular.' She breathed in. 'I'm sorry, I forgot you were still here.'

'Miss Penultimate, we shall be going shortly, of course, but, well, needs must ... May I ...' he paused here, as if finding it hard to go on. 'May I ask one final question of you, before we leave you?'

'Of course, Mr Crepuscular. You know you can ask me anything, of course.'

She didn't look at Simon.

Nancy squeezed her hand, as a moment's coldness passed over her eyes. Perhaps it was jealousy, or perhaps it was merely the ghost of jealousy. It was swift and then it was gone.

'When was it, Miss Penultimate, that you were journeying in the Amazon?'

'In the Amazon?' Penelope thought back, trying to calculate the years, before suddenly turning to Nancy. 'How old are you now, my dear?'

'Twenty-four Penny, you know that.'

'Of course, I forgot the numbers for a moment. There you are Mr Crepuscular, twenty-four years ago was the last time I was there. I lost my little toe to some piranha on that journey. A most invigorating experience really. Oh, I lost one of the girls to them too, not so much fun that ...'

'I'm sorry to hear it.'

'The insurance was quite comprehensive, but all the same, it was infuriating.'

'Now, Miss Penultimate, can I just check. That would have been 1893, is that right?'

'Yes, I guess it must have been.'

'And it was on that journey, am I to infer from your method of calculation,' he held a hand toward Nancy who grimaced inwardly, 'that you discovered the baby that grew up to be Miss Walker here?' The younger woman looked at his hand again, where it now hung in the air and something deep in her hindbrain flashed and sparked. She ever so briefly felt the unbelievable sensation of lightness, of flying through the air; she thought she might faint, but then, in an instant, was sat back on the doorstep, just looking up at his gnarled old hand.

'Yes,' said Penelope, 'that's true.' There was a question sketched out in those words which she completed by asking, 'What is this, Mr Crepuscular?'

'In 1893, Miss Penultimate, I lost something.' As he began to speak Simon suddenly understood where his father was heading with this. He looked at Nancy, at her dark hair, her dark eyes, at that profile that had aroused his heart so with a pulse of recognition, and he shuddered in a combination of love, surprise and revulsion. 'What I lost was my wife. She was beautiful and wise ... and a pirate. I would like to think, Miss Penultimate, that had you met, that is to say had you and she ever had occasion to meet, you would have been, could have been friends.'

He stopped.

'Mr Crepuscular, I think I know what you're saying.'

'What? What is he saying?'

'Nancy, shush my sweet.' Penelope pulled her girl closer, hugged her tighter. 'I think Mr Crepuscular lost something else that day, besides his wife. Am I right?'

'Yes.' He breathed deep. 'In that jungle ... in that bloody, stinking jungle ...' Here he sat down heavily on the bench, silent tears already in his beard. 'We were lost, you see. We hadn't meant to take so long crossing it, the rainforest. It hadn't looked so big on the maps I'd studied ... But close up ... oh, close up it was so confusing. There were circles and routes and paths that wound around and about each other and I failed to find my way through. They all trusted me, Miss Penultimate, they trusted me and I failed them. Do you understand?'

Simon stood behind his father and laid a hand on his wide back, fuzzed as it was with a white fur. 'Dad,' he said quietly, 'you don't need to go on ...'

'Mr Crepuscular.' This said with a sort of emptiness, as a word of empathy.

'She fell, Miss Penultimate. She fell and I lost her forever.'

'Your wife?'

'Both of them, Miss Penultimate, both of them.'

Penelope looked at Simone and then at Nancy. Was there something akin about the nose? Take away the beard and was there a similarity? Even as she wondered she knew the truth. She glanced up at the younger Crepuscular.

'My wife and my baby girl. My daughter. My tiny baby girl, Miss Penultimate. I watched her falling, falling away from me, spinning ...'

'And I found her?'

'The dates are right. I can't think how many other little white babies may have been lost that year in the forest there ... but I suspect, by looking, by feeling these things ... that we have stumbled, blindly, into the truth.'

'What? Wait?! Hang on?! Him? He's my father?! Is that what you're all saying? Is that what you're saying?'

She stared at Simone, and then she stared at Simon.

'Oh ... oh dear,' she said, understating her feelings remarkably well.

This was quite a lot to deal with all of a sudden.

'I'll go put the kettle on,' she decided out loud, standing up. 'I think we could probably all do with a nice cup of tea.'

As the others agreed and as she stood and placed her hand on the doorknob, Quirkstandard and Spiggot appeared at the foot of the garden returning from the river and a voice was heard at the garden gate.

'Don't anyone move from where you are, I'm holding a gun,' said a small man, perched on the gate's bottom bar, holding a gun.

30

The Lawyer and the Frying Pan

Love is a force for good in the world, but it has a darker side too. It can drive normal, well-balanced people to extremes: those of devotion, those of foolhardiness. At times love walks hand in hand with fear: fear of loss, fear of rejection, fear of insufficiency. Jealousy and pride and obligation stalk the lover, and then, unexpectedly, he finds himself being unwarrantedly brave. He steps out of the shadow and stands up to the bully, not for himself, but on behalf of the one he loves, for love is sometimes selflessness – unexpected, unnecessary selflessness.

Epitome Quirkstandard did something then that he would remember proudly for the rest of his life. As he took in the scene from halfway down the garden he raised a finger, pointed and shouted.

'Mr Funicular? Are you pointing a gun at my Aunt?'

At these words a spark of recognition flashed in Miss Penultimate's mind. She'd been wondering, for the long moment the silence had lasted, just who this little man was, with the gun and the dandruff. His face had tinkled a distant bell, but she wasn't sure that wasn't just the church bells signalling the arrival of noon. Mr Funicular? Ah, she thought. After she'd left his office, fourteen years earlier, she had spared him no more than a pair of thoughts, and even that, at the time, had seemed overly generous. And here he is now, almost in my garden, she thought, maybe he's discovered another clause in Sarah's will.

Of course she knew that was unlikely.

'It was true, I'm afraid,' the lawyer said, directing his words toward Quirkstandard, 'but now,' he continued, changing the pistol's aim as he finished his sentence, 'it's pointing at you.'

Epitome thought of saying, 'Oh,' in a sort of surprised and meek way and then being quiet again, which seemed to be what he suspected he really ought to do. It was certainly what his brain expected of him, and also what Funicular expected too. If he did this, his brain was telling him, he would aptly acknowledge that his question had been answered clearly, exhibit a benign stupidity and be, most likely, ignored for the rest of the episode (however it unfolded). And that's exactly what he didn't do.

'Well,' he spoke, surprising everyone, except Spiggot, and perhaps his Aunt, who always knew that he had something special in him, 'I think that's much better, Mr Funicular. I don't much appreciate people threatening my Aunt. I mean, sir, just how dare you? How bloody dare you? (Excuse my language, Auntie.) Look – she's just a meek, harmless, defenceless, charming little old lady. And you point a gun ... I mean, a *gun* of all things ... Oh, Mr Funicular ...' (Had the circumstances in which he said these most inapposite things about Miss Penultimate been different there would have been the unmistakable accompaniment of people stifling incredulous giggles, as it was Penelope just smiled wryly and not without a small touch of pride, though at the same time she felt a trickle of ice water down her spine.) 'She only has me left to protect her, Mr Funicular. You knew this ... you know this. And here you come, to her own home, waving a pistol around as if it were a sandwich you felt like sharing with everyone ... and what I want to know, sir, is ... is this ...' he'd begun to bluster, his cool having evaporated, and he began to undo his shirt cuff with a view to rolling it up, 'is, just, well ... how dare you? Just how bloody dare you point that damned pistol at her?'

Funicular had not expected this turn of events. In fact he hadn't expected anything quite like this. He'd come to this cottage expecting that a brave display of strength would finally win Miss Penultimate's approval. If he could show her that he was a man of action, a man with spirit and spunk enough to match her naturally wild demonic nature, then, he had felt certain, she would automatically be his. A gun, he thought, the most perfect of oiled and tempered machines, that would be the most powerful thing he could handle – imbued with both symbolic and practical properties – to show he was a thinker as well as a doer (and vice versa). It had taken him a while to save up to buy such a beautiful device (it was thirty-years old but the man he'd bought it from had promised him it had been cared for diligently by its former owner who had only ever taken it out on Sundays) – and he'd spent a few evenings lining crockery up on the lawn of Hyde Park and after running through a score or two of bullets he'd almost hit every piece. (He'd then practiced his sprinting and tree climbing in response to the policemen's whistles – and they had also proved to be more than adequately effective.)

But he hadn't thought that there'd be other people here when he waved his gun and made his simple declaration ('I love you, Penny') to Miss Penultimate. He'd never imagined she'd have other friends, people clustered round her; he'd assumed, somewhat naively he'd be the first to admit, that she'd be alone, bored and waiting for him (even if, perhaps, she didn't know it). Now these other people just made him nervous, and he was slightly furious about being threatened by this idiot aristocrat.

His gaze flickered from Penelope to Quirkstandard several times, and when at last it settled on the boy, as he still thought of him, he began to worry further. Quirkstandard had removed his jacket and was rolling the sleeves of his shirt up, and with the ugly mark of a faded black eye shining darkly in the noonday sun he looked, surprisingly, quite competently pugilistic.

'I don't know,' Quirkstandard continued as he fiddled with his sleeve, 'why you're waving that pistol around, Mr Funicular, and to be quite honest with you I don't rightly care. As far as I'm aware there is no explanation that would be adequate, nothing that could convince me that you're doing a Good Thing and so my interest, my curiosity to discover what's in your mind, sir, has shrunk to zero. I am, however, willing to deal with this like a gentleman. Put the pistol down, after all it is the weapon of a coward, sir, and we can step out into the lane together and deal with this man to man.' He said this with remarkable fluency and presence, with a conviction in his voice and a squareness to his jaw which was only slightly undercut by the difficulty he was having undoing his right cufflink with his left hand. This difficulty was made more difficult by the fact that he refused to take his eyes away from where they were locked with Funicular's tiny, but alert, pair. But, eventually, the links fell to the floor and the sleeve was rolled up.

'Epitome, dear, do be careful. I'm not sure this man is entirely sane,' said Penelope as she stood up. While the gunman's attention was away from her she pushed Nancy into the cottage through the half open kitchen door and quietly pulled it to behind her. At least, she took a second to think to herself, at least she's going to be safe now.

As Quirkstandard began to walk towards Ivor Funicular, Spiggot trotted by his side, excited to see his friend displaying such quality, his little head looking from one man to the other, with little alternating doggish looks of pride and hatred.

Funicular glanced nervously around. The large half-naked man (what the hell, he thought angrily, was Penny doing sitting around with large half-naked men?) was sat quite still on the bench watching everything, breathing deeply. He couldn't be read at all, Funicular simply couldn't guess what he might do: he was an unknown quantity. Behind him stood a young man, about the same age as the Quirkstandard boy, whose face had drained pale and who looked quite awestruck. Funicular didn't think he'd be causing any problems. And, ah, he thought, glancing at Penelope stood beside the door, the sun catching her hair, making her look as radiant as an avenging angel. Her face was frowning, but he knew underneath that she was stirring with admiration for his brave display of power – she knew he was only doing it for her, that over all the years he had followed her, years during which he had collected the newspaper clippings of her doings and her advertisements; she knew that his heart hadn't wavered; she knew, he knew, that he'd simply been waiting until he was worthy of her and now he was. A trail of crockery in Hyde Park and a resignation letter on his desk said that. His life was hers now, just as hers was about to become his.

'I'm not here to fight, boy,' he said, refocusing on Quirkstandard. 'I'm in love.'

'Good for you,' said Epitome. 'I do so like a happy ending, but that doesn't explain the old gun, you know.'

'Ah, well, really, that's just incidental to my plan. Maybe it's even unnecessary.' He turned to face Miss Penultimate again, while leaving the gun pointing at her nephew. 'Penny,' he said, 'will you come away with me? Will you marry me? We can live anywhere, I have some money tucked away and a contact in the P&O offices who owes me a favour for some paperwork I looked over for him … Just say that you'll be mine and that I'll be yours forever and this situation in the garden can come to an end.'

Of all the things Penelope had been expecting this was the one thing she really hadn't expected at all. However, the shattering crack of the explosion that erupted immediately afterwards had.

Epitome Quirkstandard had clearly crossed some invisible boundary line that existed in Funicular's fuddled little brain. As one man stepped across the line, the other man's finger tightened into a squeeze on the stiff trigger. Neither man had been expecting that to happen, and, indeed, Ivor Funicular looked just as shocked as anyone else at the fact that it had. He clung onto the gate as he was jerked backwards by the blast and when his mind cleared he realised that another line had been crossed, one that meant whatever happened next he really couldn't go back to his office, he couldn't tear up that letter of resignation he'd left before the senior partner found it on Monday morning – he would be an outlaw from now on.

The report of the gunshot echoed back from the Downs, quieter and softer, more like far off thunder. And a chorus of ducks honked their noisy way up in a flurry from their river.

Epitome stopped walking forwards.

A narrow blue-grey twist of smoke drifted upwards and across the garden in the slow afternoon wind.

He stood for a moment before collapsing to the lawn with a hollow thud.

Everyone watched him fall. They stood still, frozen as if they were painted characters in a classical tableau. Only the crump of his body on the grass, which seemed an age in its coming, snapped them out of their dreams. Penelope shouted something wordless, her surface cool cracking for a moment. Simone stood up with a calm, yet violent look of horror on his face, reliving as he was, all the losses he had experienced before, tying himself to the wheel of incarnation with yet another blessed attachment. Behind him Simon picked up an empty wine bottle from the table and hefted it in his hand, thinking that if only there were a way to get round behind this little man on the gate he could crack him one on the back of his head. But there was no way round so he stayed where he was.

And Nigel Spiggot leapt at Funicular.

Like a mythical Fury, with tooth and claw bared and juddering, he pounced. For such a short gentleman it was a most remarkable leap. His eyes glowed with pain, and foam flecked his jowls, which drew back from terrifyingly, surprisingly sharp fangs. And he howled, in grief, in fear, in confusion, in violent hatred; from his throat rose a terrifying, high, inhuman war-cry. But, unfortunately, Funicular's gun had settled back in the direction it had been facing before and the hammer had rotated ninety-degrees to meet the next of its four chambers and the second bullet hurtled from the barrel with more intention than the first, in the passion of rabid self-defence, and dog and lead met in mid-air and the old man fell to the floor like so much bought and sold meat. One of his little hind legs quivered twice as he lay before the gate, his eyes already glazing over, and then he was still.

'This has gone far enough,' shouted Simone Crepuscular, pulling himself up to his full and rather impressive height and stepping towards Funicular.

The gun swung easily to face him, and since there were still some yards between them both, Crepuscular stopped where he was.

'Put the gun down, sir. Violence doesn't become you and doesn't aid any of us. It is nothing but a pointless vent of emotions that could be better utilised by harnessing them through channels of creativity. Put the gun down, man, and let us talk.'

'Oh do be quiet,' snapped Funicular. 'I didn't come here to listen to some weird old man. I came here to finally be with the woman I love. I came to her with a proposition, don't you see? I came to propose, to give her the man she has been searching for and has never yet found. I've read the papers every day fearing I'd find some announcement of impending wedding bells, but every day I have been justified in my love ... she has saved herself for me. I came here for her, not for you, sir,' he said this last word with such a recognisable sneer that it collected in an oily puddle at his feet. 'Don't any of you understand? Why is it so hard to grasp? Why do you all insist on interfering with our finding, with our unfolding, our love?'

Simone took another step forward, albeit a very small one.

'Love, sir,' he began, 'is a large word, and indeed a large world, and is a good thing, but ...'

'Oh shut up, will you? Love is only four letters, it's not a big word at all ... what are you talking about? Penny, what is he even doing here? I mean ... what are you doing having men sat around in togas at your house? I don't like it. It doesn't make me feel good ... I think you ought to stop it, now.'

'Please, let me go on, Mr ...?' Crepuscular looked to Miss Penultimate for help.

'Funicular,' she said.

'Please, Mr Funicular, let me just say this. Love shouldn't be a goal to aim at. Love, sir, is not a destination that you arrive at.' Here he held a hand out, palm forward, between himself and the gun, which was being waved angrily in his direction, as if he believed he could catch any bullet that flew out before it touched him. 'If you are living your life in that belief, if that is what you are searching for, if you believe that finding love will solve all problems, will be like arriving at a solution to your life, then all your actions are being commenced for the wrong reasons, sir. Love is two things, and only two things. Firstly, it's not the destination, not the place you end up, love is the origin, is the source, is the place where all journeys begin. When you fall in love, sir, that is the beginning of everything, of a whole world. And secondly,' he hurried on, because Funicular wasn't looking very patient with this lecture, 'love is the way you travel, love is how you move from one place to another. Love is both the origin and the road on which you walk, the mode of transport on which you ride, the stick in your hand, the sandals on your feet. Knowing this, believing this, you will begin, I believe, to do the correct things, for the right reasons ...'

'Oh do stop talking,' shouted Funicular. 'I am growing so bored of this. I've not devoted the last fourteen years of my life to this woman without knowing what I was doing. I have followed her across the globe, always one ship behind, I have slept in hotels the day after she's been there, I have collected cigarette butts and railway tickets ... do you think this isn't love? Do you think I'd dedicate my life, when I could've been happily enjoying my holidays in London like everyone else or by motoring out to Richmond with my mother ... dedicate my life to traipsing the globe for nothing? I've heard the stories told about her by tribesman on the frigid plains of Siberia (I didn't understand them of course because the idiots don't speak English, but the gestures were most instructive) and I read the newspaper reports of her appearances in small outback towns. She impresses wherever she goes, always leaves some sign of her passing. Legends I expect will be made ...'

'Mr Funicular?' said Penelope in an attempt to distract his attention from Simone, at whom he was rather agitatedly waving the pistol. She'd never liked guns, didn't own one herself, but she recognised the Lancaster. It had four barrels and could stop a tiger if aimed well. He was halfway through his complement of bullets and had shown no compunction about using it. If she'd had her wits when he'd first fired she'd have used that moment of shock when he shook on the gate with the thing's recoil to jump him, but Epitome had fallen (she didn't want to think on that right now) and she'd been distracted. Besides the gate was yards away from where she stood and she couldn't be sure of crossing the gap before he aimed and fired again. And now Mr Crepuscular was stood half in the way. If she could only get to the lawyer she could snap his neck, or go a good way to doing so.

'Yes, Penny?' Funicular answered, glancing at her but still aiming at Crepuscular.

Her nose wrinkled at his familiarity, as if a foul stench had gusted into the garden.

'Mr Funicular, I remember now that I warned you, a long time ago, away from the path you appear to have followed.'

'And I, dearest Penny, took that warning to heart. I have often repeated, to myself, those sweet tough words you spoke. I have caressed their breathy vowels between my teeth and loved each consonant. It took a while, but I came to understand their true meaning, the hidden meaning inside them. It was like poetry, it required unpacking, but I found the challenge you had set me, the promise you had made.' He looked at her coyly. 'You are a temptress, madam, and you won my heart that day.'

'Their real meaning, Mr Funicular ...?'

'Ivor, please, my sweet ...'

'Their real meaning, *Mr Funicular*, was that I didn't like you, and the implication was that if we ever met again, I would kill you.' Simone gave her a glance of shock. 'I'm sorry, Mr Crepuscular, but I'm not quite the lady, perhaps, that any of you imagine me to be. There seems to be a lot of this going on. Now, Mr Funicular, seeing what you have done to my nephew and his friend, and seeing the way you are still holding that wretched weapon, which, as Epitome rightly said, is the tool of a coward, I am afraid that I shall have to follow through on my promise. This, I must point out, gives me no pleasure at all. After all,' she said as an aside, 'who enjoys squashing flies?' Even as Simone Crepuscular gave her a pained look she wondered exactly how she might get the opportunity to follow her words with her actions, without endangering anyone else. 'I simply can't let a pathetic, creeping, creepy creature like you get away with this.'

In the moment that followed four things occurred simultaneously.

First, Penelope reached down to her boot where she kept her knife. She wondered whether she would be able to unsheathe it and throw it before the gunman could fire again. She knew she couldn't cross the space between them in that time, and the knife was made for flensing and whittling, not for throwing – it was weighted all wrong and she didn't even know whether she'd be able to hit Funicular with it, let alone injure him. But maybe a distraction was all she needed at this point. Her hand unbuttoned the cover and gripped the haft.

The second thing was that Simone Crepuscular took a step towards Miss Penultimate with the intention of stopping her from doing anything foolish. He couldn't let her be party to an act of murder, even against so desperate a little man as the one they faced. He would rather have killed him himself than let her do it. But he had no intention of anyone else killing anyone else at all.

The third thing was that Nancy Walker cracked Ivor Funicular very hard round the back of the head with a large and very heavy cast iron frying pan.

And the fourth thing that happened was that as Ivor collapsed, his occipital lobes already mushed beyond cognition, his gun-hand impacted against the gate's upper bar and fired off one final bullet that careened directly into Crepuscular's beard.

In the following moments: Penelope let the knife fall back into its discrete boot-sheath; Simone and Ivor Funicular each fell to the hard earth, one with a slight bump, the other with a much heavier thump as coins spilt with a glittering tinkle on the paving stones; Nancy let the frying pan drop from her small hand, with a muddy clatter, and stood stock still shivering in the lane, pale with panic and fright; and Simon dropped the wine bottle and hurried to his father's side.

Penelope was torn. Epitome *and* Mr Spiggot *and* Mr Crepuscular each lay on the earth in their own little separate worlds, and Nancy stood in the middle of the lane, crying and turning paler and paler. How could she be expected to choose to go to just one of them in a moment like this? Always, in the past, she thought, decisions had come to her so easily, but now they all looked like this ... like a big bloody mess. There was a smell of cordite and bloody iron in the air and the sound of that last shot still rang in her ears.

She had been quite prepared to kill him and now she was standing in shock in her own garden. As long as he had been there holding the gun at them, there had been a focus to her attention, something to aim at and to be concerned about. Now that the threat had been removed she had to make a decision.

The decision was made for her when Nancy began wailing.

'My boots,' were the words that were contained in that ghastly wail, although whether one could have disentangled them from the hurt, animal sounds that carried them along, would be hard to say.

When Penelope reached her she discovered that Mr Funicular had bled somewhat. The frying pan, which had been the heaviest item in the kitchen, had done a lot of damage to the man's skull, which was clearly more concave now than before, and a puddle of thick, dark blood had poured out. It had seeped along the lane and surrounded Nancy's feet, lapping at the sides of her boots, staining her soles red-black.

Penelope put her arm around Nancy's shoulder and led her away, taking small half-steps. Up the lane they walked, and in through the front door of the cottage, retracing the steps Nancy had taken just a few minutes before. Penelope sat her down in the front room, tucked her up in the blanket she herself had slept in the troubled night before (how long ago that seemed!) and after smoothing her brow and kissing her, made her way down the hall into the kitchen.

There she met Simon who was washing his hands in a bowl of red water. She didn't even think to mention his gender and location, but simply looked at him. He shook his head helplessly, but spoke assuredly.

'The bullet hit my father's purse, where he kept his money, Miss. You know, his wallet …'

She nodded, understanding the concept of purses and money perfectly well.

'You know,' he continued. 'You know, how you always hear those stories about bullets being deflected by the lucky Bible or cigarette packet? And how you never quite know whether to believe them or not … he wrote a pamphlet about such stories once, there was an Icelandic Saga where Snorri Someoneson (I forget the details) was left for dead, but the axe of his attacker had struck his … oh, I forget, anyway … but you know the stories …?'

She nodded again. It had happened to her once. The locket with the picture of her father was in a box upstairs somewhere, bent out of shape by a Papua New Guinean arrow.

'Well, I always thought they were just folktales ... too good to be true, you know?'

'And ...?'

'Well, we never really had lot of money, and he didn't carry much with him and the bullet passed straight through. I think it hit his heart. I can't tell, I'm not a doctor.'

Penelope was caught between raising her hand to her mouth and raising it to touch this boy's cheek. She stopped halfway between doing either.

'I tried everything I know to revive him ... but I don't know much. Oh, Miss ...'

He wiped his hands on his trousers as he stopped speaking and started crying. It was a bizarre moment of politeness: he didn't want to dirty Miss Penultimate's towels with his bloody hands.

'Epitome?'

'I think he fainted,' Simon managed to say, his voice wobbling with swelling grief. 'I don't think he's actually shot at all.'

'Mr Spiggot?'

'Dead.'

They stood together for a few seconds, then he stepped forward into her arms.

'Just hold me for a moment, ma'am,' he said, not really offering her any alternative. He'd never had a mother, not for twenty-four years, and it was right now that he really noticed the lack. So they stood in the middle of the kitchen for several minutes, him sobbing on her shoulder and she stunned, silent, thinking to herself, I have inherited so many boys, how will I ever teach them right from wrong? How can I protect them all?

She looked up, unlikely tears in her own eyes, to see Nancy stood in the doorway looking at them. Penelope was pleased to notice that she'd regained some colour in her cheeks.

When the first rush of his tears had worn themselves out, Simon stepped back and stared into her eyes. It was quite dark in the kitchen, the sun having moved round to the front of the cottage by this early part of the afternoon (it wasn't even one o'clock yet), but he could see those silent, pale tears rolling down her cheeks and he turned away, knowing they'd only set him off again.

'What will I tell Rodney?' he said. 'How do I explain this?'

But it was a resigned question – no anger, only weariness powered his voice.

Nancy filled the kettle from the tap.

'Oh, Auntie,' said Epitome coming into the kitchen. 'Spiggot's lying down, he's not moving … nor is Mr Crepuscular … Auntie?'

'My boy,' she said, folding yet another man up in her arms, feeling unqualified for this.

'Oh, oi! Bloody hell … Christ almighty,' shouted a voice from outside.

Penelope recognised the voice and felt a slight shift of relief. Nerrin, her gardener, was a good man. He saw no nonsense and didn't talk much, just took his shirt off, put his muscles to work and did as he was asked. She liked him as much as she liked any man, and knew he'd be of help clearing this mess up.

'Miss P., are you in there?' he asked, poking his head through the kitchen door, but not stepping in.

'Yes Nerrin,' she said over Epitome's shoulder. 'We've had rather a spot of bother this weekend, I wonder if you'd be good enough to help us out?'

'I see ... shall I go get a shovel?'

'I think that's best,' Penelope said as the kettle began to whistle on the stove.

31

'Competent fellow required for philanthropic act'

A fortnight later Quirkstandard was wandering slowly around the Zoological Gardens in Regent's Park. He was by himself and was wearing a black armband over the sleeve of his heavy coat. The summer had turned seasonably cold and wet[24] and the hot days that had marked his unfortunate weekend in the country had long gone. The weather seemed to have changed to match his mood. The sun was hidden behind black clouds and although it wasn't raining now the pavements and paths glittered with puddles.

Underneath the coat his shoulder ached where the bruises were still fading. He had banged it badly when the bullet missed him and the lawn caught him. In fact it had been dislocated. His Aunt had mended it, but it still hurt when he moved it. He tried not to move it very much, but sometimes he forgot and a sharp numb wince of pain reminded him, not only of his shoulder, but of that dreadful afternoon.

He stood outside the polar bear's enclosure and as he watched one of the massive beasts climbing out of water,

[24] This being England.

bedraggled and gigantic, he thought of the two friends he'd so recently lost.

The bear seemed to share something of Simone Crepuscular's gait and shape. Although the animal was so big, it had a grace about it that was familiar. It wasn't hurried, it didn't rush about anything, but when it put its paw down or turned its head, he knew that it was just right. He found it hard to believe he had known Crepuscular for less than a week before he lost his friendship and his guidance. Through the medium of the pamphlets, through Crepuscular's storytelling, it seemed he had been a part of his life for just forever and ever. But Epitome had checked his appointments book and that had the dates in and he knew that time really had been that short.

Now the bear shook its wet, hanging, dirty fur and a great shower of silvery sparks of water leapt across the empty stony pen the animal lived in. How could he not be reminded, in this vision, of his old friend Spiggot? How often, over the years, had he been soaked by an unexpected vigorous shake of his friend's hair? When they were lads sitting up of an evening in Quirkstandard's little study at Eton, he'd sometimes come in from the cold and shake just like that all over the buns they'd saved up for a midnight feast and they'd have to dry them out over the merry little fire his man would build for him. They discovered that they actually tasted better like that, and so, after that, they toasted them even when Spiggot hadn't made them wet. The other boys learnt about this new fad and Quirkstandard and Spiggot shared their only moment of popularity at school because of this toasted bun trend. But like all trends it passed and in time they were quietly forgotten again. Neither of them had ever much minded anonymity.

It was only the dirty condition of the bear's hair and the vast, deep and satisfied groan it emitted (plus the fact that it weighed half a ton) that made Quirkstandard remember that he wasn't with his dear, dear friend anymore. He was in fact alone.

He consoled himself, as he had done from time to time over the last two weeks, with the thought that Spiggot had been getting on. After all, they'd met more than fifteen years ago, and for a gentleman of Spiggot's standing (which had always been quite low to the ground) that was a very respectable length of life to achieve. Although this thought was consoling in some ways, still it didn't begin to fill the hole in his heart that Nigel Spiggot had left.

His thoughts drifted then, from the bear, back to his Aunt's garden. His Aunt had told him, afterwards, how brave Spiggot had been in his defence of him, and Quirkstandard shed another quiet tear. If he hadn't been such a fool as to faint then maybe they'd still be together. If only he'd been braver. He'd been being very brave up to the point the bullet knocked him down. He was still a little deaf on one side and had woken up in the middle of several nights feeling the whipcrack of air pass by his ear. He hadn't mentioned this to anyone.

His Aunt's gardener had dug a small grave at the far end of the garden and they had laid Mr Spiggot to rest in it. By his side they had placed the India rubber ball he had brought with him and a stick he had become particularly attached to on Saturday's walk. Quirkstandard had said a few words, thinking of something he'd read in a pamphlet a few days earlier about how Anglo-Saxon chiefs were buried with all their important possessions, the things that would show just who they were and how important they were when they reached the afterlife. He hoped that Spiggot wouldn't get into trouble for only having a ball and a stick, but he knew that he wouldn't have really wanted anything else in heaven. When he'd finished his thoughts he threw a handful of earth onto the little body, which still looked so much like his friend, and the gardener had shovelled the rest over him to make a tiny tumulus and they'd gone away.

His Aunt had written a letter to Mr and Mrs Spiggot which didn't tell them the truth, but which did express her sincere commiserations with Nigel's final illness – a tale of over-exertion and over-excitement, followed by fatigue and a pneumatic cold, and finally ending with the expiration of a quite elderly and well-lived and well-loved dog.

Quirkstandard hadn't been to see them yet.

The younger Crepuscular had driven him back to London. They brought Simone's body with them in the back of the car, under a sheet and some blankets. It wasn't the most dignified return home a father's corpse has had, but they couldn't think what else to do. Once in the capital the two Crepuscular boys made the arrangements for their father's funeral. Quirkstandard provided a little cash for the bribe they needed to pay to the borough coroner to not mention the bullet. The body was cremated in a short service a few days later.

His Aunt and her housekeeper had gone off on one of their travels very shortly after the cremation. Epitome couldn't remember where she'd said they were going, he was such a dunce for place names, but he knew they would be away for some time, because they always were. He expected a postcard to arrive at Mauve's any day now.

The zookeeper came along just then and nudged Quirkstandard out of the way with his bucket. Reaching into it he pulled out a dozen fat silvery dead fish and tossed them over the fence into the bear's enclosure. The bear padded its slow way over to where the piscine feast had landed, swaying its head from side to side and sniffing deeply. When it reached the scattered fish it was visibly disappointed, presumably because (a) lunch was already dead and (b) it wasn't lovely blubbery seal. After looking up at the zookeeper with a pair of deep lazy hateful eyes for several seconds it ate the fish anyway.

A few days after the cremation, and after his Aunt had left, Quirkstandard had a meeting with the two remaining Crepusculars. They were selling *Crepuscular & Sons* and wondered if he'd be interested in it. Neither of them had the heart or the desire to take on the responsibility of continuing their father's work. It had been his baby, his love, his endeavour far more than it had ever been theirs, and now that he was gone, as sad as that was, they each saw different worlds open before them, they wanted to at least try their hands at other things.

Rodney had a wife to support and, as it turned out, a baby of his own on the way. He'd already been offered a job as Assistant Chief Assistant in the Amphibian House of *Burton's Travelling Menagerie & Miniature Circus*, a position he'd heard about through a friend at the Charing Cross Road (& Area) Toad Fanciers' Group. He hoped that a position like that would only be temporary, that given time and hard work he might even make Chief Assistant. In actual fact within six months he would be understudying for the girl in the sequined leotard who rode the great white horses,[25] but that's really a history to be told at another time.

Simon, on quite the other hand, moved, at Penelope's rather unexpected suggestion, into her cottage. Or, at least he was staying in the cottage while she and Miss Walker were away. In the meantime he was working with Nerrin to convert the shed into a comfortable residence for his more permanent dwelling. He'd had enough of the city and despite what had happened at that house, or perhaps even because of it, he felt some need to be there, among the trees and near the river. He had taken to this refitting and redecorating task with a surprising amount of gusto and for the first time in ages found he was doing something he more than enjoyed.

When he had rushed to his father's body, in that same garden some weeks before, he had found, underneath the old man's great grey beard, not only his father's split and spilt purse, but also, hanging there on a thin cord, his mother's hook. He knew what it was, obviously, but it had been two decades since he'd seen it. He didn't even

---

[25] There was something in his blood which meant he had a natural affinity with the horses – they liked him even when they were complete bastards with everyone else. He would hum a lullaby his father had hummed to him, but which he thought he'd long forgotten, and they would calm down and rub his face with their big damp noses. A talent like that could make a man indispensable to a circus, especially one that kept horses.

know that his father still had it, but clearly he'd kept it hidden and close to his heart for all those long, long years, though not quite close enough to have deflected Funicular's final shot.

Simon took the multi-purpose hand, on its bit of cord, and hung it around his own neck. He showed it, later on, to Nancy and told her what he knew about her mother ... about their mother. There wasn't a huge amount to say though, she having died when he was so very young, and his father having been so reticent, through the barricade of his own remorse and sorrow, to talk about her over the years. They sat in the garden, at the table, touching the silver hook in silence for some minutes before Nancy spoke again.

'Was she a good woman?'

'Oh yes.'

'I'm pleased to know that.'

'Yes, she was good.'

'I never really much wondered about her before, you know?'

'She was a pirate though.'

'I mean, I didn't ever know anyone, when I was kid, who had a mum. We were all orphans, you see ... I mean, in the orphanage.'

'So she did kill a few people, and rob them.'

'And Penelope's there for me now. She can be quite motherly sometimes. You'd be surprised.'

'And she did sink some ships, probably with all hands on board. That sort of thing.'

'I've not had a bad life, you see, I mean, with not knowing her. I've done alright.'

'And she did steal a lot of treasure. Dad said she was dead good at her job, though she gave it up when she met him.'

'But it's nice to know a bit about her, to hear where I really come from. Though I think more of me comes from the orphanage than her … I mean the things I know, you see?'

'In fact, somewhere she buried her treasure. I think father said it was on a small island off the Ecuadorean coast, though there's quite a lot of coast, so that doesn't really help. He mentioned a map once, but I don't know where it is. Some beautiful jewels apparently, that's what he said she'd said. Well, I'm glad I could tell you something about her, I'm just sad that neither of us really had the chance to meet her properly.'

'Yes. I'm sorry too. Mostly for you, but a little bit for me too.'

'I've got to go into town now, I have some wallpaper to pick up and I'm meeting a Mrs Althrope to discuss some curtain designs she did for me, though I'm not entirely happy with them.'

'Goodbye Simon.'

'Yes, cheerio then Miss Walker.'

He'd discovered an attachment on the hand which worked as a very serviceable wallpaper stripper, though it might have been a machete, with which he took down the garish, tasteless paper Nerrin had originally had on the walls. The paper Simon pasted in its place was much more to his liking, a delicate pale yellow, with small lilac flowers arranged in geometric patterns. He ran this halfway down the wall and, beneath a discrete distinguishing dado rail, he painted the lower half of the wall a speckled duck egg blue. To his eyes the shed was one step closer to being a pleasant place to live.

Quirkstandard bought the Crepuscular's pamphlet stock and, since they owned the freehold, the brothers rented the shop out to a barber at a fair but healthy price. Epitome collected the pamphlets with a pair of taxi cabs and they now sat in his drawing room. Although he wasn't actually happy, per se, he had at least been happier at home this last week because Cook had come back, having been invalided out of the Great War within days of joining in. Although he had no legs now he could still boil an egg just the way Quirkstandard liked it, and he even laid the soldiers out, cut and buttered as they should be. His hand trembled a bit as he did so though and he was lucky he had no feet because the amount of boiling water that splashed on the floor was prodigious. Cook and he weren't alone in the house though because he had offered the role of housekeeper to Miss Dawn, since she wasn't to be let with the shop premises, and she brought a feminine touch to the place that had long been absent.

Although the stack of pamphlets in the drawing room was large and even though Quirkstandard had only ever penetrated the smallest corner of them during his few days of delving under Mr Crepuscular's guiding eye, he found it difficult to pick one up now. Looking at them saddened him. He couldn't help but think of Mr Crepuscular when he did. He simply couldn't muster the same enthusiasm he'd once had for them. Too much, he said to himself, has happened, even if he didn't understand exactly what most of it had been about. Heigh ho.

Today, which was a Sunday, he had come to the Zoological Gardens in Regent's Park for the first time in years. After his Sunday dinner he had felt overwhelmed by a wave of nostalgia and desire to indulge it. He had used to come to the Zoo as a young gentleman, recently out of school, with good old Spiggot. They'd spend hours outside the wolves' cage, watching them pace up and down, staring out with those great golden, amber lupine eyes. Spiggot hoped that the bitch at the back would one day notice him, though she never did, or never looked like she did. Even Epitome had to admit, as Spiggot vocally commented, that she was a most beautiful creature.

He walked now from the polar bear's enclosure towards that of the lions. He didn't want to go and see the wolves today, thinking that that might be too much for him. But cats, he thought, and big ones at that, would be just as beautiful and less memory-stirring to look at. As he approached the iron bars that separated the public from the animals he stopped. A hand had touched his arm.

'Lord Quirkstandard? Ah. What a coincidence!'

'Oh,' said Epitome, recognising the man after only a moment of thought. 'Mr Pybus, fancy seeing you here.'

'Indeed, eh? I'm here with the wife and the nippers, they're off in the Lizard House, but I thought it was you over here and then I saw that it certainly was you and so I decided to come and speak to you. Ah. Just to say 'hello', as it were.'

'Well, hello then!'

'Hello, back to you, your lordship.'

'Well, Mr Pybus. It's been lovely seeing you, eh?'

'Indeed Lord Quirkstandard, sir. Yes.'

They looked at each other for a moment, each real-ising that maybe conversation wasn't the easiest art to master.

'So, Mr Pybus,' said Quirkstandard at last, 'any news?'

'Oh. Ah. Yes. As a matter of fact, yes. I've got the Aeolian Hall booked, that's in Battersea, for next Thurs-day evening.'

'Wonderful, I look forward to it.'

'Yes, that's good. I've talked some pals of mine into putting up some posters round the place, like you sug-gested, do you remember? Ah. And hopefully that'll bring a few people in. I mean it's early days isn't it? But I'm hopeful. I told some chaps who sounded interested, but sometimes people are just polite, aren't they? Ah.'

'Yes, some people. But then some people are inter-ested. It's hard to tell. But like you say, Mr Pybus, it's early days now and from big oak trees little acorns come, as they say.'

'Yes, I guess that's not half true, Lord Q.'

Albert Pybus had answered an advertisement that Rodney had helped Quirkstandard place in the *Evening Standard* – 'Competent fellow required,' it had read, 'for philanthropic act.'

One evening Quirkstandard had been sitting up late at night in the drawing room, unable to sleep, and leaf-ing idly through the pile of pamphlets. 'I can't see myself getting much out of these,' he'd said to the room. 'My days of learning have passed. But,' he continued out loud to anyone who might be listening, 'there are all sorts of people out there in the world who might still want to know things, who might have horizons that do still need expanding.' And so he pulled out a pencil and piece of paper and jotted down some cursory notes for the establishment of what he called The Common University – right down to the name. Well, to be honest, only down to the name, but he liked the name and behind it lurked a vague idea of how it might work.

When Mr Pybus called round to discuss the advertisement they thrashed out some more details between them. The Common University, they decided, would run free lectures, subsidised by Quirkstandard's fortune, for anyone who couldn't afford the normal fees charged by the established universities. They could be sure of reaching the neediest areas of society that way. The subjects of the lectures would cross all categories, originally (at least) taking their inspiration from Crepuscular's work, but maybe later, they speculated, they could expand and cater to all and any areas of learning that were requested of them. Pybus had the dream of eventually running it like a real university, and not just a fancy mutual improvement society, and they'd issue certificates and degrees to those who'd completed the requisite number of courses ... but such plans and such ends were far off in the future.

They agreed that the first lecture would be on the subject of *Victorian India & The Circus* and would be based on the very first of Simone Crepuscular's pamphlets. Quirkstandard had thought this only right and fitting. Pybus agreed to give the lecture, since he claimed to be a competent public speaker (something that pleased

349

Quirkstandard no end, since he had been terrified that someone would ask *him* to speak in public which always was just, well, not exactly, well, you see, not exactly … yes, well … just, sort of, a bit like this …).

'I'm looking forward to it very much, Lord Q. I've been reading through the pamphlet you gave me – lord, if I don't remember reading it as a kid, oh, donkey's years ago?! It all came flooding back – and I've taken the essentials, boiled them down into what I think's going to be a very neat little talk. I think you'll be proud and we'll make your friend proud too, I hope.'

'Friend?'

'Yes. Ah. I mean the late fellow who wrote the thing. Mr Crepuscular.'

'Oh yes. I hope he's proud. But I won't blame you, Mr Pybus, if he's not. I mean it sounds like you're doing your very best.'

'I hope so. I hope so. It'll be fine. No, it'll be better than that. Ah. Assuming anyone turns up to hear it.'

'Well, let's hope so, Mr Pybus, let's hope so. You're very kind, thank you. So, I'll see you on Thursday?'

'Yes, Thursday, about six o'clock at the Aeolian Hall.'

'Jolly good, I'll be there. Cheerio then.'

'Cheerio, your lordship.'

The two men gave each other a little wave and parted, Albert Pybus heading off to the Lizard House and Quirkstandard turning to face the lions.

'Oi there, mate – watch out!' shouted a stout, red-faced zookeeper, walking slowly in Quirkstandard's direction.

Epitome looked at him and wondered what he wanted. He was waving and saying something, but a growl behind him covered up the gist of the chap's message.

And then, all of a sudden, he was knocked to the ground and pinned there by a great weight. Warm breath struck his left ear and a low roar, rumbling up into the lowest ranges of human hearing, almost deafened him. Oh, he thought, it's a lion. And indeed it was, the cage door had been left open after the lunchtime feeding and it was just as Quirkstandard stood there that the lion noticed and decided to take advantage.

Now he understood what the chap in the uniform had been saying.

The warm breath in his ear, the crushing weight on his back and the pinpricks of claws he could feel pressing through his heavy coat, had him paralysed. He thought of everything that had happened to him recently, he thought of all the things he still had to do, and he wondered, quite calmly – surprisingly calmly – if this was how things really ended.

At any moment he expected the jaws (he could see them in his mind's eye, he knew what a lion looked like when it yawned, how pink its tongue is, how yellow those teeth) to clamp down on his neck and he thought, well, maybe this is for the best. My friends are gone, and I've started my legacy, my own university – Mr Pybus is a good chap, I'm sure he'll make a go of it. But it's a shame that Miss Dawn's only had her new job for a week and then she's going to have to look for a new one; and Cook, what's he going to do? And Auntie Penelope, who's going to tell her that I've been eaten by a lion? Oh dear, he thought. And then he thought of Spiggot.

He could actually see the little chap barking in front of him, stood there on the macadam path, his ferocious jaws open and a mean glint in his eye as he faced up to the king of the jungle, as he barked angrily as if he were guarding Epitome from harm. Quirkstandard smiled to see his old friend again, smiled to see him so vigorous in the face of overwhelming odds.

'Don't worry Spiggot, old chap,' he wheezed out of lungs only able to half fill under the lion's weight. 'Don't worry about me. I'm doing all right. But thanks for coming back. I've missed you, you know. Oh, it's good to see you ...'

But the lion's jaws didn't close. The zookeeper arrived just as Quirkstandard fainted from lack of air and he prodded with his pointed stick and spoke in his special stern zookeeperly voice.

The lion was smart enough to recognise the man who fed him three times a day and promptly stepped off the prone gentleman and padded quietly back into his cage. He had grown up in there and although his brief adventure in the outside world had been fairly interesting, all he had learnt from it was that he was, after all, the sort of creature who preferred the familiar. He liked his meals served cold and not all wriggly and warm; and although his instincts had instructed him to pounce, he hadn't really known what to do next.

The zookeeper apologised to the old lady and her little dog who had been minding their own business by just passing by when they were growled at by the lion and he offered her a pair of free tickets to Madame Tussaud's by way of compensation. All staff at the Zoo carried a pair just in case something went wrong.

Only then did he kneel down beside Quirkstandard and feel his neck for a pulse. It was there and it was beating quite regularly. The zookeeper breathed a sigh of relief. Fatalities in the Zoological Gardens always brought crowds the next day and several annoying pieces of paperwork and all a zookeeper really wants is a quiet life tending his animals.

This gentleman, he judged from his breathing, would be fine if he was given some air and a bit of space and maybe a cup of tea in the zookeepers' lodge. He rolled him over and sat him up and after a few minutes Quirkstandard was able to stand. He had the cup of tea and though he didn't say anything while he drank it the zookeeper got the impression that he was probably quite all right and so he went to get back on with his duties and asked Epitome to shut the door after him when he left the lodge.

Quirkstandard sipped his tea – it was strong and sugary and did him good.

When the cup was empty he sat for a while and looked at the calendar on the wall – it had a picture of a giraffe for this month. Giraffes didn't remind him of anything.

He sat looking at it for a few minutes, savouring the feeling.

After a while he slipped out of the lodge, made sure the door was shut properly behind him, passed the polar bear as he left the Zoo, glanced at it quickly, smiled quietly to himself and walked all the way home.